# BEAUTIFUL SOLDIER

## THE HEIGHTS CREW
## BOOK THREE

By

E. M. MOORE

Manufactured in the United States of America
First Edition June 2020

Edited by Heather Long

Cover by 2nd Life Designs

Huge thanks to my beta readers: Bibi, Ashton, Lisa, Jorden, Summer, Jennifer, and Angie!

<u>Also By E. M. Moore</u>

**Saint Clary's University**

Those Heartless Boys


**The Heights Crew Series**

Uppercut Princess

Arm Candy Warrior

Beautiful Soldier

Knockout Queen


**The Ballers of Rockport High Series**

Game On

Foul Line

At the Buzzer


**Rockstars of Hollywood Hill**

Rock On


**Spring Hill Blue Series**

Free Fall

Catch Me

**Ravana Clan Vampires Series**

Chosen By Darkness

Into the Darkness

Falling For Darkness

Surrender To Darkness

**Ravana Clan Legacy Series**

A New Genesis

Tracking Fate

Cursed Gift

Veiled History

Fractured Vision

Chosen Destiny

**Order of the Akasha Series**

Stripped (Prequel)

Summoned By Magic

Tempted By Magic

Ravished By Magic

Indulged By Magic

Enraged By Magic

## Her Alien Scouts Series

Kain Encounters

Kain Seduction

## Rise of the Morphlings Series

Of Blood and Twisted Roots

## Safe Haven Academy Series

A Sky So Dark

A Dawn So Quiet

## Chronicles of Cas Series

Reawakened

Hidden

Power

Severed

Rogue

## The Adams' Witch Series

Bound In Blood

Cursed In Love

## Witchy Librarian Cozy Mystery Series

Wicked Witchcraft

One Wicked Sister

Wicked Cool

Wicked Wiccans

The physical therapist digs his hands into my neck.

I cringe at the flare of pain that radiates from his rough touch. I don't pull away, even though I mentally curse him the fuck out. If I have to do this sick torture, the guy could have the decency to be hot. Or sociable. Hell, I'd even take a smile. One measly smile.

Breaking news: He's neither good looking nor friendly, and I'm fairly sure the only lip movement I'll ever get from him is his ever-present sneer.

From my first PT appointment, I could tell he had his mind made up about me already. I'm just some gang bitch delinquent who shot an innocent girl.

My stomach tugs at the thought and then does a nasty flip. When I was a little girl and thinking about my future life, I never imagined this scenario playing out. First, my parents would be here. Second... Well, fuck. The second is easy, right? I wouldn't have been accused of murdering a young girl. It's fucking insane.

PT dude digs deeper, and I suck in a breath. He doesn't ease off, and in the mirrored wall in front of me, a smirk crawls over his face.

Fucking asshole. If Johnny were here...

Fuck it, if any of my guys were here. None of them would let this douchebag do this to me...and take pleasure in it.

I grip the side of the table I'm sitting on, squeezing tightly so I don't turn and clock the asshole accidentally. Accidentally on fucking purpose, I mean. No matter how badly I want to, I'm already skating on thin ice. I don't need an assault and battery charge added to the one I already have.

"Ray," a sweet voice calls out.

The guy's touch loosens. This is the first time I've even heard his name. It's been four weeks of pure silence and torture for an hour every other day with metaphorical chains around my wrists, preventing me from doing anything about the mistreatment.

"What's up?"

"Boss said I should work on this patient."

Ray steps away. They share a look, and I'm already beginning to think this new chick isn't going to be any better. I know what the news has been saying about me, while not bothering to get to know the real me. I mean, that's just...appropriate? Normal? Human decency?

When you've been accused of such a heinous crime, I guess you lose all that.

"Have fun." Ray chuckles darkly as he passes the new girl, flipping the door open to the hallway outside the PT room.

During my appointments, no one else is here. I guess they like to keep the people who are accused of murder separate from other patients. There's no guard, though, which I thought was uber strange. No guard at the facility where I'm staying at either. Greenlawn, a halfway house for cons. A place where the police can keep an eye on me while they figure out if they're actually going to press charges.

That part's on me though. I agreed to stay at the place. It was either that or have them expedite a trial of some sort. Detective Reynolds doesn't like me very much, so it seems he's trying to hang me for something I didn't do. He even has an eyewitness to my supposed murderous rampage, which is fucking outrageous.

Instead of moving toward me, the girl takes a seat on the furthest table away and studies her nails.

A prickling sensation skitters up my neck. "Umm..."

To my left, a knock on the exterior window sounds. I turn too fast, and a sharp pain radiates down my spine. The pain isn't too much to take usually, but sometimes, PT makes it worse for a while before making it better.

I narrow my gaze, trying to see past the different torture device equipment in here to peer out the window. My heart thumps in my chest.

"You better get that," the woman says, bored. Her voice isn't cheery anymore. She's either dropped the sweet act, or I just bring this behavior out in people. "You don't have much time."

I scramble off the table. I haven't heard or seen any of my guys since the nurse in the hospital gave me the message from Johnny to not say anything. With all the shit that's gone down, I get it. I don't fucking like it, but I get it. I knew they'd find a way, eventually.

I hurry to the window. A smile breaks over my face when Finn's grin greets me. He hikes his thumb toward the sky, and I fumble with the window until it opens. It's difficult with the damn cast on my arm, but I manage. I can't wait to get the damn thing off.

"Princess!"

"Shh!" the lady scolds behind us, casting a worried glance toward the main door of the room.

Finn rolls his eyes, and then moves to the side, revealing his brother, Jax, who looks far less pleased to be here.

"What are you two doing here?" I whisper, unable to hold back the smile at seeing familiar, friendly faces.

"We've been jonesing to see you for a month."

I search Finn's face for the lie automatically. No one has wanted to see me for a month. I'm not talking about Brawler, Oscar, Magnum, or Johnny, I'm talking about at the shithole place I've been staying in. No one likes anyone there. No one here likes me either.

However, in Finn's face, all I recognize is raw honesty. It's nice to be around people who actually like me.

"You're not scared of me?"

Jax snickers. I guess if he thinks I'm a murderer, he's not intimidated by that fact.

"Only of your right and left uppercut." Finn winks.

I curl the fingers in on my right hand, testing how my bone is healing. It actually feels fine. It's been four weeks since the accident, and they said it could take six to eight weeks to heal. My money—and hope—is on six.

My former trainers don't make a move to come in, so I hop up on the spacious windowsill in front of me, pulling my knees to my chest. I bite down on my lip. So many questions come to mind, but I'm not sure where I want to start first. Images of my guys flash in front of me. Yes, *my* guys. Just because I haven't seen them doesn't mean they're still not mine. Shit must be serious if they haven't contacted me before this.

Finn reaches through the window and places his hand on my shoe. "I didn't realize how fucked up things were for you, Kyla."

I give him a wobbly smile, but Jax's ticking jaw says he

doesn't have the same caring thoughts as his brother. Hell, I know I got myself into this. The Heights isn't for the faint of heart. Shrugging, I put on a brave face. I'm well used to it by now. I've been making this same face since I was twelve. "It's all good." I glance between the two brothers and hold my breath. "You know I didn't do it, right?" I like these guys. I hope the fact that they came here means they like me too and that Johnny didn't have to threaten them to do it. With Jax's reaction, I can't be sure though.

"You're kidding, right?" Finn asks. "Of course we know you didn't do it."

Jax scoffs, and Finn glares at him.

"Out with it," I sigh, eyeing Jax. There's nothing he could say that would make me feel less about myself than I already do.

"Not sure that's a good idea..." Finn starts.

But Jax has been bottled up since they got here, or before, it seems, so he doesn't give a shit when his brother warns him off. "It's what you get, I guess." Jax shrugs. A smug, tight-lipped grin covers his face, making his condescending ass look even more condescending.

"Oh, I know. Holier than thou Jax has entered the building," Finn mimics, glaring at the brother who looks so unlike himself. One taller and leaner. The other a bit shorter and stockier. The only attribute they share is the muscles from fight training.

I place my hand on Finn's to stop him from retaliating.

"Go on," I tell Jax, squaring my shoulders for the worst of it. It was my decision to come here. It was my decision to get into the Crew. It was my decision to fall... Actually, that wasn't a decision at all. Falling for the guys in the Heights wasn't planned, but there's no way in hell I would ever take it back.

"What did you think was going to happen when you got yourself mixed up with them?" His hands ball to fists at his sides. "Nothing good comes from being mixed up in their shit. The fact that you're here is testament to that. You fucked up your body," he sneers, dropping his gaze to my cast. "You fucked up your life."

I hug my knees tighter as the onslaught of Jax's words wash over me like a gray sky. I totally get it. Everything he says is correct. "I have reasons," I tell him, shrugging. I give Finn an awkward smile. "I guess it's a good thing you got that picture of me you wanted before I ended up broken." I prop my chin on my knees. "Unless you had to take it down." I don't know why I care about that stupid Uppercut Princess poster in their gym right now, but I do. It reminds me of how strong I can be.

Closing my eyes, I breathe in. *One Kyle and Anna. Two Kyle and Anna.*

"Please, girl," Finn says. "It's still up. You're still a hot commodity in the Heights. In fact, I think it's gotten worse because now you're like the poster girl for the wrongly accused." Finn arches an eyebrow at his brother. "People in the Heights know about that."

Jax's lips thin. He glares at his brother before turning on his heel and stalking off.

Finn and I watch him go, his inked hands dropping to his sides as he walks off toward the parking lot.

Finn sighs. "Don't worry about him."

"No offense, Finn, but I've got a lot of other worries on my mind."

Finn eyes me, then mumbles, "Fuck it" before heaving himself up on the sill next to me. He leans over, pulling me to his chest. I let my legs slip down, his muscled arms swallowing me in a hug.

"I missed you," I say, trying to hold back emotions rushing to the surface.

"I missed you too, Princess. We've got to get you training again."

My eyes burn with unshed tears. "Yeah," I croak out. To think fighting was a lifeline to keep me grounded while I was here. If I go to prison for this murder, I'm fucked. I won't have a life at all. No fighting. No guys. No anything.

"Shh," Finn says, comforting me. He pulls away. "As much as I would've come to see you myself, you know I'm here for a reason, right?"

My heart stutters to a stop in my chest and then leaps forward in a motion that steals my breath. I've been waiting for news, and it's finally come.

Finn returns his hand to my shoe, squeezing me. "Everyone had to go into hiding after what happened. When I say everyone, I mean—"

"The Crew?"

He nods, his face solemn. "The bodyguard, Magnum, he slipped underground until they fixed shit for him."

I breathe out a sigh of relief, but a hiccup of air hangs tight in my chest. I won't let it go until I know everyone I care about is safe. "Was he hurt in the accident?"

"Not as bad as you. Just some scrapes. But the police had the footage of him shooting someone. Of course, it's turned up missing now."

Even if the footage hadn't gone missing, what happened to self-defense? Gregory's guys were trying to take me. Who knows what their plans were?

"Rocket..."

I glance up, meeting Finn's gaze. Everything stops. I heard his voice that night. He was there. He was so close, but he just couldn't get to me.

"That guy is one scary motherfucker."

I press my lips together to keep from smiling. I can only imagine how Finn and Jax would see Johnny.

Finn squeezes my shoe. "He wants me to tell you that he's handling this. He's driving himself crazy with how long it's taking, but I guess being accused of murder is no easy thing to get rid of."

Especially because the gun used was most likely my

gun. My prints were all over it, but I want to know how they actually got my fingerprints. Detective Reynolds must be sneakier than we gave him credit for.

"He doesn't want you to worry about anything. He thinks it'll be over soon. They had to find that eyewitness." Finn gulps. "I'm not privy to all the information, and that's probably a good thing. He just said it would be soon."

Tears stick to my lashes. I can't remember the last time I felt so much vulnerability. It's terrifying. "Soon?"

"Yeah, Princess," Finn says. "Fucking soon. And I have a feeling if it doesn't work out the way Johnny's planning, he's just going to kidnap your ass out of that place you're living in and run away with you."

I smile. I can see him doing that. Hell, every last one of my guys has threatened to take me out of the Heights.

Okay, maybe threatened isn't the word for it. They're all trying to keep me safe while I've tried to do the same for them. Keeping Brawler and Oscar in the dark for so long about my true intentions was as much about keeping them safe as it was about me. Now that they know my plans, they're in as deep as I am. It's not what I wanted to happen.

I lick my lips, dread settling in my gut. "What about Brawler? And Oscar?"

Finn shakes his head. "I haven't seen Brawler, and I'm not sure I know who Oscar is."

I think back, wondering if they've ever met, but I guess it

doesn't matter. "So, you've just been talking to Johnny then?"

"He needed someone who was close to you, but not close to him. Someone who would come here for him." Finn runs his hands through his hair. "He approached Jax and I, and I jumped on the opportunity to help you."

I arch a brow. "But not Jax?"

"He's just a little overprotective," Finn says, flicking a piece of lint off his jeans.

I snort at that. "It's fine if he doesn't like the Crew, Finn," I tell him. "I mean, I wouldn't go saying anything to Johnny, but...I'm a different story. Jax doesn't have to be afraid of me." Finn gives me a look. "Okay, maybe not afraid of me, but he doesn't have to be afraid of getting mixed up in Crew business. I don't want that. For either of you. I'm well aware of why I'm here."

Finn sighs. "Jax likes to play the tough guy, but he's worried about you too. If he wasn't, he never would've shown up."

"Tell him I appreciate it. I really do." I stare into his eyes, knowing that this brief interlude in my current life is about to come to an end. Finn has given me Johnny's message, which means he can't stay. He'll have to heed the girl's warning soon. "Thank you for coming."

He dribbles his fingers across my shoes. "What do you want me to take back to Rocket?"

Without thinking, I lean forward and press a kiss to Finn's cheek.

The flirty trainer's cheeks blaze, crimson blooming everywhere until it hits the tip of his ears. "You seriously want me to kiss Rocket?"

I laugh, placing my hand over his. "It's your funeral. I'm sure you'll figure out a way to get the message across."

Finn slides back through the window, laughing. When he peers back, he's stoic again. "Stay safe, Princess. Soon, okay?"

"Okay," I mimic back.

He walks away, jamming his hands into his pockets with his stare aimed at the lush green grass. I watch him until he disappears around the side of the building. My heart squeezes painfully, but I get up, force the window back down one-handed, and then retreat back to the table.

The girl comes up behind me. She doesn't say a word, just starts where douchebag PT guy left off.

Meanwhile, "soon" is like a chorus through the chaotic mess of my brain. I wonder how soon *soon* is.

I guess I'll just have to wait to find out and pray to God I get out of this mess.

The chances God listens to someone like me are slim, but I think good thoughts anyway.

2

wo weeks later, the sun shines directly into my eyes as I step outside the PT building. I squint, momentarily blinded before taking my sunglasses out of my small bag and putting them on. Luckily, the tinted lenses let me case the surrounding areas. It's routine now. I'm not dumb enough to think Gregory's guys won't come for me again. However, since Finn and Jax came to see me, I've been extra diligent about checking the perimeter in case another familiar face shows up. Someone just waiting for me to notice them.

As has been the case for the last thirteen days, no one's waiting or watching.

I walk over the crack-laden sidewalk to the bus stop right outside the building. Leaning against the rusty sign, I breathe in the fresh air, knowing I'll be spending another night at the halfway house.

That's not what it's called. They've titled the place Greenlawn Reformatory. It's not winning any awards. Not for names, cleanliness, or hospitality. It's a place to stay, though, and the Wi-Fi isn't too bad, allowing me to keep up with school through distance learning.

The mechanical whine of a monster engine rings in my ears, and I peek left to find the city bus accelerating around the corner three blocks away. I can't even remember what it's like to drive my car. I keep telling myself that when I get out of the halfway house, I'm taking my car for a nice, long drive. Just to get away.

It probably won't happen, but it's a daydream that keeps me sane, especially when I feel like throwing my hands up at what's become of my life.

At least I can say I did one part of my job really well. I definitely got into the Crew. I'm all the way up in it. Being framed for murder doesn't just happen to normal people, so perhaps I should be patting myself on the back for doing that one thing really, really well.

I mean, I would, except I still can't rid my thoughts of the girl's picture Detective Reynolds showed me. Knowing her life is gone... That's just something I can't take pleasure in.

The bus comes to a stop in front of me, and I climb aboard, dropping the bus money in the slot I've earned from doing various housework at the Reformatory. We're all on a schedule, and as long as we do our share, we're given twenty bucks a week. The older residents have actual jobs, but they're still mandated to help out around the house, as well.

Greenlawn Reformatory is a temporary arrangement for everyone who has to stay there. I'm just hoping it's even more temporary for me, and not because I'm getting my ass carted to prison.

*Soon*, Finn's voice reverberates in my head again.

Johnny must've run into a snag because I doubt he'd send Finn if he wasn't sure of the timeline. He knows I'd be going crazy here, me and my anti-Kardashian ass. The only thing that's ended up in my favor is that the distance learning schooling I've been doing is far better than the shithole they call Rawley Heights High, but that doesn't mean I miss school any less.

The bus vibrates as it runs its normal route through the streets of Haddonfield. The small, mostly industrial town is forty-five minutes away from the Heights, a stipulation of Detective Reynolds. He didn't want me anywhere near Rawley Heights. His men trail me every now and then. I'm not allowed to leave the county, let alone the state. I'm not even allowed to contact anyone in the Heights. In fact, I don't have access to a phone since mine was either lost in the accident or taken as evidence. Brawler has the only real phone I worry about, though, and I'm sure he's keeping it safe for me. The phone I'm allowed to use is in Greenlawn's living room. Fifteen-minute cap per night, and the house manager parks her ass on the threadbare sofa to listen to everything that's said. I haven't used my time yet. The only people I would call are currently off-limits on Detective Reynolds' orders, and the last thing I would do is call my aunt and uncle to bring them into this mess. Since Reynolds has my finger-prints, he's most certainly tracing the calls made out of the house.

After ten minutes of motoring through the city, my stop comes into view, so I stand, arching my neck. Today, they hooked me up to some sort of contraption that used elec-trical stimulation. I preferred it to the massage even though the areas where they hooked the lines up burn like hell. The best part about it was I wasn't subjected to that douchebag PT guy today, so I'm counting it as a win whether it helps my neck or not.

I reach up, pulling down on the cord to signal my stop. The driver doesn't need to look up because we've been doing this same routine for over a month. He pulls over to the side of the road right in front of a dilapidated, overgrown bus stop with glass that's milky white from nature's elements. The driver nods, and I work my way down the steps and start toward the block Greenlawn is situated.

I smooth my hands down over my pockets, checking to make sure my knife is in a good position should I need to use it. My cast is off now, thankfully. I don't think it's ready for me to start punching bags, but I sure as fuck will use my fists in self-protection if I need.

In my room at the home, I took my bed off the cinderblocks it was raised up on and have been using the hunks of concrete to keep in shape as much as I can. It was difficult with the cast on, but I haven't let up now that it's off. My arm gets sore from time-to-time, but it's healing nicely. I only hope the whiplash tweak in my neck goes away permanently. I can't complain though. All in all, I'm lucky I'm not more injured from the accident.

I walk up the private sidewalk, avoiding the vibrant rainbows the daughter of a Reformatory resident has drawn all over the cement. I kick a hot pink chalk piece out of the way, so no one trips and falls on it and take the stairs to the rundown porch. The porch door creaks as I yank it open and then crashes behind me, the door having long since lost the contraption that lets it ease closed. I have a feeling the house manager, Jacinda, did it on purpose. No one is sneaking out of the front door of this house. Not with that noise. Windows, however, are another story. Not that I've tried, but I've thought about it a time or two.

Jacinda peeks out into the narrow hallway as I head for the stairs. "Hold up there, Samson."

That's Jacinda's thing, too. She calls us by our last names like we're already in jail.

I clench my jaw. If she thinks I'm pitching in on the housework for one of the older residents because they were pulled in to take a double shift again, she's out of her mind. Keep in mind, I'm nearly always pissy on days I go to PT.

I move back around the corner, waiting for her reply. She motions to the kitchen, a sharp nod encouraging me to step inside as her dark eyebrows pull in severely.

I steel myself and walk forward. I've been trying to stay on this woman's good side. Not that it has made a difference because she's miserable to every last one of us no matter what our attitudes are. "Got someone here to see you," she says, eyeballing me.

My heart kicks into gear. I try not to seem eager, but I pick up the pace, moving quickly to the outdated kitchen, decorated in sunburnt orange. Trust me, it's as unfortunate as it sounds.

I turn the corner but pull up when I find a businessman in a suit, and not the kind of suit guys like Johnny wear in the Heights. This suit is off the rack. Probably from JC Penney's. It's a means to an end, not a fashion statement.

The guy's head moves toward the sound of my footsteps skidding to a stop on the linoleum floor. He smiles at me and stands. His eyes are sharp, even if he does look like he should be living in a different decade.

"Kyla Samson?"

"That's her," Jacinda says in a sickeningly sweet tone I've not heard uttered past her lips yet.

I glance up at her, brows furrowed, but she doesn't give me the time of day. She only has eyes for the stiff. "What's this about?" She tries to smile, but it just looks awkward on her face. The frown she constantly wears is more her style.

The guy removes his gaze from her and greets me again. "Kyla?" he asks again.

I nod, hesitantly. I don't know who this guy is. It could be one of Gregory's men, a cop, or someone the Crew sent, but my money's not on the latter.

The gentleman turns an alarming smile on the house manager. "I need to speak with my client alone."

My back bristles at the same time a swarm of confusion settles over me. *Client?*

"Samson's not allowed to have visitors."

The guy in the suit grins. He's all teeth, and warning bells ring inside my head. The suit is a cover-up or just poor fashion taste. "I believe you'll find it's alright. Feel free to check in with Detective Reynolds on the matter. Kyla?" the suit says, motioning toward the kitchen doorway.

I step through, back bristling still. I don't like giving people I don't know my back, so I look over my shoulder at the man following me down the narrow, dimly lit hallway.

"Your room?"

I give him an incredulous look. If he thinks I'm going to take him to my room alone, he's crazy.

"Ahh, yes. How about we just step out onto the porch then?"

I open the porch door, listening to it scream in protest before taking a seat on the wide railing that boxes in the small porch. He stands in front of me, clasping his hands together at his waist. The first thing I notice is that he doesn't have anything with him. No briefcase. No bag. He called me his client, yet he has no evidence that we're doing business here. I sweep him again for any bulges that could be a telltale sign of hidden weapons, but I don't see any.

Comforted a little, I try to unlock my muscles to appear relaxed. "It's time you told me who you are," I nudge after he doesn't say anything for the first few moments.

The wind tracks a piece of hair over my face, so I bring it back around, tucking it behind my ear and wait for his response.

"I'm Mr. Lordson, attorney for Rocket Enterprises."

I recognize the name—obviously—but I don't show any outward signs to that fact, even though my heartbeat starts to pick up. "You're going to have to do better than that, Mr. Lordson."

"He'll be pleased with that response." Mr. Lordson reaches into one of his interior pockets, a smile playing over his cracked lips.

I still, unable to figure out if he's reaching for a weapon or something else.

He notices my reaction, so he lifts a finger to tell me to hold on a second. My fingers itch to grab the contraband knife I won off another resident from my pocket, but I resist. Finally, it pays off. Mr. Lordson pulls a white packet from his pocket. He takes it in his hands, smoothing it out. With a grin, he passes it over to me.

I take it, instantly recognizing the logo of the hot chocolate I love. I crush it in my fingers and slip it into my pocket. I nod at Mr. Lordson to go on, instantly relaxing. This guy is a friend.

"Now that we got that settled..." He takes a seat on the wide railing with me. Taking a handkerchief from his pocket, he runs it over his forehead before putting it away. "I've been working with Mr. Marx from the beginning of your...delicate situation." He takes a deep breath, resting his hands casually on his thighs. He's older than a lawyer I would've pegged the Crew hiring. His hands are weathered and wrinkled, but with those wrinkles probably comes a hell of a lot of knowledge. "I'm here to tell you that not thirty minutes ago, DA Schneider has decided not to press charges against you for the death of Dominique Jenkins due to lack of evidence."

A whoosh of air releases from my lungs, and I grip the railing with my hands. I'm not being charged with murder. I don't think I've ever heard more glorious words.

Mr. Lordson nods. "They had your fingerprints on the murder weapon, however, just because your prints were on the weapon doesn't mean you pulled the trigger. The eyewitness—"

"Bogus eyewitness," I interrupt, silently seething. There's no way there could've been an eyewitness because I definitely didn't shoot that poor young girl. The whole thing has reeked as a setup from day one.

The corners of Lordson's eyes crinkle. "Well, he has changed his tune, much to the dismay of Detective Reynolds and the DA."

I can't even feel bad about the possibilities that come to mind regarding how the Crew handled that situation, considering the fucker was lying in the first place. "So, not enough evidence?"

"Not at this time," Lordson says. "In cases such as this, they'll usually wait to acquire more evidence. They don't want to charge you formally if there's any possibility a jury wouldn't convict."

His words burn my brain. Something similar was uttered to my aunt and uncle about Big Daddy K murdering my parents, though I suspect that was just bullshit. They were too scared to go after him and what he represented. As far as my case goes, I suspect it's a lot more accurate. "So, it's not over?"

Lordson shakes his head. He glares at the peeling paint that surrounds the picture window. "I'm afraid not, Ms. Samson, however, since they've decided not to pursue you at the moment, you're allowed to leave this place. In fact, I believe—"

The attorney cuts off just as a sleek black car pulls up to the curb. My mind whirs. He's here. One of them is here. *Someone* is here.

For me.

The car parks and sits there, idling. The damned tinted windows don't give any indication in regard to who's inside, and I can barely keep myself together.

I stand on shaky feet, and Mr. Lordson stands with me. "Just one last word, dear. That Detective Reynolds is one persistent SOB. As your lawyer, I need to inform you to stay out of trouble. I have a feeling he'll use anything he has against you, and you're not out of the woods yet. Should other evidence arise, you could be right back here. Or worse." He waits until I move my gaze away from the car to meet his. "Do you understand?"

I hold out my hand. "I do, Mr. Lordson. Thank you for your work on this." He keeps his gaze on me like I should be promising him to stay out of trouble, but I can't possibly promise that, can I? Sitting in that car—no matter who it is—is trouble. Just for the very fact that I'm probably on my way back to the Heights tonight means I'm moving back into the fire.

But I'm doing it anyway. I miss them. All of them.

The time away has made one thing very clear to me. My initial goal is still at the top of my list. Big Daddy K will suffer at my hands; however, I have a dream that comes in at a close second. I want to leave here with all of these guys who are too good for the Heights, whether they know it now or not.

Which means, I have to share some hard truths with

Johnny. In time. If I walked up to him now and told him I had feelings for other guys, he'd kill them. I know it as much as I know the truth in my heart that I can't walk out of the Heights without him either.

Now I just have to figure out how to do everything I came here to do, while keeping my budding relationships intact.

## 3

I walk down the porch steps, my knees quaking so hard that my legs are unsteady. Mr. Lordson moves ahead of me. He ducks his head to look in the front seat and then straightens again, moving to the back of the car, his hands on the door handle.

I gulp in several breaths of air to try to wrangle my heart under control. I didn't run back into the house to grab my things because nothing up there is mine anyway. Let the assholes still stuck here fight over the clothes I was able to scrounge together and the radio alarm clock that's been keeping me company.

If Jacinda knows I'm leaving, she's not hollering after me like a crazed lunatic, so she must've verified this with Detective Reynolds.

I'm free. I'm actually free.

My body shudders at the thought of his name though. The walk to the car is like being stuck between my current life and what's waiting for me. Reynolds won't back down from here on out. I don't think that for one second, but I'll be a hell of a lot happier rolling with the punches with my guys at my side.

"It's okay," Lordson says, as he opens the door.

The interior of the car is completely black inside. It's sunnier than all hell out here, but the minute I get a leg in the car, it takes forever for my eyes to adjust to the lighting. It doesn't help that Lordson slams the door shut as soon as I'm clear of it.

I blink as if doing so will clear my vision faster, but I'm not sure that's actually true because I'm still staring at a dark shadow on the opposite seat from me. My stomach twists like this was a bad idea, but as soon as I think that, a voice croaks on the opposite side. "Kyla."

His sure tenor coats me in protective warmth. No wonder why I couldn't see Magnum. He's wearing his signature all-black outfit. The more my eyes adjust, the creases in his forehead deepen until he scans every last inch of my body. It feels as if he's tearing me apart piece by piece but knitting me back together again with his reassuring gaze. "I was worried about you," I say.

He looks away, his jaw ticking at my honesty.

The hot cocoa packet in my pocket makes a lot of sense now that Magnum is sitting across from me. I knew it was a sign I could trust the lawyer, and that even if Johnny had sent it, it was because of Magnum.

"You shouldn't have been."

The car takes off, and I slide back in my seat. I hurry to put my seatbelt on, and I swear Magnum's gaze darkens even more while he watches me make sure I'm restrained.

"Your cast is off," he says softly, staring at my arm.

"You knew I had a cast?"

He runs his hand down his copper scruff. "We were watching you. You were never alone."

I don't need to push buttons, but it sure as fuck felt like I was alone. None of their faults though, so I can't even get mad. It's a fucked up world we live in.

Magnum opens his mouth, but then shuts it again. The move is so forceful his teeth clank against each other. Tension swirls between us, though I'm not sure why. "Finn said you had to go underground until they figured out how to get you off the hook for shooting that asshole?"

"I should've shot him in the fucking head. He got off too fucking easy."

I lean forward, but the seatbelt locks into place and pulls me back. I scowl. "It wasn't your fault they came for me."

"It's my—" He shakes his head, lips pressing together like he refuses to say whatever words were about to come out of his mouth. "I was supposed to keep you safe and instead, you were in a car accident, almost got dragged off by

Gregory's henchmen, and were accused of fucking murder." A guttural sound passes his lips. "Kyla, fuck."

His voice does something to me. He locks his hazel-green eyes onto mine, staring deep inside like he can see right through the armor I've already had to pull back on. He moves forward, hitting the button to release my seatbelt before moving next to me. Magnum hikes my leg over his lap until we're sitting facing one another. My heart pounds in my chest like a crazy thunderstorm that has less to do with the fact he took my seatbelt off and more to do with him touching me. "I'm so fucking sorry I didn't keep you safe that night." I open my mouth to interrupt, but he barges ahead like a reckless soldier. "Don't you fucking say it wasn't my fault. You're not my job, Kyla." He licks his lips, fingers tightening on my legs. I don't think he realizes how tight he's holding me, and fuck me, I'm not going to tell him to stop. "From the moment you came here, you haven't been a job to me."

My throat dries up like I've spent all this time away in the scorched desert, and I crave Magnum's next words like a tall, cool glass of ice water.

"I wasn't going to say anything," he concedes, warring emotions fighting it out across his features. "I was going to sit back and do my job. I told myself the reason why I was so invested in you was because of the job, but I've been lying to myself for a while. The moment that fucker wrapped his hands around you and tried to drag you to his car, I admitted to myself what was really going on. Fuck me. Add me to the list of guys Johnny's going to end up killing because I can't fucking stop."

He's captured my gaze in a way I can't look away from. The green in his normal hazel eyes is deeper, darker, swirling with the truth he's just admitted.

"I think there's something here but tell me there isn't and I'll never speak of this again."

I open my mouth but slam it closed again. My jaw hurts from keeping it shut tight. Words beg to be said, but I hold them back. I started to realize the increasing tension between Magnum and me before that night. I tried to ignore it because I already care for three men at the same time, and I'm not sure this is one of those scenarios where "What's one more?" works.

The truth is, I can't lie to another guy I like. I can't sit here and tell him I care for him and then hold back the reason why I'm here. I can't do that to Magnum like I did with the others, and there's no way in hell I can tell Magnum the truth. He works for the Crew. He's literally trained to take out threats, and I'm going to be K's biggest one.

Magnum loosens his hold on me. "I guess I misread...everything."

I watch as he slowly pulls his hands away from me. My heart breaks inside. Motherfucking shit! "Don't."

I bite my lip at the word that just forced itself out. Fuck

me sideways. I literally have no restraint at all. It's not my fault. A life filled with love is in my grasp, and I just can't fucking let it walk away. Sure, some people might not understand me, but if they lived life in my shoes, they'd get it. They'd understand the longing for something that was ripped away. I want it back, but I want it ten thousand times greater. I want it to knock me off my feet. I want to be swept away because only that will make what I've gone through worth it.

I lay my hand on his to stop it from retreating. I close my eyes. "I made a mistake with Oscar and Brawler." *Johnny, too*, I think, as I lick my parched lips. Though that one was far more unavoidable. "One I don't want to make with you."

His fingers tighten on me, bunching my jeans in his grip.

"I'm keeping something from you." I have to force the words out like I haven't spoken in ages. In all honesty, I haven't, really. I haven't had a friend. A lover. No one for six weeks. "I can't tell you what it is, and I'm not sorry about it either." What I'm doing is risky. Maybe. I hope not. Gang ties are deep. They're supposed to be everlasting, and I'm here mixing things up. Asking them to trust me and not the institution they grew up in.

Magnum does that thing with his gaze that makes my insides display like an open book. "You don't think I see you?"

My lips part. Nerves skitter over my skin.

"I see the real you," Magnum says. His words set fire to

my heart. Or deeper. My soul. I want to lay everything bare, and at the hint that he might see the real me, I'm lost. "I know you're hiding something." He swallows, looking away briefly before finding my gaze again. "You came to the Heights for a reason, and I get that it means more to you than you ever let on. I'm here for you." He tightens his grip on my jeans again as if he's holding on for dear life. "I'm too fucking greedy to stand by and watch anymore. You want to know what I see when I look at you? Someone who's trying to save everybody. Even herself. I thought you were playing with Johnny at first, but I realized quickly you weren't. You like him. You like his messed-up parts. You want to show him a better life the same way you want to help Oscar and Brawler too."

My eyes itch. Tears work their way to the surface, but I refuse to acknowledge them. "Johnny's going to hate me when he finds out."

All the fears I've had over the last several weeks rise to the surface like I'm on a rogue wave about to crash. I'm going to hurt him. I've wanted to help him, but I might even send him further into a downward spiral of hate he won't be able to recover from.

"Johnny's..." Magnum pauses, his throat working. "I told you he'd burn down the world for you once. Do you remember?"

I nod as the first tear falls. Magnum reaches out, smearing it over my cheek before it runs down my face.

"I think you're the only one who could make him see."

One by one, he catches the tears with his thumbs, flicking them away. It's been a long time since I've cried. It's an emotion I hold back because it's weak. A display that symbolizes how completely overwhelmed I am.

"You just have to show him. We all do."

My heart skips a beat as Magnum leans in. He licks a tear from my face, then rests his lips against my skin. Not doing anything more, just staying connected.

I like the sound of what he's said. In fact, I love it so fucking much. Magnum cares for Johnny. I'm not sure I would've received the same reaction if I'd said those words to Brawler and Oscar, but Magnum has an understanding of him I'm not sure many do. Maybe he sees what I do.

His eyelashes flutter over my skin as the chaste press of his lips turns into more. He trails his bottom lip over my jawline until he reaches the sensitive spot behind my ear. He closes his mouth over my skin, kissing a trail down my neck that has my core tightening.

"I see you," Magnum breathes. He kisses my collarbone. "I know you." He presses his hand to the center of my chest. "This right here is all you need to know about anyone."

God-fucking-damnit, I'm a goner. As if I had a choice in the matter. Feelings don't work like that.

His lips linger on my collarbone before he pulls away, situating me in his lap with his strong arms around my waist.

I glance at the divider securely in place, my heart

thumping so hard it thrums at my wrists. Thankfully, we're alone back here.

Magnum presses a kiss to my shoulder. "How's your neck?" He pulls my collar down, and my neck heats at his inspection.

"Better," I tell him, moving back to rest my head on his shoulder. "I had electrical therapy today."

I turn to the side to look at him, and he lifts his brows. "Does that even work?"

"I'll tell you tomorrow." I smile. "The doctors tell me I'm healing perfectly, but they know I want to get back into fighting, so they're doing everything they can to heal me until I'm brand new."

He closes his eyes for a brief moment, and the guilt coloring his features is unmistakable.

The car hangs a left, and Magnum holds onto me tighter. "Where are we going?" I ask, peeking out the tinted window.

"You're headed back to the Heights to continue on as normal."

Just the way he emphasizes *you're* makes me hesitant. "And everyone else?"

"I haven't seen Brawler since that night. Oscar, I've seen a few times, mostly when the Crew was discussing how to get you back."

I'm sensing he led with the easy parts first. "Johnny?" I ask.

He breathes, and his chest expands underneath me. "He's hanging on by a thread." Magnum kisses my neck as if that will soften the blow. "K wants him to stay in Chicago where they've been holed up, but he's adamant he's coming back to the Heights."

"They've been in Chicago?"

"They left that night." Magnum rests his chin on my shoulder, his scruff pricking my skin. "He arranged everything from there, talking to the Crew here via video conferencing."

"So, he won't be in the Heights when we get back?"

Magnum shrugs. "It depends on who won. Johnny or his father." The usual steady bodyguard shifts underneath me. I turn my head and catch uncertainty in his gaze. He looks over. "K's not used to having something as important as the Crew vie for Johnny's attention."

A smug smirk threatens to come out, but I hold it back. "Let me guess, Big Daddy K isn't happy?"

Magnum shakes his head. "Not at all." He hugs me closer to him briefly. "If it was just a father-son spat, that would be one thing. But you're Crew business now, and at the moment, Johnny's acting like you aren't. He's acting as if you're a separate entity he gets to have for himself. Something he's using his own mind on."

Uneasiness sweeps over me, raising the hairs on the back of my neck. Big Daddy K runs a tight ship. This won't go over well with him. He likes to have every aspect of Johnny and the gang planned out himself. That's why he made up the no sex rule, using me as Johnny's prize for when he moved up.

"I need you to be extra careful," Magnum whispers hoarsely. "The last thing we need is for K to see you as a threat rather than an asset. Johnny's smart enough to know this, too, so if he doesn't come right back to the Heights, don't put his balls in a vise for it."

Interesting choice of words, though not far off from where my mind was headed. However, it's unfair of me to think that way. It's only because I want to see him so badly that I want him on the next plane out of Chicago.

The car starts to slow, so Magnum slips me off him, creating space between us. "Be very careful. Trust no one but me, Brawler, and Oscar."

I lift my brows. "Johnny?"

Magnum strokes his facial hair. "I fucking hope so, Kyla." He glances out of the car. "From this moment forward, you be the good little Crew girlfriend. Got it?"

Before I can answer, he opens the door and stretches his legs out into the familiar underground parking lot.

Emotions tumble inside me. Some hopeful, some laced with anger, but mostly, I do as Magnum says and paint the face of a Crew girl on the outside.

## 4

Disappointment slows my feet, making me stop in the middle of my tower apartment when I realize Johnny's not here. The whole building is suspiciously quiet. No hum of energy on the upper floors. No security personnel walking around. Magnum and I didn't see a single soul on the way to our floor.

As if reading my expression, which I have no doubt he can, Magnum says, "Most everyone went to Chicago. There's just a few key people here to talk with the lawyer and—"

"What about Finn? He said he spoke to Johnny."

"He called him. He had their number because of the gym charges on his credit card."

I blow out a breath. "Hopefully, that's the last time we'll need them. I don't want them mixed up in this shit."

"Agreed," Mag says, wrinkles appearing between his nose. "The fewer the better." He scans the place, but keeps on coming back to me, almost like he can't bear to look away. The discussion we had in the car makes my skin prick. His arms around me felt so right. Like, I don't understand what we were waiting for before.

I glance around the place, noticing everything is just as it was when I left. The housekeeping staff must have been through like usual. There isn't a speck of dust inside the place. My bedroom door is open, and I peek through the entryway to find my bed made with what are probably fresh sheets even though I haven't slept here in weeks.

Magnum's phone goes off in his pocket, and I almost jump. He takes it out, immediately bringing it to his ear. "Yeah. I got her." Magnum moves his stare to look at me. "Sure."

He holds out the phone. I raise my eyebrows, and Magnum nods.

I take the phone, hand shaking a little no matter how hard I try to calm it down. While I was gone, I tried not to think of this moment because I didn't know if it would ever happen. "Hello?"

Johnny expels a breath that sounds as if the weight of the world has been on his shoulders. "Babe."

I bite down on my lip. I secretly love it that he calls me babe, and I freaking missed it. "Yeah." I smile but smooth it out afterward. I'm caught between happiness and sweet relief.

"Has Magnum checked your rooms yet?"

I glance up to find Magnum walking through the apartment. He disappears into the bedroom, pokes his head into the bathroom before coming back out and looking in the front closet. "Yeah. We're all clear."

Another sigh passes his lips. "I'm sorry I'm not there. I'm sorry— Fuck, I'm sorry for so many fucking things right now."

"It's not your fault."

He growls, the sound ripping from his throat and almost knocking me on my heels. "I brought you into the Crew. It *is* my fault."

A hot sweat breaks out over my forehead. If he only knew I wanted to be brought into the Crew. "Well, I'm not playing that game with you, so you can stop it. What's done is done. You got me out." I wish I could see his face right now, but I imagine he's chewing his lip, going back and forth between continuing to argue with me and wanting to hold me.

"Did Magnum fill you in?"

"I think so," I say, peeking at Magnum who's taken up a spot by the door. He crosses his arms, legs spread wide in that authoritative stance I love.

His voice comes out strained. "I want to be there with you. You know that, right?"

"I know."

"I'll be there as soon as I can. In the meantime, Magnum and Oscar will be watching over you. The tower is safe. No one will be coming for you anytime soon. We took out a couple of Gregory's guys even though we haven't been able to fucking find him yet. We've been gathering as much intel as we can, and I'm trying to convince my father to get our asses back to the Heights so we can do more. I'm hoping now that the charges against you have been dropped, he'll relent."

The animosity coming through the line isn't veiled at all. He's clearly pissed at his father. "You know I'm with you one hundred percent."

He groans. "God, I just need to see that you're okay. I'm dying here—" A voice calls for Johnny on the other end of the line, and Johnny snaps. "I said give me a fucking minute."

A short pause silences the line before the same person says, "Are you finally talking to her? Thank fuck. Your morose ass is unpleasant." I pin the voice as coming from Jiko Cardinale immediately. It's an easy deduction knowing they're in Chicago and Johnny doesn't let just anyone talk to him that way.

A glass shattering breaks the connection for a second.

"Alright, alright," Jiko says, cracking up like it's any other day. The asshole is fucking laughing. "Hey there, Kyla," he shouts. "I'm glad you didn't end up in an orange jumpsuit. It wouldn't suit you." I roll my eyes, but there's a yelp and a slammed door on the other side of the line.

Fucking good. I hope Johnny hurt him. "What did you do?"

"Just pulled my knife on him."

I cock my head to the side, wishing I could've seen that one. "I thought Jiko was your friend."

"He talks too goddamn much."

Now that makes me smile, which makes the tears threaten again. I haven't smiled at all in the last six weeks. I've been going through the motions, doing what I've been told, but losing the guys was like missing pieces of myself. I'm already all the way down this road and then some. "Johnny, we have a lot of talking to do."

"I know," he says, agitation still lacing his voice. "These were the worst weeks of my life, Kyla."

My heart nearly splits in two. They were up there for me, but I've had worse. Sadly.

"When I come back, we'll talk, okay?"

"Yeah," I tell him, voice raspy. I don't want him to hate himself for what's happened. It's not his fault. He's blaming the wrong person.

"I have to go." He sighs reluctantly. "Oscar will get you another phone since RHPD won't cough your other one up."

"Okay."

"Um, Kyla?"

"Hmm?"

"I... I um..." Another silence descends, but eventually he says, "I'll call you soon."

"Okay, Johnny. Bye."

"Bye."

I hang the phone up and hold it out to Magnum. He crosses the length of the floor to take it from me. After pocketing it, he reaches up, brushing his fingers under my eyes. "Why do you look so sad?"

I swear my heart clenches. Like literally squeezes like it's going through physical pain. "Johnny really cares for me."

Mag nods.

Everything I'm doing to this guy compounds. I blink up at Magnum. "I think I'm going to break him."

Magnum pulls me close, wrapping his strong arms around me. "I'm not so sure about that. Johnny's stronger than you know. A strength that has nothing to do with the Crew, Kyla."

I swallow, keeping my emotions at bay. I have to be strong right now. "Care to elaborate?"

He runs his hands through my hair. "I think that's a conversation you and Johnny need to have."

I'll add that to the list of things I need to say to him, including the fact that I care about three other guys. Oh, and I want to off his father. I mean, what could go wrong with that conversation?

A knock sounds on the door, and Magnum steps back. I jump, holding him to me briefly before remembering that I'm in the tower, which is the safest place for me.

"I have a surprise for you," Mag says, peeling my fingers away from him. He walks toward the door, pulling it open to reveal two figures. Seeing them immediately glues my feet where I stand.

Brawler nudges Oscar out of the way. Amid a spewed line of Oscar-esque profanities, Brawler rushes toward me.

"Stop," Magnum orders.

Brawler halts, but his jaw ticks, looking torn between obeying and just coming for me anyway.

Mag holds his hand out, wiggling his fingers at both guys. I watch on in surprise as Oscar and Brawler pull out their cell phones and hand them over to Magnum who holds a small device. He runs the handheld piece of technology over both phones and then hands them back.

"You check the place?" Oscar asks.

"We're clear," Magnum announces, nodding.

"What the hell is that?" I ask, pointing to the thing Mag is just now putting in his back pocket.

I barely get the words out before I'm squished against Brawler's hard chest. He rains kisses down on the crown of my head, holding me lightly in his arms as if he doesn't want to hurt me.

"Back off, Big Man," Oscar says from behind him.

"Fuck you," Brawler growls, only holding me tighter.

"Then you're about to feel my arms...and a very happy dick."

Brawler groans, moving so Oscar has just enough space to wriggle his arms around me. He tucks my head under his chin, fingers gripping me. I reach my hands under his shirt to pull him toward me, and he hisses when I hit a spot on his side.

I pull away, eyeing him. I immediately get drawn into his handsome face. His black ballcap hides his tuft of black hair, but his dark eyes are laser sharp.

"What's wrong?"

He shakes his head, but Magnum throws him under the bus without a second thought. "Gregory's guys ran him off the road before they hit us."

"The fuck?"

Oscar glares Magnum's way before turning to me. "It's just a bit of road rash. It's practically healed already."

I move forward, snatching his shirt up. I don't know what it looked like before, but mottled bruising mars his side. His beautiful, chiseled abs side. "Oscar..." Anger scorches through me as I look at what they did to him.

He pushes his shirt back down. "It's nothing."

"I'm so sorry."

"Are you kidding me?" he snaps. He roams his gaze all over me until he's inspected every square inch of my skin. "How are you feeling?"

"Cast's off," I say, lifting my arm lamely. "It's not too

bad. I don't think I should push it, but I might be able to start some light training. My neck still hurts every now and then. I should probably find a PT place closer to the Heights. The guys at the place I've been going to are dicks, looking at me like I, you know, murdered someone."

Brawler growls.

"On it," Magnum says. He takes out his phone, fingers moving over the screen. He's probably texting Johnny right this second about what I need, unless he's taking care of it himself, which I wouldn't put past him, now that he's let himself feel what he does for me.

"Princess," Oscar starts, eyes pleading with mine already. "I would've come."

"I know," I tell him.

"I was going to," Brawler laments, sliding a furious glance Magnum's way.

"I know," I tell them both. I take one of their hands in each of mine. "You couldn't have, anyway. Reynolds had eyes on me, and not seeing anyone was part of the stipulation I was given."

"You didn't have to follow their fucking rules."

I squeeze Oscar's hand and then bring his palm to my lips to place a kiss there. "I didn't kill anyone. I just wanted to show I was working with them. That I didn't have anything to hide by returning to the Heights and masking myself behind the Crew."

"But you put yourself in danger," Magnum says, speaking up.

I was surprised Johnny didn't say anything about that. I have no doubt it's coming. "It was my decision, and I made it. Besides..." I lift an eyebrow in his direction. "You told me I was never alone."

"That's where you kept going, wasn't it?" Oscar asks, crossing his arms. He shakes his head. "I fucking knew it." Magnum shrugs unapologetically. He opens his mouth to say something, but Oscar cuts him off. "If you say it's because Princess is your job, I'm calling bullshit."

I peer at Magnum. Neither one of us talked about how to approach the subject of him and I with the group. Of course, Oscar Drego is perceptive as shit. He had it called right from the beginning.

Magnum's not one to back down though. He only holds my gaze for a moment before turning to Oscar and Brawler. I think he's going to tell them he likes me too and to shut the fuck up about it, but instead, when he opens his mouth, the purest honesty comes out. "I suspected I might like Kyla, but I wasn't sure. When they stole her out of my car, though, my world tilted." He balls his hands at his sides. "I knew then the feelings I had for her were more than just friendly. I was going to say something to you guys, but I felt I should say something to Kyla first."

Three sets of eyes move to me. I squirm under all their gazes. "And what did Princess say to that?"

Fuck me, but I actually missed Oscar pushing my buttons by calling me Princess. I hope he never stops, which means I have to keep pretending it bothers me. "Princess says you should stop fucking calling her that." A messy ball of emotion crawls up my throat, and I'm not sure I'm fooling anyone.

"Kyla..." Brawler says. I glance up at worried turquoise eyes.

"This is just as awkward for me as it is for you."

Oscar barks out a laugh. "You sound like you're about to have the sex talk with us. Christ, we know about contraceptives, we want to know who else is sticking their dick inside you."

"Classy, Drego," Magnum mutters. "I haven't stuck my dick inside her."

The weight of their gazes makes my skin clammy. It's not that I'm not going to tell them. I want to tell them, but I just never figured on having a conversation that starts with, "Yeah, so I really want to jump four guys." Does anyone think they're going to have a conversation that starts like that? If they do, maybe they should run with that in sex-ed class instead of how to put condoms on bananas.

I'm sick of hiding behind secrets. I match their gazes, looking into each of their eyes. "I like Magnum. I like Oscar. I like Brawler," I say, smiling at him. Then, I hesitate briefly before I say, "And I like Johnny Rocket." I stick my chin in the air because it's that name that I think could ruffle some feathers. Mainly Brawler's because Oscar and Magnum already know.

Brawler turns away, running his hands through his blond hair. "Johnny Rocket? Are you kidding me? He's going to get you killed, Kyla!"

"If anything, it's me getting myself killed, and you know that," I say, piercing him with a glare. He knows it was my decision to come to the Heights, to get stuck in the Crew. No, I hadn't planned on Rocket claiming me, but I wouldn't take it back at this point either.

I'm in deep with him. Not the Crew.

I look at each of the guys in turn. Brawler and Oscar only tolerate one another. Magnum might be Switzerland. At least, he was before, but I'm not so sure now. Johnny is the wild card, but it became clearer to me while I was away that I'm not giving him up. He can choose not to be with me, but I'm sure as hell not pushing him away. This isn't an either-or scenario. I'm not picking and choosing the guys based on who each of them tolerate. It's because I like them. It's because I care for them. It's kind of like I'm an animal tamer with a whip. I want them to fall in line, but I can't make them do it either. Ultimately, it's their choice whether they want this with all of us or not.

"I care about all of you, but I'm not the only one involved in this," I finally say. Nerves rush through me, and I'm a dorky teenage girl again wanting to ask her crush to the dance. Fear sluices through me that one of them might up and walk away because of this, but I can't let that emotion hold me back. I won't let it. It's better that they know now what they're getting into. "A relationship like this wouldn't be conventional, but neither are any of us," I say. "I'm in it. This is it. It's us five for me. No one else." I bite my lip. "Are you guys in?"

## 5

The silence fucks me up. Each passing moment sounds like a nail in my coffin. I've already had my heart set on all of these guys, but I understand the notion is ridiculous. Crazy, even. I mean, who do I think I am taking four extremely fuckable guys off the market at once?

I'm going to get lynched in the court of able-visioned women, ages eighteen to seventy-three.

I don't expect Oscar to be the first to speak up. "I already suspected you had it bad for Johnny." He grits his teeth. "I've had to live with a fuckton of shit, so I know when a good thing comes along." He steps toward me, stooping down to claim my mouth in a heated kiss that sends shivers all the way to my toes. "I'm in," he says over my lips. Pulling away just a fraction, he gives me one of his salacious grins. "I don't know how Johnny's going to take it, but I'm looking forward to that playing out. As long as he doesn't kick my ass again."

"Yeah, let's hope that doesn't happen again," I agree. But who am I kidding? It could get much worse than that. Johnny isn't the type to share, which is why I've kept my mouth shut this entire time.

I start to turn toward Brawler, but Magnum speaks up next. "I knew what I was getting myself into from the beginning." His hazel-eyed gaze ricochets through me. Heated promises linger in his depths, and my nipples peak under his scrutiny. I try not to fall down the rabbit hole of wondering how Magnum treats his loved ones. If it's anything like his personality, he'll care with an unguarded intensity. I wasn't expecting to have this conversation so soon, and already, I feel like shit because Brawler and Oscar know something he doesn't.

"Johnny?" Brawler asks again, his tone definitely giving off a case of *What the fuck?* The apprehension weighing his shoulder is tough to look at.

I move toward him, taking his hands in mine. "He can be saved, Brawler. I know it."

"That's assuming he wants to be." His cold gaze twists my stomach.

Magnum hits Oscar in the shoulder, and despite Oscar looking like the last thing he wants to do is walk away, they both go into the kitchen to give us a little privacy.

"You're mad..." I start.

Brawler runs his hands through his hair again. "I don't know what to think. Maybe I refused to see it. I don't know. Every time you were with him when I was around, you seemed off. I thought it was because you didn't want him to touch you."

I bite down on my lip. It wasn't that. I just thought *he* would hate seeing it. "I was scared to say something. I thought you... Well, you hate the Crew so much."

His jaw snaps shut. "I thought we had that in common."

"We do. Fuck. You'd hate them too for what they've done to him. It's all he knows, Brawler."

He searches my gaze, shaking his head. "Oscar was forced to join. I get that, but—"

"Johnny didn't have a choice either. He was brought up in it. He knows no other way. I've seen the good parts of him," I plead. If Brawler walks away, it will break me. Not that I wouldn't deserve it. I keep turning the tables on him. I'm fucking everything up. "None of you were a part of my plan," I tell him. "God, none of you, but pieces inside each of you match up perfectly with me." Oscar laughs in the kitchen, and I smile, tentative at first before turning back to Brawler. "The Crew's his family right now, and he's loyal and caring. Imagine what he would be if *we* turned into his family, Brawler?"

His hard edges soften. "Is that what you want? A family?"

A breath expels from my chest. Goddammit. I do. "More

than anything. We all deserve it." Our backgrounds flit through my brain like a photo album. Brawler, whose mother is lost to depression because his brother and sister were murdered. Oscar and his mother who can't care for him, let alone herself, because of her addictions. Magnum, whose father was killed while he was in the Crew, and whose mother won't have anything to do with him because of it. We're all missing that most vital piece that makes us human.

Maybe I'm talking out of my ass, but I think we can have it with each other.

Brawler must follow my line of thought because he laces his fingers with mine. "I trust you. I'm putting one hundred percent of my trust in you. If you think Johnny can be saved..." He shakes his head. "...I'm in."

"I won't let you down."

Brawler scoops me up. I wrap my legs around his waist, holding him to me as tightly as possible. He breathes into my neck. "Who am I kidding?" he murmurs. "These last several weeks, I was already contemplating what I would do without you, Kyla, and it wasn't pretty. I finally realized why my mom—"

A shiver runs through me. He better not mean what I think he means. I pull away to stare into his dark blue depths.

He shakes his head, lips firmly closed, telling me he doesn't want to talk about it. I slant my mouth over his.

Where words fail me, my touch will make him see. Hopefully, I can ingrain in every fiber of his being that he is worthy of everything he's never had.

"Is this what we have to look forward to?" Oscar deadpans. "Watching our girl makeout with one of us?"

Brawler deepens the kiss, palming my ass in his big hands until my toes straight up curl. I'm pretty sure he's grabbing my ass for Oscar's benefit, but I'm not stopping him. I've missed him—all of them.

When he pulls his lips from me, he lets me slide down his torso, his arousal pressing into my stomach like a dirty promise. No matter how much I want to lean into him, there's more that needs to be discussed right now. I turn to face the rest of them, a little dazed. They're both staring at me with their brows raised. Confusion slithers through me like I've missed something. "Um, what?"

Magnum chuckles from his spot on the couch.

"Focus, Princess." Oscar snaps his fingers, and despite it being all sorts of wrong, it works in bringing me out of my funk. Only because now I want to slap his smug face. "You got what you wanted, so now what?"

I glance between all of them, but something still isn't sitting right. They've pledged their allegiance to me, so it's only fair.

I slip away from Brawler and kneel at Mag's feet. He edges the cup of cocoa he got for me closer, like that's the reason I'm sitting here. I ignore it for the time being even though it smells divine. I haven't had hot chocolate in exactly six weeks.

"You're with us, right?" I ask.

Magnum's brows furrow.

"Me. Us," I tell him, motioning toward Oscar and Brawler. "Not the Crew."

"More than you know," he says, lips thinning.

I press my tongue against my teeth as I contemplate how to say this. This is one giant fucking leap, but since I'm getting real with everyone here, it needs to be done. I can't leave Magnum out of the loop. It's not right. I wouldn't even do it to Johnny if I knew he wouldn't just go ape shit and kill us all.

"Oh shit," Oscar says, already knowing what I'm going to say. I don't dare look at him.

Magnum peeks a look over his shoulder at him before turning back to me. "Is this the secret you told me about?"

I nod. "I just need to make sure you're with me."

I stare into his eyes while Oscar says, "Maybe you should teach him the secret handshake, Princess."

I glare at Oscar because this is fucking serious, but he's always unapologetic about his actions. Instead of returning my look, he rolls his hand over like I should get to talking. It's good if he thinks we can trust him.

"I'm with you," Mag says, ignoring Oscar's jibe as well. He cups my chin and forces me to look at him again. He's so ruggedly handsome. His facial hair ages him into hot older man territory, even though he's technically not that much older than me.

I wait until his words coat me. I let them fill me up until I feel the rightness of it, and then I'm not scared to tell him. Licking my lips, I say, "Big Daddy K murdered my parents when I was twelve, and I'm going to kill him for it."

Mag blinks. Then, he pulls me up to straddle his lap, placing his hands on my cheeks like I didn't just announce I was going to murder his boss. He stares into my eyes for a long while before saying, "Thank you for telling me your secret."

"Why does the new guy get to hold her?" Oscar whispers.

"Shut the fuck up, Drego," Brawler barks back, clearly exasperated.

Oscar shrugs, but I turn my full attention back to Magnum because he took that admission like a champ. I raise an eyebrow. "That's it?"

"That's it," he says. "I knew it had to be serious since you refused to leave the Heights." He drops his hands to my shoulders, squeezing me briefly.

I eye him, waiting for the moment where he tells me it can't be done. Or that it's too dangerous, but Magnum doesn't utter any of those words. He just turns me around in his lap so I can lean over and grab the cocoa he made me.

I look around, watching each of them take the moment in with a quiet confidence, and it warms my heart. This moment had been scaring the shit out of me for the longest time, but now that we're here—together—a little piece of the other side comes into view, making me crave it even more.

One day, we're all going to be out of the Heights, and I'm going to love every single second of it.

## 6

It turns out the thing Magnum used to scan Oscar and Brawler's cell phones is a device used to detect bugs—listening and recording technology. Apparently, he's been using it all along, checking my apartment since the moment I got it, as well as the cars we use.

I have a lot to learn about this life. It never dawned on me anyone might want to hear what I'm saying or see what I'm doing unless it was to get to Johnny and the Crew.

Magnum's relinquished his hold on me. I'm sitting on the floor in front of him, legs crossed at the ankles. Brawler's in front of me, our feet rubbing against one another while Oscar eye fucks me from his spot on the couch. I swear every time I catch him looking, it's as if he's undressing and doing naughty, naughty things to me.

Magnum runs his hand through my hair. "It's not just

other people I was worried about," he says, continuing our conversation on what's been going down since I left. "I did it in case Johnny was spying on you."

I still. Brawler stops playing footsy with me. I tweak my neck back.

Mag shakes his head. "He never did."

A sense of relief coats my suddenly buzzing skin. I'm going to come clean with Johnny about everything, but I need to bide my time. If he saw anything between me and the other guys, he would get the wrong impression. I'm not with them and not him. I'm not playing him. I'm with *all* of them. A family, like Brawler said. I get that from his point of view he might not think that, so that's why I have to make him get behind the rest of the guys, or die trying because that's probably exactly what it will come down to.

"Thank fuck for that." Oscar runs his hands through his dark hair and then puts his ballcap back on. Have I mentioned I think it's so damn sexy when guys wear baseball hats? Especially when they look like Oscar when they do. He owns that shit. When Oscar lifts his gaze, he smirks at me. "You've got a little something," he says, pointing to the side of his mouth.

"Ha. Ha." I wipe my mouth anyway in case I was drooling because I wouldn't put it past myself. I've been away from them for six weeks. I give myself a mental high five to the face to keep myself on track. "Where are we at with Gregory? Johnny says he got away, but the Crew got a couple of his other men."

Magnum traces the pad of his thumb over my neck. "We did. I shot the one guy. He didn't die, but a couple of the other guards were able to chase their car after they left the scene. They found where they were hanging out and took a few of them out. Gregory got away though. He never made the stop back to their safe house."

"So, that's why Johnny and K are staying in Chicago? They don't want to be traced back to the killings?"

"It's just better all-around if they stay away," Mag tells us. "They don't want to be implicated, and every time there's something big like this, something public, the media and the police make a big show about trying to do something about the gang problem."

I bite the inside of my cheek. That's not always the truth. Sometimes they're more than happy to look the other way as my family well knows.

"Interesting that he didn't come back though," Brawler offers. I already know he's judging Johnny for staying away. For not being here for me.

Magnum halts his touch on me. "It's not his fault. It's K's. I know all of us have some weird shit wrapped up in the Crew, but I'll be the first one to say that Johnny cares for Kyla. One hundred percent. I've never seen him like this. Parts of him that I thought were long gone are coming out. He's furious with his father that he's not back here right now. He's staying away to help Kyla at this point because if he comes here for her, K won't be happy about what Kyla's doing to the guy he's had his sights on for taking over. He won't take it out on Johnny. It'll be Kyla who suffers."

Brawler's ears blush to a deep crimson, and the rest of his body goes rigid like the calm before a storm.

"Don't kill the messenger, man," Mag says. "I'm just saying if you're doubting that Johnny actually cares for Kyla, think again." He rubs his thumb just under my ear. "I think she might just be his savior."

Goosebumps sprout over my skin. The thought should terrify me, but instead, I'm ready. Bring it on. All of us can help Johnny. All of us can help each other. Johnny might need it the most right now, but this is going to be a long road for every single one of us.

"I just don't understand how she's going to do that," Brawler says. He pulls his feet back and sits cross-legged. "In case any of us are missing the point, she also wants to kill his dad, which I don't think he'll just take lying down."

"He's got a point," Oscar says. "Maybe you're working on something that just won't happen. Can you give up killing K if it means being with Johnny? Because I sure as fuck would like to get out of the Heights as soon as possible. Football's over. Fucking—"

Oscar's rant has me squeezing my nails into myself. "Nope. No. Not happening. Big Daddy K is going to pay for what he did to me. I'm not leaving the Heights until it's done." I meet Oscar's gaze. When I see him, I see his body wrecked by more than just football. His mind, too. Growing up anywhere else, Oscar would've been someone. Colleges would be knocking his door down. I saw it enough in the fancy little prep school I used to go to. No wonder why he's so damn ready to get out of here. "I don't want to keep you here," I tell him, meaning every word.

Oscar gets to his feet, stepping around me and storming to the other side of the room. "I'm not leaving."

I move to my feet and pad over to him. He's staring out the window, arms crossed. I slip my arms around him from the back, pulling him to me. "We're not giving up our dreams. It's like, what, December?"

Oscar laughs, the sound pained and lost. "So, after you kill K, you're just going to what? Continue on at another high school? Go to college like nothing happened?" He places his hand on my arm to soften the blow.

I step in front of him, lifting my head at a slight angle so I can look him in the eye. "I am. It's about living the rest of my life just as much as it ever was about killing K. To me, if we all don't get out of here and start living those lives we wanted before the Crew, killing K won't have mattered. I need you to dream, Oscar. I need you to apply for colleges where you can play football."

He shakes his head. "No one's looking at me, Kyla. Scouts won't even come to the Heights."

"Then you make them look. Didn't you tell me about some scholarship before?"

He grimaces. "The All-State? It's not happening."

"Then we'll do something else. We'll get you some aid and you can be a walk on. You can play a year at a community college and then get recruited to a bigger one. You must have film of you playing, right? I'll help you send out copies to every school in this state. Hell, to any schools in this country. You're good, Oscar Drego. You deserve to be seen."

Oscar takes my hands and moves them off him. He gives me a half-hearted smile. "I lost the fight in me somewhere along the way, Princess." He squeezes my hands. "I mean, I'm just a druggy prostitute's son." He drops my hands and turns.

I don't let him get far. "No. No, fuck that," I say, eyeing all three of them. "I don't care who we are here. Here, in the Heights, I'm a soon-to-be murderer. Oscar, you're the would-have-been star quarterback. Brawler, you're the bareknuckle fighter who fights for the local crowd when you should be in an octagon in the UFC. Magnum...I don't know. Fuck." *Reminder to myself to find out what Magnum would be if he left here because I'm dying to know.* Surely, his goal isn't to keep the Heights Crew alive anymore. "This is just something I'm doing right now to get to where I want to be. It's like braving the storm to get out the other side unscathed."

"What do you want, Kyla?" Magnum asks. "When all this is over?"

I swallow to keep my emotions in check. What I want is so basic. I don't dare to think beyond that. I don't know about college, though I think it's a good idea. I don't know about fighting, even though I'd love to. But all that would be icing on the cake because what I really, really want is to just be surrounded by people I love. That's all I've ever wanted since I was twelve. "You," I say. "All of you. Around me. Being there for me. Caring for me." The L-word is on the tip of my tongue, but fuck if I can say it right now. I don't want to put a name to the emotion because what if I lose it all again? It will eat me from the inside out next time.

Brawler rises to his feet. My heart lodges in my throat as he prowls forward, not giving me any time to think. He dips, capturing my lips with his, kissing me thoroughly. His tongue presses against my lips until I relent, giving him access to all of me. Whether he's meaning it in this way or not, his kiss is like a balm to my soul. When he pulls away, my lips feel swollen and worshipped. "I'm there," he says. He turns toward Oscar. "I'll help you, too. Kyla's right. You shouldn't give up on football because we got dealt shitty hands with a deck no one cares about anymore."

Oscar rubs the back of his neck. He hits his cap, making it sit awkwardly on his head. He grabs it off, turns toward me, and puts it on my head. Leaning down, he kisses me. "I need a moment. I'll see you tomorrow, okay?"

I grab his hand to hold him back. "Don't go."

He wiggles out of it. "It's okay. I'm good. I just...I'll be here tomorrow, alright?"

Oscar makes it to the door before Brawler leans over to kiss my temple. "I'll go after him. Don't worry. We got this shit handled."

I watch them both go, the door closing behind them. Magnum gets up to lock it as I blow out a breath. "He's not used to having people stick up for him, not even in front of himself."

"Which is why we need to get out of here." I rub my temples, and Magnum moves up, placing his hands on my hips. I love how he's gone from staying away to touching me like it's natural.

"Sorry," he says, like he's somehow heard my train of thought. "I just don't want to stop touching you now that I can." He drops his forehead to mine. "I was sure Johnny would be able to get you back, but...it didn't ease my worries any."

My heart squeezes in my throat. His presence looms over me, dousing my body in sensations. Curiosity pricks at me. Magnum and I were friends first. Countless hours spent with each other in his apartment and in the car while he carted me everywhere. We became easy talking buddies after a while, but after the weeks have passed, this seems like a giant leap I can't wait to take, but it's still a leap.

"I will go as slow as you want," he breathes.

My body hums in approval, a slight vibration that automatically moves me closer to him. His arms wind around my back, and I have to remind myself to breathe. "If you're with me, what do you want after this, Magnum?" I smile, remembering that day in the hospital when the detective let the cat out of the bag about Mag's name. "Detective Reynolds told me your real name."

The corner of his mouth teases up. "I *am* with you." He leans over, his lips brushing against mine. "And you can call me by my real name."

"Jacob," I say, testing the sound of it on my lips, but only serving to increase the friction between us. My mouth buzzes, tingling with excitement as it moves over Magnum's plump lips.

"Say it again." His demanding voice sets fire to my core.

"Jacob."

He covers my mouth with his own, teasing and prying, spreading my lips apart, so he can dive his tongue inside. I moan hard, leaning my hips into him until he pulls me that much closer, removing all distance between us. He reaches his hand up my back, tangling in my hair until he holds me in place while he ravishes me. He plays my mouth like a kissing prodigy, knowing exactly what and where and how to have me gasping for breath.

"I miss my real name," he says finally. His chest slides against mine as we both compete for the same air.

"Magnum is pretty badass though."

"I just miss being me," he admits. "Not an arm of the Crew, but Jacob Cotton—" He presses his lips together.

I swallow. "You didn't tell me what you wanted after all this."

"Just to be me again," he says. "That's what I want. To be me again. With you. To let everyone see me."

"That's pretty vague." I don't even know the words coming out of my mouth right now because I keep staring at his lips and trying to regain a state of steady breathing.

"It's all I got." He groans when I arch into him. "I have to go before I take you into that room and screw up everything I just promised you."

He leans my head back, searching my face.

"Don't," I tell him. "I don't want to be alone again."

He kisses my cheek, hand massaging my neck before he finally speaks. "Okay."

Magnum follows me into my room. He leaves me to get ready for bed, getting comfortable in a chair in the corner. When I come out of the bathroom in one of Johnny's shirts and nothing else, his eyes blaze, but he stays where he is. I'm okay with this.

I slip under the covers, telling him goodnight. He whispers it back, and that's the last thing I'm conscious of as I drift off to the most content sleep I've had in the last few weeks.

## 7

Without the threats surrounding me, I sleep most of the day away. I never let my guard down at Greenlawn's. Most of the people there were supposed to be there. Unlike me, they'd actually done the shit they were accused of. I tried to stay out of their hair, but by refusing to involve myself with any of them, I made myself a target that I was constantly looking over my shoulder for.

That's not to mention Gregory or Detective Reynolds.

I don't know if Gregory ever tried looking for me while I was at Greenlawn, but he had a prime opportunity to find me there and do what he wanted. The RHPD said they were keeping my whereabouts top secret, and the Crew obviously didn't tell anyone either. Thankfully, I came out unscathed with an unhealthy addiction of watching my back. Most nights, I barely slept, so knowing Magnum was in the room last night gave me my first restful sleep in a month.

When I roll out of bed, I stumble to the windows and open the blinds, letting the warmth of the sun shine in. Greenlawn was so gross—even worse than the apartment I had in Brawler's building—so I'm never letting this place go to waste again. The tower is like living in a fancy hotel.

"God, you look beautiful in the morning."

I start, my heart already in my throat. I hate I'm like this now, always wondering what's about to get me.

"I'm sorry, Princess." Oscar moves behind me, clasping my wrists in his hands, rubbing soothing circles along my pulse point.

"It's not you."

He spins me, taking me in. I'm sure I look like I've slept for sixteen hours, but he's wise enough not to say anything.

"Something's up. K wants a video chat with all of us this morning, so you should get ready."

I close my mouth so tight I'm afraid I might break a tooth. "What time?"

Oscar moves hair off my shoulder, still watching me intently. "You got about a half hour."

I nod.

He pulls me to him abruptly. "I'm sorry for leaving last night. Everything you said, I want it. I'm just so fucking scared to want anything anymore because the only thing I've ever wanted that I've been able to keep is you. I keep waiting for that to blow up in my face, too."

I snuggle into his neck, kissing the slight curve lightly as I breathe him in. He's freshly showered and smells like a rainforest. "You got me," I tell him. "Nothing is going to change that. And you will play football again, Oscar. I promise."

"Why is it whenever you say it, I believe it, but every time I try to tell myself the same thing, it sounds like a load of shit?"

I pull away, fingers just grazing his chin. "I hear I'm quite convincing."

His eyes change, switching from adoration to something much more primal. "There's so much dick in this apartment."

"What?" I laugh. Totally not what I was expecting him to say.

"I'm just wondering how we're ever going to have time for one another. I want my sexy cheerleader."

I make a mental note to buy an actual cheerleader uniform. Better yet, I can steal one from school. Oscar would probably jizz his pants to see me in Heights colors.

"Fuck me. Don't look at me like that." He turns me away from him and taps my ass. "Shower. I'm sure the Crew wants their princess looking like royalty."

I do as he says, hopping in the shower, taking an even quicker one than I ever did at Greenlawn despite the fact that there's zero soap scum in this shower, and I don't have to worry about any of the pervy residents walking in on me.

Well, that's probably not true, but I wouldn't actually mind any of the guys here walking in on me, so there's the difference.

When I get out of the shower, I find everything right where I left it. I run a brush through my hair and put on a minimal amount of makeup before moving out into my room to dress. My closet is stocked with the same skimpy outfits, so instead of pulling on any number of those, I grab some joggers and a cut-off t-shirt. Once I'm dressed, I run my fingers through my still wet hair, but it'll have to do because I'm sure my half hour is up.

I haven't heard a word out of the guys since I've been in here, so I walk out. It turns out Brawler is the only one in the apartment. He lifts his head from his phone when I walk in. Rising to his feet, he pulls me in for a quick hug before saying. "They're next door in Mag's place. You better go."

He leads me to the door, opening it. Mag's door is open, and the copper-headed bodyguard is sitting facing the door, so he waves for me to come in and then gestures for me to shut the door behind me. Brawler stays where he is, which makes sense because this is Crew business, and luckily, Brawler isn't Crew.

"She just walked in," Oscar says.

Oscar moves over, allowing me space on Mag's couch. I sit, facing the laptop that's open in front of us that holds

Johnny and his father. I trap a breath in my chest after seeing Johnny. He has a fresh black eye, and I immediately ball my hands to fists. Whoever touched him will fucking pay for that.

I'm about to open up my mouth and ask when Magnum butts in. "What do you need me to do?"

Big Daddy K smiles at Magnum approvingly. Subtle differences differentiate this Magnum with the Jacob of yesterday. This one looks like a giant steel rod is shoved up his ass. He's so tense. His face not only impassive but serious. It's a far cry from the guy who hugged me yesterday, but I understand the role each of us need to play. I wish I could play it better myself sometimes.

"I'll get to that shortly but let me take a look at Kyla here."

I take my eyes off Johnny. Other than a sad smile he gave me that I didn't return, he's super stiff next to his father, and I'm immediately on edge thinking it was K who hit him.

"I'm glad to see you back at the tower and safe."

*Focus, Kyla. Fucking focus.* I need to act the part, and with the way Johnny's eyes are begging me right now, I know he's thinking the same thing. "Thanks to you and Johnny," I say. "Let me know what I can do to make it up to you."

"Nonsense," K says, though it doesn't look like he believes the words at all. "That's what family is for."

My stomach heaves, and I throw up a little in my mouth.

After just imagining my family being the ones surrounding me right now, the thought that Big Daddy K would even be in the vicinity is physically making me sick.

"I just can't figure out why your fingerprints would've shown up on the gun."

I swallow and take a leap. Heights kids own guns, so this shouldn't be a revelation. "Probably because it's my gun," I tell K, locking gazes with him. He tilts his head just off-center, so I continue. "My gun was in my apartment, but it got ransacked after the shootout that night. What I don't understand is how the police knew they were my finger-prints. It's not as if I've ever been in trouble before."

"Fucking Reynolds," Johnny curses. "I told you he was after her for some reason."

His father sneers at him, but Johnny doesn't back down.

"He probably got your fingerprints from that school. Didn't you have a meeting with him in the principal's office that one time? He could've gotten it off anything you touched."

A meeting? If he means browbeat into talking to him, then yes, I guess it was a meeting. Either way, his explana-tion makes sense. It's one I came up with myself and even had my fingers crossed so damn tightly that it wouldn't get traced even further back to Joanne Ridley. Because I didn't know how they'd gotten them, I wasn't sure who knew what, and I still need to keep that part of my life separate from this one.

"Don't worry about the charges, Kyla," Big Daddy K says, and if I didn't know any better, I'd think he actually meant every word that was coming out of his mouth. His voice is like butter, and he's so put together that looks are definitely deceiving in his case. He's a monster in an expensive suit. "The lawyer took care of them, and we're going to make sure they don't stick."

I bite my lip, wondering if that's what someone told him six years ago when he killed my parents. They patted him on the back and told him not to worry about a thing because Crew people don't go down for their crimes. The only difference between us is that I actually didn't do what I'm accused of.

"Alright, plans," K says. He sits back, crossing one leg over the other while Johnny still sits stiffly beside him. "I need everything to return to normal ASAP. We're bleeding money here, and people are starting to get restless with what's gone down on the street."

"What about Gregory?" Magnum asks.

"I'm hoping he'll go the way of Roza Fonz's band of dimwits, but we've got our ears to the ground, trying to sniff him out. I haven't forgotten what he did to you and Kyla, and as soon as we find him, he'll pay just like Dunnegan."

I try not to think about the life draining from Dunnegan's eyes. Not that he was a good person, but I'm not judge, jury, and executioner. Big Daddy K fancies himself just that, though.

"Magnum, I need some of the guys still there to check something out. We got wind that a junior guy might have been found in the old fight warehouse this morning."

Oscar sits forward. "Junior guy?"

"Farmingham," Johnny explains.

"Farmingham? We never recruited him."

"But we were, and I don't think Gregory's guys ever got the memo. We think it's a retaliation killing."

Oscar's leg jumps up and down. "So, you don't think they're backing down?"

K shrugs. "We've got to find that out, but I can't let them think they're getting to us, so everything is back on as of now. Start the fights again. Get back into the school, recruit, recruit, recruit. I'm sending some guys home today, and we'll follow shortly. Everyone else is getting the same instructions. Johnny's returning early to run Candy's in Dunnegan's..." He smiles. "...failure to remain alive."

I can't help it. I drift my gaze toward Johnny. His shiner doesn't detract from his good looks, and now I'll be seeing him soon. He's going to take Candy's over. He should since the new club aspect was genius. He took a high-class strip joint and made it into the place to be. He deserves to take that business over.

What the hell am I thinking? It's a Crew-owned business, and he needs to get as far away from it as possible.

"Keep me updated," K says, before leaning forward to

shut the video down without giving me the chance to look at Johnny one more time.

Mag leans forward and shuts the laptop.

"Who's Farmingham?" I ask first. I have a lot more questions, but they'll wait. This seemed like the biggest piece of news since it might be directly related to Gregory.

Oscar's jaw hardens. He runs his hands down his thighs. "He's the guy you called out that day in lunch." He turns toward me just a fraction. "You slammed his head into the table."

I gasp. "That's Farmingham? He's dead?"

Oscar gets to his feet. "The guy was a fucking dumbass, but shit."

Guilt seeps into my skin like a wet blanket weighing me down.

The door opens behind Oscar, and Brawler walks in. He catches my face, and immediately asks, "What's wrong?"

Oscar turns toward me. What he sees makes him move forward. "You didn't do this."

"You didn't recruit him because of me," I say, knowing already that it's true. They don't even have to tell me.

Magnum takes a quick second to update Brawler before Oscar's jaw starts ticking again. "Yes, and it still didn't matter. He still wound up dead even though he wasn't a part of the Crew."

The guy was an asshole and a douchebag, but I didn't want him to die. "What are the chances this is a message?"

Magnum speaks up now. "We treat every time someone in the Crew dies as a possible message from our enemies. Especially if they died under suspicious circumstances. I don't know anything about this kid's death yet though."

"Gregory probably got antsy because everyone left, and he couldn't find anyone important to send the message, so he started at the bottom."

"The bottom? He wasn't even on the bottom," Brawler says.

"If he's starting at the bottom, I need to put the word out at the school."

I grab Oscar's hand before he can turn away. "How many Crew members go to school?"

"It's not just the members," Oscar says, clearly distracted. "It's apparently anyone who wants to recruit in." He motions toward the side of the laptop. "I got you that phone. Johnny's orders. I already gave out your new number to everyone. I'll call you later."

Oscar pulls the keys to his bike from his pocket as he exits Mag's apartment.

"To answer your question," Brawler says. "So many recruits. More than half the guys at school want to join. For some of them, it's their only choice for anything. But there's about ten junior members who are already in."

My head spins. I'd only looked at major players when I researched the Crew. I don't know why, but I never thought about all the little guys. The young ones, like me, getting caught up in this life when you could have some psycho like Gregory decide he wants to take you out to send a message to the higher-ups.

Coward.

"I'm coming with you," I say, getting to my feet and facing Magnum.

He sighs. "I knew you were going to do this."

"Johnny will get pissed," Brawler offers.

I shrug. "I want to know what happened to Farming-ham. Plus, I'm in the Crew now and K gave us an order. I'm rolling with it." I head toward the door. "Be ready in five. I just need to change."

Mag and Brawler exchange a look, but I ultimately win, and it's mine and Brawler's asses parked in the back of the car as we make our way to the old warehouse.

## 8

We arrive at the rundown warehouse, and a flood of emotions almost bowls me over. For starters, this place looks a lot shittier in the middle of the day. Little things stick out, like the litter of human waste on the sidewalk leading toward the alley. Cigarette butts, empty McDonald's fries pouches, plastic wrappers, and just general trash dropped and forgotten.

When we step inside, though, it's back to normal. The place looks the same as I remembered it, except it smells a little better without the raging fighters' sweat and blood pooled over the ground. The same dim lighting leaves the shitty pallet-like seating in a haze. The place lacks the raucous crowd, making the area feel both bigger and void of life.

My heart squeezes painfully. I miss this. Brawler's

fingers tangle in mine momentarily, and I glance over to find him staring. His resolute blue eyes shine, and I know he's following my train of thought. From what I've gathered, they shut the fights down. The cops were out in full force, so they didn't want to dangle the underground fights in their faces like a carrot. A snowflake can turn into an avalanche quickly.

"Any idea where this...body is supposed to be?" Brawler whispers. His trained eye searches the interior. He knows this place better than anyone.

Magnum shrugs but moves forward on confident legs. He's stealth, hands at his sides, eyes darting everywhere. "I don't know much about the kid, but he was here, and he wasn't supposed to be. Where do you think he'd be if that's the case?"

Brawler's gaze tracks upward. At once, we all look with him at the box they built for Johnny and the other higher-ups in the Crew to sit while watching the fights. I've spent my fair share of time up there, too, and yeah, it's by far the most comfortable spot in the building. Why Farmingham would be up there, I don't know, but he certainly wouldn't find a better spot unless he likes chipped tile in bathrooms.

Magnum takes his gun out of the waistband of his pants and edges forward. His knees are bent, arms outstretched in front of him with his finger already on the trigger. "Watch her."

Brawler moves me behind him as we follow Mag up the

steps. There's no getting around the creaks of our footfall on the old wood, so hopefully, whoever killed Farmingham is long gone, not waiting around to watch this play out.

"How did someone even find him?" I whisper.

Brawler reaches back for my hand, and I put mine in his. He gives it a squeeze. "I'm not the only one who comes in and out of here. Anyone with a key could've found him and reported it."

Magnum crouches as we approach the box with its face full of windows. We're staying just under the ledge to remain hidden. He climbs to the landing then turns to look at us. "I'll check the place out. The vantage point isn't ideal, so stay back until I tell you it's safe."

Brawler and I both nod. My stomach tumbles over itself as Magnum prepares to enter the room. He knows what he's doing, but that doesn't make it any less scary to find someone you care about seconds away from potentially putting himself in danger.

Magnum reaches out with his left hand to turn the doorknob. The catch releases, and he steps back, letting the door open on its own. He waits until there's just enough space to allow him through before he lifts himself to full height and charges in. He cases the room like I've seen Navy Seals do on TV. I can't lie and say watching him doesn't turn me on, but that's doused in a fraction of a second when he calls out, "Stay the fuck back."

Just the tone in his voice, I can tell he's not talking to us.

Before I can even think, Brawler moves. He doesn't wait for Magnum's orders. He charges in, pulling me in behind him, shielding me with his wide body. I'll always want someone like Brawler on my side. He may get annoyed with Oscar, but he went after him last night. That wasn't the first time either. And now, he's just charged into a room to help out another one of our guys.

I squeeze his hands tightly, and he pulls me against him from behind, mistaking my show of emotion for fear.

"Mag..."

"What are you doing here?" Magnum demands. He hasn't lowered the gun, so this person must not be a friend. He's tense, shoulders bunched, still lining up his shot with the barrel aimed in front of him.

I peek around Brawler's shoulders, which is a feat in and of itself since he's twice my size, but I'm too curious about the man who's shown up at the warehouses on the day Farmingham's dead body was found. It can't be a coincidence. Before I find the intruder, though, my gaze freezes on the prick who bullied me the first day at Rawley Heights. His arrogant expression is wiped from his face now. There's a hole in his temple, his prone body half on the leather couch and half off. A small blanket bunches at his waist as if he was sleeping here when someone came up on him and shot him. Congealed blood puddles on the sofa and where it subsequently dripped to the floor. A smell in the air filters through my nostrils. Repugnant, but not terrible yet.

"Mack?"

Brawler bristles, and along with him, my back straightens. I peer up to find the guy they've both been staring at. He looks to be between Johnny and Mag's age. Brown hair, shorn closely to his head. He has earrings adorning his ears and the flames of a tattoo licking up the side of his neck. Not to stereotype, but he definitely looks like the gang member type, so why Magnum hasn't lowered his piece yet is beyond me. The air thickens with tension the longer the standoff continues. With my hand inside Brawler's, he tightens his fingers to fists, almost crushing my small finger bones. Thankfully, it's the hand I didn't hurt in the accident.

"Did you do this?" Magnum barks, gesturing toward Farmingham's lifeless body.

The guy has the audacity to roll his eyes, even though he's barely spared a glance away from Brawler since he's recognized him. If Brawler knows who he is, he hasn't confirmed as much, and with the bunching of his muscles, I'm not sure he has. It has to be someone from the past though. No one calls him Mack anymore.

"Simmer down, Magnum," he spits. "I knew you'd show up, and we need to talk."

"You know I don't like talking."

The guy ignores him. "Aren't you going to introduce me to Kyla?"

"I'd just as soon put a bullet between your eyes."

The guy leans coolly against the bar in the back as if he

was truly just waiting for us to show up. "You know, that hurts. We were always friends."

"Friends don't walk away from each other."

The guy's gaze moves to Brawler's, and true regret lies there. "I agree."

Brawler can't stand it. "Alright, what the fuck is going on?"

Magnum moves toward us, gun still outstretched. "Take Kyla and get out of here. I'll clean up the mess."

"For fuck's sake, Magnum." Cold exasperation laces the intruder's words. "I'm not going to hurt you. Or Mack. Or Kyla. I came here to talk. Isn't that why you came here? To find out what happened to your recruit?"

Magnum's jaw tenses. "We don't need your help."

A quirky smile turns his lips. "The fact that Rocket's girlfriend was almost kidnapped and then framed for murder says you do." He turns to look at me. "Hello, by the way. I'm Cole."

I step out around Brawler, making sure to drop his hand. Whoever the guy is, he obviously has history with the Crew, and he knows I'm Johnny's girlfriend, so holding Brawler's hand won't do. "Sounds like you already know me, so I won't bother introducing myself."

"Wait...Cole?" Brawler asks, his voice dipping a few octaves.

Sadness washes over Cole's face. "Yeah, Mack. Cole."

Mag moves forward, his gun still raised in Cole's direction even after we've pretty much already solidified that they used to be friends—or at least know each other.

Cole raises his hands in front of him in a motion of surrender. "I'm not going to hurt you."

"Not that you fucking could," Mag scoffs.

Cole licks his lips, looking slightly keyed up, but mostly bored. "I won't try anything, Mag. I came here to talk and to talk only. I don't even have a weapon on me, and I know how good of a shot you are with that thing, so I'd appreciate it if you lowered it the fuck down." Mag doesn't relent, and Cole sighs. "I didn't kill your recruit, but I know who did. I knew you'd be coming here looking for info, and I have it. That's the only reason why I'm here."

Mag drops the gun to his side hesitantly, but even so, just that motion lifts weight from my shoulders. So far, Cole hasn't shown us that he means any harm, and I'm willing to take him at his word. For now. Mag must be too, otherwise he never would've lowered his weapon.

"I remember you," Brawler says, his voice far away as if stuck on a memory and not like we're also discussing murder and gang shit.

Cole rubs his neck, his many hoop earrings tinkling against one another for a surprisingly gentle tone that defies the moment.

"Who is he?" I ask.

"He was my brother's friend."

Cole takes a deep breath. "And Johnny's," he says,

locking gazes with me. Then, he moves his stare to the copper-headed bodyguard. "And Mag's."

"We're not walking down memory lane. You defected, and by right, I should be killing your ass right now."

"You won't do that, though, will you?" Cole asks, smirking. He crosses his arms, showing off more ink on his skin. He laughs, and it's not friendly. I don't understand the power struggle going on, but Magnum isn't happy about it. "I mean, we are family after all."

I blink, then swing my gaze over to Mag who expands like a bomb ready to detonate.

He peeks at Brawler and me from the corner of his eye. "Cousins," he elaborates. His face when he looks back at his family is this side of terrifying. "Start talking."

"It was Gregory's guys sending a warning."

"We figured as much," Mag says, his tone biting.

"But you weren't sure."

"How do you know?"

"Hearing things," he shrugs. "It doesn't matter. You'll find Gregory's calling card in the recruit's pocket. He wants you to know it was him. He wants you to know he's not going away as easily as you'd like. He's also actively recruiting in your area, so be careful. The Heights Crew has always had a lot of supporters, but they also have people who hate them. Right?"

He eyes Mag, and it might seem like he's just asking a question, but it looks like a hell of a lot more than that, too.

Since he defected, he's probably talking about himself and others like him. I know more than anyone how people can end up hating the Heights Crew. Even Farmingham's dead body on the couch is proof of that. How will his family react? Will they hate the people who did it? Or blame the Crew because they're the linking piece?

"I want to help," Cole says. "You know why I left."

But I don't, and I'm sensing that's a major part of the story that I'm missing. "And why's that?"

Cole goes to answer, but Mag shuts that shit down. "Is that all you've got for us?"

"For now."

Mag lifts the gun in his hands again, lining up his shot. His finger steadies over the trigger, and Cole pales.

I take in a steady breath, wondering if Mag is actually going to do it. His own cousin. "Just get out of here," he says, eventually.

He trains the gun on him the whole time he walks toward the door. Cole stops briefly before addressing Brawler. "Don't get involved in Crew shit, Mack. Your brother wouldn't have wanted that for you." He doesn't wait for an answer, just turns and walks away.

We wait, his footsteps thudding down the stairs until the bang of the exterior door sounds, signaling his retreat from the warehouse.

Magnum finally puts his firearm away, sticking it back in the waistband of his black tactical pants. He moves forward, patting down Farmingham's pockets. In his front right, Mag sneaks his hand in and pulls out something. He peers into his palm, shaking his head. He turns, and Brawler and I slide closer.

"Seriously?" My brows raise. "Fucking Runts?" A small package of Runts candy lies in the middle of my badass bodyguard's palm like some cosmic joke.

"Our intel said Candy's was more his than Dunnegan's."

"But his calling card is fucking Runts?" I can't tell if I should laugh my ass off or be impressed that a bad guy is willing to use such an inferior candy as his calling card. Like, what the fuck do we do with that? I mean, he could've used Skittles if he was going for something sweet. Or better yet, chocolate. Dark chocolate. Dark chocolate with nuts. That's a hell of a lot more sinister than candy shaped like fruit.

Brawler doesn't say anything to this, and upon closer inspection, he's retreated inside himself. Mag looks at him warily. "You okay?"

The dark angel wings on his neck catch my attention. They're for his brother, and I'm sure that's who he's thinking about right now. He gives himself a shake. "Fine. I just didn't expect to run into someone from the past today."

Mag moves over, placing his arm on Brawler's shoulder. "We can't trust Cole." He locks gazes with me. "I don't care what he says. Yes, he knew your brother, and he was friends with Johnny, but we're not trusting him. Okay?"

"What happened to him?" Brawler asks.

Mag drops his hand. "He left after your brother died. Defected. No one's heard from him since, but there are rumors he hooked up with another gang. I wouldn't be surprised. I saw the hint of a fire tattoo on his neck."

I'm almost afraid to ask. "And that is?"

"Not from around here," Magnum answers as he glares down at what's left of Farmingham. "But there's a gang in the tri-state area called the Dragons."

Fire. Dragons. It makes sense. I peek up at him. "How much trouble are you going to be in because you didn't kill him?"

"We keep this to ourselves for now," Mag says, eyeing us both. "We'll tell K we found Gregory's calling card ourselves, which I would've. I don't trust the fact that he showed up here, regardless of what he's said."

Mag is thorough. He didn't need to be told to check Farmingham's pockets. The only thing Cole succeeded in doing was popping up out of nowhere as if he was trying to throw us off. Or offer help. He knew Magnum would show up at the scene and used the opportunity to talk to him. The reasoning behind it is the only thing that remains in the dark.

Whatever his reasonings, I'm with Mag. We hold him at arm's length if he decides to show up again with vague answers. I don't care about his history with the Crew or my guys.

"I'll call in our cleanup team," Mag says.

I drift my gaze back to Farmingham's dead body as Mag moves to the side of the room, bringing his phone to his ear.

"He wasn't even our recruit," I say, dumbfounded at the whole thing and trying not to look at all the blood pooled on the floor. I thought the guy was sleazy—an ass—but there are worse people who deserve to end up like this.

"It doesn't matter," Brawler says. "Everything the Crew touches dies."

## 9

In the back of the car on our return trip to the tower, Brawler traces lines over my thigh absentmindedly. Goosebumps spread over my exposed skin, settling in the base of my spine. It's been so easy to come back to the Heights and fall into everything again. Everything feels so natural.

And no, I'm not talking about the dead body. I'm talking about working with the people I care about.

Magnum's been quiet since the warehouse. As natural as it is for him to be self-reflective and listen rather than talk, he's doing it for a whole other reason right now. His cousin showing up threw him for a loop. "You have a lot of history with him, huh?" I ask.

Mag blinks, looking into the rearview mirror. He nods.

"That's an understatement. We came into the Crew at the same time." He runs a hand over the side of his scruff. "I didn't think I'd see him again."

"K?" Brawler guesses.

Mag turns left down a side street, grabbing the steering wheel from underneath. "K wasn't at the top then. It was Mayhem."

Now that's a name I haven't heard yet. "And Mayhem was where Big Daddy K is now?"

"Top dog," Magnum says, his words coming out on a breath. "But it doesn't matter who gave the orders. Anyone who defects is shot on sight."

"That's...a little harsh." I entwine my fingers with Brawler's. One day, we're going to defect. All of us. We'll have to make sure they never find us. "I don't know why they won't let people get out if they want to."

"People know too much. They can be used against us— them," he says, correcting himself with a shake of his head. "Not many would go away quietly. Not many wouldn't break under pressure from a rival gang and release as many secrets as they know. That's why when you're in, you're in."

"You make it sound like we won't ever have a chance."

Mag meets my gaze in the mirror again, but he doesn't say anything to alleviate my worries. My stomach twists.

Brawler hugs me to him. "Don't lose hope."

"Hope is one thing I've never lost," Mag says. He returns

his gaze to the road then leans forward. "Shit. We've got a problem." He pulls over.

My heart rockets up my throat, lodging there until Mag has the car safely parked. Brawler and I follow his line of sight. "Shit."

Mag throws the car door open, and I scramble out of the car on the street side, leaving my door open. Magnum's long strides eat up the cracked road so fast I have to jog to keep up with him, but eventually, we flank Oscar who's getting shit from some guy.

The thug pulls back, eyeing the sudden entourage Oscar has. For Oscar's part, he doesn't look perturbed at all. He's still wearing that shit-eating grin like nothing in the world bothers him. I know that's not true now, but it's the image he likes to display for the world.

"Is it true?" Blue bandana wearing a-hole asks. "My boy dead?" He doesn't wait for an answer like he's only interested in hearing himself talk. "We're supposed to be kept safe. Chill and shit. Now word is we got a retaliation killin'. My boy," he adds, pumping his fist against his chest.

"Calm down, T," Oscar says, bored. He kicks off the telephone pole he'd been leaning against when the guy got in his face and approaches him. "You know what it's like in the Crew. No one ever sugarcoated it for you. Your boy is dead. Taken out by people with no regard for human life. That's why we need to be in the Heights, and all the other pieces of shit competitors stay where they are. You feel me?"

"But Farmingham, man? It ain't right."

"It's not, but bitching about it won't do us any good either. We stopped recruiting him. He shouldn't have been on their radar, but those pieces of shit didn't give a damn about that."

Whoever this T is grinds his jaw. He doesn't go to our school, not that I've noticed, anyway. He looks older. Mag's age or even older than that. He's got a tattoo of a tear coming off the edge of his eye.

I see why. He's a whiny bitch.

"Now," Oscar says. "You good?"

The guy's jaw ticks, but he's done complaining. He nods, hiking his pants up his hips.

"Good." Oscar's fist flies through the air, clocking the guy in the jaw. The guy stumbles until his back hits the side of the building. The guy's eyes round as Oscar stalks after him, suddenly taller and getting in this guy's face as a red mark brightens his skin. "Don't ever get in my face again, T." He takes the collar of his shirt and throws him back. T's head hits the brick wall behind him. Fury ignites in T's eyes, but he stays where he is, gaze darting to the rest of us surrounding our friend. Oscar runs his hand over his face. "Your fucking drunk spittle hit my cheek."

Oscar steps back, and the guy takes it as his cue to leave. He does so in a hurry, holding his jeans up as he goes, otherwise he'd be showing us his ass crack.

I put my hand on Oscar's shoulder. "Hey. You okay?"

He shrugs me off him, sending me a warning look over his shoulder.

I back off, only because we're in public. I hate seeing him this angry, whether he's putting on a show for the Heights or not.

"Did you talk to everyone?" Mag asks.

Oscar slowly turns. His hard mask is on, the one that grows wary when we're alone, but is stuck messing up his perfect features when we're anywhere else. "People are afraid. First Kyla, now Farmingham."

"K will make it right. He always does."

I can only imagine what that means. More bloodshed. Bringing someone in and killing them at the dinner table like he did with Dunnegan. Shooting someone point blank in the face. *Someone* will pay for taking out Farmingham. That's how Big Daddy K runs this place.

Oscar starts to walk away. His bike is parked up ahead, pulled right up onto the sidewalk.

"Where are you going?" I call out.

"Someone told me my mom is passed out a couple of alleys over. I have to get her and drop her off at home. Is that okay with you, Princess?"

My blood boils underneath the surface. I stalk after him, calling out over my shoulder. "I'm going with Bat."

"Whoa, whoa," Mag says, jogging up to meet me by Oscar's bike. "What are you doing?" he whispers, gaze darting around.

"Oscar needs help, so I'm going with him."

Oscar looks at me with a challenging stare, eyebrow raised. He wants me to come with him. He's practically salivating for it even though he's trying as hard as possible to look aloof.

"Johnny..." Mag starts.

"I'll deal with Johnny," I tell him. He told me Oscar and Mag are watching over me. I'm sure he didn't mean like this, but I'm not technically wrong. Besides, before the fight that never happened, Johnny was getting used to the idea of other people around us. I suspect he was even beginning to like it. I don't know what a month of being isolated with his father has done to him, but I don't think he'll freak over this. Oscar is perfectly capable of taking care of me. "I'll see you guys later?"

Brawler and Mag both look resigned as Oscar holds a helmet out to me. His sly grin jumps as I slide in around him. I pull him tight, tight enough that he expels a breath. "Remember where we are," I breathe.

"I'm not an idiot."

"Just to look for your mom and then back to the tower," Mag orders.

"Yeah, Pops," Oscar says, his chest rumbling with laughter at the look Magnum sends his way. "He's touchy," Oscar says to me as he starts the bike, the engine gunning to life underneath us.

"It's hot as hell," I deadpan, sliding my gaze to Jacob's.

"Hold tight, Princess. I'll show you hot."

Oscar takes off, shooting down the dead city streets. People are likely staying in after what happened to Farmingham. No one wants to be the next easy victim.

A sickening feeling twists my gut. Farmingham had to be sleeping in the warehouse. I wonder if he was homeless. Or if he was just trying to escape something.

But also, who knew he was sleeping there? Or was someone following him?

A lot of unanswered questions flip through my brain as Oscar hits the side streets. He slows as we keep our eyes peeled for his mom. She wasn't the nicest person the last time we met. In fact, she straight up scratched my face, but that was the drugs in her system. I don't know what we'll find today, if we find her at all.

The first couple of alleyways are a bust. There's nothing. No one is out and about, except for a few homeless men living in cardboard boxes lined with newspaper. Oscar bypasses them, the roar of the motorcycle kicking up around us and echoing back tenfold as the noise bounces between the buildings surrounding us.

"Fuck," Oscar roars. Under my hands, his heart beats fast, pounding out a frantic rhythm. Now that Gregory has retreated, I wonder what's happened to her. The streets are worse than the upstairs room in Candy's. If she's here, maybe she isn't being prostituted out anymore. That should be a relief, but somehow, it doesn't feel that way.

Oscar guns it, and I hold on tight, my arms snaking around his abs to get a better grip. He takes a few more turns before we slow in front of a corner grocery I recognize. Oscar lives above the store with his mom, even though I get the feeling his mother isn't there very often. He stops the bike and turns it off, the vibrations of the engines cease, but my muscles are like Jell-O. I swing my leg over, hopping off the bike while Oscar helps guide me. He gets off next, much more gracefully, and opens a metal-corrugated door next to the door to his apartment. Inside, there's a small storage room. He walks the bike in and then holds out his hand for the bike helmet I took off. He watches as I run my hands through my hair and then locks the place up again.

"I thought we'd try here. Maybe she stumbled her way back home." He pulls the door to the apartment open and holds it open for me as I follow him up the narrow steps.

"What's been going on with her since I've been gone?"

"I haven't heard from her much. I tried asking her about Gregory since she kind of remembers we saw her that day, but she doesn't remember all of it. I don't know if she still sees him or not, and I haven't said shit to Johnny or K about what we saw. I don't want them bringing her in. It's possible she was too damn high to remember anything, and I don't want them getting trigger happy because they think she's holding back on them."

I swallow a lump in my throat. I would hope they

wouldn't do that. Johnny wouldn't. I know that from the very depths of my heart, but K is soulless.

He opens the door at the top of the stairs. He's cleaned the place a bit since the last time I was here. I wait just inside as he walks around the apartment, checking everywhere. When he comes out of his mom's room, he punches the wall.

I walk up to him. "Hey, hey. It's okay."

His hands turn to fists. "It's just so fucked up." He turns ravenous eyes on me. "Everything is fucked up in this hell hole, but you."

The intensity of his words strike me. I crack a smile. "I don't know. I'm kind of fucked up too."

"Not like me. Not like the rest of the Heights. I don't even deserve to touch you."

My head snaps back as if he's punched me. "Don't do that."

His jaw ticks. "It's fucking true, and you know it. Out of all the guys you've chosen, I'm the one you went slumming for. I'm a piece of shit thug who hits someone for accidentally spitting in his face right after I told him his friend died. My mom's a whore and a drug addict. I'm no one, Kyla."

Shit's real when he uses my actual name.

"You need a lobotomy if you think that's true."

He watches me like a man starved. He's barely holding it together. His chest rises and lowers with the ferocity of his breaths.

"You're no one? You don't deserve to touch me?" I start to strip. I pull my shirt off, dropping it at our feet. My breasts jiggle as I stand upright before him, and he takes his eyeful. I kick off my shoes and then shimmy out of my skinny jeans, kicking them to the side as well until I'm standing in front of him in my bra and panties. "Do you want to hear how many times I've thought about your cock sliding inside me?" I arch a brow. "When I was away at Greenlawn, I had a lot of time on my hands." I stalk toward him, wiggling my fingers. "These fingers have gotten a work-out, but I'm done with that. I want you to touch me."

Oscar's gaze zeroes in on my cleavage. I have to say, this bra is doing a banging job. No wonder he's looking at me like he could jump me right now. He swallows. "You'd let me do that. A street rat?"

I back him up into his room. "*Let* you do that? I'd beg you."

Oscar groans. I don't know what shit other bitches did to him, but he's no one's slut to keep around only when it suits them.

"You're not my dirty little secret, Oscar."

A spark fires in Oscar's gaze, and he moves forward, hands cupping my ass as he grinds his erection into me. I've worked myself up for this moment. Dreamed about it in a fitful sleep. Daydreamed about it with my fingers coaxing my clit into submission.

Oscar drops to his knees, nose nuzzling my pussy, but

we're not going there this time. This isn't about me, it's about us.

I lift him with one finger under his chin and order him to the bed. "You're too dressed," I tell him.

I watch like a greedy bitch as he whips his shirt off, throwing it to the other side of the room. His abs ripple in front of me. His darker skin pulled taut over the dips, signaling every last football workout he's ever done.

The remnants of his road rash pain me, but he starts on his belt next, and I help him, pulling at it while he works on his zipper. I take a handful of his jeans in my fists and tug down, revealing his tented black boxers.

He kicks his jeans off, and I don't give him time to stop me. I push him to the bed and crawl over him, arching my body into him until his cock rubs against the apex of my thighs. "Fucking Christ, Kyla."

I reach under the band of his boxers, running my fingers down his hard shaft. He pumps his dick into my hand at the same time. My panties are soaked, and my core throbs, aching for me to feel him.

I move down his body, kissing his taut stomach. I remove his boxers as I kiss the angle of his Adonis belt, licking up and down the curved surface. I could eat my next meal off here and be one happy lady. The glistening pre-cum on his dick is too much to bear. I reach out, running the tip of my tongue over his slit. He watches everything I do with heightened anticipation. "Now look who's wearing too much."

I reach around, unclasping my bra until my breasts fall heavily in front of me. They always feel like they weigh more when I'm turned on, and right now, I'm turned right the fuck on and they're as heavy as boulders.

Oscar moves his hand lower, cupping my mound. He moves the fabric of my panties aside, fingers trailing over my slit. "Wet for me."

I'm mesmerized by his touch. I keep still as his fingers play over my clit until he gives me a quick pinch. A startled cry pushes past my lips.

He locks gazes with me. "Are you wet for me?"

"Fuck yes," I breathe.

He pulls me toward him, and at the last minute when I should be collapsing on top of him, he twists until he's hovering over me. He grabs the back of my panties with one hand and pulls them down. I lift my hips, so he can drag them down over my ass and past my thighs and calves. His cock bobs between us while he traces his gaze over my skin.

"Touch me," I pant.

He reaches out, agile fingers plucking at my nipples and smoothing over the swell of my breasts. He leans over, taking a nipple in his mouth and sucking on it until my core burns with need.

"Get inside me," I plead. He reaches for a drawer at the side of the bed, but I wrap my legs around his hips. "Now."

Oscar drops his forehead to mine, breathing heavily. "Kyla."

"I want to feel you," I tell him.

He groans, the tip of his dick pressing against my entrance. I angle my hips, taking just the tip in, rocking up into him over and over.

"Fuck, fuck, fuck." He slams into me, and I cry out.

My walls close around every last hard ridge. He presses his lips together, staring down at me in awe. "Please move," I gasp.

He doesn't need another invitation. He pulls out, sliding back into me, grinding his hips. I press my fingertips into his ass, holding on while he starts a panty-melting rhythm that has me spasming around him in no time.

He rides my climax out and then retreats. Intense pleasure ripples through me as Oscar gets a condom out of the drawer, rips the package open, and slides it over his cock. "As much as I loved every second of that, I care about you more."

He gets back into position, pushing into me with ease, filling me up again as my head falls back onto his pillows. With stroke after stroke, he fucks me into oblivion. I swear the neighbors can hear our loud pants and guttural moans, but I'm unashamed of Oscar Drego. Or who I am when I'm with him. I want every last part of him. The jagged edges. The strong masks. The vulnerable side.

He starts to shake, giving me one more facet of him as he pumps into me harder. He slams into me one last time on the heels of a moan that has me coming again right alongside him.

I let out a breath as I hold him to me.

"I think I love you, Princess. And that scares the shit out of me...because everything I love turns to shit."

## 10

*A* while later, Oscar drops me back at the tower before going out to look for his mom again. I offer to help him, but he turns me down. He'll be going into some seedier parts of the city and doesn't want me involved in any of that shit. Especially since I've gone and "cracked like porcelain".

When I get to my apartment, a surprise waits for me. I do a double take because the swinging heavy bag in the corner of the room was most definitely not there when I woke up this morning.

I walk up to it, admiring the quality. A steel bracket mounts it to the ceiling. I give it a good push, and it swings back. The damn thing is solid. Even as heavy as it is, it won't pull out of the ceiling. The tower is probably made with reinforced steel. I doubt there are any wooden studs in this place. It was built to keep high priority targets safe.

Brawler texted me earlier to say he was heading home, so Magnum must be behind this. I stroll to his apartment, knocking on the door. He opens it, visibly relaxing when he sees it's me and that I'm safe. I hike my thumb over my shoulder. "Did you do that?"

He shrugs like it's no big deal. "I thought you could use it to heal your arm. Since K wants the fights back on, he's going to want you headlining, so you need to recover as soon as possible."

I was afraid K would do that. I want to fight more than anything, but the last thing I want to do is injure myself getting there. If I start too early, I could potentially cripple myself permanently. Something tells me K won't want to hear any excuses though.

Magnum gestures with his chin. "Here. Let's go into your place."

He shuts his door, and we walk across the hall. The bag in the corner is still softly swaying back and forth with minimal sound, which is perfect. "I guess I should have Brawler set something up. Maybe some easy opponents just to get me in there."

Mag strides over to the bag, admiring his handiwork. "That's a good idea. I can't imagine the money the Crew has lost over the last several weeks. The fights and Candy's were their big moneymakers. Since Gregory ran off and Dunnegan—"

"Got a bullet in his head?"

He nods. "Got a bullet put into his head, they had to shut Candy's down. Johnny will come back and get it on its feet again in no time, but I'm sure K's not happy with how everything turned out."

I hit the bag with my left hand. "Did you notice Johnny's black eye?"

Mag side-eyes me. "I did."

"Big Daddy?"

Mag holds the bag for me, and I throw a couple of punches with my left. "If I had to guess? Yes. He hasn't hit him in a while though."

I stop, my hand falling to my side. "He's hit him before?"

"In school. I remember him coming to school sometimes with some bruising, but it hasn't happened since..." Mag trails off and blows out a breath. "...I think since he started training under K."

"I fucking hate him," I growl. The thought he would beat his own son is worrisome. Johnny's supposed to be his number one. He's grooming him for his position, right? Why would he make an enemy out of him?

*Because he's not*, I realize. At least not in his mind. He's making him fall in line. He's making him into the perfect little protege he wants him to be.

It's disgusting.

Mag doesn't say anything, and I raise a suspicious eyebrow at him. He didn't bat an eye when I told him I wanted to kill Big Daddy K, but he hasn't spoken out against them either. I know he's with me, but why do I feel like there's another story in here somewhere?

"Why are you looking at me like that?"

I shake my head. "You haven't said much about what I told you yesterday."

"What do you want me to say?"

"It's kind of a big deal," I say, feeling him out. "I told you I wanted to take out the biggest leader in the gang world. Someone you've sworn to protect."

Mag lets go of the heavy bag and comes around, standing in front of me. "Death threats are commonplace in the Heights. My whole job is based on someone planning to kill someone else or keeping someone who's at a high risk of getting taken out safe. You telling me that yesterday was just another day in my life."

"It's so fucked up," I blurt. Even now, I can't believe the shit that goes through my head sometimes. And the shit that's been going through my head started six years ago, but a lot of these guys have been dealing with this stuff since they were little kids. They didn't grow up right in it like Johnny did, but they were around it. How many families sitting in the Heights right now know that a high schooler was shot dead today? How many of those families have little kids and just shrugged it off because stuff like this happens all the time?

This just reinforces my decision that I need to end K sooner rather than later. I don't care. I'll kidnap Johnny in the process, get him out of the Heights, and then tell him what I did to his life. At least he'll be out of here.

I sigh because it'll never work out that way. I need to save Johnny, then kill his father. Since I won't leave without him, that's the steps now. Even if I had an opportunity to kill Big Daddy K tomorrow, I can't take it. Not until Johnny is completely on my side.

"When the time comes, will you help me take him out?"

Mag could be a wealth of information regarding K's whereabouts. Not only that, the Crew trusts him whole-heartedly. They've staked their lives on him. He could be a tremendous help in this.

"You want me to help you kill someone?"

The tone in his voice makes me look up. Hesitation sits in the corners of his eyes, festering. "Yeah." I wrap my arms around myself. "I do."

"There's one problem with that, Angel."

My heart lurches at his pet name. I've never been some-one's angel before. He's told me I might be Johnny's saving grace, but angel is so much more... I don't know. The name tugs at my heartstrings.

"What's that?"

He licks his lips, and I watch him, mesmerized.

Magnum is still mostly an enigma to me. I know I'm attracted to him. I know he's a good person, and the feelings that bubble up inside me when we're together are the same heartfelt feelings that rise to the surface when I'm around the others, so I know what I feel for him is legit despite not knowing much of his past.

He cups my face. "I've killed people before, Kyla. I know what that's like. I know what each one does to a part of my soul, and I don't want that for you."

His words should melt me. They should turn me into goo at his feet, but all he's succeeded in doing is pissing me off. "I will kill Big Daddy K." No one is taking that from me. I've set my life on this path. It was my choice. My decision.

"I'll keep you safe. I'll support you, but I won't help you murder someone."

My mouth unhinges as I stare at him. He's completely, one hundred percent, no doubts at all serious.

He traces his thumbs over my cheekbones. "Don't get mad."

"Don't get mad?"

He gives me a small smile that's so unlike him. "You're better than us. I understand that you want to do this, but I'm not going to walk you into the fire, Kyla. I don't want to take your hand and lead you into something you won't be able to just shake off."

"But K is a piece of shit. The world would be a better place without him."

"I've killed many pieces of shit, and yeah, that's the reasoning I use, but it doesn't make a difference. You'll replay the same shit every day. You'll remember the look in his eyes, and even worse, you might even remember the spark of joy you felt when you were taking his life." Magnum's demons darken his hazel eyes. "It's not something you do and you're done. It haunts you, and what's worse, you can't move on, the ghost of what's happened staying somewhere else. The tragedy of what happened is in your own mind. It'll forever be with you. Every morning. Every night. Every—"

I raise my hand and press it to his lips. I turn my face into his palm that's still cupping my cheek, and I kiss his hand. "I get what you're trying to say, I do, but I am doing this, Magnum. You're not going to be able to talk me out of it. I'm not just going to wake up one day and decide I can't risk my soul or my mind. He never gave my parents a chance. He solidified my life when he murdered them. I'm not backing out because I don't want to." Vengeance has slithered in my veins and rooted. A bunch of pretty words aren't going to kill off the vines.

He pulls me forward, pressing his lips to my forehead. "I get it." He brushes his lips over my skin as he talks. "I understand. Just please understand when I say I'm not going to help you do it."

I bite down on my lip. Even if it does feel like he's chastising me, I can't fault him for it. This was always my destiny. My fucked up murder adventure. I don't need Magnum's help. I don't need any of the guys' help, and honestly, it would probably be best not to get them involved. If this all goes to shit, they can continue without me.

I take a deep breath. I should probably put some safeguards into place, so that if something does happen to me, they can leave. I should show them where my car is. I should tell them how to access my accounts. I can even tell them who my aunt and uncle are and, in turn, tell my aunt and uncle if any extremely hot men show up on their doorstep that they're there to help them at whatever cost.

It pains me to think about this because if that ever happens, it means I didn't make it. But it also comforts me to know that they'd be taken care of. Maybe Oscar could use some of the money I have to pay for college. He could show someone who cares what he's really made of. He could make it all the way to the NFL.

And Brawler, he only needs money to continue training. I can talk to Jax and Finn, and even though they might not be able to train him directly, I'm sure they could point him to someone who can.

Johnny? Well, if I don't make it, it might be because of him, huh?

I change my train of thought because I just can't handle that. Instead, I glance up into Mag's eyes. "When you said you wanted to be yourself, what did that mean, Jacob?"

He shivers, and I have to admit, I used his real name

intentionally. His walls are always up, barriers barricading him like a fortress. Calling him that makes them shake a little. He kisses my forehead again and pulls away. "I just want to be the person I was meant to be before the Crew entered my life and upended it."

"Do you know who that person is?"

"Pieces, maybe," he admits. "Finding yourself is hard to do when outside forces demand you're something else."

"So, when we leave the Heights, you just want to go all hippie and travel where the wind blows you?"

He smirks. The last thing I can imagine Mag doing is being a hippie. Although, all that glorious red hair would be nice. He chuckles. "No, not exactly, but it would be nice to see different things. Experience different things without the confines of the Heights and the Crew."

"I think you might just be a hippie yet," I tease.

He groans and buries his head in my neck. "Far from it."

I hold him to me, loving the feel of the warmth of his body next to mine. "We need to come up with a way to get to know each other. Actually, scratch that. You know everything there is to know about me. I need to get to know you better."

He shakes his head. "I have a feeling none of us have even scratched the surface yet when it comes to you, Angel."

I shiver at his pet name. I really, really like it. It's the way he says it too. Like a purr that rolls off his tongue.

"Why don't we start with asking each other questions?"

"Hmm." The rumble from his lips vibrates the nape of my neck. "Since I really want to kiss you right now, let's start there. First kiss?"

I cringe. "I was thirteen, and it was awful," I tell him. "I was so nervous I thought I was going to throw up. I had it built up in my head that it was going to be the best thing ever because I'd had a crush on the guy for the last few months. Well, it was slobbery, and the boy ended up telling everyone I tasted like fish." Fucker. I was vulnerable in the new, rich kid school my aunt put me in. My classmates knew I didn't come from money, and it turned out this boy was just playing me.

"You definitely don't smell like fish. You smell like..." He breathes in deep, dragging the tip of his nose across the arch of my neck. There's something so sensual about it that my toes nearly curl in my shoes. "...a garden in the summer."

My knees go weak. It's true that things get better with age. Magnum must have experience. Not that I want to know the ins and outs of said experience. I shiver. Fuck. I really don't want to know the ins and outs because my jealousy will flare again.

Come to think of it, it's kind of fucked that I want four guys to share me, but I don't want to share. I shrug because, well, that's me, so whatever.

"Don't distract me," I tell him.

"You're easily distracted."

I smile because it certainly seems like I'm easily

distracted around them. I put some space between us, pulling back a little. "Your first kiss?"

"There was a girl down the road when I was six. I pecked her cheek."

"No, no, no. Real kiss. With tongue."

He groans. "Why don't we just say that my kiss with you —with tongue—was the first one I've ever really enjoyed."

He full-on distracts me then, moving in to cover my mouth with his, sending sparks of electricity through me as he claims my lips over and over again until I can't even remember the boy's name who pissed me off when I was thirteen.

## 11

Murmuring seeps into my consciousness. I extend my legs out on the bed, stretching like a cat, working the kinks out from the turtle position I'd been sleeping in.

Silence fills the room, which is odd, since I'm sure I heard something loud enough to wake me.

I make myself relax, tucking the pillow back under my head. Magnum fell asleep in the corner chair again. Maybe he talks in his sleep, even though I doubt he even falls asleep. The guy must be working on zero hours. Guilt coats my sleepy haze. I shouldn't have asked him to stay here again.

The whispers start back up, and this time, I'm sure of it. I listen in case Magnum does talk in his sleep, curious if he's dreaming about me. He's starred in a few of my dreams, so at least we could call it even if that's the case.

My heart freezes in my chest when another voice joins his. I suck in a breath, but I stop myself from reacting even further. Johnny's here. Not on the phone, in my head, or staring back at me from a computer screen, he's in this room. I'm sure of it.

"Thank you for watching her," he says.

"She's special," Mag whispers, and my heart squeezes at his words.

I lay there dreamily. If I wasn't positive they were actually having this conversation, I wouldn't believe it. Last time Johnny caught someone in the same room with me alone, he beat the shit out of him. Now, Magnum is legit in my bedroom, and Johnny is thanking him. Mag even called me special, and so far, Johnny hasn't reacted to his words.

"I would've been back before..."

"Don't even mention it," Mag says. "We know. We get it."

Johnny sighs. The edge of the bed depresses, and I bite my lip. "Shit's all fucked up." The somber, edgy tone in his voice makes me want to wrap my arms around him, but I don't want to give myself away yet. Plus, if he's finding someone to open up too, that's even better. He and Magnum have been close. I don't know if they've ever had a relationship where they talk about shit, but Johnny needs those kinds of people in his life. People he can talk to about anything without repercussions. "I thought I was going to lose her, man. It was worse than her dying because at least then I would know she could never be around. But being sent to prison? She'd be alive, but we couldn't have the relationship we both deserve. Even worse is knowing that I put her there."

The chair Magnum is seated on creaks. "You know you can tell me shit, right? We came into the Crew at the same time, that makes us brothers. I mean this respectfully, but I don't give a shit if you're K's son, I support *you*. You don't have to isolate yourself on the way to the top."

I hold my breath, waiting for Johnny's reaction as my mind swims. If Johnny and Mag joined the Crew at the same time, how come they're not closer than they are? They took two different ways, but even so, Magnum's right. They should be more like brothers.

"It's hard to put into words," Johnny says, frustration lacing his voice. "Dad thinks all the Marx's need are each other."

"But then he hits you."

"Don't fucking say it out loud," Johnny seethes.

"She's not dumb," Mag says, voice lowering. "I noticed her expression when she saw you on the video."

"I'm not weak."

"No one said you are. No one will fucking say you are."

"I just have to do better," Johnny says, as if the bodyguard isn't even responding to him. Magnum's trying to pull him into a conversation, but it's as if he's only responding to himself.

Mag sighs. "I'm not sure *doing better,* in the way you're proposing, will help Kyla." The chair creaks again. "I'm only saying this because I know how you feel about her. Your dad's not going to like it if she pulls you away from him. You've got to be smart about this. You've got—"

"I know," Johnny growls.

Well, that's my cue to act as if I've just woken up.

I sit up on the bed, the sheets pooling at my waist. Johnny looks over his shoulder at me, and the joy that surges couldn't possibly be faked. I don't care that he has a black eye his father gave him because he's a soulless, unforgiving bastard. I don't care that he's attached to the system that took my parents. Because Johnny is Johnny, and despite all that shit, there's a real man under his Crew armor.

"I didn't mean to wake you."

I hold my hand out, and he puts his in mine, squeezing my fingers carefully. "Are you kidding me? You should've woken me up as soon as you got here."

Mag stands from the chair. He and I exchange a look over Johnny's head, and all stealth-like, he winks at me while Johnny's back is turned.

Johnny slips his hand from mine and turns to Mag. He holds his hand out, and they give each other a firm hand-shake. "Thanks again for watching her."

"I meant what I said," Mag says again, and they share a

prolonged look. I hope it's sinking into Johnny's head that other people care for him, and not the kind of care his father gives him. I mean real caring. The kind that doesn't come attached to thinly veiled brainwashing and abuse.

"Thanks, Mag. It means a lot to me that you stayed."

"Whenever you need it," Magnum says, Adam's apple bobbing. He turns and leaves without giving me another look. The front door opens and closes, and with that, Johnny and I are alone after all these weeks.

I move to my knees and Johnny meets me, kneeling on the bed. "What's this?" I ask, my fingers brushing against the dark coloring around his eyes.

"Are you okay?" he asks at the same time. His voice breaks, and my heart literally wrenches in half.

"I'm so much better now," I tell him. "Magnum, Oscar, and Brawler have been taking good care of me, and I missed you and them, and now we're all here."

He cups my face, staring deep into my eyes. "You're right where you should be."

He has no idea.

"I'm going to kill those assholes. Gregory and his men are dead. They tried to take you from me. Twice."

I tilt my head.

"The murder rap was a backup plan in case they couldn't get to you."

That makes a whole hell of a lot of sense. I briefly considered that it had to have been Gregory who set that one up, but it sounds as if Johnny's confirmed it. What a bunch of dicks. They killed an innocent girl and then blamed it on me.

"We think what was left of Roza's guys joined up with them."

My heart sinks. Of course they did. Because that's what happens when you're getting your ass kicked. You team up with someone or something bigger to help retaliate. "They think if they get to me, they'll break you, but that's not going to happen."

"They won't be getting anywhere near you again."

"If they do, we got this," I tell him. I need him to not be so hard on himself. He couldn't have predicted that it would go down like this. Shit like this isn't normal.

But even as I'm thinking it, the other part of my brain is saying that it's normal for the Heights. Shit like this happens here all the time. Fight after fight over power and control. It never ends.

"You've got yourself a good team, and we're all going to make sure nothing happens to any of us," I tell him.

He bites his bottom lip until it's swollen and plump. He's so fucking kissable right now, but the fear dancing in his eyes tells me he wants to say something. "You're not going to leave me then?"

I reel backward. "Leave you?" The force of his words almost knocks me on my ass. I shake my head. "That's not happening. Johnny, I care for you."

He drops his forehead to mine, then picks my hand up and brushes kisses over my knuckles. He closes his eyes. "Let me get this out because it's the most selfless thing I've ever said, and I don't want to say it, but fuck, I think I finally know what it means." He pauses for a beat. Underneath his closed lids, his eyes dance, and I wonder what's lurking in the depths there. "I'll get you out." His gaze opens, staring straight into my eyes. "I'll get you out of the Heights. You'll be safe. I'll set you up for life. I'll—"

"Stop."

He presses his lips shut, and damn if there aren't unshed tears in his eyes. *Just fuck me. Fuck.*

"I'm not leaving you here."

My heart is a puzzle made up of pieces of Johnny, Brawler, Magnum, and Oscar. I know it because all of them offered to get me out. They've all risked life and limb—K's, and even Johnny's ire—to make sure I'm safe. The moment I told him I wasn't leaving him here, another puzzle piece shifted just slightly into place. I meant exactly that. I'm not staying to kill Big Daddy K anymore. I mean, yeah, I'm still going to, but right now, I'm staying for Johnny. I'm staying for him because he said he'd get me out with no thought of escaping with me. He thinks he's stuck. He'd stay behind, knowing his father would give him more than a black eye after finding out I left. K's evil knows no boundaries.

Johnny drops his head to my chest and loses it. He clutches my t-shirt in his fists, pulling the fabric tight around me. The noise he makes breaks my heart. I run my hands through his hair and down his back, holding him close. His bowed back, his bent head, it's as if he's praying at my altar, which only makes me love him more. Johnny doesn't submit to anyone or anything, but the fact he feels comfortable enough to do this with me means I know just where he stands in his feelings for me.

"I was hoping you'd say no because I'm a selfish asshole, but even though I'm happy, I hurt too. I don't want to be like my dad." He peers up at me. His face contorts in pain, and I hold my breath. "You asked me about my mom once. She left. She got out. She started a new life, and I've hated her ever since. The moment she left, she changed my dad, or at least that's what I thought. I thought she turned him into a monster, but the more I learn, the more I realize he's been a monster all this time. That's why she left. She didn't change him. She ran from the person he is."

I pull him to me and lie back on the bed. We hold one another, and even though my heart breaks for Johnny, it soars for him too. He's breaking down his barriers. He's letting me in. He's letting himself think outside of the Crew box.

"Hey," I say, threading my fingers through the back of his hair and making him look at me. "I'm not running from you."

His eyes close, and he draws in a ragged breath. He tries

to dip his head again, but I hold him tight, making sure we're looking at one another.

I smile, a small one that only teases the corners of my lips. Hesitation almost closes my throat, but I'm through pulling punches with him. No, it's not the time to tell him I'm going to kill his dad, but I'm not going to sugarcoat his father's personality either. "You're not like your dad. He's mean and uncaring, and if your mom left, I'm sure she had a reason. A damn good one."

"I didn't understand it until I almost lost you. When I was thinking how much I wanted to get you out so nothing else could happen to you, it dawned on me that my mom did the same thing. She took her future into her own hands, and after that, I just got it. It's like a switch turned on in my brain. I thought she was a horrible person. Someone who would leave us behind. Selfish and low." He shakes his head slowly. "I don't think that anymore, Kyla. If you were to leave, I wouldn't blame you. I'd help you hide. I'll give you everything."

"Shh," I soothe him. "I'm not going anywhere."

"But why?" He swallows. "This place isn't for you. I can't keep you safe all the time even though I'll try like hell."

My throat dries. My tongue sticks to the roof of my mouth, so I lick my lips to bring life back to my parched skin. "Because I'm not going without you."

Just like he said a switch went off in his brain about his mother, it happens again now. Johnny reaches for me, kissing me like a crazed man. He parts my lips, delving his tongue inside like he can see my soul from here. He wants to torture it. Soothe it. Ravish it and put me back together.

I moan into him and grab his shirt. "Johnny..."

I'm so caught up in his stare, I don't notice the slight shake of the bed at first. The rattling of the windows doesn't register. It isn't until the loudest explosion I've ever heard goes off, rocking me to my core that I hold on to Johnny with a fierce grip as the foundation of the tower shakes.

A violent tremor rolls through the building. The door to the apartment opens, and Johnny jumps, clearing my body and the bed as he lands on his feet closest to the bedroom door. He fists his hands at his sides.

Magnum rushes inside, yelling, "Bomb! Get out. Get out. We have to get out."

I leap from the bed next, putting my hand in Johnny's outstretched palm. Magnum ushers us forward, taking up the rear as we sprint toward the apartment door. Once we clear it, Johnny pulls me to the right, the opposite direction of the elevators. My bare feet pound the carpet as we run. At the end of the hall, he opens a cleverly disguised Emergency Exit and we spill out into a stairwell.

The building vibrates beneath our feet, along with sounds I've only ever attributed to knocking or creaking that rip through the building.

"Watch the exit!" Mag calls out behind us. "It could be a trap."

After sprinting down the stairs, we explode out into a landing that leads to an exterior exit door. Magnum moves in front of us. He pulls a gun out of a foot holster and hands it to Johnny. Then he takes a knife from the same holster and holds it out to me. "Do not wait for either of us. Run to Oscar's. Don't turn around."

Magnum whips the door open. A blaring alarm goes off, but I hardly hear it because all I see is Magnum running from the concealed cover of the building into who knows what.

"Mag!" I call out.

A thousand different scenarios flood my brain. What if he gets shot, and I just wasted my last moment? What if he doesn't make it? What if—?

Johnny pushes me toward the door. "Do as he says. Do not look back. Stay low."

Cool air hits my face, and the dark night sends shivers down my spine as I take my first step toward uncertainty.

## 12

A rapid succession of gunshots ring out, and I can't tell who is shooting at who. My feet skid along the pavement as I take off to the left. It's so disorienting because I've never come out this side of the building, and I have no idea where I am in relation to the street.

*Go to Oscar's house they said. Ha. Ha. Ha.*

Deliriousness must be setting in. I really shouldn't be laughing at a time like this.

Through the faint moonlight, a hedgerow comes into view that looks as if it dips into a bit of a ravine.

I head that way, hoping I can hide in the brush as guns fire behind me. My shirt snags on a branch and tears. Cold seeps underneath until my body goes numb. It's a battle of cold versus hot within me as my adrenaline surges at the same time.

I skid down an embankment when a shadow leaps out of concealment. His surprise attack shocks me into freezing. His massive arms move around me, bear hugging me from the side.

His rank breath coats the side of my neck. "You're not so tough, are you?"

*Well, now, he really shouldn't have said that.*

I lift my foot and slam my heel down onto his foot. His growl turns into a yelp in my ear as I elbow him in the gut to create space.

He reaches out, his hand grasping for me. He catches hold of my shirt, and the sound of it tearing rips through the air.

Wonderful. I'm literally now wearing a scrap of clothing, that doesn't hide anything, and panties.

I punch the interested look off his face as he basically drools over my chest. I give him a left cross. Blood spurts from his nose, coating me in it from the top half up. A stomp kick to the gut has him dropping back, falling on his ass. "Not so tough, huh?"

He spits out a ream of blood. He bares his teeth at me, and in the dim moonlight, he looks feral. Like some sort of animal that's been washed up to take me out.

He tries to get to his feet again, but I lift my foot to round kick him in the head. Unfortunately, it doesn't land. He grabs it, twisting until I fall to the ground.

He crawls toward me, deflecting my attempts to kick him

away until he's on top, unloading all of his weight on me as if he's a sack of potatoes. I draw in a shaky breath, trying to wiggle my arms between us to give me some space, but he's like a wet piece of clothing conforming to every available nook and cranny. It wouldn't surprise me if the guy has trained in Jiu Jitsu.

Lucky for me, so have I.

I elbow him in the face until he gives me enough space to get my arms inside. Then I hook my arms around him and push up while I use my feet as leverage to slide out. Once I'm free, I scramble to my feet, turn, and kick him in the chin while he's on all fours.

He collapses onto the ground, moaning.

Fury rushes through me. I give him a few solid kicks to the ribs, hoping to incapacitate him so I can catch my breath.

I search the ground for the knife Magnum handed me, and by some dumb luck, I find it propped on a stone near where I skidded down the embankment. I grab it and hold it to the guy's throat, pressing the tip in to let him know I have no qualms about killing him.

I mean, he probably already gathered that but I'm not going to let him get the jump on me. "Listen here," I growl. "Who sent you?"

He coughs. Blood splatters over the pebbles where we are. His breathing doesn't sound so hot. Shallow and gurgling. I probably broke a rib or two, which he fucking deserves.

Up over the ridge of the ravine, the gunfire ceases. If I was certain Magnum or Johnny were around, I'd yell for them, but if there is anyone up there, it might be this asshole's buddies, and I don't need him having backup.

"Who are you?"

"Fuck you, Princess," he spits.

My lips curl. I actually kind of like it when he says it like that. All distasteful. Filled with fury. It felt like I deserved it. "I'm not asking you, I'm fucking demanding you tell me who you are and who you're associated with." Let's get real. This isn't some random...what? Bombing? And then subsequent gunfire? Come on. You'd have to be a total ditz to believe that.

Plus, it's awful fucking suspicious that it felt like an explosive went off the day Johnny got back from Chicago. He's called the Rocket for that reason.

"What are you going to do? Kill me?"

I slip the tip of the knife in further, a stream of blood coating his neck. "Think I won't?"

"I think it doesn't matter because I believe in what I'm doing, and I'd rather die than give anything up."

Well, Christ. That's completely nuts, but also impressive. I haven't been properly trained in interrogation techniques. Everything I know I learned from movies, so here goes.

I reach under him and grab his balls. He howls.

"Tell me everything you know, or your sac is the first thing to go."

He thrashes around, and I have to kick him in the ribs a few times again.

Voices sound above the ridgeline. It's too dark, and the brush is too thick to see who it is. I crouch low, wishing the asshole here could breathe a little more quietly.

"Did you see where she went?"

"This way," Johnny answers.

Footsteps skid against pebbles, and it sounds as if they're going right by me. I have to make a split-second decision to give my position away. I don't know who else is out there, but if Johnny and Magnum are having a conversation, it must be fine.

I hope.

"Johnny! Mag!"

Footsteps crunch in the gravel. "Did you hear that?"

"Mag," I call out.

"Over here!" Johnny yells.

The asshole coughs, and I move the blade back to his neck. I eye the shrub line and then glance back to the guy, darting between the two threats. Finally, a figure steps through the branches at the spot where I came down. Two shadows descend the embankment. The one in the back aims a gun at dipshit's head.

"Kyla," Johnny says, feet working over the uneven terrain as he makes his way over. He assesses me, pulling his shirt off and handing it to me when he sees what I'm left wearing. He gently takes the knife from my hand, and I pull the shirt over my head, covering my body again and ripping the already shredded shirt away from me.

"Did he...?" Johnny asks, scanning me for evidence.

I shake my head. "Not sure he could have. Seems like a pussy to me."

The guy does this weird sort of cough-laugh that's more gurgle than anything else. "Bitch."

Mag cocks the gun. "I'd watch what you say if I were you."

"He told me he'd rather die than tell me who he's working for."

Johnny bends, grabbing my scraps of shirt before placing his knee into the small of my attacker's back. While Magnum holds him at gunpoint, Johnny ties his hands together behind his back, and then kicks him over until he rolls onto his back. "Recognize him?"

Mag peers down, brow cinching. "No."

"Me either," Johnny huffs. "We've got to blindfold this asshole and get to the safe house."

Safe house? This is news. I thought the tower was the safe house. An impenetrable fortress. What ever happened to that idea?

"I'll get us a car," Mag says. He lifts his shirt, putting his gun in the back of his waistband. He walks by, gaze sliding over me. He, too, searches for injuries. Other than some cuts and scrapes, my right arm is a little sore. I'm pretty sure I used it to catch some of my fall when I came down the ravine.

Johnny beckons me forward, and I move toward him. He puts his arm around my shoulders, and I place my palm on his chest. His skin is cool to the touch.

"Did he hurt you?"

I shake my head, and he kisses my temple. "Looks like he got the worst of it."

The guy is keeping his mouth shut. Smart move.

I find myself looking at him, searching for clues as if I'll be able to find out who he's working with. He has to know he's pretty well fucked right now. Johnny has him, and he's not getting away.

A short honk comes from the opposite side of the bank. Shortly after, Mag skids down the ravine, and then he and Johnny wrench the guy up, dragging him under the arms up the slope. I scramble to the top. Dirt and mud cling to my hands. Idling on the side of the road is a small car. When he and Johnny get to the top of the ravine, Mag takes his shirt off and wraps it around the attacker's face, covering his eyes. Looking at a shirtless Magnum and Johnny, I would think I was at some sort of Chippendale show, but the bleeding asshole takes away the effect of that. I knew I hated this guy. I hope this isn't the only chance I'll get to see Magnum and Johnny shirtless in the same room at the same time because if it is, I'm going to kill this guy for ruining it.

"I'll get in the back with him." Mag drags the guy to the backdoor, shoving him inside none too gently. The two of them in the backseat look like packed sardines because the enemy asshole is easily as big as Magnum.

Johnny opens the passenger door for me, and I slip inside, pulling my seatbelt around me and making sure it locks in place.

Once in the driver's seat, Johnny starts the car. He places his hand on my thigh and squeezes. When he looks up, he makes the shh motion to me, and I nod knowingly. He doesn't want the guy to figure out where this safe house is in case he gets away, even though I highly doubt that's happening.

We ride in silence, which is an opportune time to get my thoughts together. Soon, my adrenaline crashes, and I start to shake. It's like coming off the worst high. Johnny rubs my leg harder as I tremble beside him. He's trying to calm me, but I either need to exercise it out or lie down with my eyes closed and zen it away.

We drive away from the city, and I can't be too sure, but I'm almost positive I've seen the same houses a couple of times, so it wouldn't surprise me if Johnny is not only taking the long way there but also driving around a few blocks in an attempt to throw the guy off. It would surprise me if the guy is even conscious beneath his blindfold, but who knows.

Forty minutes later, we're in the thick of the forest when Johnny hangs a right, slowing the car. The ruts in the dirt drive bounce the car around, but eventually, we pull into a much more level gravel area.

A few black-clad bodyguards jog down the wood steps, approaching the car with guns drawn. Johnny turns the interior light on in the car, and they stow their weapons away, coming toward us in earnest now that they know we're friends and not foes.

A guard wrenches my door open and hauls me to my feet. I step away from him as he does a cursory once-over, injury shopping. I wave him away, and by then, Johnny is beside me, pulling me to him.

The guards take over from there, leading our captive to a barn-like building to the west. I can't imagine the horrors that await him there as I'm sure they're way more adept at interrogation.

"Let's get you cleaned up," Johnny says.

The structure in front of us is a beautiful two-story log cabin. It's so homey looking that the backdrop highlighting all the bodyguards stands out. This could be any family's weekend cabin. Especially since it's deep in the woods where no one else is around. I can't even imagine where the nearest neighbor is.

Johnny leads me up the front stairs to a wrap-around porch. He pulls open a storm door, and I'm greeted with more wood inside, coupled with soft lighting and rustic fixtures. Don't get me wrong, everything is new, it's just designed to look old and lived in.

I immediately fall in love with the place. It couldn't be more different from the tower. Instead of the sterile white and steel, it's warm and inviting.

"Where are we?"

"Our safe house," Johnny explains. "We only use it in emergencies, such as when we can't access the tower."

I run my hands through my hair, my fingers getting stuck in a rat's nest. I give up and toss my hair over my shoulders.

"Up here," Johnny says. He takes my hand, gently holding my fingers. "We'll get you washed up, so we can see your injuries better."

"What about you?" I ask, looking him over from head-to-toe. "Did you get hurt?"

He shakes his head. "Mag drew all the fire. I backed him up, trying to pick people off, so you could get away."

"I tried," I tell him. "The guy jumped me."

He pulls open a door at the very end of the hall on the second floor, and we move into what must be the master bedroom. The huge space boasts an enormous bed in the middle of the room. Behind me, Johnny turns the light on and a fan whirs overhead. Beyond the bed, sliding-glass doors lead out onto a back deck.

"It's pretty, isn't it?"

"Gorgeous," I tell him. It's the perfect place I would've conjured up for myself when I just want to get away. To escape somewhere where no one knew me.

After a moment, he pulls me in the opposite direction. The harsh light of the bathroom illuminates a modern bathroom that somehow goes with all the other rustic design elements. Johnny drops my hand and moves to a whirlpool tub that looks big enough to fit three people. He turns the faucet on, checking the temperature, before turning toward me.

"I'll grab you some clothes," he says. "And I have to make a few calls, but I'll be right here if you need me."

I nod, and he moves forward, pressing a chaste kiss to my forehead. "I'm so glad you're okay."

I wind my arms around his waist, dropping my head to kiss the top of his shoulder. "I'm glad you're okay," I say over his skin.

"One of these days, I'm going to tell you that you don't have to worry about anything and mean it."

I close my eyes, wondering when that day comes, what that point in time might look like? I can only hope it doesn't include people trying to kill us but does include three other gorgeous men.

That's what I would call perfection.

After lingering in the tub, scrubbing down from head to toe until all the dirt and grime has disappeared and my hair is finally untangled, I find a towel on the edge of the tub, wrap it around my body, and emerge from the water.

It's been a hot minute since I've taken a bath, and I have to admit it was relaxing and perfect.

I pad out to the master bedroom and find a stack of clothes on the bed. They're just joggers and a plain shirt, so I pull them on even though they're a couple of sizes too big. I cinch the ties around the waist and roll up the hem, so the pant legs aren't dragging over the floor as I walk.

Sticking my head out the door, I listen for Johnny. He said he had to make a few phone calls, but he never came back.

I retreat down the stairs, but no one is in the house. It's empty. The ticking of the second hand on the clock above the living room mantle sends shivers up my spine. I hug my arms to myself as I peer out the front door. The lights are on in the barn where Mag took our captive. The functional part of my brain warns me that I won't like what I see in there, but the dysfunctional part of my brain tells me it doesn't matter. I'm just as deeply involved as the rest of these guys, and I don't believe for one second it's a coincidence that the moment Johnny gets back from Chicago, someone tries to blow up the tower.

The driveway pebbles sting my feet, but I walk crisply over the gravel, anyway. The side door is unlocked, so I let myself in. Voices, as if coming from a tunnel, sound from the corner of the room. There, another doorway looms, and it leads to a descending staircase. I take the steps, my foot hitting the bottom cement, where the voices are crystal clear now.

A single light fixture dangles in the middle of the room. The floor is tiled, and a chair sits in the center of the space with a halo of light surrounding it. Encircling the guy who tried to take me out is a ring of Heights Crew men. Johnny's in the middle, looming over the asshole, watching as streams of blood run from a cut on his forehead. The captor's eyes are badly bruised and swollen now. He can barely see out of his right eye. It's so puffy it's gross. The guy acts as if he's not in the worst shape imaginable though. "The girl was better at this than you guys. At least she threatened to chop my dick off."

"Actually, it was your balls," I say, moving forward. "And there's still time."

Johnny and Mag both turn, catching a glimpse of me. I give them both small smiles of reassurance. Honestly, for as terrifying as the moment was, I'm not severely injured and neither are the guys. That's all we can ask for.

Johnny leaves the circle, and the other bodyguards close rank around the chair, blocking us out. "I'm sorry," Johnny says, giving me an apologetic smile. "I had to take care of this."

I peer over his shoulder. The guy is leering at me between two solid bodies. Magnum whacks him upside the head with the butt of his gun, which is probably how he got the cut on his forehead in the first place now that I think about it.

"I know," I tell him. "We have to figure out where the threat is coming from."

Johnny runs his hands through his dark hair, exhaling. He's exhausted. He only just got home from Chicago, had an intense conversation with me, and then the building started shaking and we got shot at. That's enough for anyone's nerves to be frayed down the middle.

"Is he going to talk?"

"He's being pretty tight-lipped. I'm guessing he's been around the block a few times."

"He told me he wouldn't open his mouth because he believes in his cause. He said we'd have to kill him because he's not giving us anything."

"It might come down to that," Johnny says, glancing up at me through feathered lashes. His light blue eyes stand out, almost like a spotlight in the grimy room around us. This room is definitely an interrogation room. The tile, the stripped walls. Hell, there's even a drain in the middle of the floor. The Crew isn't playing around. The safe house is as well stocked as the tower. Maybe this is what the basement of the tower looks like.

"We got a crew checking out the tower right now. Whoever this guy belongs to, they set off explosives, but it was a piss-poor job. The bark was bigger than its bite. We'll call in the builders to check the foundation, but it's probably still livable. The team is also bringing the device here, so I can take a look at it. I might be able to find some clues as to who placed it."

I tell him my thoughts on the attack being deliberate based on him coming home and his nickname. A small smile crosses his face. "I thought of that too, babe. It wouldn't surprise me."

The sound of clothing ripping splits the air. Johnny turns, and we both find Magnum in front of the asshole, ripping the shirt from his body. He's inspecting a tattoo on his right side.

He rears back, punching him in the face and then turns

to stalk toward us. The other guards, once again, close ranks to shield us from the captive's eyes.

Mag drags his fingers over his scruff. A honey brown permeates his irises with a sour look of concentration. When he joins our small circle, he says, "He's got a dragon tattoo."

He's talking to Johnny, but he's looking at me. My stomach twists. That's the second guy today who had a dragon tattoo. I wonder if Mag thinks this guy is in the same gang his cousin is, and if so, why his cousin would try to "help" us. Or even fake it, when hours later, someone else is trying to take us out.

"Can we be sure?" Johnny asks, not needing Mag to confirm his suspicions. "Dragon tattoos are popular."

"I think we need to have a talk," Mag says, lowering his voice. "The others can handle this guy overnight. He's not budging, but give him a couple of days down here, and we'll see if he changes his tune. There's no point in killing him right away."

Johnny's gaze darkens as he looks back at the guy who tried to hurt me. For a moment, I wonder if he's going to be as reckless as his father and just whip his gun out and shoot the guy. He doesn't. He turns on his heel, grabs my hand, and leads me up the stairs with Magnum following close behind.

My bare feet scruff against the cement in the upstairs barn area. Right as I step outside, I barely get two paces before Magnum scoops me up in his arms and walks me over the gravel driveway.

My face flushes a terrible crimson that I hope doesn't ruin everything. I meet Johnny's gaze as he looks at us, but the expression on his face is indecipherable.

As soon as we get to the porch, Magnum lowers me to the well-kept floor, and Johnny once again puts his hand in mine without a word.

It might be me, but I think we're making progress. Johnny is either lessening his natural caveman tendencies, or he just really likes Magnum. Both work for me.

The clock in the open plan living room reads four in the morning. Soon, the horizon will light up over the trees of this canopied forest. It's been a long night, but I'm with Magnum. This needs to be said. How can Johnny make decisions if he doesn't have all the information?

Johnny sits on the couch. I go to sit next to him, but he pulls me to his lap, arms wrapping around my middle. He sets my feet up to the couch and starts rubbing the dirt and tiny stones from my feet before massaging my heel.

Mag sits opposite us in a chair just beside the fireplace. He's only a few feet from us, and normally, I would say he seems so far away with Johnny in the room, but right now, it doesn't feel that way. It feels like we're all on the same page, which gives me even more hope.

Mag runs his hands through his hair. "I kept some-thing from you, and I'm sorry. I didn't think it was relevant, but now that it is, I'm making sure you know everything."

Johnny stiffens underneath me, and it's so subtle I doubt Mag even notices.

I silently cheer Magnum on, urging him with my eyes to just tell Johnny. Underneath his hard facade, he's a decent human. He may do things for the Crew that are decidedly indecent, but that's not who he truly is. I know it in my heart.

"Earlier, when I went to check on Farmingham's body, Cole was there."

Johnny's hand stills on my feet. "Cole?"

Mag nods. "He didn't tell me anything I wouldn't have been able to find out for myself, but he acted as if he was there to help, telling me about the Runts in Farmingham's pocket."

"Like you wouldn't have checked his pockets anyway..."

"Exactly."

"So, how does this intersect with the guy in the barn?"

Magnum presses his tongue against his teeth. He doesn't look over at me, but I feel like he wants to. "They both have a dragon tattoo. His was on his neck. I didn't ask him about it, and he didn't offer up any information either, but it just seems like too much of a coincidence right now."

"And the Dragons are, what?" Johnny pinches his nose in thought. "Three? Four hours away?"

Mag nods. "There are different chapters in a few of the

surrounding states, but the closest one is about three and a half hours away."

Johnny shifts on the seat, holding me close to him. "We've never had a problem with them before."

"It's hard to know what's going on, but Cole showing up was a red flag. He knew I was going to check out the body, so he beat me to it."

"Do you think he killed him?"

Matter-of-factly, Mag answers, "I can't say yes, and I can't say no. Is he playing the Gregory angle? Is it really the Dragons? Cole knows I'm not stupid. Part of me believes he really was trying to help, even though—"

"He was never smart," Johnny says, sighing. He takes a deep breath. "You're aware there's a kill order out on him."

I try to relax even though the way Johnny said it is threatening. Accusing.

"Anyone who defects is shot on sight."

"I know," Mag says, straightening in the chair. He faces him like a man. He's not cowering or shying away from the subject. He made a decision, and he's dealing with the consequences...on his own. He's wisely keeping Brawler and I out of the story.

"Why didn't you do it?"

"He's just...dumb," Mag says. "He didn't pose a threat. He wasn't even armed."

"And he's your cousin."

"And he's my cousin," Mag solidifies.

Johnny chews on his lip, and the palpable tension in the room beats its own rhythm. With each ticking second of the clock, it ratchets higher and higher.

For Mag's part, he doesn't look disturbed. A lesser man would. He just admitted to his gang leader that he kept vital information secret. He put family above Crew.

What Johnny does with this information will tell us a lot about how his mind works.

"Kyla, can you go upstairs please?"

I don't even register the words at first. It isn't until Johnny places my feet softly on the carpet that what he said actually seeps through my brain. I want to balk, but I have no reason to, and I also don't want to get Johnny in a pissy mood now that he potentially has something on Magnum.

"We'll sleep in the master bedroom tonight. Why don't you lie down, so I can talk to Magnum alone?"

Johnny squeezes my hand lightly as I stand, his reassuring hand on the small of my back. I lock gazes with Magnum, but the look I receive back tells me nothing. He's just empty. Waiting.

I walk toward the beautiful ornately carved banister and glance back. They're still locked in a staring match. Apprehension crowds me like a stocked subway train with no room to breathe. This is a moment on the precipice. I don't even know if Magnum has ever defied an order before, or what Johnny usually does to people who do, though I can take a guess. If I was lining up a shot on a dartboard, I'd aim for the big circle that says, *He makes them pay*.

Before I'm caught staring, I move to the top of the stairs and stop. I sit, making sure I'm out of their view, but can still hear them when they begin talking again.

"You know what I'm supposed to do, right?" Johnny asks.

"Punish me," Magnum says. "That's at your discretion."

The sofa creaks, and my heart lodges in my throat. Images flicker by of Johnny pulling out a gun and shooting Mag point blank in the face just like Big Daddy K did to Dunnegan and Roza. I'm on the point of thudding down the stairs and calling out to him to stop.

Only, it turns out I don't have to. "When someone has a secret, that makes them friends."

Magnum doesn't say anything.

"When two people have secrets on each other, that makes them allies."

"I've heard the terms."

I smile because I'm fairly sure Magnum said almost the same thing to me once.

Johnny blows out a breath. "We were talking before Kyla woke up, and you told me I could talk to you."

"Anything," Mag says.

"I was once in your position." Johnny's voice sounds off, and I don't think I've ever heard the same tone come out of his mouth before. He's sad, confused, and lost. Everything all wrapped up at once that what comes out is a tenor so lonely it makes my heart break. "I found one of my family members before. Someone who defected. I didn't kill them either." There's a long pause before he speaks again. "I wanted to, and I almost hate myself for it now."

"Who was it?" Mag asks.

"My mom."

My body trembles with the ache to go to them. To both of them. His mom got away, so yeah, she defected. He told me as much earlier, but he didn't tell me he'd found her. He'd only told me he hated her for it.

"She was living with a new family. A new life. They had a house in a posh neighborhood just on the outskirts of a quaint town. It was perfect...and I was bitter."

"That would've been a lot to take in, man," Magnum says.

"I left her there. To lead her new life. I walked away." The ticking of the clock extends. "But it didn't matter because he killed her, anyway."

I gasp. I'm so thrown by his admittance that I don't cover my mouth until it's too late. Then, I'm just sitting there with my hand over my face, my lip tucked between my teeth.

"My dad found her, and he wasn't as nice as me," Johnny continues. "He killed her. I just want you to know that I know how that feels, and I would never do that to anybody. Your secret is safe with me."

My heart drums so loud it's like there's a concert going

on in my chest cavity. I pull myself up to shaky feet and retreat into the master bedroom, sinking down into the insanely comfortable mattress and curling up into a ball.

That bastard killed his own wife. He killed his son's mom.

He deserves everything coming to him.

## 14

When Johnny finally makes it to the master bedroom, I pretend to be asleep. I don't want to look him in the eye and pretend I don't know anything. I spend the time lying next to him getting my game face together. A time will come when I will ask about his mom, but it won't be right now. He can tell me when he's ready, and besides, we have current things to worry about right now.

The next morning, I slip off of the mattress and head into the en suite shower. Getting ready for the day when you don't know what you're going to face is awkward. At least when I was at my aunt and uncle's, I knew I'd have to deal with petty bitches and guys who think their shit doesn't stink at the prep school. In the Heights, everything is a toss-up. It could be school, it could be training, it could be getting fucking shot at.

Regardless, since it's called a safe house, I'm hoping for an easier existence here. However, I don't know if that will be the case considering we're holding someone captive against their will. Someone who'd tried to take me out yesterday. I have a feeling it won't be a quiet, reserved day in the middle of the woods.

I leave the shower followed by a billow of steam. Tying the towel around my chest, I walk into the enormous bedroom to find Johnny sitting on the edge, shoulders tight with his head hung low. He looks as if he's carrying the weight of the world. I move to him and thread my fingers through his hair. "Hey..."

He peers up at me. He takes a moment to watch me like I'm his favorite work of art. He doesn't say anything, just roams his gaze all over me. "I don't know if I said this before, but this is my favorite time with you. In the mornings when we haven't had to deal with the day yet."

A smile peels my lips apart. "And what is today going to bring?" I ask. "More interrogation? Bloodshed? Clandestine meetings?"

He chuckles. It's a deep sound that catches me off guard. Surely, I've had to have heard him laugh before, right? Maybe this time is different. "Do you think I have clandestine meetings?"

"Oh, all the time," I whisper. "When I'm at school or training."

He tangles his fingers with mine and brings my hand to his face, brushing a soft kiss against my semi-sore knuckles. I got a couple of good shots in on the guy yesterday, so it's no surprise. A grimace crosses his face. At first, I think it's because he's seen how red my knuckles are, but instead, he says, "My dad's coming back today. He wants to see this guy in person." He slides his gaze to the nightstand. "I heard this morning that the damage to the tower was inconsequential."

My eyebrows shoot up. "Inconsequential? The building shook, Johnny."

He smirks. "It's rated to shake, babe. It's meant for shit like that. We just didn't want to go there last night because of the shooting, and in case they did some permanent damage to the building's structure. Being there when it decided to fall would be a terrible idea."

"So, we're going back to the tower?" I ask, hesitation whipping through me.

Johnny shakes his head. "Not yet. Some of my dad's men will take the guy to the tower, wait for him to return. I might have to sneak out to be there when that happens, but I'll come back."

A flicker of hope passes through me. "We're not going back to the tower?"

He snakes his arms around me. The knot in my towel

loosens with the contact. His gaze flicks to it and then back up to my face. "You really like it here, huh?"

"Am I that easy to read?"

"Not usually, actually." He locks his light blue eyes on me, and a shiver crawls up my spine. "I'm happy you like it though. This is one of my favorite places." A distant look flashes in his eyes. "I'd live here if I could, but we have to live in the Heights. We can't just stroll in and expect people to respect us when we're not even living in the city we control."

"Well, it's not like you're truly living like everyone else anyway," I tell him. I get his logic, but it isn't as if he's living in the threadbare apartments everyone else deals with. The tower is posh. It's a mansion compared to the holes everyone else lives in.

"Yeah, but that's what makes our life so enticing. People see what we have and then they want it. They recruit in during high school. The dream is to work their way up through the ranks. For some it doesn't happen, but for others... Look at Bat," Johnny says, animated now. "He was just a nobody until we took him off the street. Now he's already made something of himself even though he hasn't even graduated yet."

I bite the inside of my cheek. I don't think my mind has gone to how deep Oscar is in yet. On his own admission, he joined the Crew because everyone was kicking his ass for leaving and coming back. He's involved in a lot of the important meetings, and he's worried about the rest of the recruits like he's the one who looks after them. Just what does Oscar do for the Crew? Johnny's insinuating he's kind of important. I press my luck and ask him. "What does Oscar do?"

"You want to talk shop?"

I point at myself. "Not a Kardashian, remember?"

Johnny chuckles again. "This and that," he says, intentionally vague, which only piques my interest further.

I act like it doesn't bother me though. Rubbing the back of my neck, I ask, "Are you going to tell your dad about Magnum's cousin?"

Johnny pulls me to the side and stands. "No, I'm not going to do that. What he did was stupid. Now it's not only his ass on the line, but mine too."

Already, a barrier starts to descend between Johnny and me. Maybe it was all the Crew talk, but the guy who chuckled a couple of minutes ago, now has frown lines creasing his mouth.

"I'm sorry," I tell him.

This makes him pull up short. "For what?"

"Ruining your favorite time of the day."

His jaw ticks as he glances over his shoulder. Whatever he sees there makes him come to me again. "You aren't ruining anything. If nothing else, you're the bright spot in all of this."

I give him a hesitant smile. "If my opinion matters, I think it's a good thing that you trust Magnum and he trusts you. You need to open up to people..." I drop off the part that should've said, *...who aren't your father*. He should trust people who don't make him pay for it later.

"You like the other guys here, don't you?"

I swallow. The lump in my throat is so big it practically makes my esophagus walls burn. "They're good guys."

I desperately want to tell him he has a whole family waiting for him. People who will accept him even if he isn't Johnny Rocket of the Heights Crew. At the same time, I know it's too soon. A red flush creeps up my neck. "It was Oscar and Brawler who I was talking about before. They're living in these small ass apartments. Their family life isn't great, and I just wondered what they—and others—see when they get a glimpse into your life."

"They should see hope," Johnny says. "It might take hard work to get here, but trust me, if it weren't for the Crew, Rawley Heights would be a joke. A lawless land of the poor and decrepit. That's what it was like before the Crew. The Crew brought jobs and a solid foundation to the Heights. The economy is booming compared to what it was."

His words drone on like he's reciting from a textbook. He's probably right though. I bet the Crew has done some good things for the Heights, but that doesn't mean everything they do is good. "There's good and bad with everything."

He latches his gaze to mine. The same insecure Johnny who asked if I wanted to leave is back.

I'm quick to reassure him. "I'm staying, Johnny. I just think we both realize the same thing. It's why you won't tell your dad about Magnum's cousin. Sometimes, the Crew isn't so good."

Johnny's gaze hardens. "I know you know this, but those words can't ever leave your mouth around anyone. Understand?"

It would be easier if I could just rip myself bare for him. Show him my insides instead of telling him. Words can be so inconsequential when they're not saying what you truly want to say. "I think you have more friends than you know." I press up onto my tiptoes and kiss him. "You're a good person, Johnny."

He laughs. The sound dark and dangerous, almost curdling my blood. "I'm not good, babe. I'm trying to be, for you, but sometimes invisible straps hold me in place."

"I've got a knife," I tell him, lifting one shoulder.

"The only good decision I've ever made is you."

He cups the back of my head and pulls me forward, sealing his lips to mine. We don't get far because the door to the room crashes open.

Johnny and I jump, and my towel completely unravels. I try to grab it, but it's too late. I flash boob everywhere, and fuck me, but standing in the doorway is none other than Big Daddy K.

"Dad," Johnny exclaims, moving his body in front of mine to shield me.

I quickly knot my towel again, holding my arms securely just under my chest. My face flushes with heat as if it's been cooked from the inside out. Anger sweeps through me. What kind of fucking asshole doesn't knock before he comes into a fucking bedroom?

Johnny's tense voice says, "I thought you weren't coming in until later."

Big Daddy K's piercing gaze goes right through Johnny as if he's undressing me. The disgusting bastard got a pretty good look too. I throw up a little in my mouth and swallow it back down.

"The Cardinale's got their private jet to take me. May I see you in the hall, please?"

Johnny goes to leave, but I reach for his hand, holding him back. He turns a surprised look at me, but I just smile and lay a kiss on him. Like he claimed me at the underground fight nights that first evening, I'm claiming him now. Johnny's mine.

When I pull away, his gaze darkens. He turns without another word and closes the door securely behind him after his dad exits in front of him.

Fuck me.

I sit on the bed, silently seething. I want to punch something in the worst way. Instead, I move to the dresser in the corner and look through the drawers until I find something to put on. I pull on a pair of gray sweats, giving them the same treatment as the joggers yesterday, and then I tug a white shirt on next, taking the extra fabric bunched at my hip, pulling it out, and tying it in a knot. At least it won't look like I'm walking around in a potato sack.

The last thing I want to do is disturb Johnny and his dad, so I stay where I am. My stomach growls for at least fifteen minutes before Johnny comes back in. I'd been staring out the glass doors, so I get up. Instead of saying anything, he walks right to me, throwing his arms around me and whispering, "You have to be careful, babe. Don't piss my dad off. Whatever you do, don't do that."

I grip him tighter. "I wasn't the one who doesn't know how to knock."

"He'll do far more than that."

"Like punch you? Like give you a black eye?"

A growl rips from his throat. "I defied him, and he made me pay for it."

"That's not a father, Johnny," I whisper.

He holds me tighter. His arms are so tight they're like a boa constrictor around my ribs. Finally, he kisses me just under the ear. "I have to go. We're taking the asshole to the tower where we can properly interrogate him. I thought you might like to stay here. I'll be back tonight. Absolutely no one knows where this place is, so you can have it to yourself while we deal with the problem."

I nod into his neck, breathing him in. I hate to let him go, but a reprieve from being thrown back into the Heights world so soon sounds like heaven.

"The kitchen is fully stocked. Netflix, Hulu, cable, whatever you want to watch. There's a hot tub out back. Think of it as a spa day, but not the Kardashian kind."

I grin, chuckling into his embrace. "Sounds perfect."

He pulls away. "I'll be back."

He pecks me on the cheek and strides from the room. I go out onto the back deck off the master bedroom and watch as they all get into cars. A black sack sits over our prisoner's face again as they load him into an SUV. Johnny, Mag, and several other bodyguards get into one vehicle while K strides toward another. He pauses near the passenger door, and I must catch his eye because he gazes up at me.

I'm tens of yards away, but the anger in his face is unmistakable. I may have just made an enemy out of K for something so damn stupid. Or maybe it's a few things compiled on top of one another because he's definitely not smiling anymore. I doubt he'd lift his glass to me at a dinner anymore either.

I raise my hand and wave, giving him a clueless smile.

He inclines his head and then gets into the waiting vehicle.

A few seconds later, they're pulling away, and I can't help but think, *Game on, motherfucker.*

## 15

Like Johnny said, I pamper myself, using the hot tub for the majority of the day. Since no one is around, it didn't even matter there were no bathing suits to be found in the house. After breakfast, I sank into the heat of the water and stayed there, watching the birds fly from tree to tree and chirp their cheerful melodies.

I could get used to a place like this. It's so apart from everything else happening that it makes for a good separation. Even K's appearance earlier left with him instead of lingering in this peaceful place.

When my skin is thoroughly pruned and wrinkled from the water, I amble out of the hot tub, letting the brisk air coat my body in goosebumps before returning to the bedroom and pulling the clothes I found this morning back on.

Johnny was right when he said the place was stocked. I

fix myself a small lunch and then work my way into the enormous living room with windows that edge all the way up to the second story.

Using the laptop I found on the kitchen counter, I Google how to start a fire in a fireplace and get one going in the enormous stone-encased fireplace that takes up one whole wall. Then, I lie down on the sectional sofa, staring at the flames as they burn brighter and brighter. I'm not close enough to the fireplace to feel the heat, but I'm close enough to enjoy the dancing flames and the somehow soothing nature of watching a fire crackle and burn.

Sometime later, car tires crunch on the stone parking area. I peek my head over the top of the couch and watch as a black car parks just short of the porch. For a panic-inducing few moments, I watch the vehicle until a familiar dark head juts out over the top.

I move to a sitting position and gaze at the entry as I wait for him to walk in. He unlocks the door and strides inside, throwing a set of keys on the counter before turning to greet me.

My mouth parts, and I immediately get to my feet at the sight of the crimson streaks and specks that coat him. "What the hell?" I run to him, grasping his hand in mine. "Is that yours?"

Johnny tears his shirt off, breathing heavy as he wipes down his arms and face with his inside out t-shirt. "No."

I sigh in relief, but it's only temporary when the gashes

on his knuckles jump out to me. I bring his hand to mine. "What's this from?"

"I had to take care of something," he says.

I shake my head, biting down on my lower lip. I don't like the sound of that. As much of an oasis as this place is, the dangerous part of it is I'm out of the loop. I don't know what Oscar, Magnum, and Brawler are up to, and my phone, as far as I know, is still in the tower.

Johnny grits his teeth and stares at his bloody knuckles. "Turns out the asshole was a lot more talkative today. Didn't say anything we wanted to hear but decided to explain in detail what he was told to do to you if he'd gotten his hands on you."

My stomach plummets.

Johnny must see the look on my face because he captures my face between his two palms. "He won't be able to hurt you, babe. I took care of it."

A shiver racks my body.

"I need a shower," Johnny says. "Stay here."

I listen to his command for about thirty seconds before I follow him up the stairs into the master bedroom. He's already stripped and in the shower, water sluicing off his chiseled form. His bloodied shirt lies in the middle of the floor, so I kick it aside. I ogle him like a creeper for a few moments before he sees that I'm watching him. Electricity charges between us. While he stares, I lift my borrowed shirt from my body and unclasp my bra. Now topless, I drag my bottoms down and step out of them before moving for the glass door. Despite the water droplets blocking some of my view, Johnny's arousal is apparent.

Steam coats me as I walk in. He wipes the water away from his eyes. The damaged knuckles catch my attention, so I move to him, grabbing his fingers lightly and forcing them under the spray. A few of his knuckles might need Band-Aids, but unfortunately, there's not a lot you can do when you have an injury in that spot. You still need the movement of your fingers which can cause the skin to crack all over again and bring you back to square one.

"I was enraged," Johnny says, watching as I do my best to clear the blood and inspect the full damage that he's done.

"I can imagine," I tell him. "If anyone said awful things about the people I love, I'd be the same."

Johnny reaches out to cup the swell of my breast. This isn't the first time we've been naked around one another, and my body reacts the same as the other times.

"You're so gorgeous," he breathes.

I let his hands go, then grab his forearms to maneuver him under the hot spray, making sure the tiny dots of dried crimson blood that spattered over his neck are gone. I trail my hands over his skin, deepening my touch until I've wandered my hands all over him. Up and down his Adonis belt, over his ass and muscular thighs. His torso is perfectly muscled, and though he lacks the build of a middle or heavy-weight, he owns his own category of hotness.

"You're killing me, babe."

His ragged voice fills the shower, matching the jolting intakes of my own breath as I find a new area of his body to admire. I haven't touched his dick yet, but I'm already heated and wanting. I'm well aware of the rule Big Daddy K put in place, but that's not what's keeping me from taking this further even though I desperately want to. I'm worried about breaking us. I have my secrets, and Johnny hasn't told me all of his either. I'm not just talking about his mom, I'm talking about the things he's done. He isn't saying it outright, but did he kill a man today? Did he beat him until he wasn't breathing?

Do I care?

"I'm not good enough for you," Johnny says, tightening as I run my hand up his thigh from behind.

"Who says I'm good enough for you?"

His ass bucks back into me as I skim his cock. I grab his hips, holding him in place because I am two seconds from saying fuck everything. Just fuck it. Johnny is a part of me now, so sue me that I want to act on these base desires. Letting him fill me, enjoying his hard thrusts because I can just imagine the way he fucks. He is called Rocket after all.

Johnny turns, reaches around me and shuts off the waterfall showerhead. He shoves the door open and then picks me up, one arm around my shoulder and the other around my knees as he carries me to the bed.

"I want you so bad I can't stand it."

He lowers me to the comforter, and I move up the bed, placing my head on the pillows. I pull him down with me so we're facing each other on our sides. We've been in this position before. It's at this point where he usually stops.

"There are things…" He licks his lips, eyes eating me up with desire. "I wonder if you knew them if you'd stop looking at me the way you are now."

It's as if he's peering right into me, pulling the words I need to say to him out. "It goes both ways," I tell him.

He skims his hand up my side, grazing the pad of his thumb over my breast. Chills erupt over me.

"We should stop," I tell him.

He rolls me over onto my back, pinning my hands above my head. "No," he growls. "I want to show you how much I care for you."

I clamp my jaw shut. He lets his hips dip, torturing me with his hard cock against my abdomen. "There are things you don't know," I force out. *What am I doing? Fuck.* A cold sweat breaks out over my forehead.

"I don't care. Open up for me, babe. I don't care about my dad. I don't care what you've done because when I see you look at me like that, I know this is right. Even when you find out about me, I'll fight for you. I won't take no for an answer."

"Neither will I," I tell him, challenging him with my stare. "You'll hate me."

"Not possible. You're saving me. You can't possibly have

done the things I've done. I never thought I'd find something like this because I'm too far gone. I don't deserve it. I'm fucked. I'm broken. But you—"

He nudges me, and my resolution slips. I want to believe in everything he's saying.

"Do you trust me?" I ask.

He nods, lust and excitement mix in his eyes, but an acknowledgment as well. He's not just on some horny high where he has to have me and will regret it later. This is the natural progression of our relationship. This is the next step in committing to one another.

It's the same for me. I slowly move my knees to the side, opening for him. I don't look away, I gaze straight through to his core, where I feel his promise to me and give it right back to him.

I breathe out. His soul is intoxicating. "I think I love you, Johnny Marx."

I bite my lip as soon as I've said it, but Johnny pushes inside with a soul-touching sound of love and claiming and promises that at first distract from how fucking amazing he feels seated inside.

He doesn't return the sentiment, but his gaze says it as he looks down at me reverently. His strong touch, the way he holds me, the way he tries to break all the way into my center tells me he feels the same way.

My toes curl as he batters my body with sure strokes. "Say it again," Johnny pleads, increasing the pace.

"I think I love you."

He groans. "You don't know how much I needed that."

"It's true," I tell him, holding his gaze, hoping he remembers this exact moment when I tell him my secrets. I hope he remembers he said he'd fight for me. I hope he remembers the way he feels right now because if he's anything like me, he's lost himself to me.

I'll fight for him. If he tries to walk away, I'll kidnap his ass and show him. I'll tell him a million times how all this is real, and if he wants to hear me say I love you, I'll do it as many times as it takes. I'll say it until my throat is raw and strained. I'll write it until my hands are weak with arthritis. I'll stare at him with the truth in my eyes for the rest of my life. He'll never have to doubt it.

Never.

His body starts to shake. I've been too busy making so many promises to him in my head that I've missed out on fully enjoying the pleasure bombarding me.

I let out a breath, and he dips his gaze to my lips. Leaning forward, he kisses me until my lips swell and rational thought leaves my brain, pleasure taking over.

I try to struggle from his grip, but he holds me in place, switching the angle of his movements until my mouth opens and I release a breathy sigh.

He kisses a trail down my neck, lips curving over my collarbone in a salacious tease.

I meet his strokes with my own and watch in awe at the

pained expressions that flit over his face. "Fuck, Kyla." He groans long and deep, a guttural sound that makes my core clench at the primal nature of it.

I test his weight on my wrists, but he still won't let up, so I continue to fuck him back, lifting my hips in the only move I can do to give right back to him.

This undoes him more than anything else. His resolve starts to teeter, and whatever shields he had in place crack. "Fuck me, baby. God."

His hold loosens, and I pull my wrists out to grab his ass. Then, I hook my leg around his in a grappling move and force my way on top. I move over him, the vulnerability on his face clear. He grabs my hips, clinging to me as I ride him. In between the short pants that stream from my mouth, I say, "I want you as much as you want me."

He moans, his movements tightening as I sink myself on top of him time and time again. He's going to come easily. He was hiding from me again. For what reason, I don't know, but not with this. Not when I'm giving it right back to him.

He reaches out and swirls his finger around my clit until I come hard, crying out on top of him.

"Yes, baby. I'm going to come." He tries to lift me off, but I lean forward, putting my weight over him. Even if he wanted to stop me, it's too late. His cock jerks, cum coating my insides. My pussy clenches, milking him until I climax again.

He pulls me forward, grinding against me until we both come down. Breathing hard, I tell him, "I'm on the pill. I wanted to feel you like that. Unrestrained. Uncaring."

His cock jerks. "Mmm, yes."

I roll to my side until we're facing each other. He pulls out, and the evidence of what we did spills out onto my thighs. I have no doubt we've made a mess of the bed, but I couldn't care less.

Johnny grabs the back of my head, forcing me to look at him. "You're always showing me the way things should be." He peers down at my lips, and I know he's referencing the change in him mid-sex. He drops his forehead to mine. "I wanted to be the bad guy in case you leave. I wanted to tell myself that I made you do it. That I forced you into fucking me so it would hurt less when you decide against me."

I pull his hand to my chest, settling it between my breasts where my heart thumps a mile a minute. "That, right here? That proves otherwise, and I don't want you to forget it."

Johnny bends, kissing me where I'd just put his hand and then pulls me to him, both of us settling against each other. I pull his arm around me and marvel that the world is still standing in the aftermath of Johnny Marx and I coming together.

That has to be a good omen, right?

---

## 16

*J*ohnny threads his fingers through mine as we make our way back into the Heights. Even though I've only been in the log cabin for two days, it was a much-needed sanctuary. A place to forget. A place to have a moment of peace. A place where Johnny and I coming together felt like the most beautiful thing in the world...instead of something wrong. Or disallowed. Or unforgivable.

Don't get me wrong. It *was* beautiful. It's what I've been wanting, but at what expense? He promised me important things, and I turned around and made the same promises back to him. We both need to hold up our end of the bargains.

Neither of us speak very much on our way back, but our fingers twined together is the only reassurance I need. If

Johnny can't forgive what's going on at the end of this, I, at least, have this memory to take with me. I'd been hoping to enjoy the aftermath for longer in our little haven, but Johnny received a call from his dad hurrying us back. Apparently, matters need to be discussed. Right now. Though, it seems as if there are always matters to be discussed that calls Johnny away from me.

The look in K's eyes when he saw me on the balcony. I shiver, even now, remembering the hard look in his gaze. I shouldn't provoke him because I know what he's capable of. At the same time, what I'm doing shouldn't be annoying him. I'm loving his son. That should never be a crime.

My stomach tumbles over itself, squeezing as I wonder what this meeting is about, considering my presence was requested. Actually, requested is too nice of a word. It was demanded, and I could tell by the stiffness in Johnny's shoulders when his dad told him he wanted me there that Johnny didn't like it at all.

We pass the sign welcoming us into the Heights. The scenery isn't bad yet. We're in the suburbs section, mostly. The houses aren't great, but they're not quite as dim and disheveled as the inner city of the Heights. We're in the calm before the storm. The shroud before the maggots eating away at dead, putrid flesh.

Johnny squeezes my hand, then peeks at me from the driver's seat. It's nice to be together, just him and me. I can be myself without worrying over who else is around, who's allowed to see what I truly feel. I have a feeling my happy place is about to get smashed to bits though. He licks his lips, dribbling his free hand over the steering wheel. "I need you to say as little as possible while we're at the meeting, okay?"

I nod.

"I mean it," Johnny urges, his icy blue eyes intense. "I don't know what my dad is going to say, but it must involve you. No matter what it is, stay quiet. If it's something we don't like, I can work on him later, but disrespecting him in front of a group is never wise."

"Neither is disrespecting him when you're alone apparently," I counter. Unease skitters up my spine, but so does a healthy dose of injustice. "So, you'll work on him later, and he'll just hit you again." His jaw ticks, and I sigh, some of the fight leaving me. It's not Johnny's fault his father is a lunatic. "I'm not going to say anything to get you in trouble, and I don't need you to fight my battles for me, Johnny. Whatever your dad has planned for me, I'll do. Okay? You're not getting hit again because of me."

Johnny slips his hand from my grasp and thuds it heavily on the steering wheel. "You don't understand the shit he could ask you to do. You're one of us now because of me. He owns you. The stories I could tell you—" He breaks off, swallowing as if he's willing all the terrible things he's seen and done back into a corner of his mind that he never has to face.

I turn in my seat, reaching out to set my hand on his

thigh. "And you will tell me someday, but you know me. I'm tough and resilient. Your dad won't break me. He can't."

The look Johnny throws my way says he believes otherwise, but I know what I'm made of. You don't do what I've done to cower at someone's feet when the time comes.

"Listen," I try again. "The last thing I want to do is hurt you, so don't worry about me during the meeting. I'm not saying a thing unless he asks me something directly." Which actually works for me anyway, considering every time I'm in his presence, I want to gouge his eyes out...or my own.

Being around my guys is easier now that I don't have to hide my distaste of Big Daddy K. Not that I'm going to up and tell Johnny I plan on murdering his father soon, but I also don't have to watch everything I say. It's completely normal to hate your boyfriend's abusive father. I shudder to think about what he's had to endure his whole life.

Fuck abusers. All they do is start a long line of abuse—mentally and physically. I'm not saying everyone learns the behavior, but it can be learned, and it does perpetuate. Take Johnny, he struggles with it. I now understand his reaction when he threw me against the wall outside the clothing shop. No, it doesn't make what he did right. It never will. I'm just saying I understand where he got it, and I can see the connections in his mind that he's made that he can be better than that. He *is* better than that.

The block the tower sits on looms ahead. As we get closer, I tilt my head to gaze up at the building. Despite the fact that I know I was in this vibrating building the other day, it looks fine. No cracks in the exterior. No missing walls or crumbled rock on the sidewalks. It withstood a fucking bomb.

"I'm positive it's safe to head back inside," Johnny says, noticing my stare. "I would never bring you back if I thought differently."

"I know," I reassure him. "I'm just shocked the building can withstand what they threw at us."

"It was made that way. Plus, they were amateur bombs. The noise of the explosion was worse than the damage, and they didn't even add the charges in the correct places for maximum damage." I lift my brows at him. When I don't immediately respond to him, he looks over at me and grins. "What?"

"You know a lot about this."

"I may have blown up a building or two in my time." He snickers, and a flash of cruel delight simmers in his gaze. "I even set the school science lab on fire once."

I laugh, the sound bursting from my chest like I can't contain it. The sound surprises me, which only makes me laugh harder. First of all, I can barely think of Johnny Rocket in a classroom setting. It seems too lowly for him. Did he sit through lectures dressed in his suit pants and tie? Second, just the fact that he set fire to the school has me rolling.

"To be fair, it was an accident the first time."

I shake my head at him. "I bet the administrators were happy to get rid of you."

"Except I keep showing back up."

My gut clenches as I think of Johnny with the school secretary. He was a little playboy, wasn't he? Unrepentant, took what he wanted, and gloated about it.

The guard at the station waves us under the building and into the parking garage. While Johnny parks, I ruminate over how far he's come. At the same time, I've gone in the opposite direction. I've backslid. Do I even have morals anymore? Did I check them at the city limits of Rawley Heights, only to get them back when I leave this town? Maybe. Hopefully....

Then again, I never claimed to be a good person. I came here to murder someone. In that way, Johnny and I are the same. We act for our own happiness, regardless of how bad those actions might be.

Now, though, the deeper the guys imbed into my life, I like to think I'm acting with *all* of them in mind. I just hope Johnny sees that when he finds out the truth.

Magnum steps off the elevator, holding it for us as we close the car doors and step up to him. He eyes me briefly before moving his gaze to Johnny. "Everyone's upstairs already."

Johnny checks his watch, but we're not late. At least not by the vehicle's clock.

"Heard any rumors as to what this is about?" Johnny questions, taking my hand to lead me to the elevator.

The copper-haired stunner shakes his head. He's dressed all in black, as usual. At this point, it would be a jolt to my system to see him in any other color. Plus, the black offsets his hair nicely and clings to his muscles, and... I block those thoughts as he answers. "No, nothing."

"Stay with Kyla," Johnny orders. "She's been instructed not to say anything, but—"

I pierce Johnny with a look, and Mag smirks. "But you're not sure she'll listen?"

"Basically, yes," Johnny deadpans.

These assholes. I do have some restraint. "While we're giving out orders, no one comes to my defense if shit starts to go down in there," I tell both of them. "Also, I promise I won't say a word unless spoken to."

"Still," Johnny says to Mag. "I don't want her left alone."

The worried look in Johnny's pale blue eyes alarms me. Does he think Big Daddy K will do something to me right now? Does he know? I shake that thought out of my head immediately. If he knew K was going to do something to me, there's no way he'd be bringing me here right now. "How worried should I be?"

Johnny presses his lips closed and all of us step into the elevator.

"I'm just saying," I continue. "I'd like to know so I can prepare myself, but in the same token, if he does do something, neither one of you step in his way. I mean it. I've seen what happens when that goes down."

Johnny's Crew mask has completely taken over him. His voice is even harsh when he answers. "You should always be worried when you're in my father's presence, and you're delusional if you think we'd just sit there."

Magnum's look tells me more of the same, and I don't miss the warning implied in Johnny's words. Big Daddy K may not do anything to me today, but the chance is always high. Not that I didn't know that already, but it's a good reminder. I've seen how trigger-happy he is—literally.

The elevator stops at the top floor, and we step off. Magnum's fellow bodyguards move forward, but Johnny waves them off. "She's one of us now."

My steps falter for a second. This is big. This is huge. If the guards are told not to check me, I could get a gun up here or a knife. Some sort of weapon I can take K's life with. Thoughts fire in my brain. I need K's schedule to figure out when he's alone. I need the key to his door. I need to figure out when I can sneak into his suite and just get it over with without the threat of getting caught. I need—

But I can't do any of that, can I? Not until I've pulled Johnny to my side.

Jesus. It sounds like I'm some mad scientist with evil plans for tempting the innocent, but all I really want for Johnny is to have a life worth living. And we all know Johnny is far from innocent.

The guards nod, and I notice Trey, the one I accidentally got in trouble before when Glo came to kill me. Seeing him is a reminder that actions have consequences.

Johnny threads my arm through his as Magnum opens the door to K's suite. Mag's presence is another balm to the quickening pulse at my wrists. Even though I said I wouldn't want them to stick up for me—and I mean it—I'm glad they're both here. The only time I would want them sticking up for me is if I was in Dunnegan's position and K's about to put a bullet in the back of my skull. Then, all bets are off. I'm not dying for the fucker. That's always been at the top of my list of things not to do.

K stands when he sees us enter the room. "There they are." His smile stretches the width of his face, and I'm not sure I've ever seen anything so fake. He moves forward. Johnny has to drop my hand as his father pulls him into a hug. I stiffen, my heart sinking into the acidic bowels of my stomach as I wait to go completely dead inside. As I feared, K releases Johnny and turns toward me. Instead of a hug, he picks up my hand like Johnny always does and brings it to his mouth to kiss my knuckles. His lips linger a little too long, and I nearly crack teeth trying to keep the smile on my face.

*Enemies close, enemies close, enemies close,* I repeat to myself. One of these days, this will all be worth it.

If it isn't, I'll just hack that hand off. No big deal.

He lets me go, and I take in a shaky breath. Mag moves

closer to me for comfort. He can't touch me. He wouldn't dare with everyone around, but he stands as close as he can without arousing suspicion. I want to hug him for it.

Actually, I'd love to do a lot more than that to the red-headed, mature hottie, but that is definitely a thought for another place and time.

I glance around at all the players in the room. Instinctually, I find Oscar first. We share a short staring match, emotions beaming between us before I sit next to Johnny. Magnum stands behind us, and even though it's stupid, I'm glad to have him there. I don't want anyone sneaking up behind me.

Other than a few bodyguards catering to K, there are the usual business gentlemen that must be in K's inner circle. His right-hand men. One of these days, I need to ask Johnny who they are to understand the inner workings of the gang. Dunnegan used to sit at this very table, and he's dead. I wonder if any of the rest of them are as scared as I am while they sit here. Do they muse over if today will be their last day?

I guess they don't have to worry if they aren't doing anything wrong.

Today, the table is set up more like a business table. The oblong silver stretch of metal we once sat at for dinner is now devoid of plates or silverware. In fact, absolutely nothing sits on the solid surface other than Big Daddy K's forearms as he addresses us.

"I thought it was a good idea to bring all of us together to discuss the incident that occurred two days ago. Firstly, the tower is completely safe despite the attempts to bring it down."

A guy across the table from us leans back in his seat. He has slick black hair, and out of everyone else here, he reminds me of the gangsters in the old mob films, complete with a red handkerchief in his suit pocket. "I'm glad we went with the extra reinforcements then," he chuckles.

"From an excellent supplier," K says, laughing alongside him. When he finishes, he peers around the room as if dissecting us all one-by-one. "Secondly, there are rumors going around about a recruit who was murdered. I'll let Bat fill you in on that."

Oscar sits up straight from his usual lazy position. His eyes widen a fraction before he catches himself. Then, it's as if I'm staring at Big Daddy K, only a couple of decades younger. He's all smirks and no nonsense statements. "Farmingham had been a recruit, however, he was just recently taken off our prospects list. The intel used by whoever killed him was old. Farmingham's death is nothing to us except, of course, the meaning behind it, presumably a message. When Magnum inspected the scene, he found Gregory's calling card. Candy," he says, in a tone so derogatory that I have to press my lips together to keep from laughing. Candy—and Runts at that—is the stupidest calling card I've ever heard. If it wasn't real, I'd think it was a joke.

K nods at him. "Rocket is getting a team together to work on this, but if anyone hears anything, let us know."

Everyone nods their agreements.

"That's everything I have for updates unless anyone has questions…" Big Daddy K inspects the room, traversing all of us with beady eyes before he starts again. "Excellent. New business." He looks over his shoulder at Trey with a smile like he'll enjoy this next part. His enjoyment and cool demeanor makes my skin prick. "Bring him in."

*Dear God. What the fuck? Who now?*

I immediately leap to the idea that I'm about to see someone's head get blown off again. Maybe Big Daddy's name should be something more appropriate. Brain Matter Splatter? Skull Destroyer?

Johnny reaches under the table, gripping my thigh with his hand. I make myself relax, but in the next instant, nothing in the world could make me relax.

Trey returns to the room with Brawler in tow.

"We have a matter to vote on," K says.

I practically leap from the chair. I don't, really, but my energy, my soul, everything, jumps from my body and runs to the blond-haired giant, throwing myself in front of him.

Somehow, K's words snake their way through the deafening moment. This is not happening. Brawler? Here? What the fuck could we possibly be voting on?

Fear and nerves rage inside me for a toxic mix. I barely restrain myself to the chair, and I don't even want to think of what K's doing with him. Or why? What could Brawler have possibly done to him? This specimen of purity with the light and dark on his shoulders couldn't hurt anyone.

Johnny's fingers tighten around me again, and I can imagine the tension I'm bleeding right now. If he only knew it's taking everything in me to stay seated.

K glances around the table, and I school my features as best I can with every ounce of my strength I have left in me.

"This is Marcus Timms," he begins. "Some of you might know him as Manning's little brother, Mack. Still more might know him as Brawler. He's been helping us run the underground fighting ring our new girl is especially fond of."

Big Daddy K winks at me, and every cell in my body locks up. My mind goes to things that make my stomach upheave. If they try to hurt him, I'm about to break the promise I just made to Johnny because there is no way on this planet I'll be able to sit still and not react if Brawler's in danger. I can't. I won't.

Time slows as K says, "Brawler came to me yesterday and wants to recruit into the Crew."

*Noooo!* I grip the table in front of me and glare at Brawler, eyes willing him to look at me, but he stands stoic.

He has no idea what he's just done.

17

I keep willing Brawler to look at me. I stare every dagger I have into the side of his face because what in the ever-loving fuck is he thinking? Join the Crew?

Magnum presses in closer from behind. My muscles are so locked up it feels as if my skin will rip apart, coating the room in my flesh and blood.

Why would he do this? The Crew isn't the place for him. He was the only one of us who could escape from this cleanly. Literally, the only one of us who could skip off into the sunset, but not if he does this. Once he aligns himself with the Crew, there's no getting out without repercussions.

*Think, think, think,* I scold myself.

"Relax," a whisper sounds from behind me. Magnum takes a deep breath and releases it. I try to match my breaths with his, but I feel like I'm going to throw up.

When I made the promise not to say anything during this meeting, I didn't know this was going to happen. I had no idea Brawler would throw himself into the line of fire for no goddamn reason.

All the happy thoughts I've ever had about Brawler not being in the Crew crash at my feet. *Well, at least Brawler is safe. At least Brawler can get out,* sit like nauseous bricks in the bottom of my stomach.

This is someone I care about. I can't just sit back and let this happen.

Johnny glances over. His gaze narrows as he takes me in. "Are you okay? You're white as a sheet."

"Just feel sick all of a sudden," I croak out, thankful for the excuse on the tip of my tongue. I do actually feel sick from the rotten turn this meeting has taken.

Johnny places his arm around me, squeezing my shoulder and rubbing his hand up and down my forearm in an attempt to comfort me.

"What's going on?" K snaps, eyeing the two of us with his anger-spitting gaze.

"Kyla doesn't feel well." Johnny goes to stand.

K slams his fist on the table and shouts, "Sit!"

For his part, Johnny hovers over his seat, flashing a look at his father. He doesn't give in, but I don't mistake the conflict in his gaze.

K pulls his suit coat together as if he's pulling himself together from his little outburst. "We need to finish this."

"At least let Kyla leave," Johnny says.

K flicks his sinister gaze to me. "I have something to discuss with Kyla afterward. Surely, she can make it to the end of the meeting."

I might not make it to the end of the meeting to kill his ass. I'm sure Magnum has his pistol in his waistband right now. I could slip out of this chair, grab it, aim, and shoot. I'd smile in the bloodshed. I'd revel in his shocked expression.

If Brawler goes through with this, Big Daddy K will have his hooks in *everyone* I care for.

I tuck my arm around my middle, clenching myself. As much as I want to tell K to fuck off, I give him a smile instead. "I should be fine. Thank you."

I use my other hand to tug Johnny back down in his seat. He's furious. His body is almost pulled as taut as mine, but we've already gathered the attention of the whole room, and I can't have this looking suspicious.

"I don't think I ate this morning, is all. It'll pass," I clarify, giving everyone in the room a small smile. Better they think I'm a sick wimp than an enemy contemplating the murder of their leader.

I think back to this morning where Johnny woke me with another round of intense sex, and then my fake grin turns into a real one as I return my stare to K. *I fucked your son, even though you explicitly told us not to. I rode his dick until he came inside me.* He can have this one, and I can have my silent one, too.

Big Daddy K does not own us.

"Well, we can't have that for our prizefighter, can we?" He turns toward Trey. "Can you get Maureen to bring our princess some snacks? Fruit, perhaps?"

I lock my jaw down. That's it. No one else is allowed to call me princess but Oscar.

Speaking of, I glance over to find him watching me. His eyes latch on as if he's trying to convey some sort of message, but my head's too fucked to figure out what it is right now. I'm already trying to calm myself down, and I haven't jumped up and killed the asshole yet, so his secret message is lost on me.

While Trey strolls into the back where the servants must hang out, Big Daddy K continues. His tone is far sharper than it was the first time around. I can imagine he's bitching up a storm about feminine shit in his head. He probably never had to feed a dude at this table before just because he wasn't feeling well. Yeah, the situation doesn't look good for me, but the other avenue was getting out of this chair and telling them all to fuck off.

Now, that would've been far worse.

"You may remember that Manning Timms served the Crew until he lost his life in a retaliation by..." Big Daddy K waves his hands like he can't be bothered to remember who killed Brawler's brother, and I know Brawler must be standing there wanting to put his enormous paws around his neck and squeeze until the life runs out of him. Fucking asshole. "Brawler, why don't you tell the group why you want to join the Crew?"

Brawler finally looks around, but his stare never lands on me. His gaze lingers over everyone in the room except me even though he must feel the hot pokers I'm burning into his huge, chiseled body. "The fight organizer position has served me well, and I believe I've brought a great deal to the Crew just as the Crew has done for me." His voice is sure, almost practiced. The only tell that he's lying through his teeth is the way his jaw ticks, and the fact that he won't fucking look at me. "I believe I can serve the Crew better if I were a full-fledged member. It's time to stop sitting on the sidelines and join things head on. I know my brother loved the camaraderie and the brotherhood, and I'm looking forward to experiencing that as well. The only family I have left is my mother, so I can commit to complete dedication to The Heights Crew."

The acid in my stomach sluices around, tossing like a ship in a storm. I don't care why he thinks he's doing this, I'm just going to kill him. That's that. I'm going to murder his ass before he even has the chance to join the Crew, which is going to end up killing him anyway. Out of everyone I've met here, Brawler does not belong.

Fuck. His fighting career. What's going to happen with that? He's giving up so much. This is going to be Oscar all over again. Dreams ripped out from under him because the priority isn't about him anymore, it's all the Crew.

The backs of my eyes physically hurt and burn with the fight to wrangle in the tears that threaten. I never wanted this for him. I'm sure he has some very thought out reason why this is a good move, but it's not. Nothing he will say will make me change my mind.

"Well, you certainly look the part," one of the businessmen boasts.

The table laughs, and it's sickening. If they only know the reasoning behind his neck tattoos. The story that made me fall for him even more.

"If the table agrees, we'll fast track him. He's already been helping the Crew out, and he's almost graduated anyway. We won't stick him in the group of this year's recruits. Show of hands?" Big Daddy K lifts an eyebrow.

Around the room, hands lift in the air like they're giving the boy scout salute. I glare at Oscar when his hand rises. Next to me, Johnny's opposite hand rises as well, and I almost crack a tooth.

K glances around the room but stops on me. I'm still sitting with my hands tucked under my thighs, so I don't accidentally jump out of the chair and throttle anyone. "Kyla?"

"Yes?"

"If you're at the table, you vote."

Dread twists my insides. "Oh, I didn't—"

He sighs angrily. "You're practically my son's wife and you're sitting at the table. Vote, dammit. Yes or no?"

I dig my nails into the chair underneath me. Everyone else in the room has voted yes. If I don't, they're going to ask questions, and I can't give them the true explanation. But voting yes is going to kill me. It won't matter in the scheme of things because everyone else has voted yes. My vote technically doesn't count, but my hand weighs a thousand pounds as I lift it into the air slowly.

My heart cracks open inside my chest. I can tell myself my vote didn't count all I want, but it feels as if I just sent someone I cared about to his death.

I'll never forgive myself for this. Never.

K's head bobs. "Excellent. We'll discuss your initiation tasks and get back to you, Brawler. If you complete those, you'll be sworn in, but not before." He gestures toward the end of the table where Oscar is sitting. "Why don't you take a seat? The next business item deals with the fight ring, so it will be good to hear your opinion."

Brawler walks around the table, head held high. He's not wearing his usual clothes. He's dressed in a polo shirt and khakis, and it's difficult not to notice how damn good looking he is in them. The sleeves of the dark green polo hug his biceps, showing off how muscular he is. He looks like he's come dressed for a job interview, which is exactly what this was, I guess. A job interview he never needed to have.

When he sits, he still doesn't make eye contact. A chill goes through me. The last person who sat in that chair got their brains blown out. Coincidence? Probably not. We've signed Brawler's death warrant.

Johnny squeezes my thigh, and I turn my attention to K again. From the back of the room, an elderly woman moves forward with a platter of fruit that she sets in the middle of the table. K's gaze flicks from me to the platter, so I immediately reach out and grab a banana. A few of the other men around the table also take an offering. I force a few bites down because I don't want to seem ungrateful even though I'm almost positive I'll probably throw all this back up as soon as I leave here. I just hope I can wait that long.

"So, The Ring. As everyone else is aware, the Crew took a beating financially over the last several weeks. The fights stopped, as well as Candy's. Those two were our money-makers, and although the other businesses are great supplemental income for the organization," he says, glancing toward the other guys in the room, "...it's not enough to sustain us. We need to get the fights back up ASAP. I want Kyla headlining. The fight has to be good. Draw in the biggest crowds. I want that place packed and the audience begging for more." He turns his gaze to Brawler. "Who's your best fighter besides Kyla?"

"Limone and Kyla are our top fighters."

K cocks his head. "Limone? She's a chick, right? I'm talking best fighter. Male, female, transvestite. I don't give a fuck. I want the best fighter opposite Kyla in The Ring."

Brawler swallows, but Johnny speaks up. "Brawler," he says. "Brawler's the best fighter we have."

"Excellent," K says. "Set that fight up." He laughs as if he's told the funniest joke in the world.

My stomach bottoms out. Fight Brawler? This can't be happening. I can't fight Brawler. The idea is ludicrous.

K taps his chin. "Hmm. I think the fight should be one of your initiation tasks, Brawler." He nods as if he's enjoying this moment too much. "Yes, I like this. Your first initiation task is to beat our little Uppercut Princess."

I grip the side of the table as the world tilts on its axis. Again. Twice within the span of fifteen minutes. I have to fight Brawler. Injured. Not only that. He has to beat me because he's recruiting into the Crew.

"Maybe we should pick a different match up," Johnny offers. Realization dawns on his face. His father has just signed me up for a trip to the hospital. He knows recruits will do anything to complete their tasks.

K zeroes his gaze in on his son. The challenge written there is enough to bring anyone to their knees. "I thought you had every confidence in the world in Kyla. Didn't she beat Roza's guy for us? Didn't she—?"

"I do," Johnny snaps. He tries to regain his composure and fails. "But she's injured."

"The Crew can't wait for injuries, Johnny. You know how important it is for us to get the businesses up and running again."

"I know," Johnny says through gritted teeth. I slip my hand underneath the table and grip his thigh. It's my turn to warn him. We can't piss off K right now. He'll hurt Johnny, and he might even take his defiance out on me. I couldn't care less about that fact. I can hold my own, but Johnny cares. He wouldn't forgive himself if his father hurt me because of him. Hell, I'm sensing this is what this is. He wants me to get taken down a peg or two. "I just thought we could give her another week," Johnny says, calming to the point where he can speak with confidence. "Have Brawler fight someone else as the headliner since he's not injured. Maybe even tease an upcoming huge fight. What will bring the crowd back if our two best fighters have already fought?"

"That's Brawler's problem, not mine," K says dismissively, though the tick in his jaw commandeers my attention. He doesn't like Johnny disagreeing with him. "He knows what's at stake, and he's never had a problem filling the fights before. Do you want to change your vote on Brawler?" He finishes with a defiant smirk as if he's caught his son looking like an asshole.

"No," Johnny says simply, the matching tick in his jaw too much to overlook.

The tension between the two is palpable and raw. A few of the businessmen shift in their seats, no doubt feeling it too. K has probably killed people for lesser infractions...like my parents.

The reminder is a kick to the gut. I lean on Johnny and

run my hands over his thigh. He's just worried about me, but he needn't be. I'll do what I have to. For all of them.

But Johnny won't understand the turmoil raking my body when I square up in front of Brawler. To fight to win. To hurt someone I care about.

Sparring is a different scenario. We never punch, kick or swing at each other with the intent to do real damage. This time, we'll have to.

I move my gaze away from the clusterfuck that is K and Johnny's relationship and peek at Brawler. He'll have to fight me to win, even though it will kill him, too. If he doesn't win, he doesn't get into the Crew.

I don't give a fuck about that, but he does. He never would've put himself in this position if he didn't think joining the Crew was the right course to take.

I bet he never imagined this would happen though.

For the first time, he glances over at me and our gazes connect. The turquoise in his eyes swirl like fall leaves. His jaw tightens, hard as granite. As is mine. To outsiders, it probably looks as if we're sizing each other up or staring one another down in preparation for the fight.

They have no idea the opposite thoughts plaguing us. *How can I hurt this person? How can I hit them with the intent to do damage when all I want to do is hold them to me and keep them safe?*

I don't know how this is going to play out, but I know

that the first time my knuckles connect with Brawler's skin for real, I'll lose a piece of myself.

That's what the Heights takes from you. Your humanity. I see it in Johnny all the time. Little by little, piece-by-piece, it takes the part of you that makes you human. It either rips it from you completely or twists it into something you don't recognize.

Hurting Brawler will do all this and more to me.

K wants a good fight, and he'll get one. I just hope that afterward, Brawler and I can soothe one another. Forgive one another. Move on from this shit thing that's just happened.

Because more than anything, I need us to.

"It's settled then," Big Daddy K says, his voice ringing with finality. "Brawler and Kyla fight Friday."

## 18

This can't be happening.

As Big Daddy K's guests leave, I stay by Johnny. I track Brawler as he and Oscar walk out side-by-side. The upcoming conversation I'll have with him won't be fun. I'm angry. I'm hurt. I'm worried about everything happening at once.

Big Daddy K sees everyone out until the four of us are left over, me, Johnny, Mag, and the douche himself. Johnny threads his fingers through mine. He whispers, "You should go."

I grind down on my teeth. There are a lot of things I need to be doing right now, but this is just as important as the others. Besides, K said he needed to speak with me. Unless that was just a dick measuring contest. A way to see if I'd stick it out in the room.

Johnny's father moves into view. He prowls forward like a dangerous predator, his eyes on Johnny. "Out, Kyla."

My back straightens. I can't leave Johnny, I can't. "I thought you needed to speak with me."

"Another time," K says through clenched teeth, gaze zeroed in on his son.

Johnny squeezes my fingers and lets them go, wiggling himself from my grip. "I thought I—"

"Go!" K roars, making me jump. His face turns a furious shade of red. "I will not be ignored."

"Magnum," Johnny pleads with his friend and bodyguard.

Magnum takes my shoulders, forcibly steering me from the room. I peek over my shoulder, watching the glaring match play out until I can't see them anymore. The first crack of skin on skin whips through the room before the door is even shut behind us.

I turn, digging my heels in to go back, but Magnum has years of experience on me. He wraps his arms around me with a vise-like grip, speaking softly into my ear. "You won't help. Johnny's got this. He's been dealing with this his whole life."

Thankfully, no one else is in the hall as he carries me into the elevator, my feet just grazing the carpet at our feet. He presses the number for our floor briefly before returning his arms to me, holding me in place and soothing me at the same time.

"He hit him again," I grind out, my mind flashing to all the terrible things K could be doing to Johnny right now. "He should put me in the ring with himself. I'll kick his fucking ass."

"I know you would," Mag says, kissing my temple. He breathes, the hot breath stirring my hair. "You have to calm down. You have to go deal with Brawler right now. We need a plan. A fucking good plan."

I go limp in Magnum's arms until he doesn't have to hold me back anymore, he has to hold me up. "Did you know he was doing that?"

Mag relaxes his grip only to stretch a soothing hand over my abdomen, making careful strokes of comfort. "No, I had no idea."

I relax against him, placing my head against his shoulder. He gives my neck a chaste kiss, but it ends all too quickly. Right before the elevator opens, he props me up. I wobble on my feet, and he puts a steady hand against the small of my back until I regain composure in case anyone is hanging out in the hall who we wouldn't want to see how comfortable we are with each other.

The doors open fully, and Oscar and Brawler appear in the hallway. I march out, eyeing Brawler the whole time.

He meets my gaze head-on, the pulse at his neck a flurry of beats visible with the naked eye.

"Everyone," Mag says. "My place. Now."

"This ought to be fun," Oscar deadpans, leaning against the wall as Mag unlocks his door and ushers us through it.

As soon as the door closes behind us, I approach Brawler. "What are you doing?"

I want to be mad. I want to scream and rage and scold him, but an overwhelming sadness attacks me first. It's not the fury I thought I would start with. I try to say something more, but I choke. He sat in Dunnegan's chair. Dunnegan's. Fucking. Chair. The dead body slumped over the table next time could very well be him, and then where would we be?

I fist my fingers in my hands. Brawler reaches down, scooping them up, his enormous palms encompassing every square inch of my tight fists. He moves his fingers just slightly so he can kiss my skin as he brings them to his mouth. "I had to, Kyla. Are you okay?" He squeezes me, and instead of looking me over in a cursory inspection, he pierces me with his gaze as if he can find all the answers he needs inside me. "This is the third time you've been caught in a crossfire, and I've been stuck not knowing one fucking word on what's happening. I can't do it anymore. I had to do something."

I close my eyes before reopening them. "But join the Crew? It's the Crew, Brawler. They murdered your brother, they—"

He kisses the end of my pinkies again, his hands warm against my skin. "Which is why I can't let anything happen to you. If I get in, I can help protect you. I can keep you safe.

Out there, I can't do shit. I just have to sit and wait. Hope you make it out okay not knowing where you are or what exactly happened. They tried to blow the fucking tower up, and I had no idea what happened to you. Talk about another Crew hit was all over the Heights, and I had no idea if that was you. Then, you're whisked away for a couple of days—days—and I still don't know if you're hurt. Or what they did to you. Or if you even got away. It's killing me. It fucking killed me, okay?"

I throw his hands away and scream out in frustration. "But this isn't what was supposed to happen, Brawler. You had an out."

He pulls me back to him with a growl. "I don't want an out without you. If you think I'm going to just one day skip off into the sunset and leave you here, you know nothing about me."

His words press into all the sensitive parts of me. "If you were smart, you'd do that now."

His blue eyes spark like turquoise fire burning through dry brush. "Not happening."

"As heart wrenching as this all is," Oscar says, interjecting his lazy humor into our moment, "Now you have to fight each other, so I'm with Princess on this one. Dumb move."

"You would've done the same thing," Brawler scoffs back. "In fact, I'm pretty sure it was you who told me to man up and join the Crew a few weeks ago. I need to know what's happening with Kyla."

"I told you what I knew," Oscar seethes. "She's alive. She's at the safe house."

"But you wouldn't tell me where it was!"

"Because I don't fucking know where it is!" Oscar lifts his hat off and then pulls it back down over his head with a hard tug. "I told you everything I knew."

"Careful," Brawler teases with a humorless smirk. "People might think you actually care."

"Fuck off. You don't think I was worried?" He points to me. "This girl is my life. My mother might as well be dead. No one cares about me but her."

"You don't think it's the same for me?" Brawler yells. His shoulders heave up and down.

"Alright," Mag says with finality, walking into the center of our spat and eyeing each of us. "That's enough. What's done is done. Brawler can't take back what's already out there, which means he needs to complete the initiation tasks K sets forth."

"Yeah, one of which is taking Kyla out."

"I didn't know he was going to set that," Brawler answers through clenched teeth.

"He's evil," Oscar says. "He takes what you love most and exploits it against you, watches to see how you handle it because if you do, he knows he has you in the bag. He knows he can mold you into doing whatever he wants. If you don't, he just discards you. The last guy who didn't make it through initiation disappeared. Did you know that?"

I bite my lip and peek at Magnum. My first thought is maybe the guy just escaped. Maybe he wised up and walked out of the Heights, but at the same time, that's a naïve person's wish. Nothing happens like that without the Crew having their filthy hands in it.

Magnum runs his hands through his copper hair and doesn't make eye contact with any of us, and especially not me.

Fuck. "What happened to him? The guy." I force out.

Mag shrugs. "It depends on how badly you fail the tests. Some are sent away. Some are coaxed into leaving, and others are just taken out," he says slowly, putting emphasis on each word like it's a stab to my gut. "They end that way because the recruit realizes in the middle of initiation that they really didn't want it. If they try to leave, they're killed. If they try to defect with help of a rival gang in exchange for secrets, they're tortured and then killed."

"Your cousin defected..."

Mag scratches his unruly scruff. He hasn't shaved in a couple of days and it's obvious. Then again, who has time to groom when bombs are going off and you're getting shot at? "They couldn't find him. That's the only reason he's still alive. But I assure you, the only people who try to initiate and don't make it, stick around because they busted their fucking asses and just came up short. If you're weak, they discard you anyway. If you try to get out, you're dead. Brawler can't go back now." Magnum looks over at the tattooed giant. The fighter's body is bigger than his own by mass, but Magnum is the one who's been around the block a few times. "I wish you'd said something. Manning wouldn't have wanted this for you."

Brawler narrows his gaze at Mag. "What would you know about it?"

Mag shrugs. "I initiated in with him."

For a few moments, silence descends over the room like putrid smoke. Brawler's nostrils flare. If any of us try to break the tension, I'm afraid he'll just end up losing it.

"Like you said," Brawler starts. "What's done is done. I will not fucking apologize. I've got two Crew guys standing in front of me right now, I'm sure both of you can give me some tips, and together, we can figure out how the fight between Kyla and me has to go down."

Magnum reaches out to squeeze Brawler's shoulder. "I'm here for you."

Oscar and I exchange glances. Red blotches reach up his neck. "We'll figure this shit out because we have to. None of us missed the fact that Kyla is on K's radar. He put her up against Brawler and made it into one of his initiation tasks. He *wants* to see her get hurt."

"It's Johnny's reaction to her," Mag says. "Johnny suddenly has more loyalty to her than him, and he's furious about it."

"We need to smooth things over with him before he decides to just take Kyla out. Fuck what Johnny wants. K will just kill her. In his mind, Johnny will find someone else. You know he doesn't give a fuck about women. He never has."

Brawler falls back onto the couch. "He won't let it go? Not even for Johnny?"

"Johnny is everything to him," Mag answers. "But this has everything to do with the Crew, and there's family dynamics at play here, too."

He killed his wife for leaving, so he won't think twice about taking me out. Johnny and Mag know that as well as me. Until Johnny comes clean about the secret he told Magnum, I'll keep that piece of information I'm not supposed to know to myself. However, with the way Magnum is looking at me, I know he's thinking the same thing. I'm nothing to K compared to his wife. Presumably, he must have loved her at one time.

I'm just as dispensable as any of the guys sitting around his table. Perhaps even more so because I have tits and a vag. I get sick during big boy discussions. I can't even control myself around his son, tempting him to the dark side with pussy.

There's no way around it. K's gunning for me. I don't fit into his plans for the Crew. Not when I'm a distraction.

"I have to head back to my place," I tell them. I need to

be there when Johnny gets out of his extra meeting turned physical abuse session.

I sneak past Magnum, but don't make it any further.

"Hey," a chorus of voices call out.

Strong, tan hands snake around me from behind. Oscar's smell engulfs me. The lithe, taut feel of his body presses against my back. "I was so worried," he whispers. "Don't do that to me again."

I turn around in his arms, allowing him to make me feel safe for a brief moment before I pop up on my tiptoes to give him a solid kiss on his mouth. "I'll try."

Brawler's next. A broken man stares back at me as soon as Oscar steps away. I make the first move. I wrap my arms around his big shoulders and kiss the light angel on the side of his neck. "We'll get through this," I tell him.

"You don't hate me?"

I take his face in my hands, making sure he's looking at me when I say, "I could never hate you. I did think about strangling you though."

He slips into a small smile. "I did it for you."

"I know," I tell him, swallowing down the bile that accompanies that thought. I never want someone to risk their life for me.

He pulls me up to meet his lips, turning the kiss deeper as soon as our mouths press together. Liquid heat fills me. I'd love nothing more than to sit back with these three and comfort one another about the tasks we have in front of us, but I need to make sure Johnny's okay before we do any of that.

Brawler sets me on my feet. He holds me steady before I turn to find Mag waiting for me. "Jacob…"

Tension leaves his body like a heavy rain washed away all the negativity. He pulls me close and presses a kiss to my forehead. "We're all here for him," he whispers. "Make sure he knows that."

I nod, and he tilts my chin up to press a chaste kiss to my mouth. Our lips linger together, just touching without going further. A tease. A promise.

"I'll tell him," I say, and then I squeeze his hand and walk from his place.

I can't keep doing this me and Johnny life versus the me, Brawler, Mag, and Oscar life. The part Johnny doesn't know is that he's already involved in the other half.

There's a spot for him. He only has to take it.

## 19

The elevator opens as I sneak across to my room. I stop in the middle of the hall, peering up as Johnny storms out. His wild hair a halo around his head. He's disheveled, the collar on his shirt stretched out, and murder radiates from his eyes.

"Where's Brawler?" he demands. "Is he in here?" he asks, pointing toward Mag's apartment. "There?" he asks, moving an accusing finger to my door.

I step in front of him, terror seizing me as I gape at his appearance. "Are you okay?"

I twist his face back and forth to see if he's hurt again, but Johnny wrenches his face from my grip. "I'm fine."

The door opens behind me, and Johnny gently moves me out of the way to step up to Mag. "Is Brawler in there?"

He doesn't leave Mag enough time to answer. He

elbows him out of the way and strides into the room. Mag follows after, and I'm right on his heels. When I get in, Johnny has Brawler pushed against the side of the couch, leaning over him, his face a mask of torture and anger that pains me. "If you hurt her, I will kill you. Do you understand me? I will fucking kill you."

Mag pulls Johnny from Brawler, allowing the latter to stand. My fighter didn't fight back even though I know he could have. He didn't because we're all on the same team, whether Johnny knows it or not.

"I'm not going to hurt Kyla. That's the last thing I want to do. I joined the Crew to help her."

Mag still has an arm around Johnny, holding him back while he breathes through his nose.

"I didn't know your dad was going to do that." Brawler shakes his head, pure agony lancing his face, and I don't know how Johnny couldn't believe him. "If I'd known, I never would have done it."

I shimmy my way between Magnum and Johnny and grip Johnny's wrist. He peers down at me.

"It's true," I tell him. "Brawler wouldn't hurt me."

"None of us would hurt her, dude," Oscar says.

Johnny roars, upheaving the table in front of the couch. It slams to the floor as he yells, "Everything is so fucked."

He's not wrong, and I don't have anything to say that will tell him any different because it does seem as if we're backed into a corner here. Brawler and I have to fight. There's no getting out of it. That damage is already done.

So is Brawler's fate with the Crew.

"We'll figure it out," I tell him. It sounds lame as fuck, but it's all the positive talk I have.

"You're all willing to help Kyla?" Johnny asks, glaring around the room, begging them to say otherwise. Whatever he had to endure in his father's suite, he looks as if he's ready to retaliate on someone else.

He won't find a fight here. Magnum, Oscar, and Brawler nod.

"Above yourselves? Above your own well-being?"

I bite my lip as they all nod again. The unity in the room makes the space feel smaller as if we all really might be able to help each other. As a team, like I'm hoping for.

"I'm not some fainting, prissy girl," I say, speaking up. "I can help myself, too."

Magnum shoots me a warning look, but I don't need anyone fighting my battles for me. Truly.

"I'd help any one of you, too," I say, looking around the room, making sure they see the truth in my eyes.

They ignore me, but Oscar steps up to Johnny. "The same better apply to you."

"I will *not* let anything happen to her."

"Your dad—" Mag starts.

Johnny cuts him off. "I know. I've seen the look before."

"You have to toe the line, man. Kyla doesn't think when

she worries about you, and vice versa. Don't let him get to you. That's what he wants. He wants you to force his hand."

"He won't touch her. I can promise you that."

I don't think anyone believes him. I certainly don't. There's no way Johnny can promise us that because his father is a loose cannon. He does what he wants when he wants. That's how he got to the top of the Heights Crew. Ruthless, unforgiving tyranny.

"Let's sit and discuss things," Mag says. "We need to be smart about this. Together, I think we can come up with a good plan."

I'm glad Mag is taking point on this. It's a natural solution because Johnny respects him, and he's the one Johnny knows the most.

They share a silent communication, but whatever Mag was trying to communicate doesn't go over as well as he'd hoped.

Johnny strides over, taking my hand. He squeezes me, then leads me from the room. I go with him instead of pushing it. Johnny needs time. The only person he's ever trusted in this world beats him and killed his mother. His hesitation is more than understood.

He leads me across the hall, stopping briefly to unlock my apartment door with his own key. When we get into my place, he drops my arm and starts to pace.

I watch him for a little while. His mind is working to fix all of this on his own. He can pull that with the others, but not with me. I walk in front of him, stopping him. He's so preoccupied he almost rams right into me, stopping himself at the last possible moment.

"Are you okay?" I ask. "I know he hit you again, Johnny. I heard it."

Johnny pulls his shirt up, looking down at the same time as he reveals every inch of a red splotch over his abs. "He punched me. Not in the face this time. I think he realized how nervous it made everyone to see me like that, so he did it some place no one could see."

My fingers trail over the mark lightly, and he shies away. "We should get you some ice."

"Ice isn't going to fix this, babe."

"One problem at a time," I tell him. I retreat to the freezer, grabbing out an actual ice pack I asked house-keeping to deliver before the night of the accident. For as much as we need it, we should buy stock in these damn things. Maybe we'd get a free lifetime supply.

I pull his hand and make him sit on the couch with me. "Shirt off," I tell him.

He grins at me. "You always want to get me shirtless."

"Stop being so hot, and I wouldn't have that problem."

Heat burns behind his eyes as he slowly shucks his shirt off, tossing it on the arm of the couch. I place the ice pack on his welt, and he sucks in a breath.

"Sorry," I cringe.

"It's not your fault."

"It's kind of my fault. It's because of me you're getting hurt."

He cringes. "I hate that you even know this. If he hadn't hit me in the goddamn face, we wouldn't have this problem. I'm not weak, Kyla. I just—"

I cock my head. "Are you serious? I know you're not weak, Johnny. Your father is beating you."

"That makes it sound worse." He lays his head against the back of the cushion.

"How long has he been hitting you, Johnny?"

His face closes off. For a moment, I don't think he's going to answer, but then he opens his eyes, staring up at the ceiling. "On and off since I was a kid. Only when I would piss him off, not do something right. My dad knows violence, Kyla. That's how he speaks. It's his language, and it's served him well over the years. He thought it would work well for me too."

"It's not right."

"I know that...," Johnny says, and it's as if he's left the word *now* off the end of that sentence on purpose. "I just don't want you to think I can't handle this."

I pick his hand up, kissing his knuckles like he always does to me. "Sometimes, the strong thing to do is to lean on people. You don't have to be a macho man all the time. You can have different facets of your personality other than ruthless son of a gangster," I tell him. "I know you don't trust Brawler and Oscar, but they're here to help us."

"Help you, you mean?"

I shake my head. "Both of us. *All* of us."

Johnny eyes me with uncertainty. "Been here a few months and already found people who'll lay down their lives for you."

Embarrassment barrages my cheeks. "No one's laying down their lives," I tell him. "Be straight with me." I hold his gaze. "I'll give you a truth if you give me one back. No getting angry."

"Sometimes the truth is the hardest," Johnny says.

I nod knowingly. The truth can hurt worse than lies sometimes. I swallow because what I want to tell Johnny right now could rip him from me. He's only known allegiance to his father and the Crew, but he has to see that he can't live like that anymore. "My truth is... I think you deserve better than your father."

Johnny's body locks up as if he's a mechanical part in a working cog that's frozen in place, refusing to work. Slowly yet surely, he relaxes, and with each breath he takes toward deflating, my heart rate returns to normal. "That's my truth, too," he admits.

The pain in his eyes is very real. "My father is my every-thing, Kyla. I understand it took a lot for you to say that to me. You feared how I would react, and you have every reason to. People have died for lesser infractions." He pauses for a moment. "I didn't see it until you. I thought my life was one gang problem to the next. An endless succession of things that needed to be fixed for the good of the Crew. You showed me something different. You showed me what life could be like. You showed me what love is supposed to be." His lip trembles, and he bites down on it like he can't stand for me to see the vulnerable side of him. Little does he know I want to see all his parts. The vulnerable part of him only makes me believe he can be saved. That he deserves it, and that I would do anything to give that to him. "Going against my father upheaves everything I've ever been taught. It feels so wrong in here, Kyla," he says, pulling his other hand up to his chest, placing his palm over his heart. "My head is telling me one thing, but my heart is telling me another." He licks his lips. "My head is whispering traitor. Traitors get gutted. Traitors don't deserve to live. It's only my heart that says anything differently."

I kiss his knuckles again. "I think you should listen to your heart more often."

He shakes his head. "My father..." He clears his throat and starts again. "My father...I know he acts tough, but if he ever heard the words I just said, it would be like stabbing him in the heart. He's wanted me by his side since I was a little kid. It's all he's ever talked about." He glances over. "You sure you don't want to leave? I can't get out Kyla. It would kill him, but you can."

I bring his hand to my lap and stroke my fingers up and down his arm. "I'm never changing my mind about that,

Johnny Marx, so you can stop asking. When you're ready to leave, I'm ready to leave."

"There's no saving me. I see it in your eyes. I know that's why you want me to work with your friends. I've done too much fucked up shit. The only life I'll know is this."

"I refuse to believe it."

He gives a quick shake of his head. "This is my life."

"The gang itself isn't all bad," I tell him, trying to reason. "Maybe you could make it better. Maybe you could..."

He's already waving my thoughts away. "He's ruined me."

"Fuck that," I growl. "You're not giving up."

Johnny wraps his hand around the back of my neck, squeezing a little. It doesn't hurt. In fact, it does the opposite. I lick my lips as need burns through me.

"My father has shit on me. He has shit on everyone in the Crew. That's why no one gets away, Kyla."

"You could change it."

"He'd have to die, and that's not happening. He's the most protected man in the Heights, and he's still my father. Family has to mean something."

I worry over my lip and cuddle in next to him. He lifts his arm so I can get closer, even though I'm careful not to touch his bruised ribs.

In a way, I understand what he's saying. I would do anything for my family. Hell, I am doing anything for my family. I'm here, aren't I? I'm making amends. I'm getting them justice.

As far as Johnny's concerned, he's doing the same. He'll stick with his father until his father does something irredeemable. Something Johnny won't be able to look past. Not even a black eye and some bruised ribs can convince him, so I don't know what it will take to get him to see that Kingston Marx is not his family. Family doesn't treat each other like that.

Somewhere deep inside, I think he knows that. But maybe like I think Johnny can be saved, he thinks his father can, too.

I lay my head on his shoulder, knowing K will never get that far. Even if he could, I'm not allowing him the chance. Just like he didn't give my parents.

The next morning, Johnny and I discuss my return to school as we sit on the couch after breakfast. We decide I should wait until after the fight is over. It's only another week, and I can keep up with my studies through the online schooling anyway, so it shouldn't be a big deal. Somehow, schooling just doesn't seem as important when bombs are going off and bullets are whizzing over my head.

Instead, we decide it's more important that I train with Jax and Finn while he calls a meeting with the Candy's workers to get that up and running as a nightclub facility again. "Be careful," Johnny tells me, squeezing my fingers. "Call me if something happens. Anything. I want to know about it."

"Don't worry," I tell him, knowing he has a bunch of shit

on his plate. "Do what you have to do. Mag, Brawler, and Oscar will be there with me. Not to mention Finn and Jax. I'll be surrounded by a bunch of badasses."

Johnny smiles, shaking his head in disbelief. "How you got so many people on your side in such a short amount of time is mind-blowing. Finn jumped at the chance to see you when you were away you know."

I give him a teasing smile. "I'm just that good, I guess."

He reaches his hand around to cup my ass over my tight training pants, bringing me close to him in a possessive move. "Mmm, that you are." He bites my earlobe and gives it a playful tug.

My breath whooshes out of my chest. Now that Johnny and I have taken our relationship to the next step, I can't stop thinking about it. "Keep that up, and neither one of us is going anywhere for another hour or so."

Chuckling, he kisses a trail down my neck, nuzzling me and breathing me in. He pauses before trailing his lips over my sports bra straps until he hits my collarbone. "I don't know. I think I should send you off with something."

As amazing as that sounds... "Magnum will be here any minute."

He cuts my excuse off, placing his hand between my legs where he strokes me through my pants. I buck into his grip. "Magnum can wait," he breathes. He pulls my shirt over my head, then unclasps my sports bra in the back, pulling the cups away until I'm bare before him.

He stares at me in wonder, his finger still igniting the fire inside me as he passes it over my inseam. He leans over, sucking my nipple into his hot mouth. He sucks and tortures it with his tongue until breathy moans escape me.

Johnny bypasses my pants and panties, sneaking his hand inside to find me wet, easily pushing a finger between my folds.

My pussy involuntarily clenches around him, and he curses. With his free hand, he pulls my pants and panties down, then leans me back onto the couch cushion as he spreads my knees, opening me to him. He watches me as he pushes his finger inside again and again, and I drop my head back to the leather. "I'm going to taste you until you cream in my mouth." He crooks his finger, and I buck off the leather, searching for him.

He tugs his finger out, then places my legs over his shoulders as he yanks me forward, right into his hot mouth. I cry out as he caresses his tongue over my sensitive nub, and I'm lost.

I run my hands through his hair, then grab the back of his head, holding him to me, keeping his mouth right where I want it. "You taste as sweet as sin."

He presses against my nub, then groans until the vibrations set sparks afire inside me. "Johnny," I breathe out, my moans mixing with his.

He gives me everything I need, licking, sucking, and

moaning as if he's eating his favorite meal. "These beautiful breasts. This perfect pussy."

Pleasure rockets through my body at every caress of his expert tongue. I urge him on, my snippets of praise invoking his deft kisses. Johnny lifts his hand to tease my nipple, and I squirm. He pulls me closer to his face in a slow, methodical grind while his tongue never lets up. It's as if he's making me fuck his face with his slow, sensual rhythm. "God, you're so good at this," I pant because hot damn he deserves the praise.

A knock sounds on the door. I tense, but Johnny continues moving me forward in easy strokes with a solid hand to the small of my back until he turns his head briefly. "Give us ten!"

"Ten," I choke out. "I'm—" He squeezes my nipple, and I explode. I let out a cry I haven't heard before as he assaults me with his tongue, riding my orgasm out until the pleasure is just too much. He doesn't let me pull away though. He keeps at it until I'm coming again. "Johnny!" Wave after wave crashes over me. I'm helpless in the undertow, a place I wouldn't mind staying if people weren't waiting on us. Eventually, the pleasure subsides, and I manage to pull back enough.

He lifts his heated gaze to me. His swollen, lush, liquid-dipped lips smile at me as he darts his tongue out and licks the coating right off him. He looks like a sex-crazed fiend with the way I've mussed his hair.

He shifts, dropping a kiss to my pubic bone before standing and dragging me to my feet with him. He pulls up my panties and athletic pants before I can protest. "Mag's waiting," he grins. He hands me my sports bra, and as soon as I have it clasped, he pulls the shirt I had on back over my head.

He doesn't even wipe his face before he moves toward the door. I hurriedly pull my hair up into a ponytail again, sure that the hair I'd had looked like we'd just went at it. I mean, I certainly took the ride of my life.

Johnny invites Mag into the apartment while I'm still buzzing from the high. My breath still hasn't returned to normal, so I turn to grab my small bag that has a change of clothes, water, and protein bars in it. I don't look at anyone before I try to escape, but before I can slip past him, Johnny pulls me into a hug from behind, plastering my body against his hard-on. He presses it into me with Mag watching. "Think about that while you're training, babe."

He's probably ruined me for the rest of the day. I won't be able to think about anything else, and Jax is definitely not going to take sex as a reason why I'm distracted.

"I'll be nursing a semi the whole time you're gone."

I bite my lip to keep from moaning, especially since Mag's intense gaze slides over me. He finally looks away, the corded veins in his neck pulling taut.

Johnny squeezes my ass. "Have a good time."

He lets me go, and I walk out the door in front of

Magnum. We ride the elevator down in silence while I try to get my breathing under control. We even get into the car without a word said. I pull my seatbelt around and lock it, and that's when Mag sighs. "I heard you through the door."

I peek over at his lap. Johnny isn't the only one with a stiff dick right now.

"Sorry," I mumble, confused at how I can stare at Mag's lap like I'd like to try his on for size even just shortly after being with Johnny. They're all enough for me individually, and it's not just about sex anyway. I care for them all. Sex is the natural progression of romantic relationships. Sure, everything else about this is unconventional, but fuck, I refuse to let myself be weird about it. I want them all. I can't deny it. I don't want to.

"Don't be," Mag says. "I'm a grown man. This isn't the first boner I've had that will end in blue balls." He wraps his hands around the steering wheel. "I'm just worried if K finds out what he might do."

I'm worried about that too, but the fact that Mag is sporting an erection seems to have hotwired my brain. "You liked listening to me?" I ask, my breath shallowing.

He adjusts himself on the seat. "I just wish I could've seen it in person."

He turns the car on, waits a few beats, then backs out of the spot in the garage. He gives a quick salute to the body-guard in the booth and drives me toward the gym. "Did you check the car?" I ask, then shake my head. He obviously did.

He already talked about things he wouldn't if he wasn't sure. "We didn't have sex just then," I clarify. "But we did at the safe house."

Magnum swallows. "Be careful of K. If he finds out, I don't know what he'll do."

I shiver at the thought. I know exactly what he'll do. He'll beat Johnny again, and that's not going to happen. "He won't find out," I promise.

At Johnny's insistence, Brawler and Oscar are also meeting us at the gym. Apparently in this case, he's of the mind that more is merrier. I don't disagree. While he's at Candy's, I'll be testing my hand. The pain from the scuffle with the asshole has gone away, so it's just the normal questions as to whether I'm okay to use my arm to punch full force. K will want to see a fight. He'll be able to tell if we're pulling punches.

"I want you to be careful because of your neck today, too," Mag says. "You have an appointment at a PT place tomorrow for assessment, so don't do too much. This is just a preliminary training and planning session."

My neck has been okay. Surprisingly, it didn't hurt the day they tried to blow up the tower despite the fight. The hot tub at the safe house did wonders afterward, just loosening the tension, so I could relax. I'm half tempted to tell Johnny he should put a hot tub in the tower somewhere, but I would also want it private because I'm not using something like that when his father or another guard could come in at any moment.

Plus, ever since I spent half a day in one, I've been wondering about hot tub sex. Hot tub sex sounds amazing. We would definitely need a private one for that.

We're halfway to the gym when Magnum reaches over, squeezing my hand. Barely moving his lips, he says, "Don't be obvious, but we've got a tail."

My heart leaps to life in my chest. The last time we had a tail, I was accused of murder, almost kidnapped, and had to be away for six weeks.

"It's Reynolds," Mag says quickly.

"The lawyer said he wouldn't be giving up," I tell him. I don't even need to look for the car Mag sees. I trust him, and it makes sense. They're trying to find evidence against me. They're trying to intimidate me into confessing, or just trying to see if I do anything else like kill someone in the middle of the street.

"I'll have to have a talk with Jax and Finn because he'll walk right up in there and grab towels, water bottles, anything that has your DNA on it."

"They won't match it to the scene."

"That doesn't mean they should have all that," Mag replies, gritting his teeth. "There are good cops and bad cops, and Detective Reynolds is an over-eager asshole."

"You're saying you wouldn't put it past him to plant evidence?"

He nods curtly, gaze still moving to the rearview mirror every once in a while. Not enough to make it obvious, but enough to be sure that it's Reynolds still following us. "We don't leave anything behind at the gym, okay? And we'll tell Jax and Finn they shouldn't trust him."

"Maybe I should find somewhere else to train," I offer, stomach flipping. I hate involving them. "I don't want to drag Jax and Finn into this. They're trying to get their business going. They're good guys."

"Brawler's already discussed coming back with them, and they want you there, Kyla," he says, looking over at me as he parks the car out front of the gym. It sits inside a strip mall, taking up the majority of the building with Boxing Gym written in bold, black letters over the door. It's pretty generic, but the place is well kept for the Heights.

I pull my phone out of my bag, hesitating before I click on the last text I got from Johnny. He told me to tell him everything, but I also don't want to bother him at Candy's either.

"What's up?" Mag asks.

"Just wondering if I should tell Johnny about Reynolds now or later."

Mag lifts his gaze to the rearview once more. Finally, I follow his gaze, twisting in my seat like I'm getting something from the back and see a gray sedan drive slowly by the gym and continuing, turning the corner at the next intersection.

"Tell him I have it handled, but he'll want to know now."

I type out the text and hit Send before we get out of the car. When we walk inside, relief shakes me. A training gym has been one of the few constants in my life. Finn jogs forward, his light hair down, caressing his shoulders as he moves toward us. "Damn girl," he says as he laces his arms around me. "You're like a magnet for fucked up shit."

"Don't I know it," I grumble, squeezing him back. "I'm glad to be here."

He pulls away, grinning at my arm. "Looks like you have better use of the hand. I was worried since the last time we met you could barely open a window."

I stretch my fingers out, flexing my wrist. "It's healing nicely. The doctor said that since I was a boxer, it might heal up faster than others would, and I think he's right. Mag hung a huge punching bag in my place, and I've been hitting it when I can."

"When you aren't in danger of dying, you mean."

"Yeah, then," I say, playfully punching him in the shoulder.

He chuckles, then looks behind us. "No boss man today?"

"Who? Johnny? Nah, he has business shit."

Finn throws his arm around my shoulders and walks me toward the middle of the gym. Brawler is already hitting a speed bag in the corner, looking like he's going to murder it, and Oscar isn't here yet.

"What's Brawler's problem?" Finn asks, tilting his chin his way. "He's been like that since he got here."

"He didn't tell you?"

Finn eyes me suspiciously. "No, what?"

I laugh with no humor. "Just you wait."

Out of the back, Jax walks toward us, wrapping his hands with bright green wrap at the same time. He puts the end in his mouth as he tapes it up then bites the remainder off. When he gets to us, he places his hands on his hips.

"Is this okay?" I ask, looking solely at Jax. He's always been the one who's unsure about this arrangement, and he certainly wasn't a fan of coming to see me at the PT place a couple of weeks ago.

"We're good," he says.

The bell above the door rings, and I stiffen. "What's up, Princess?"

Oscar comes up on my other side, poking me with his elbow. "Same old stuff," I tell him, having to shut my mouth before I drool. He's wearing a tank top with overly large armholes. His tanned football chest muscles peek through the sides. He's paired it with black athletic shorts that stop at his knees, showing off amazing calves.

"Just people trying to take you and kill you? That kind of thing?"

"You know it."

"And spy on her," Mag says, bringing the conversation around to Detective Reynolds and completely ruining the light mood.

"What?" Oscar snaps. The good humor that was on his face just evaporates.

"Let me get Brawler," Mag says. He calls him over, having to yell his name several times before he catches his attention.

He lumbers over to us, and the strain in his body and face is apparent. I couldn't comfort him enough yesterday. I couldn't tell him everything was going to be okay as much as he needed. I hate that I couldn't do that, and guilt lays over me.

"I have a feeling I'm about to eat my words," Jax complains, looking between all of us. Lines form between his brows.

"Knock it off," Finn chastises, pulling his shoulder-length hair around his ears. "They're our friends."

Brawler finally reaches us. "What's up?"

I can't keep my gaze off him. I want to go to him—hug him—but I can't do any of that right now. Not with Jax and Finn here, and certainly not with Detective Reynolds spying on me. For all I know, he could be ogling us right now.

Mag launches into a spiel about what we witnessed on the car ride here, explaining why it's a big deal though I think anyone with half a brain could figure it out. Everyone listens intently, Oscar cursing when he learns the news.

"So, you want to take back that invitation now?" I ask Jax. "I won't be offended."

"*I'll* be offended," Finn says, speaking up for me. "Nothing's changed. The cops are trying to threaten you, and that doesn't fly with us, does it, Jax?" His brother doesn't respond, but Finn keeps going anyway. "We'll continue like usual, only be more careful." I admire his easygoing nature, and the lengths he'll go to help me. He gives me a wicked grin. "Now, let's hear it. Who are you fighting next?"

I lock gazes with Brawler, my tongue darting out to lick my lips. "Him."

"Him?" Hesitantly, Jax and Finn follow my gaze, but return back to me. "Him, who?" Jax asks, gaze narrowed.

I shrug. "They're putting me up against Brawler on Friday, and needless to say, both of us have to win for different reasons. We need a plan."

Finn's brows shoot up just shy of his hairline as he gawks between the both of us.

"A plan?" Jax asks, scoffing. "Two people can't win the same fight. If that's the case, you need a goddamn miracle."

Yeah, that would help too. I wouldn't turn one of those away, but I already know God doesn't listen to me.

## 21

*B*rawler sits out during training. Hugging the sidelines like a spectator. Well, I guess what we're doing is called training even though it isn't hardcore training. I take it easy for the day, only hitting the pads with fifty percent force to make sure I don't injure my hand. In between rounds, Jax insists on massaging my wrists and lower arms, his tattooed fingers working over my skin in sure movements.

We both sit on the bench just outside the ring as Oscar decides he's going to get in with Finn and try to go toe-to-toe with him. It's not that Oscar isn't badass. He one hundred percent is. He just doesn't have the training Finn has. Though, he does have the power, strength, and force necessary to be good, along with that straight-up brutality instinct he learned from growing up in the Heights. I watch the show as tension pours off Jax while he works his fingers over me. He doesn't care for me very much. Well, maybe it's not even that, but he definitely doesn't like the affiliation I have with the Crew.

He shouldn't like it, and I don't blame him one bit.

I glance down, watching his hands. I have my arm lying lazily over my knee while he works, and since I'm this close, and his hands aren't flying through the air at my face, I can finally see what's tattooed on his knuckles over one hand. FREE.

"What's that about?" I ask, nodding toward his tat.

He stiffens and turns his hands to the sides to hide his tattoos. "You ever heard of the expression nunya?"

My forehead crinkles. "Um, no…"

"Nunya business, Princess."

I glare at his hard features. I guess that's what I get for trying to be conversational.

Jax drops my hand and sighs heavily. He leans his elbows on his thighs, dropping his hands between his knees. "Both of you can't win the fight," he says, changing topics.

"Obviously," I snap back.

"Why do you *both* have to win?"

I shake my head. "Once, a very sarcastic, very miserable fighter told me a saying…" I smile in his face. "Nunya."

His gaze sparks like he's going to rage at me. Instead, the corners of his lips turn up into a slight smile. Hardly noticeable. In fact, I don't know if it can even be called a smile at all. Maybe a cross between a grimace, a sneer, and a reluctant compliment. He purses his lips. "Let's just say at one point in my life I wasn't free. When I got free, I decided to tattoo it on my knuckles to remind me to fight for my freedom every damn chance I got."

Goosebumps skitter up my spine. The sentiment is one I know all too well. I don't know how or what happened to make Jax feel trapped. There are so many ways you can feel that way, and freedom is always the better option. It's something to fight for.

That's why I'm here.

I mirror his position, leaning over with my elbows on my knees. A drop of sweat rolls down my spine. He told me a truth, so now it's my turn. "I won't go too much into it because I know you don't want to get involved in Heights Crew business, which I think is extremely smart and important that you don't get mixed up in it, by the way," I tell him, locking gazes. "But I need to win the fight so shit doesn't go downhill for me. Brawler needs to win it for the same reason." I glance over at Brawler while he sits in the corner by himself. He has his feet pulled up in front of him on the wide bench, his arms wrapped tightly around them. The hood of his sweatshirt is up, hiding his face. He's been sitting there with his back against the wall ever since we broke off to start training.

"Or else?"

"Or else we're fucked."

Since Brawler's recruiting into the Heights, he needs the win. If he doesn't get it, we don't know what the punishment might be, and I don't even want to think about it. As for me, K is already fed up with my existence. If I lose this fight, therefore losing the fight audience, he may not have a use for me. Not even Johnny's feelings can save me now.

"I take it this is Big Daddy K's doing?"

It doesn't surprise me that Jax knows K's name. Everyone knows it.

I nod.

"Why?" he asks. For someone who doesn't want to get caught up in my shit, he's asking a lot of questions. "It doesn't make any sense. Finn follows the underground fights more than I do, and he says you guys are the best fighters the Crew has. I don't know why he would put you up against each other so quickly."

I pull my shoulder blades back to stretch then test my neck, working it from side-to-side while I figure out how to answer or how much information I should give him. "I think it has to do with me," I tell Jax finally. "He's not very pleased with me at the moment."

"So, he's doing this to fuck you over?"

"Or to test me."

"And the problem is...you like Brawler."

His gaze seers me like a hot press. I push my tongue against my teeth as I figure out what to say. "He's my friend," I say finally. "I don't want to hurt him."

Jax studies me for a little longer before standing to stretch. The bottom band of his tank pulls up over his abs, and I look away to see Oscar and Finn still trading friendly blows amidst laughter. It's good to see Oscar so carefree.

I peek over my shoulder to find Magnum still staring out the glass double doors leading out to the parking lot, but when I look away, my gaze stops on Brawler again.

"I'm going to need a little break," I say to Jax. "Mind if Brawler and I talk privately somewhere?"

Jax cocks his head toward the back of the gym. "You can talk in the office."

I nod, stand, and make my way over to his sullen form. He lifts his gaze when he sees me approach. His sad eyes stand out the most, and I just want to crawl into his arms, but I have to be mindful of where we are and what I'm allowed to do. "Let's talk," I tell him, motioning toward the back.

He stands, and I turn to lead him toward the office. Oscar watches us, but then Finn throws a punch he almost eats, so he's immediately pulled back into the pretend match he has going on.

When we get into the back office, a cracked leather two-person seater that looks as if it could have originally come from a doctor's office that went out of business awaits us. A huge steel desk sits in the middle of the room. One side neatly arranged while the other is a complete mess with paperwork and receipts strewn everywhere.

I close the door behind us. The blinds over the small window in the barrier bounce off a couple of times until they still again.

I reach up, pulling Brawler's hood back to reveal his full face. "Hey."

"Hey," he says.

I told myself I was going to be smart about being with each of the guys, but I'm truly a goner for all of them. The desperate look in his eyes beckons me forward. I press against him, kissing him on the lips. A soft brush at first, tentative, exploring, until my baser instincts take over. This is the guy who's fought for me from the beginning. The one who threw caution to the wind first, despite Johnny's public claiming, and I'll be damned if I let him swim in turmoil over this.

He pushes me away, tearing his lips from me. "How can you even kiss me after what I did? I fucked this up. Fight you? *You?*" He slams his fist into the wall by my head. "I won't."

"You will," I tell him. "And it'll be okay."

"God, I fucking hate him," he growls.

"I don't want to talk about that. We'll figure out something, and even if we do have to get in the ring together, it won't matter. I'll pretend your punches are kisses."

He drops his head at me, looking as if I'm completely insane. Brawler's fists aren't lips. That's for damn sure. But they can have the same effect on my body. Both want to tear me apart.

"I'll let you pummel me over and over," I tell him, trailing my hand down his taut torso. His body locks up when I get to his hips like he wants to pull away, but he doesn't. I explore lower, palming his hard dick through his athletic shorts. "Every hit I take will be worth it."

He moans as I stroke him. He's on the border of giving in despite the conflict written all over his face.

"Or maybe I'll just let you take me out," he says, voice betraying all the emotions he's trying to keep back.

But he can't do that, can he? He's committed to the gang. I've had the answer in the back of my head this whole time. No one else is saying it out loud, so neither am I. Brawler has to win. There's no point in arguing about it. He has the most to lose at this point.

I drop to my knees in front of him, and his gaze darkens. "Don't."

I reach up to his shorts, slowly removing them, pulling them out and around his erection as it levels in my line of sight. The sight of his cock turns me on even more. I push his shorts to the floor and inch closer, my hands reaching up the backside of his thighs. I press my fingertips there, and he jerks forward. I take him inside, moaning at the feel of him in my mouth.

"Fuck..." Brawler grinds out. He leans against the wall, peering at me with hooded eyes.

Here, I'm his. He can say he won't hurt me, and maybe that's what this is. A desperate need to tell him it's okay. To tell him it doesn't matter what happens next. We'll still be each other's.

I suck hard and pull back, letting him pop out of my mouth. I wrap my fingers around his base, stroking him again, eyeing the pre-cum that's seeped out greedily. "Do you remember that day you wrote on my mirror? I saw it you know."

I lick the salty liquid with the tip of my tongue, and he shudders.

"Fucking beautiful," I say reverently, letting the sparks fly over my skin just like they did when I first saw his message. He had some huge balls to go against Johnny then. To tell me he'd help me get out.

He reaches down with one hand, pulling his fingers through my hair. He fondles a few strands before I move my mouth over him again. This time, he doesn't hold back. He places his hand on the back of my head fisting a handful of my hair, but I'm the one in control. The one making Brawler lose his resolve. This is what he needs.

"I keep thinking about you," he confesses. "I want to be inside you every night. To feel you under me, hear your cries."

Intense heat settles in my core, which only spurs me on. I take him in further, pressing my lips against him tighter.

"Everything about you is fucking beautiful, Kyla. Everything."

He tightens his grip in my hair as he rocks in and out of me. He starts out slow until a strangled cry releases from him that has more liquid heat dampening my panties. "Let go," I urge, and then I'm right back on him again, stroking him toward the back of my throat.

I sink my nails into his ass as he fucks my mouth. The masculine noises of pleasure he makes coats me with pure need. Without warning, he rips my mouth from him as he places his hands over the tip of his jerking cock. Cum spills into his hands as I sit back in satisfaction. Watching my big man lose control thrills me. He took what he needed, and I let him. He doesn't always have to be the knight in shining armor. He can be the one who defied everything despite the consequences.

Do I think he should've sacrificed himself to keep me safe? Fuck no.

I understand why he did it though.

He reaches behind him to the desk and grabs a few tissues to clean up with. He holds them tightly in his hand while he pulls his pants up and then helps me stand, pushing me against the concrete wall at my back. He kisses me, this time throwing himself behind the kiss until I'm in a daze, captured by the full force of his feelings. He doesn't seem to give a fuck that he can taste himself on me, and my pussy throbs.

"Johnny's a damn fool if he won't share you with us." He breathes heavily. He waits until I lock gazes with him until he asks, "What happens if he says no?"

I blink at him. Worry lines his features as if this question has kept him up at night. "If you're asking if I'll give you up, the answer is fuck no. You and Oscar are a part of me. Magnum, too. He won't like the answer if he makes me choose." My mouth dries. Fear coats me, and I look away, trying to keep my breathing under control. Just the thought of losing any of them sends me into a spiral.

"That's if he doesn't kill us first."

"He won't kill you," I promise, gritting my teeth.

It's a dangerous thing to promise, but if Johnny cares for me like he says he does, he won't kill the people I care about. If he wants someone to rage at for what's happened, he can rage at me. He can take his anger out on me. I'm the one who deserves it. I'll gladly take all the punishment before he even faces the others.

"He doesn't deserve you. Hell, none of us do, but he claimed you like you were property. He hacked his way into your life, and you know damn well what he did to you in the beginning." I open my mouth to say something when he cuts me off. "He hurt you, Kyla. Don't you remember that? The bruises I saw. The bandages I had to apply." His body shudders in thought as I wince. "I get when you say he doesn't know any better, but if he decides he wants in on this... You, me, Oscar, Magnum. We're having words with him. He doesn't treat you like that. If he does it again, I don't care who he is, he answers to us."

The reminder of past Johnny sits like a dead weight in my stomach. It doesn't change the way I feel about him. I can acknowledge the person he was, but still see the man he is right now. "He doesn't treat me like that anymore."

"He beat the shit out of Oscar for touching your wrist. He's a loose cannon. Don't you think it's a little suspicious he offered me up, Kyla? When we were at the meeting, K asked who the best fighter was. He could've said anyone. Instead, he said me."

"Well, you are," I say, brows pulling together.

"He also knows we're friends," he says, disgust at the word lacing his tone. "He should also know that the last thing we would want to do is fight each other."

I shake my head. I get Brawler's suspicion. Johnny doesn't have a great track record when it comes to me. No, I haven't forgotten the bruising and the physical pain he inflicted, but I'll maintain that was from a scared boy. Now, he's a man, coming into his own. He's not his father's puppet any longer. He's not in his father's shadow, doing as he does. He'll make his own decisions here on out, and hopefully, that decision will be joining the family I'm trying to build for us. One that will love him for who he is, background scars and all. "I love that you're concerned," I tell him. "But I think what happened there was just Johnny falling into a routine. His father asked a question, and he answered truthfully. He didn't think about the consequences."

Brawler looks like he wants to argue, but he doesn't. This fighter has the biggest heart out of everyone I know. He'll forgive Johnny, eventually. If only because I ask him to, he will.

"Well," he finally says. "If you'll stop distracting me. Your phone is in my gym bag. You need to call your aunt before we leave here. I've been texting her. I hope that's okay. I was pretending to be you, but she wants to hear your voice. I figured pretending to be you was better than having her send the police, considering you were gone for a long time."

I move to my tiptoes to kiss him on the lips. "You're the best." I grip his shirt in my hands, tugging him even closer to me. Leaving my phone with Brawler was the best decision I could have made. I knew he would handle it.

I walk out of the office with a weight lifted off my shoulders. Connection is what we all need. A place for us to fit in. To feel like we belong somewhere that's different than the shitstorm surrounding us.

## 22

Brawler rocks at texting because for once, the conversation I have with my aunt isn't strained with accusations about how I'm not talking to them or how they're worrying about what I'm doing. When I get off the phone with her, I have an actual smile on my face. So different from my normal wave of guilt that plagues me for the rest of the night.

In fact, I'm in such a good mood that I invite everyone over for dinner at my place.

"Um, Princess?"

I turn my head toward Oscar, just knowing by his asshole smirk that he's two seconds from making me want to slap him. Lovingly, of course. "Yeah?"

"Aren't you forgetting about Johnny?"

I crack an even bigger smile. "No, in fact, I'm thinking about Johnny and all of us. I'll make dinner. We'll watch movies and talk. It'll be great."

Brawler gazes at his feet while Oscar still stares at me as if I've lost my head. "Johnny isn't one to have people over."

"That's because he's usually up his dad's ass. If we want to help him, we have to separate the two. Insert...us."

"Insert *us*?" Oscar grins. "That's your grand plan?" His voice takes on a high-pitched female quality as he says his next words. "Guess what, babe? I found you a new family, and now we can all be together." He drops his facade. "That's what's going on in that pretty little head of yours?"

I barely contain the laugh bubbling up my throat, but I do. I also step forward and give him a playful shove in the chest. "Yes, asshole. The sooner he finds out he actually likes you guys the better. *If* he actually likes you guys."

"Please," Oscar scoffs. "I'm downright lovable."

I roll my eyes into the back of my head. Literally. Well, okay, not literally, but I roll them as far as I fucking can. That Drego, always so full of himself. "Then you'll have no problem winning him over." I move to peek at Mag. "This is a good idea, right?"

He scratches his scruff. I'm beginning to think he does that when he's nervous, or thinking, or hell, basically any time. "It could go either way."

Footsteps approach us, and I glance at Finn who's come

out of the back room with fresh clothes on. They're about to shut down the gym, and he's dressed like he's about to head out for the night. "What could go either way?"

"I'm inviting everyone over to my place for dinner. I'm cooking. You in?"

Finn beams, but Jax speaks up from behind him. "No."

Finn spins. "What? Why?"

"We're not going to the tower. Are you fucking crazy?"

"We were there to pick her up for the last fight."

Jax shakes his head. "That was before someone tried to fucking bomb it." He glances over at me. "Thanks for the invitation, but we'll pass."

I nod at his answer. I honestly can't blame him for his reaction. He's just trying to keep them safe. "I understand. Maybe some other time? We can all go out to eat or something."

Jax throws his arm around Finn, discreetly squeezing his shoulders. "Yeah. Sounds good," Finn says, though he doesn't appear to agree with his brother at all.

I step up, throwing my arms around him for a quick hug. "Sometime, 'kay?" He nods, and I pull away. "Thanks for the training sesh."

"Same place, same time tomorrow, Princess," Finn says, replacing his frown with his coach exterior.

Automatically, my gaze veers to my poster on the wall. Honestly, it's fucking badass. I look fierce and determined.

Basically, everything I hope I look like when my opponent stares me down from the opposite side of the ring just before the bell rings.

Finn follows my gaze. "Our enrollment is up thirty-five percent."

Jax hits him upside the head. "Jesus. We don't talk business in front of customers."

"They're not just customers, asshole," Finn says, rubbing his head. "They're our friends."

Jax grinds his teeth together. He stops when he realizes I'm looking at him, and we stare one another down. I get his hesitation. I do. I'm just not used to it. Being feared in this way kind of sucks. "Well, we're getting out of here," I tell them. "See you guys tomorrow."

We walk out. Oscar jumps on his bike, and Brawler gets in the car with Mag and I, taking up the backseat while I ride shotgun with the copper-haired badass hottie.

"We need to make a quick trip to the store," I inform them.

Forty minutes later, we're inside my apartment. I've already texted Johnny to tell him I'm cooking dinner for everyone tonight. He hasn't written me back yet, but I'm not counting that as a tick in the "I shouldn't have done this" column yet. There's no telling why he isn't writing back.

I make the guys sit in the living room while I start cutting up potatoes for scalloped potatoes and ham. My mother used to make this dish. Call me nostalgic because it sounds amazing. Magnum keeps sneaking into the kitchen while Oscar and Brawler find something to watch on TV. Every once in a while, they chuckle, and it makes my heart lift in my chest as if it's suspended by bungee cords.

"So, real talk," I say, staring at my phone again and not finding a response from Johnny. "Good idea or bad idea?"

"Good idea," Mag says with authority. He reaches over and takes the knife and potatoes from me before cutting them just like I was. I smile up at him and start making the sauce that goes over them. "Johnny needs this. You think he's ever known a family dinner that didn't involve a bullet in a guy's head? Like with Dunnegan? If he ever had it, he was probably too young to remember."

"Do you think he'll accept you guys?" I ask, gut twisting. I'm not sorry for what I'm doing, however I'm sorry that it might hurt Johnny. Even though, I don't know, I believe he can be turned around. Everything that's happening can't be for nothing. It's not as if I'm with Brawler and Oscar with the intention of leaving Johnny behind. I would never do that. It's not even like I'm keeping the others from him because I'm trying to be a shady bitch. I'm not. This is just how it has to be right now, and I'll fucking fight anyone who says otherwise.

"Don't feel bad," Mag says, glancing over at me. "I can tell it's been eating you up lately, but don't let it. You're doing what needs to be done. I've been on the outside for most of this, and I've never once thought you had ill intentions. Never. That's not you. Johnny didn't give you a choice in the beginning. He never does. He's dickheaded and stubborn. He's done shitty things to you." He licks his lips. "But then I saw the gradual change in how you acted around him, starting with the shootout. I think it scared you that you might lose all of them, so you just let yourself feel what you wanted to instead of holding back. To me, that takes a lot of bravery." He puts down the knife and brushes his fingers across my cheekbones. "My gut feeling tells me..." He blows out a breath. "My gut feeling tells me Johnny belongs with us, but I don't know if years of indoctrination will win out."

I close my hand over his, pressing his palm into my cheek. "You care for him too."

"Like a brother. I always have. When you initiate in with someone, you're tied for life. No matter if that guy is now the leader's son or someone who defected or..." He peeks out the kitchen at Brawler and lowers his voice. "...someone who didn't make it."

I bite down on my lip. "Brawler has a lot of mixed feelings about his brother. He blames him for his sister's death."

Magnum squeezes my hand, then lets go and reaches for the knife to start cutting the potatoes again. "I know he does. I'm not sure there's anything I can say that would make him think otherwise."

"Do you blame Manning for his sister's death?"

Magnum gives a quick shake of his head. "I blame the Crew."

Magnum and I finish up, then place the scalloped potatoes and ham in the oven, which still looks brand new. I don't know if that's because it's cleaned a lot or if it's from lack of use. I'm not that much of a cook. In fact, I don't particularly like it even though I love home-cooked meals. However, maybe cooking is something I could use to try to bring us all together.

What Mag said about Johnny is probably true for all of them. How many times did they have home-cooked meals when they were kids? Did they sit around a table telling stories about their day? Did they laugh and joke?

I only have those memories from when I was a kid. I cherish them, hold them inside because that's the last time I've ever felt truly at home. Hopefully, I can make a new home now.

I'm sitting on the arm of the couch, being drawn into the comedian Brawler and Oscar are watching after setting the table when the door to my place opens. I peek over my shoulder and find Johnny walking in. He's not alone. Jiko Cardinale follows him. Both of them wear dapper looking suits while the rest of us are still in training gear. Well, aside from Mag who's wearing his usual black tactical outfit.

"Hey," I say, popping up from the couch to greet Johnny.

He gives me a quick kiss on the cheek. "Jiko's in town to

help me get Candy's settled. Since you said you were making dinner, I invited him."

"If there's enough," Jiko interjects.

"Yeah, there's enough," I tell him. I hold out my hand, but Jiko bypasses it. He steps forward, grips my upper arms, and kisses both of my cheeks.

Stunned, I just kind of stand there while Jiko laughs. "That's how we greet each other in Chicago. It's an Italian thing."

I clear my throat. "I'm afraid I didn't make an Italian dish, so I hope that doesn't matter." Uneasiness crawls over me. I don't know why I don't like this guy. Whether it's just the usual being wary of someone or if there's something behind it, I don't know. "I'm making scalloped potatoes and ham."

Jiko cocks his head. "Never heard of it, but I'm willing to try anything."

Johnny glances around me and is greeted by a round of masculine voices. Apprehension pricks at my skin, but Johnny nods at the rest of them. So, that must mean he's cool about having them over, right? I mean, he's not beating Oscar up for being in my apartment, so that has to be a good sign.

If you think about it, Brawler and Oscar have every reason not to like Johnny. So, if they're willing to try for me, shouldn't Johnny do the same?

I fucking hope so.

"How did training go today?" Johnny asks, pulling up my injured hand.

I shrug as he works his fingers over my skin. "Not too bad," I confirm. "I'd say I went fifty percent on the bags, and no issues thus far."

Shadows crawl over his skin. "Except for Detective Reynolds following you."

"Yeah, there was that," I admit.

Johnny runs his fingertips down my arm while he looks at Mag.

"He didn't come back around again," Mag informs him.

"Make sure you're doing bug sweeps from now on and be careful what you talk about in there."

Mag nods. He's been doing all of his bug sweeps in front of me now. He checked the apartment when we got here, and every time we see one of the guys, he checks their phones like someone may have slipped something inside in the middle of the night. Honestly, it could be coming from two sides. Or more. Detective Reynolds, who wants to see me go down for a murder I didn't commit, and Gregory's people, or the Dragons, or K. Literally, everyone.

"You should rub some Arnica gel on that," Jiko says, motioning toward my hand. I raise my eyebrow at him. I actually have it down on my grocery list of things I need, but that's usually a fighter/martial artist remedy. He smirks. "What? Didn't pin me as a fighter?"

"Not exactly," I say.

He shrugs, brushing off my slight. "I hear you have a big fight coming up."

I don't know what Johnny's said to him, so I just nod. "Yep, Brawler and I are going at it, and I think I just might kick his ass."

Without looking away from the TV, Brawler raises his middle finger in the air. It's so unlike him that it makes me laugh. Not that he wouldn't throw someone the bird, but me? That seems like something Oscar would do. Who, by the way, thinks Brawler's *fuck you* to me is extremely funny, considering he's doubled over on the couch.

Johnny snickers beside me. He gazes at the scene, and I would give anything to see it from his point of view. What does he think in that devilishly handsome head of his? Is he wishing I hadn't done this? Is he timid, like stepping into the ocean for the first time with the waves crashing over one another mere feet away?

Me? Having them there, like this? It only solidifies that I'm doing the right thing.

"We still have twenty minutes until dinner," I tell them, grabbing Johnny's hand and pulling him closer to the living room. "Let's hang out."

"Looks like we're going to need to get another couch," Johnny says, voice low. His tone is indecipherable.

I squeeze his hand though, and he squeezes back. "There's that chair in the bedroom I can bring out," I offer.

"I'll get it," Johnny says, kissing my temple.

He strides toward the bedroom, and I waver about going after him. I'm about to take a step his way when Jiko Cardinale's voice stops me. "He's got it bad for you, girl."

Despite the fact that I don't like those words coming out of his mouth, they make me smirk. "Yeah?"

He peeks toward the door and then leans in conspiratorially. "I've never seen him go against his father's wishes like he does for you."

I swallow hard. This conversation is suddenly taking a turn for the worse. "Yeah, and he's got the bruises to prove it," I say before I can stop myself.

Jiko blows a breath out of his nostrils, making them flare. "Par for the course."

"Well, that's a pretty fucked up game then, isn't it?"

"You don't know the half of it," Jiko says, his ominous tone stoking apprehension inside me.

Darkness overrides his features. Shadows dance over his face, making the red tints I saw in his hair at the dinner where Dunnegan got shot stand out even more.

Jiko's handsome. They both come from the same type of families, and if what Jiko is insinuating is true, he's probably gone through the same shit Johnny has. It's not shocking Johnny found a friend in him, if that's what they are.

Johnny's told me he's cool, so maybe I should let my guard down around him. Paranoia in the Heights, however, is something that jumps out at you and clings like a bitch in heat. It's hard to trust anyone around here.

Johnny comes out carrying the chair, winking at me as he settles it beside the couch. My heart fills just watching him.

I shake my paranoia away. I've already proved to myself there are good people here. I just wonder at the end of all of this, which way the scale will tip? Good or evil?

## 23

Johnny watches as I say goodbye to Magnum. Jiko left first, claiming he wanted to get to bed early for tomorrow. He actually hadn't been all that bad during dinner...or afterward. Brawler left after him. Hesitation slowed his movements to the door like he didn't want to leave me, but he had to get home to see his mother. He rarely misses a dinner with her, so he knew she would be worried he wasn't there. Oscar left just five minutes ago, staying and—I don't think it was my imagination—actually enjoying a conversation with Johnny.

Mag stayed just long enough for he and Johnny to talk about Detective Reynolds and how he'd followed us to the gym.

I close the door behind Mag's retreating form, catching a

glimpse of the way his pants hug his ass. Sue me. The guys are hot, so yes, I'm going to catch my fill when I can.

I spin, leaning against the door to look back at the dark prince before casually locking the deadbolt.

"You look happy," Johnny muses. He darts his tongue out to run across his lips in an almost mesmerizing way. "I wasn't sure you'd look like that again after we got you back."

"Is that why you're going along with my crazy ideas?" I throw out. "Or did you actually have fun tonight?"

Honestly, the night couldn't have gone better. We all sat around the table chatting like normal human beings. Johnny and Mag even talked about their younger days, even though talk of the Crew life came to a grinding halt. The particular story they were telling involved Brawler's brother, so both guys were hesitant to finish it in front of him.

"I have fun anywhere you are."

I stride forward, pushing my palm against his chest. "Talk to me," I tell him, eyes begging him the whole time. I reach up to undo his tie, loosening it and pulling the fabric out of his collar before unbuttoning the first few buttons of his shirt. I don't understand how he can wear a suit almost all the time.

"You just want to know all my secrets..."

"Is that so bad?" I challenge.

He nips at my lip, dragging it through his teeth before it pops back to me.

Fuck. I hadn't meant this to go in a sexual direction.

Honestly. Not that I fucking mind. "Don't distract me," I chastise. He grins. I take a step back, peering at him suspiciously. "You were trying to distract me?"

"To be fair, you're easily distracted around me."

I give him a teasing swat. "There's your arrogance. I can't say that I missed it."

"You fucking love it," he says, letting me back him up until he hits the leather couch. He sits and pulls me after him onto his lap.

I situate myself on top, playfully grinding over him—accidentally on purpose—until he's squirming beneath me and nursing a semi. "You and Jiko seem to get along well. We can trust him?"

Johnny settles his hands on my hips, stopping my movements. "Yeah, we can trust him. My dad and his dad have been friends for a long time. He's my oldest friend, even though he lives far away. He also has to deal with the same stuff I do, you know?"

I nod. "I wasn't sure if we could talk freely around him," I confess. "When we were talking about Brawler, I didn't know if we could discuss our plan for how the fight should go down."

"That's easy," Johnny says with a quick lift of his shoulders. "You're going to kick his ass."

I swallow, my throat suddenly tight. Considering I'd come to the exact opposite conclusion, I don't know how to react. "What happens if he loses?"

"None of your concern. He brought it upon himself when he decided he wanted to fast-track it into the Crew."

I stare into Johnny's ice-blue eyes. Despite the words coming out of his mouth, I detect a hint of hesitation on his side. He has to think of Manning when he sees Brawler. He's just saying all this for me because Johnny would literally give up everything for me. "It is my concern," I say. "Brawler's not going to get hurt because of me."

Johnny's jaw ticks, and he moves me off him. He stands, hands perching on his hips as he glares down at me. "So, you're willing to let him beat the shit out of you, so he can get his way? That's what you're saying?" A chill creeps through me. It's the sudden lack of him that's the problem. Couple that with the daggers that are now being sliced through me, and I sit on the couch like a chastised child while he continues. "It's not happening, Kyla. Brawler's not going to touch you, and if he tries, I'll—"

I stop him before he can make that threat. I don't want to hear it, and I don't want him to put it out there either. He's better than that. We're better than that. "Your father did this. Not Brawler."

He gives me a look like he's telling me to get real. "My father's running the Crew like he always does. You think him making this fight was just a spur-of-the-moment decision? It wasn't. He knows you're friends. When people want into the Crew, we tear them down. We make sure they know the only family they have is the Crew family. You guys in the ring will show him what Brawler's about. If he tries to take you out, he gets a plus sign in the Crew column. If he wusses out—if he phones it in—that's all the information Dad needs to make his decision." He glares at me. "The same goes for you, too. You need to fight for your own survival."

His words harden my bones. I get to my feet, not letting him glower over me any longer. "We can figure something else out."

Johnny shakes his head. "He won't be satisfied until you're both shedding blood out there. I let you have your little dinner. I didn't kick his ass out, but from here on out, Brawler is not your friend."

Johnny turns, but I stop him in his tracks. "No."

He peers over his shoulder, his shocked gaze biting, as if threatening me to disagree. "No?"

"No, Johnny. That's not how this works. I care about Brawler, and I'm not going to just kick his ass and not give a fuck what happens to him. We can come up with another plan."

"He'll kick your ass without a second thought."

"Bullshit."

"Not bullshit," Johnny growls. "That's the way things happen here. It's everyone for themselves."

"You have got to get that notion out of your head," I growl right back. "That's not how the real world works. Brawler's upset we're fighting. If you took two seconds to look at him, you'd see it written all over his face. He joined so he could help keep me safe just like you want to. He's worried your dad might actually try to hurt me."

Johnny's jaw ticks.

"So, I'm not going to just turn around and screw him over before he screws me over first. I'd rather be wrong than do that to someone I care about."

Johnny turns, exploding. His hands ball to fists, and a ball of rage detonates from his chest in a scream that makes my heart stop. The tension in the thick air burns hot. Goosebumps skitter up and down my skin. He turns slowly. "You keep saying you care about him. What's that mean, Kyla? You keep saying you care about all of them. What are you saying?"

My heart wrestles for control in my chest. It's hard to know if this is the right moment. I have to go with my gut. He's asking me a direct question. If I lie to him now, it'll hurt even worse when he learns the truth. I send a silent prayer that I'm not signing anyone's death warrants and then turn pleading eyes to Johnny. "It means I like them," I say, voice as even as it can be given the situation.

He drags his gaze down me. My body flushes at his inspection. He moves forward with purpose. He's so close his breath brushes over my nose. "Does he make you hot?" His hand moves to cup my mound before I can say anything. His finger works between my legs, stroking me. "Does he turn you on?"

I moan.

Johnny snakes his hand under my leggings, past my panties, and thrusts a finger into my wet heat. "Does he make you feel like this?"

He pumps his finger in and out of me while his strong arm pins me to his side.

"Johnny," I gasp, trying to push him away, trying to wrangle my emotions under control. Out of everything that could've happened, this is not what I ever imagined.

He removes his finger only to thrust two deep inside. A low mewl purrs from my throat. I grip the sides of his unbuttoned shirt, holding on as he drives his fingers in and out. It's as if he's battling for control over me. Like he thinks if he can do this it means he still has me. Maybe he's caught on to the way I am with them. Maybe he's seen right through me all this time.

Or maybe he's just being Johnny. The commandeering, demanding asshole he can be. Taking something from me I don't want to give him right now.

We don't say anything as he drives me higher and higher, my breathing practically tumbling over from one breath to the next. He doesn't kiss me. He doesn't give me secret, sweet thoughts. There's nothing intimate about this moment.

As much as I wish I could lock my body down and not give it what Johnny is demanding, it doesn't happen.

I spiral out of control, my core clenches around his

fingers. He doesn't even wait until I come down. At the first feel of my climax, he withdraws his fingers, leaving me swaying on my feet, my pussy clenching around nothing while I finish my orgasm.

Without a glance back, he strides toward the door. "You're winning, and that's final," he barks as he pulls my apartment door open. He walks out without looking back, slamming it behind him.

I fall back onto the couch, tears pricking my eyes. Desperate loneliness crowds around me. I have no idea where we stand right now. What was that even? My instinct says it was a power struggle, but for what? Over me? Against me? Against *them*?

I stay where I am for a few minutes, just staring blankly ahead, not knowing what to do. I could go after him. But should I?

What he did was wrong regardless if my body liked it or not.

I groan, and a soft knock sounds on the door, snapping my head to attention.

I don't bother getting up, and I don't have to either. My phone buzzes on the table in front of me. It's from Mag, telling me he's coming in.

He must have a key to my door too because after a moment, he steps inside, shutting the door behind him.

I don't look over. I'm sure I already know what this is about. Johnny left, but he sent Magnum to watch me.

"You guys argued?"

"I guess?" I answer, lifting one shoulder helplessly. I still don't really know what it was. "He told me I had to beat Brawler, and I told him I wasn't going to do that."

Magnum bites down on his lip and then brings his phone out.

I eye him. "What are you doing?"

"Warning Brawler in case he goes over there."

Shock races through me. I get to my feet. "You think he's headed over there?"

Mag puts his phone away and looks at me. "I don't know what he'll do, Kyla. Sending Brawler a warning is the smart thing to do though."

I shake my head. "This was supposed to show Johnny what the real world is like. Somehow, it fucking backfired on me."

"Maybe it did show him," Mag says, placing his hands on my shoulders. "Maybe it did, and it scared him. No one said this was going to be easy."

"But what's he going to do?" I ask. "Lash out? If he goes to Brawler's, what the hell is he going to do to him? If he hurts him—"

"Brawler can handle himself," Mag says, trying to soothe me.

I know the guy can, but that doesn't mean that the son of the most powerful man in the Heights could be on the way to his place right now.

"He's probably not headed that way, okay?"

I bear down on my teeth. "Now you're just saying that to patronize me."

He pushes me further away so he can look at me. "For the record, it's been a while since I've looked at you like a girl, so patronizing isn't the word for it. I'm—"

"So, you've finally realized my past and maturity level makes up for our age difference?"

His face heats. He drags his gaze down me, firing my skin up in a delicious way that melts away the feelings Johnny just invoked. "What age difference? I see a brave, sexy as fuck woman who has too many crosses to bear."

I pull my shoulders back and lift my chin, emulating the woman Mag thinks he sees. I need my strength now more than anything. I take several breaths. "I'm not beating Brawler in the fight. He needs to beat me to keep him safe."

He frowns. "I was worried you were going to say that."

"Tell me another way this works out," I beg. I'm desperate for another option. I don't want to do this.

"Short of having you fight someone else, I don't see a way out of it. The problem is that it has to be convincing. I'm worried you could get seriously hurt on top of the injuries you already have, and I worry Brawler won't be able to do it."

"Leave Brawler to me," I say. "What I really need help with is convincing Johnny. He can't hate Brawler right now.

Johnny's going to need all of us when his life implodes, and that's going to be sooner rather than later."

I hope I'm right. Pushing Johnny into this could be forcing him right back toward his father. But he's come so far. He's opened up to me. He's told me about his past. He hasn't hurt me in a long time. He's done everything he can for me.

"You know him better than anyone..." I start. "Tell me he'll end up on our side. Tell me he won't do anything crazy."

"Anything crazy?" His eyebrows rise. "No one can promise that when it comes to Johnny Rocket." He worries over his lip. "Whatever just happened in here, scared you, didn't it?" His gaze hardens. "Did he hurt you?"

I swear his hand twitches toward his back where he usually keeps his gun. "He didn't," I say, leveling my voice as much as I can. He didn't hurt me physically, but as always, there's more than one way to hurt someone.

Sure, he brought me to orgasm, but it wasn't in a way that told me he even wanted to. It was about control. It wasn't about the act. Hell, it wasn't even hate fucking. At least then, you're fucking your aggression out. The way he left afterward said it all.

"Did he tell you he'd be back tonight?" I ask, not able to help how needy I sound.

"He didn't say."

"Then I want to go to his apartment," I tell Magnum. If

Johnny is upset—if I've pushed him too far—I don't want him retreating into other habits he might have had before.

Mag nods, and he takes me up through Security. The guards just off the elevator nod at us as we walk by, and when I knock on the door, Johnny doesn't answer.

Thankfully, Mag doesn't make me wait out in the hallway like a thrown-out piece of trash. He lets me into Johnny's place with a key of his own, and I walk toward the bedroom.

"Kyla?" Mag calls out, the desperate tone in his voice makes me turn to face him. "If Johnny doesn't choose you, he's the dumbest man alive."

I smile at his compliment, then retreat into the back, slipping under Johnny's covers in his empty bed, relishing in the fresh sheets that still have that little hint of him on them.

Maybe I've gone completely mental. Someone on the outside might say I've lost my shit. They might even say I have some sort of Stockholm Syndrome. My answer to them would be a giant middle finger in their face.

I know someone who deserves to be fought for when I see it. We already promised we wouldn't run away from each other's secrets, which includes this. So, yeah, when Johnny gets back tonight, he's going to find me waiting for him. And if he ever docs it again, I'll be in the same fucking place because Johnny never had anyone who fought for him, and for once in his life, he fucking deserves it.

## 24

The next thing I know, a door sounds as if it's being torn off its hinges. A guttural curse whips through the air, making tiny hairs stand up all over my body. Ragged breaths fill the room as I jolt up in bed at being woken up like a bomb went off in the apartment.

Johnny stands in the doorway to his room. The door bounces against the wall and returns to hit him in the shoulder. He's not even aware of it. He's staring at me with wide-eyed confusion, apprehension, and relief mixing into one intense gaze.

His clothes sit askew. His shirt is all the way unbuttoned, lying open in a crooked mess. His jacket is nowhere to be seen and more than a few wrinkles mar his perfectly tailored pants.

Johnny strides toward the bed with authority. I just stare

at him, not backing down, but sitting up straighter as he approaches.

He drops to his knees by the bed, his hands gripping the side of the mattress with such force that his knuckles turn white. "I thought you left." His voice is surprisingly less hostile now that his previous curse has increased the tension in the room tenfold.

"I was waiting for you," I tell him. "I didn't like the way we left things."

His heated eyes blaze with a fire hotter than the earth's core. If I were a lesser person, I'd be consumed by flames right now, combusting from the inside out until I was a pile of ash in front of him.

He crawls into bed next to me, and I move back to make room for him. He doesn't let me move too far though. He pulls me to him. His whole body shakes in wild tremors that seep into my skin until I'm gripping him, hoping I can make us both stop.

"I just tore apart your rooms," he breathes. "I destroyed everything inside it. I thought you'd finally had enough and left. I thought you walked away like I told you to. I thought—"

I tighten my grip, my head resting against his thumping chest. "I told you I wouldn't do that to you."

"I pushed you away. I think I was trying to provoke you."

"You'll have to do a hell of a lot more than that to push me away, Johnny Marx."

Like the masochist I am, Johnny pulls me back under his spell. He feathers kisses over my hair, his hand gripping my head to his chest is almost painful, but I understand the need to be close. He wants me near. Closer than this even. If he could, he'd probably consume me.

As for me, I'd rather wipe away the mess that happened between us earlier. The old him crept in. I have no doubt it'll happen again as he struggles internally with what he's learned his whole life and what he knows now, but he can restrain it.

"Babe," he breathes. "I need you."

He winds his hand under my shirt, reaching up to palm my breast over my sports bra. He teases my nipple until it peaks at his touch.

I lean on my forearm at the same time he does, meeting in the middle as we kiss each other greedily. Bruising, punishing kisses that I have no doubt he doesn't mean, but have me yanking his shirt off his shoulders and my fingers shaking as they work on the clasp of his suit bottoms.

He takes my hand and puts it on his hard cock right through the thin material. He pumps his hips forward, gasping in my mouth. I give him a quick squeeze before I'm tugging his pants and boxers down to free his cock.

He does the same with my leggings until they're just past my knees before I swing my leg over to line up our bodies. He grips my hip, and I lower on top of him with a low moan.

With a hand on either side of my legs, he moves my leggings down until he can tug them off. My panties are a little harder, and I'm fairly sure he tears them in the process, but within thirty seconds, I have room to move over him just like we desperately need.

He lifts his ass, spearing me, and I cry out. He grins, and it's hot as fuck as he maneuvers his suit pants down. I help him shimmy them off when I realize what he's doing. We kind of went about this all wrong. Usually, you undress before you start fucking, but this is what it's like when you just want to feel someone inside you right this fucking second.

I whip my shirt off next while moving over him. He runs his hands up my body, palming both breasts, teasing the edge of the cup where it meets my skin.

"Show me you want this as much as me," he pleads.

I place my hands on his chiseled abs and ride him. I ride him straight into an orgasm that curls my toes. I fucking love this position. The friction on my clit. The view of him as he watches me fuck him. It's everything.

He grabs a hold of the bottom band of my bra, yanking me forward, pulling my panting body down. He reaches behind me, unclasping the bra hooks in the back, and I'm so thankful I use the best of the best bras and not just the flimsy sports bras other women wear. It's not because I have huge breasts, it's because I don't want them bouncing around when I train, but they're also useful for easier access in moments like this.

He pulls the straps down my arms and tosses the fabric to the floor as he sits up, changing the angle. "Oh, fuck," I breathe.

He lifts his hips, and we grind against each other, kissing like our lives depend on it. Like his lips are the only thing giving me oxygen to breathe and I'm a woman suffocating.

He kisses a trail down my neck, pausing at my collarbone before taking one of my nipples into his deliciously hot mouth. He tugs and pulls, teasing. My head falls back, giving him all the access he wants. He takes it, worshipping each of my breasts in turn while he fondles the other with expert fingers. The sounds in the room of just our bodies moving together and our harsh breaths commingling drown me in need.

We stay that way until my body is so locked up tight in anticipation of my orgasm that I start to shiver. He reaches between us. "Give it to me, babe." His thumb grinds circles into my clit. "Give me all of it. I want to feel you come on me again."

My mind obliterates. His other hand wraps around me tighter, making sure my movements increase against him.

"I want to see that orgasm face you have. I want that plastered in my memory for eternity."

I desperately work myself over him as he presses down

on my clit. The sounds coming from me sound animal-like, primal as I finally reach the catalyst and scream his name.

I collapse against him, and he rolls me onto my back. He doesn't give me time to recover. He hikes my leg up over his shoulder, pumping in and out of me. Unbelievably, this new position awakens my body again. Just when I thought I was done and didn't have enough for anymore, I'm desperately kissing him again, holding his face to mine, so I can ravish him like he's ravishing my cunt.

"Tell me what you want," I breathe in between kisses. "Tell me all of it."

"You," he sighs. "Just fucking you. I won't always do the right thing." He draws in a harsh breath. "Fuck. You feel incredible."

I moan at his words. "I won't always do the right thing either," I admit. "But I will always be here for you."

He pumps inside me, hips working overtime. Still, lines crease his forehead. "I don't want to lose you," he breathes, his nostrils flaring. "But I think I'm too late."

In his eyes, a lost boy appears. A look I imagine he would've had when he was younger lingers. It's far from the confident Johnny Rocket I'm used to seeing.

"I'm right here," I tell him, taking his cheeks in my hand and pulling him down to wash those thoughts away. He can have me. All of me. He's not late for anything.

He fists the sheets beneath us. "You like Brawler. I can tell." He fucks me harder. His hips slamming into me until I can barely draw breath. "You want him like this, and I don't want to share you."

Separating what's happening between our bodies and minds is almost impossible. "I like both of you," I grunt almost on a cry. Fuck, he's so good at this. Why do all of his truths come out when we're like this? Desperate for each other?

"I'm going to kill him," Johnny says, glaring down at me.

It's a half-hearted threat. I don't know if it's because he's balls deep inside of me, or if it's because he doesn't really want to.

"You're just scared," I tell him, arching my back. "But my feelings for anyone else have nothing to do with my feelings for you. They'll always be the same."

He grinds against me, a swirl of hips that has me gasping. He slows the pace as if he's teasing me. "I'm going to fight for you." He locks gazes with me, and I see the unsaid promise there. "This is all my fault, but I'm going to win you over. I'm going to treat you like the queen you are until you drop them and come back to me."

He fucks me slow, hands wandering over my sensitive flesh. An almost maddening amount of pressure crescendos until I squirm beneath him. My orgasm hits me out of nowhere, and I gasp as the pleasure rocks my body.

He pinches my nipple, and a jolt rockets through me. "Is that what this is about?" I ask. "I told you before that no one owns me."

He pulls out, and I groan at the loss of him. He sits up on his knees, stroking his cock in front of me like a dark god. He makes a twirling motion with his free hand. "Flip onto your knees."

I stare at him stroking himself, pleasure leaking between my thighs before he grows impatient and flips me himself. In one stroke, he enters me from behind, and I pant out his name.

"It *sounds* like I own you, Kyla. It sounds like I own this pussy, this incredible body," he says, hands smoothing up my spine. "It sounds like it's calling out for me. Am I wrong?"

He pounds into me so hard I can't answer. It's onslaught after onslaught of pleasure.

"Tell me I'm wrong," he boasts. "Tell me you don't want to be owned like this."

No such words would ever cross my lips. "Fuck yes," I grind out instead, moving back into him as he spears me.

He holds my hips in place. Sweat drips down my spine, and he leans over to capture it with the tip of his tongue. Oh fuck. My thighs are jelly. My core is thoroughly fucked in all the right ways.

Johnny moves his hands to my ass, squeezing me there to the point of pain. He releases, and I let out a breath only to feel the palm of his hand slap me in the same spot. Pleasure spikes, sinking into every pore, every thought. He does it again, and another orgasm rakes my body, torturing it in the most beautiful way.

He grips my hips as he loses control, ramming inside me until he comes with a low grunt, his cock jerking inside me as my pussy clenches around him. He collapses over me, chest heaving. I can't keep both of us up, so I fall to the bed and he falls with me like we've just taken a giant leap to an unknown place with each other.

His hot breath stirs my hair when he finally speaks. He's still sprawled over my back, cock seated inside my sated walls. "This is all my fault, and I'm not mad. But I will fight for you, Kyla. I thought you left, and the bleak existence I would have without you flashed in front of my eyes until all I saw was pain. I don't deserve this, but I'm not fucking giving up either. It's not in me." He lets out a breath. "Tell your boys it's game on."

I wait for a beat, but the only thing that comes is the rapid beat of his heart against my back. Fuck, he's really serious. I turn toward him, catching him before he slips from the bed. I sit up, kissing his shoulder as he swings his legs over. "I never meant for this to happen," I tell him. "I wanted to tell you. I want you to know them like I do."

He hangs his head. "I have no one to blame but myself."

"Don't do that," I plead. "I didn't realize what was happening with all of you until it was too late."

His jaw ticks. "Just so it's clear. Who are we talking about here?"

I watch his face. Either he has the best poker face in the world, or he really isn't planning on killing them. He says he's going to fight for me, but we're going to fight for him too. "Brawler."

"I know that one," he says, jaw clenching.

"Oscar," I tell him, ignoring his response.

"Fucking Bat?"

Jesus. Oscar never gets any love. Johnny just mirrored Brawler's reaction. I know he's a smart mouth, but he's so fucking good underneath it all.

"And—"

"There's another?"

I take his arm, pulling him until his back is on the bed and I'm straddling him. "I'm being open with you, babe," I say, letting his nickname for me slip out. It works this way, too. He is my babe. He's my gorgeous Crew leader. My torn bad boy with a heart underneath it all. "My feelings grew for everybody at the same time. I've never felt like this before," I tell him, letting my soul ooze out between us. With this information, he could make me bleed. He could ruin me. He could turn my life into a total rotting mess, but I'm trusting him with everything. "Jacob," I breathe, using Mag's real name and letting my last secret in regard to this finally slip out.

A low rumble starts in Johnny's chest. "Now I don't feel bad for punching that fucker earlier."

I still. "You punched him?"

"I thought he left you alone so you could run away."

I lean over him, making him look at me. "He let me up here. Magnum cares for you, Johnny."

"Yeah, cares for me enough to take my girl from me."

I pin his hands above his head and loom over him. "No one is trying to take anything from you, Johnny. We all want to work together. We all want to be together."

"And everyone knew but me?" I prepare for an explosion, but a smirk crosses his face instead. "They're all terrified I'll kill their asses, aren't they?"

"They are, and I'm trusting you not to do that."

"No promises."

He tries to shirk me off, but I press my body against his. "Johnny," I warn. I know he could get me off him if he wanted, but he probably wants to have this conversation as much as I do. "It's not about liking them better than you or you better than them. Or any of you better than the other."

"So, you want us to...share you?" His brow rises like he can't believe what he's hearing.

I nod, words getting stuck in my throat.

"I don't share," he says, "but I will fight my damndest for you. You can tell them to relax. Killing them would be too easy, and besides, I'd lose you in the process. I'll win you though," Johnny says, the sound a dark promise. "At the end of this, you'll want me and only me. I'll show you I'm enough."

"You're already enough," I tell him. "This has nothing to do with something you're lacking. I told you the other day that I thought I was falling in love with you. I'm fucking in love with you, Johnny. There's no falling. I'm already there."

A shimmer of pain flashes in his eyes, and I recognize the hurt there. He thinks he's completely fucked this up for himself. "I should never have fucked that random girl. I should never have hurt you, and I'll be paying for that shit my whole life. Don't give up on me," Johnny pleads, his hands flexing against my hold. "I'm not my father. If I can promise you anything, I can promise you that."

I let him free his hands and wrap his arms around my body, pulling me toward him. We lie there in an embrace. All in all, considering what could have happened, the only thing that would have made this better was if he agreed to share from the beginning.

That's not Johnny Rocket though. He's a fighter through and through, and a part of him still thinks I'm his and only his no matter what.

And I'm fine with that. As long as I can be the others' too.

*J* wake in Johnny's arms and settle into his warmth at my back. Maybe it's a shit thing to do to feel hope in the midst of all this, but I do. It surges inside me like a gallop of faith. No, it's not like Johnny told me he was committing to all of us. He only promised me...well, him, basically.

I wrap his arms around me tighter. What he must have gone through when I was at Greenlawn. He must have buried himself in a massive pit of blame. I don't know how to get it through his head that there's nothing he could have done to stop me from falling for the other guys, too. It's as if this was supposed to happen.

My phone buzzes on the nightstand. Jacob appears on the screen, and I watch as a text scrolls across. REMEMBER: PT APPT.

Damn, this guy. I shake my head and smile.

I slip out from Johnny's grasp and tiptoe to the bathroom. I text Mag back that I'm in Johnny's suite still, then I take a shower and ready myself for the day. I wrap a towel around my chest as I do my hair, then send a quick text to Magnum, asking him to bring me some clothes to wear. Considering I'm not supposed to be sleeping in Johnny's apartment per his father's orders, all of my clothes were moved to my place when I was moved out. I bite my lip. I'm not only not supposed to be sleeping here, I'm not supposed to be fucking him either.

A few minutes after I've dried my hair as best I can and run my hands through it, a soft knock sounds on the door. I hold the towel around me as I run out to the main room to let Magnum in.

"Hey," he says whispering. He holds out an outfit to me, and I smile when it's black leggings coupled with a black shirt. We're totally going to match today. "I didn't know what you wanted."

"This is perfect," I tell him, stepping back so he can come inside.

He inspects me, gaze lingering on the towel for a little longer than the rest of me. Then, he asks, "How did last night go?"

"Well..." I say, drawing it out. He steps in, and I close the door behind him.

I don't get the chance to tell him what happened though.

"I ought to kick your fucking ass, Cotton."

I freeze, and Mag's gaze darts over my head. The hostility hitting my back is potent. Mag moves me out of the way. Like, physically takes my shoulders and shuffles me to the side, giving me a warning look to stay out of this.

Mag stares at his friend. "I'm sorry," he says, and there's a real apology in his voice.

"You're sorry?" Johnny seethes. "You know I fucking love this girl. You know it." He finally gets to Mag and shoves him against the door.

"Johnny..." I start.

Mag gives me a withering look that makes me stand straighter. "Just go get dressed. We'll handle this."

Johnny's gaze drops to the clothes I'm holding in my hand and my towel-dressed state. If he could get any madder, he does. His cheeks flame, and the look he sends Mag's way would make me shrivel.

All of these guys have balls of steel though. They respect each other, but that doesn't mean they're going to bow down to one another either.

Neither will I.

I do walk into the bedroom to get dressed, but I leave the door open to hear their conversation, so I know if I need to step out in Magnum's defense.

"I take it you know?" Mag asks.

"Yes, my fucking girl told me, which is a hell of a lot

more than you fucking did. Or any of those other fucking punk asses."

"You should see the way they care for her," Mag starts.

"I *have* seen. What do you think tipped me off in the goddamn first place?"

"Don't be mad at her."

"Mad at her? I'm not fucking mad at her." Another loud thunk comes, and I can only imagine Johnny has shoved him up against the door again. I find a pair of black silk panties in the pile of clothes he brought for me and slip them on while letting the towel hit the floor. Then, I pull the leggings on, all the while listening to their conversation.

Johnny screams in frustration. "It's my fault. I'm a big enough man to admit that, and don't even say you didn't mean for this shit to happen like some goddamn soap opera. You knew how much I cared for her. You fucking knew, Cotton."

After putting the bra on that Mag chose for me, I slip the shirt over my head and frown at Johnny's use of Mag's real name. I can't remember ever hearing him call him anything but Mag or Magnum. Maybe this means it's more personal for him. It's not about the gang. This is about them being friends.

"I know," Mag says, voice deepening. "Fuck."

I bite my lip as I lean against the wall next to the door. The crack in Mag's voice hurts.

"When I said do anything to keep her safe, it didn't

mean you could fucking fall for her too. The one thing in my life I've ever had that actually means something. That was actually *for* me. Only me."

A quiet growl rips from Jacob's throat. "Don't you think she's that for all of us? I told her I thought she was your savior, but what if she's all of ours? God knows we don't fucking deserve one."

"No, you don't deserve mine. My savior."

"You're going to have to stop thinking of her that way," Mag counters. "She's not just yours."

"She will be. By the end of all this, she won't even remember your fucking names. I told her I'd fight for her. Right after I made her come on my dick five fucking amazing times." His voice lowers. "Ahhh," Johnny practically purrs. "I can see in your eyes you haven't done that yet. But you want to. Let's see if she feels the same way now."

Johnny's whispered threats simultaneously turn me on and piss me off. I walk out of the room while they stare at one another. "I'm ready," I announce.

"Mag and I aren't done."

"Oh, but you are," I say. "Magnum's taking me to my PT appointment for my neck."

"I'm coming with you," Johnny says, not even looking at me. He still has Mag pressed up against the door.

"Don't you have to deal with Candy's? We'll be fine."

Johnny finally turns toward me. He's shirtless in a pair of low-slung sweats, and if he just wore that forever, I'd be the happiest woman alive. He lets Mag go and comes toward me. Reaching out his hand, he pulls me against him as soon as I put my hand in his. He turns me so my back is facing Magnum and then takes a handful of my ass. "That's why Jiko is here. He can handle it. Your appointment is important."

This is about more than my appointment, but it will also be a good test to see how Johnny will get along with the rest of the guys. Right now, it's not looking too good.

"Just let me get dressed." He pauses and glances back at Magnum. "Do we have time to do that, Dad?" Johnny sneers.

I smirk, hiding my face in Johnny's neck. He's trying to throw Mag's age at him, but what he doesn't realize is that his maturity is sexy as fuck.

Mag doesn't answer aloud, but Johnny kisses my temple and swaggers his way into the bedroom. I turn, hesitantly. Mag glares daggers into Johnny's back. It's a look I've never seen him give the heir to the Crew before. "So, um...Johnny knows," I say. Stating the obvious is kind of my specialty.

Mag barely lets the words get out of my mouth before he yanks me toward him and winds his arms around me. "Did he hurt you? Are you okay?" His gruff voice sends shivers down my spine.

"He didn't hurt me. He was surprisingly cool with it. Way cooler than he was with you."

Mag shrugs. "I deserve it."

I pull away to stare into his hazel-green eyes. Specks of gold greet me. "Do you really think I'm all your saviors?"

"I think you're that and so much fucking more."

His words are like a tractor beam leading me forward until my lips press against his. He's hesitant at first, but when I don't give him the opportunity to pull away, he throws himself into it, kissing me nice and slow like we're basking in our own private spot in heaven.

Moments later, a shuffle sounds behind us, and Mag tears me away from him. I reach up to touch my swollen lips, knowing Johnny saw that. I don't want to hurt him. I don't want to hurt any of them. That's the last fucking thing I want to do with all of this. Is it naïve to think this is all some divine intervention though? I wasn't supposed to come to the Heights. These guys definitely don't fucking belong in the Heights. Yet, somehow, by pure accident of circumstances, we're thrown together. Five lost people. Five humans with misguided morals and pasts. What if coming together saves all of us?

I pull my big girl panties on and glance over at Johnny. "Ready?"

Determination dawns in his gaze. "I'm always ready when it comes to you, babe. Let me just grab my gun."

My eyes widen as Johnny goes into the closet to pull out his piece. I never know where he's hidden the thing. I swear he tucks it away in different places all over the apartment, and I don't know if it's on purpose or if it's just something he does.

"Ready," Johnny says, brandishing the Glock with a glint in his ice-blue eyes.

Jesus fuck. I may have just declared war between a bunch of guys who are literally weapons in and of themselves.

Despite their spat, Johnny and Mag talk business on the way to my PT appointment, and I'm glad they can put their personal differences aside and still work on Crew shit. With how Johnny acted this morning, I wasn't sure if he would just fire Magnum, but that's in the same box as killing him. He can't do anything to the guys without hurting me, and he won't do that.

Sly thing, isn't he?

Johnny traces his thumb over the skin of my hand. "Detective Reynolds was probably following you as much as he was Kyla yesterday. You did punch him."

Mag's jaw ticks. "He knew he wouldn't get anywhere with that, though. No cameras, and everyone in that hall would've taken my side."

"Wasn't there another police officer there, too?" I ask, trying to remember. "Yeah, he handcuffed Oscar."

Mag smirks. "Apparently, he's someone who thinks Reynolds is a fucking dick. He also has a brother in the Crew, so..."

I shake my head at how far the Crew's reach is. Well, I

already knew they had the cops in their pockets. Obviously not Reynolds, but they have to have at least someone higher up in their pockets for Big Daddy K to get away with my parents' murder among the others. "Who's on our payroll?" I ask as discreetly as I can. This shouldn't seem weird since I am one of them now. Mag meets my gaze in the rearview mirror. I can't decipher his look, but I push on anyway. "In the police, I mean. You have people turning a blind eye to illegal activities. Magnum shot someone and didn't get in trouble for it. Like, who is it? It must be someone big."

Mag clears his throat. "Technically, I got out of that because their phony witness disappeared."

Oh, right. I forgot about that.

Johnny stops moving his thumb over my hand. "That's one of the most closely guarded secrets my father has."

"So, you don't even know?" I peek at him, finding that hard to believe. I thought Johnny was involved in everything the Crew did.

"I have my suspicions, but no, I don't know."

The finality of his words makes me pause. It doesn't really have any effect as to why I'm here. I'm here to kill Big Daddy K and get the fuck out. With my guys. I don't care what happens to the Crew after that. My beef was never with the whole Crew, just the fucker who took my parents from me. I do think it's crazy that they can get away with so much stuff though.

Mag pulls up to the PT office. I stare at a building filled

with windows. They're not see-through though. They're the kind that just reflect back whatever is in front of them. So, right now, our car's profile is mirrored back to me. "I hope this place is better than the last."

Johnny turns toward me, brows pulling together. "What?"

"Those guys hated me," I say, actually dreading walking into this new place. I don't want another repeat of that PT asshole. "Dicks."

"Who was it?" Johnny grinds out.

I turn to him and pat him on the leg. "It doesn't matter. It's over now. Plus, I can't really blame him. He thinks I killed a little girl." Even though the "evidence" against me was shotty at best. Reynolds just wanted to peg me for something, and whoever put my prints on the gun, handed me to him on a silver platter.

"I'm going in with you," Johnny says.

Johnny throws the door open, and I get out after him. I give Mag a small smile as he frowns. As soon as we close the car door behind us though, Mag whips the car into a parking spot and joins us.

Johnny's whole body locks up, and he squeezes my hand tighter.

Though I walk hand-in-hand with Johnny into the PT place, I'm with both of them, which makes me that much happier. No one will treat me like shit with both guys by my side.

A nurse waits for us as soon as we get inside. She's all smiles, which immediately puts me at ease. She, however, looks at Mag and Johnny with wide eyes like she's impressed I have such a brood of men surrounding me.

First, she takes me into a separate room where I get some x-rays, and then I'm escorted out in their hideous gown to a private PT room where Johnny and Mag are already sitting. Johnny has my shirt and bra in his hands, and I bite my lip to keep from thinking how domestic this all looks. It's like I'm here with my husband or boyfriend, except that there are two boyfriends and not just one. Oh, and my other two boyfriends are sitting at home with probably zero idea Johnny knows what's going on. Unless Mag has told them.

I sit on the table, and we don't wait long. A doctor in his mid-forties strides in. His silver-streaked gray hair is handsome, silhouetting a boyish face. He shakes hands with me first, without the added extra grip strength of showy masculinity that I appreciate. Then, he shakes hands with Johnny and Magnum. Johnny introduces himself as my boyfriend, leaving Magnum to say friend with a scowl. He wants to say he's my boyfriend, too, but what we're doing is all so different from how others walk around. We don't need to be drawing added attention to ourselves.

"Let's see what we got here," the PT guy says. He opens my gown in the back and peers at my spine. He thinks for a moment. The mirror in front of me shows the furrow of his brows. "You know what, let me have you sit in a chair for a second."

Magnum immediately jumps out of his stool and rolls it toward us. The PT guy grabs my hand to help me off the table and then I sit, giving him a better view of my neck. His hands massage into my spine, asking me to tell him when it hurts. When I don't say anything at all, he asks me the last time it did hurt. "It aches every now and then," I tell him.

Two short raps sound on the door, and Johnny jumps into an offensive stance as it opens. The nurse on the opposite end screams as Johnny fills her line of vision.

I press my lips together to keep from laughing. Johnny apologizes profusely, giving her the lame excuse that she startled him, but I saw his hand dip into the waistband of his pants. He was two seconds away from pulling a gun at the intrusion, and I'm not sure Magnum was far behind him.

The nurse giggles warily and hands the doctor a folder. He quickly shoos her out of the room and then places my x-rays on the wall, flipping on a light so they illuminate from behind. He studies the pictures for a few minutes while we all look, too, acting as if we know what we're looking at. I mean, they look good to me. I see vertebrae that move into a neck that holds my skull. That's good, right?

"Huh," he says. He turns, his finger pressed against his lips as he regards me. "Honestly, you seem fine. You don't have much pain. Your x-rays look good. I asked your previous PT place if they could send over your previous images. The ones they sent were from when the accident occurred. You say you've been going to the specialist all along?" he asks.

"Yes. When I moved back here, they'd just started this electric shock therapy, as well as the exercises I was doing previously."

The PT guy shrugs. "What they did worked." He turns to peek at the x-rays again. "What I see here, and based on my examination today, I don't believe you need to see a physical therapist, Kyla." He launches into a spiel about doing the exercises they showed me if my pain ever flares up again, including what kind of pain medicine I can take when —or even if—that happens.

"Are you sure?" Johnny interrupts.

"Quite sure," PT guy says. "Your girlfriend is well. That doesn't mean you can't come see me again if you have increased pain that lasts a few days. That might be a trigger that you're regressing, but as of right now, no, I don't see a reason to treat her. I'm honestly surprised they treated her for so long."

Mag and Johnny share a hard look. The doctor shakes all of our hands again and walks out the door. In his absence, I release a breath. Johnny hands me my things, and I turn away from Magnum to put my bra on. Not that I wouldn't mind getting dressed in front of him, but the next time he sees my breasts, I'd rather it be because we were two seconds from jumping in the sack together.

I pull my shirt on next just as Mag says, "Reynolds."

"Huh?" I ask, turning.

"Reynolds," he says again, moving his glance from Johnny to me. "Reynolds kept you in PT so he could keep an eye on you. It's the only thing that makes sense."

"Fucking asshole," Johnny spits.

"No wonder why those guys hated me," I muse. I imagined it was because they saw me on the news or read my file or because they'd been briefed on who they were dealing with, but maybe the Crew isn't the only group who has people in their pocket?

The police do too.

Johnny plants me on his lap in the backseat while Mag drives us to Jax and Finn's boxing gym after the PT appointment. If anything, he's being more touchy feely than usual, which is fine by me. Except, I don't like knowing *why* he's acting like that. It's as if he's trying to provoke Magnum, who, as always, is as cool as a cucumber. Johnny won't be cracking that tough exterior anytime soon, try as he might.

Magnum pulls into a parking spot in front of the gym, and Johnny follows me out of the car. I turn to say goodbye, but I run right into his chest before backing up. "You're not heading right to Candy's?"

Johnny threads his fingers through mine with a small grin. "Jiko's going to pick me up here, so Magnum can stay with you."

"And that's okay with you?" I ask, lifting a brow. It's always been okay with Johnny that Magnum stays with me, but the dynamic has changed now. He's been claiming his territory all day, but now he's going to willingly leave me with him?

"Despite the fact that he should've fucking told me he'd grown feelings for you, I do trust him with you. Trust him to keep you safe, that is." He watches Magnum as he walks around the side of the car toward the door. He doesn't wait, almost as if he's trying to give us some space. "It's odd though," Johnny muses, the cute little crease in his lip showing up. "I don't think I've ever seen Mag with a girl before."

"He stays pretty busy keeping you safe," I tell him, reminding him of Magnum's loyalties. Nothing's changed. Well, other than the fact that I have a few boyfriends. But I mean, no other aspect has changed. The guys are as they always were. He doesn't have to worry that Magnum will act differently.

A pinch forms between Johnny's brows. "Or he's gay," he offers.

I press my lips together. His desperate attempt at trying to steer me away from his friend is comical. "If he's gay, I should hang out with more gay men because he's a hell of a good kisser."

Johnny reaches down and squeezes my ass to the point it's almost painful. "I deserved that one," he grits out.

"And more," I say teasingly, wiggling out of his punishing grip. I pull on his hand, and we walk toward the glass doors. Johnny surveys the surrounding area, no doubt looking for Reynolds. He's extra pissed about what just transpired at the PT office, even telling me he's going to take me to see the Crew's doctor to make sure they didn't do anything to me that they shouldn't have.

I don't think they did, though the electrical pulse therapy could've been a way to stick it to me, but I don't think it gave me any lasting damage. Who knows if I was even seeing actual PT qualified medical personnel? They could've been random people in Reynolds' pocket.

When we walk into the gym, Mag has his bug detector out, sweeping the area while Finn watches him, clearly impressed. The badass bodyguard then orders everyone to take out their phones, using his device to check them, too. Oscar and Brawler are used to the treatment, but Jax and Finn haven't been subjected to this yet. While Finn asks a bunch of questions, Jax just looks pissed as all hell.

Yay. This ought to be a fun day training when Mr. Morose is even grumpier.

Johnny walks me right up to the group, a smile on his face. Oscar and Brawler immediately look on edge. He threads his arm around my waist and teases the area just above my waistband. Then, he slips two fingers just under the top edge, massaging my skin just over my hip bone.

"I'd like to talk with these assholes for a couple

minutes," Johnny says, giving Jax and Finn a warning glare. The look in his eyes and the tenor in his voice are at complete odds with the grin on his face. I don't know what he has planned, but I'm a little nervous to say the least.

"Cool," Finn says. "Just call for us when you're ready, Princess."

He gives me a wink, and Johnny immediately turns toward me, gaze narrowing as if he's wondering if Finn's made it on my whore list. Honestly, he wouldn't be a bad addition looks-wise, but just fucking no. I'm not adding guys to the list because they're handsome. I have a real connection with the four who are standing in front of me right now.

I give him a dubious look and move my shoe to press down on his foot, giving him a warning.

He shrugs as if he was only curious, but I could already tell the gears in his head were working overtime to see how he could take Finn out.

Brawler glares at the spot where Johnny's touch meets my skin. I start to burn under the heat of his gaze. Johnny must notice, but he doesn't give a fuck. If anything, he holds me tighter. "I just thought you all should know I'm aware of your shady asses, and if you think you're going to steal my girl away from me, you're even dumber than you look. She's *mine*, and I'm fighting for her. All of her."

Oscar takes the scene in, his dark eyes shadowed. Brawler actually growls though. A low hum in his throat that is mighty impressive.

"Got a problem with that, initiate?" Johnny asks, immediately pulling rank.

I step on his toe again. He can't be pulling seniority on these guys. We're all equal in this aspect.

Johnny only smirks. "Don't worry. I'll help my father pick out some of the best initiation tasks we've ever had."

"Bring it," Brawler says, not losing face at all. "I did all of this for her, and I'll continue to do it all for her. You can throw whatever you want at me. Hell, you can even try to kill me—"

"No one's killing anybody," I say, answering that right off the bat.

"Look at you pathetic assholes," Johnny says, mirth clear in his voice. "You all agreed to what? Share her?" He laughs, and my body locks up.

"Yeah, I guess maybe we should've claimed her and pushed her around a little first," Oscar deadpans.

Johnny's laughter cuts short, and the viciousness in his gaze cuts me. "Fuck you, Bat."

Oscar steps up to him. "I mean this in the most disrespectful way possible. Just fuck right the fuck off."

Well, this is going well. Perfect, actually. Couldn't have planned it better my-fucking-self. "Guys..."

"No, fuck him," Oscar seethes. "Selfish prick. He thinks he's better than us because we're trying to do what's best for everyone. For you." He turns back to Johnny. "You don't think I want her to myself? I'm just not a raging asshole like you. I want what's best for her, too, not just to get my dick wet more often."

Johnny moves so fast, I'm not sure any of us see it coming. He punches Oscar square in the face right after giving me a quick nudge out of the way.

Oscar doesn't take it though. Not like the last time. He lunges at him, getting in retaliatory shots.

Mag and Brawler step back, watching this play out with glee on their faces. I glare at them incredulously as Johnny and Oscar roll on the ground, trading blows and each trying to get the upper hand. Finn and Jax peek out of the back room but disappear just as quickly.

I glare at Magnum and Brawler. "Seriously?" I ask them.

Brawler grins like the fight-fueled man he is. "What? I'm enjoying it. Bat took the words right out of my mouth."

"For fuck's sake," I grumble. I tear at the first shirt I can grab, which happens to be Oscar's. I pull him back while Brawler reluctantly steps forward, yanking Johnny to his feet. Both guys square off with one another, chests rising and lowering.

I go from annoyed to mad to upset in like point two seconds, and no, I'm not on my fucking period. It's just everything that I thought could be is chipping away in front of me. What I want seems like an insurmountable task now. Killing Big Daddy K will be easier than this.

Mag moves forward, fingers tracing along my jaw. "Hey, it's okay."

I squirm out of his grip and face the rest of them. "When you guys hurt each other, you hurt me." I turn my gaze toward Johnny, and my shoulders droop. I'm pretty sure we already had this conversation. He said he wouldn't hurt them. Unless that was just to sweet talk me. But Oscar's not in the right here either. They can argue all they want. Get shit off their chests, I don't care. I just don't want them physically fighting.

Johnny growls. "Fucking fine." He lowers his voice as he approaches me. "He just caught me off guard. I'm sorry." Louder, and with authority, he says, "What's happened before and what happens in the future is between Kyla and me. It's not up for discussion."

"Same for us," Brawler says, voice even, taking up his fighter stance that makes him look huge and deadly—not to mention hot as fuck.

Oscar arranges his shirt back over his body. "So, how is this going to play out now that big bad gang boss is here?"

"I don't know what you fuckers are doing, but I'm fighting for her."

"Expect the same," Brawler says, eyeing Johnny up and down like he could take his ass on right now, leaving him unable to walk for a week.

I'm only used to seeing him this menacing during fights. I kind of want to throw myself at him right now.

"I think Kyla should have a say," Magnum says, speaking up for the first time. He has a hint of a shiner that I've just noticed because he's standing in the direct sunlight streaming in through the windows of the gym. Johnny must not have gotten him all that good last night in his chaotic state.

"I still want what I wanted before," I say. "All of us. A family."

Johnny's jaw clenches at that. "I don't share. I have no qualms about competing with them. Three dicks against one. I'm confident in my abilities. I'm sure I'll be able to measure up."

God. If he brings up the five-orgasm thing again, they're definitely going to be on the floor fighting. "Can we just train?" I plead. "Everyone knows everything now. We don't have to dissect it all right this second."

Well, no. Fuck, they don't. I shoot Mag, Oscar, and Brawler a glare, hopefully telling them that obviously Johnny doesn't know shit about the fact that I want to kill his father. That's just another hurdle we'll have to tumble through. At the end of all this, he might not even want to fight for me. He'll probably curse the day I walked into his life.

Just fuck me. One step forward and two steps back.

Before I let my thoughts spiral, I yell out loud enough for Finn and Jax to hear, "I'm ready!"

Finn waltzes out of the back room at once. He was probably eavesdropping on all of us. Not that the guys were trying to be quiet when they were fighting. I move to the bench, and Finn follows me there to wrap my hands in royal purple wrap. "That was interesting," he murmurs, peeking up at the other guys in the room.

The others have dispersed, keeping their distance from one another...and me. "The scary gang guy looks like he's going to murder everyone but you."

"It's been an interesting twelve hours or so," I sigh.

"Let me guess," he says. He waits until I meet his gaze before saying, "They all want you." I shrug because I'm coy like that, and I don't know how much anyone else should know. "Girl," Finn says, laughing with his best gossipy girl voice on. "I see the way they all look at you."

I smile. I've never had a really good friend-friend. I started out having friends here, but then they turned into more. "Have I mentioned before that I like you?"

"Are you trying to get me killed, Princess? Fuck. Whisper that shit."

I burst out laughing, and every single person in the room with a cock glares over at us.

He turns back to me with wide eyes. "Okay, I was joking, but now I'm fucking serious. Look like you're not having any fun." He finishes my right hand and starts on my left. He doesn't talk again until the glares leave us. "Jax and I will always be here for you."

I scoff at that. "Jax doesn't even like me."

Finn laughs, but he doesn't deny it. "Don't feel bad. Jax

doesn't like anybody. He doesn't even like me most of the time and I'm his flesh and blood."

I sense there's a story there, but it's not Finn's to tell. It's Jax's. No matter how much of a distraction a good story could be, I can't really afford to be derailed right now.

The door rings overhead, and Finn looks up. "Who's this? Number five?"

I turn to find Jiko Cardinale striding into the gym like he owns the place. "No, that's Rocket's friend from Chicago."

Finn smirks. "Jax is going to have an aneurysm with all the gang guys we have in here. This could be fun." Without giving me a chance to respond, he stands. "Ready, Princess? We have to figure out a way to kick the ass of...one of your boyfriends?" He shakes his head. "You're in a world of shit, girl. I don't envy you at all."

"Same," I say, standing after him and heading toward the ring. "I'm not going to take it easy today. I think I have some aggression to get out."

Seeing us get up, Jax walks toward the ring from the opposite side. "I got her."

Like before, Brawler holds back as Jax and Finn get into the ring with me. I wish he would just come up here. He already wants to throw the fight, and it's not happening. Fighting is his future. Regardless of the fact that we're fighting one another in a few days, he still needs training for every fight after that. He's going places in the fight world as long as we can get the fuck out of the Heights unscathed.

Jax starts some drills with me. Defense first, and then a punching and kicking combination while we move around the ring. I'm not taking it easy today like I did the other day. I should probably only hit at seventy-five percent, but I don't really have the time to baby my arm into this. K needs to see a good fight, which means I'm bound to get hurt, even if I am going to let Brawler win. And really, "let" him win is just a turn of phrase. He can kick my ass.

Probably. Maybe. I don't know. It would be a toss-up. But for the purpose of this fight, he's beating me.

After five rounds, each one with a different challenging combination, sweat drips from my face in rivulets and hits my chest and back. I take off the thin sweatshirt I'd put on over my shirt and wipe my face with it, tossing it over the side of the ring. I pause when I notice Johnny and Jiko are still standing just outside the ropes. I thought they'd be long gone, dealing with Candy shit.

Johnny's gaze is pure hunger while Jiko's looks apprecia-tive, but not in the kind that makes me feel as if I'm about to get jumped. Johnny's, however, screams that at me, sending a chill down my spine. He really did give me all those orgasms the night before, and it was fucking amazing. Not that I want there to be a competition between him and the guys, but a competition about how many orgasms they can give me sounds like the one to have if, you know, that was going to happen. We could all race to the finish line. Again. And again. And again.

"Easy, killer," Finn whispers in my ear as he hands me a water bottle. "Your eye fuck game is on point. Jax and I are going to get sent away again."

I elbow him in the ribs and smirk, but I shake those thoughts off anyway. "Right. I'm ready. Let's go again."

Jiko jumps onto the ring, leaning over the ropes before we can start the next round. "I'll hold pads for her."

I eye him warily.

Below us, Johnny chuckles. "Just can't stay away, can you, Jik?"

Jax and Finn look to Johnny and when Johnny shrugs, Jax hands the pads over with a deep smirk on his face. I hope that means he thinks I'm going to take his ass down. I'd hate it to mean something else since he is my coach, after all.

Jiko enters through the ropes and shrugs his suit coat off. He rolls the sleeves of his white button-down up and kicks his shoes off. He grabs the thai pads, shoving his hands through and getting into position like he's done this before.

*Okay...*

"Cross, cross, cross, uppercut," he orders.

Finn rings the ring-side bell, and we start. I don't hold back, and Jiko doesn't either. He gives me just enough pressure back with the pads that I know he's done this before, and he's quite good at it too.

When the round is up, Jiko straightens, and several droplets of sweat form in his hairline. "You're good, Kyla. I'll give you that."

"You don't have to give me anything," I throw back.

He holds his hands up in surrender, the black thai pads still surrounding them. "Just a figure of speech." He hands the pads to Jax and walks past me to pick up his discarded stuff. He walks backward toward the ropes. "Can't wait to catch your fight on Friday."

His gaze lingers on me, and I stop to watch him leave the ring, wondering what the hell that was all about until Jax calls out, "Heads up." I look up in time to find a water bottle careening toward my face. I catch it with my gloves on and then have to re-catch it as it slips through, but eventually, I tear my gloves off and am able to suck down some refreshing cold water.

When I peek back, Jiko and Johnny are gone. Unease crawls over me. I still don't like this Jiko guy. Since Johnny seems to trust him, I hope I'm wrong.

Clearly, training doesn't erase the feelings I have about Jiko Cardinale because as soon as we get in the car, I grumble, "I don't like that guy."

"Finn?" Magnum asks, brows pulling together.

"No," I tell him. It's not surprising where his mind went, considering Jiko and Johnny have been gone for a couple of hours, but I haven't been able to let it go. There's just something about him that rubs me the wrong way. "Jiko."

He nods slowly. "I hear he's into their crew's underground fights as well. It was odd he wanted to hold pads for you though."

I shrug. "Johnny told me we can trust him, but I just get a weird vibe off him. I don't know."

Magnum reaches over, threading his fingers through mine. Instantly, my mind swirls with better thoughts. No more trying to figure Jiko out when I can sit back and think about the heat engulfing my body from Magnum's touch.

"So, um, did that go as bad as I thought it did?" I start, worrying my lip over the scene from earlier today. Johnny and Oscar fighting. Brawler speaking his mind.

Mag's lips thin. "It could've gone better, but I don't know what I expected. Honestly, what happened is true to Johnny. He's not used to losing, and he's used to always getting his own way. The only person he ever loses to is his father."

I like that I have Mag to talk to about Johnny. Brawler and Oscar will only tolerate him right now. Well, maybe not even tolerate him, but they're trying, and I have to give them credit for that. But Mag also wants the best for Johnny. He knew him before Johnny was practically second in command of the most powerful gang in town.

"What was Johnny like in high school?"

Mag runs his hand through his copper hair as he turns out of the gym. "Kind of the same. Intense. Quiet, but mouthy if he needed to stick up for himself. His dad wasn't top of the Crew yet, so there's a bit of a difference there. Everyone pretty much figured K would take over though, so that made Johnny heir to the throne. Much like now, girls swarmed him, though that was pretty much par for the course for any Crew guy when we were in school. I'm sure it's the same for Oscar. He could probably pick any girl he wanted." He shoots a quick apologetic glance over to me. "Not that he would."

"So, it was the same for you in school?" I ask, trying to be all nonchalant about it, but I know the least about Magnum's past compared to the others. Surely, he's not as black and white as he grew up, his father died, he initiated into the Crew, and then worked as a bodyguard ever since. "You had girls crawling all over you?"

His grip on my hand tightens. "Yeah, but I don't know. I never took too much stock into that sow your wild oats mantra. I'm not perfect by any means, but I'm not a manwhore either." His cheeks glow a pretty color red, flushing his skin and highlighting his hair. God, he's sexy. "I don't mind being alone. I like my space. I like my own thoughts. In fact, I haven't thought about women in a long time. Not until I met you."

I swallow down the anticipation that sticks in my throat. I place my other hand over our entwined fingers. "I'm sorry Johnny punched you."

"I deserved it."

I shake my head. "We all deserve to be happy, Magnum, and we can be happy in whatever way we want. None of us went about this in the right way." The truth is, there was no right way. By all odds, none of us should've ended up together, but here we are.

"What are you going to do if Johnny won't...I don't

know? Get involved? What if he gives you an ultimatum in the end?"

My heart skitters, the fast pumps of the beating muscle go off with a flurry inside my chest. "Johnny has to make his own decisions," I say around a messy ball of emotion. "But I've made mine already."

I can't force Johnny into what the rest of us have. Do I hope he sees it our way? Fuck yes. My feelings for Johnny run deep. But am I willing to give up Brawler, Magnum, and Oscar for him and only him? No.

Maybe Johnny's right. Maybe it would have been different if he'd not been a dick in the first place. Maybe I would've been all about him and no one else. If he'd treated me like he treats me now, I would've gotten lost in him, but I wouldn't take any of it back. No way.

However, Johnny had a disadvantage the others didn't from the very beginning. He's the son of the asshole who ruined my life. He may not have ever had a chance to sweep me off my feet.

Mag pulls over to the side of the road. I hadn't been paying attention to where we were going, so I look up at the house we're parked in front of now. "Where are we?"

He places his fingers under my chin and moves my face to look at him. "I'm happy to hear you say that, Kyla." He moves to kiss me, and I let him. He takes control, sliding his mouth over mine in a determined coax until my toes curl in my sneakers. I'm sweaty from training, but I don't think about that when Magnum deepens the kiss, threading his fingers through the hair on either side of my face.

I moan into him, and he pulls away with a small smile. "I love those little noises you make."

My face flushes with desire. "You should keep going to see what else comes out of my mouth."

His gaze flares with interest, but he shuts it right down as stoic as ever. He's a master of his own emotions. I envy him that. Mag stares past me toward the building rising up after the curb. "This is the house I grew up in."

I turn, breaking his hold on me and stare up at the two-story building. The shutters are crooked and falling and the white paint is peeling, revealing weathered wood underneath. "Where are we?" I ask, looking up and down the street to get my bearings.

"Just on the outskirts of the main city. Believe it or not, this house used to be really nice, then my dad died."

I reach for his hand on the seat and squeeze. I love that he brought me here. That he wants to share a bit of him with me. If I could, I'd take them to the house I grew up in. Hell, if my parents were still alive, I'd be introducing these guys to them by now. One of these days, when it's absolutely safe, I'll introduce them to my aunt and uncle. When we're out of the Heights, and we don't have to worry about bringing our fight to them.

"Does your mom still live here?"

He shakes his head. "She moved as soon as I graduated."

A flash of pain clouds his hazel-green eyes. He said he doesn't talk to her anymore because of the Crew. "Is that a relationship you'd like to get back?"

"Eventually," he says, smiling softly at me. "I want everything to go back to the way it should have been. Eventually."

"Do you still own the house?" I ask, turning back to the structure and inspecting it for signs of life. It doesn't look like anyone has been in it recently, but most of the buildings in the Heights look the same way. Forgotten.

"We do," he says.

"But you don't ever go in it?"

He shakes his head. "No. I haven't been inside in years. I'd have to face a lot of demons to step back into that house."

I squeeze his hand. "You let me know when you're ready, and I'll be right here."

He takes a deep breath. "That's one of the things about you that draws me in. You're selfless. You have so much going on, yet you're talking to me about this old wound. You went to as many of Oscar's football games as you could because you knew how much it meant to him. I think it's time you let someone take care of you for a while."

"You already do," I say. "You saved my life...what? Twice now?"

"I want to do so much more."

His words have me reaching out for him again. I release my seat belt and kiss him with everything I have. It's awkward with the cupholders and gearshift between us, but we make it work. I kiss Jacob until I'm breathless and needing more. He hauls me into his lap. My ass presses the horn on the steering wheel briefly, and he grins into the kiss before moving his seat back to allow me more room. I settle over him and gulp at the bulge in his pants pressing against my thin workout attire.

I grind against him, and he freezes. After several beats, he pulls away, both of us breathe heavily. "I'm sorry," he says. "We have to stop."

"Not impressed with the car space?" I ask, going for humor to cover up the fact that I really don't want to stop.

He chuckles, but a layer of tension tightens his body. He helps me sit back in the passenger seat. "Not ideal, is it?"

He licks his lips, staring out the window for a moment while I arrange myself in the passenger seat, feeling like a little kid. Maybe it's just because I know the age difference between us, but whenever something like this happens, I feel as if he's chastising me. Like, I'm the one coming on to him, and he has to be the one to stop it because he's oh so mature with years and years of wisdom.

Or, I'm reading too much into this because as hot as a car fuck could be, it's maybe not the best for our first time.

"I should applaud you for your restraint," I say, dropping my head back to the seat.

He moves his lust-filled gaze to me. "The only thing you

should applaud me for is my grip strength when I jerk myself off tonight with thoughts of you."

Well, hot damn. I squeeze my thighs together. Okay, I'm petty. I know it, but I damn well needed to hear that.

"Johnny seems to be keeping you well satisfied anyway," Mag says as he adjusts his seat and pulls the car away from the curb.

My cheeks bloom a deep rose color. "He should never have shared that with you."

He shakes his head. "I signed up for this. I knew you cared for all of them when my feelings grew. You never have to apologize about what you do and who you do it with, Kyla. Never."

Man, it's a fucking turn on to hear that. "Thanks," I tell him sincerely, a simmering burn spreading through my limbs. Jacob may be able to hold off screwing me, but I'm not sure I can. Well, I'm sure I can, but I'm sure I don't fucking want to. Besides, now that Johnny's aware of my feelings for everyone else, there's no reason to hold back anything.

It takes us about ten minutes to get back to the tower. Magnum nods toward the security guy in the booth, but he holds his hand up to stop us from just driving straight through. "Big Daddy K wants to see Kyla as soon as she's in."

Mag nods and waves, but as soon as we're away from the booth, he swears, "Fuck." A quick check tells me the muscle in his jaw is feathering with this information.

I'm in the same hesitant boat. What the fuck? What does he want to see me for?

"I don't like this." He pulls into his usual parking spot and slams his hand against the wheel a couple of times.

"Maybe it's about the fight," I say, trying to reason this out with a level head.

"Yeah," Mag says, voice gruff in a sound that says he's hardly agreeing at all. He doesn't know why I'm being summoned, but it must scare the shit out of him. He pulls his cell phone from his pocket and hits Johnny's name. The phone rings and rings. No one answers. "You try."

I take my phone out and do the same. It rings until it goes to voicemail, and I shrug.

Mag sighs. "Hopefully, he's up there."

He pushes his door open, and I follow. Apprehension floods my stomach, and it's like I'm walking on a cruise ship as we make our way to the elevator that will take me up to the suite floor. I try to brush off the dread because this legitimately could be about anything. My fight. Brawler's initiation tasks. Me and Johnny. Gregory?

I pull my shoulders back and plaster on my game face. It doesn't matter what it is, we got this. If it's something awful, well, that's what I've trained for. I shake myself out on the elevator and stretch my arms.

Mag bends and pulls his pants leg up. He pulls at a strap and takes off his knife holder. "Here, put this on."

The knife itself is slim and not super bulky, but I'm

wearing leggings. It's a good thing they're black, so there's less of a chance for it to stand out. I pull up the material on my left leg and attach the strap so that the knife is on my inner right calf just above my ankle. When I pull the leg back down, you can see it there, but it's not a neon sign or anything.

"Use it only if you absolutely have to," Mag says quickly. "If Johnny's up there, let him do all the talking. He'll protect you. With his life."

Fear crawls over my skin like a million spiders walking up my body with their gross, spindly legs. I want to ask if he thinks he'll be coming in with me but the elevator dings and the door opens. I lose my chance.

Taking a deep breath, I walk out like I've done dozens of times before. The guards don't pat me down or use the wand on me, so we stride toward K's door with the knife still strapped just above my ankle. The guard there at the door greets Magnum. "What up, brother?"

"I hear he's waiting on Kyla," Mag says, keeping his voice even and calm.

I envy him that facade.

"Yep." The guard glances at me and gives me a small smile. "She's to come in immediately," he says, stretching the word out. If this is serious, K hasn't let anyone else know. They seem to be in decent moods, even joking a little.

"Is Johnny in there?" I ask. "I can't get ahold of him."

The off-hand question shouldn't come as a surprise. I hope, anyway.

"Yeah, he's in there. He and the guy from Chicago." The guard kicks the door open behind him and moves out of our way as we walk in. Pressure swarms me, and it feels like the first time when I came into this suite to meet him. I thought I was going to throw up then, and I might just do that now. No matter how hard I try to not be afraid of him, I can't. That doesn't change the fact that I'm going to take his life one day, though, but I'm woman enough to admit he scares the shit out of me.

Magnum and I step farther in, and the guard who let us in closes the door behind us with him on the other side.

My ears perk up, but I don't hear any noises, and I don't immediately see anyone either. It isn't until we get even farther in that Johnny's slumped form strapped to a chair, blood running down his face, pulls me up short. My stomach threatens to expel at the sight.

"Johnny," I say almost hesitantly, like I can't believe it. Then I yell his name, running forward. Magnum tries to grab me, but he just misses. Johnny's right eye widens as he takes me in. The other is swollen shut. His usually crisp white shirt is bloodied from the gash on his cheek and nose.

His gaze says everything though. He looks at me with a heart full of apology and regret and love.

In that moment, I know I'll take so much happiness in

killing Big Daddy K. Not only for what he did to my parents, but for this moment right here, right now.

A deep growl rips through my throat, and I turn.

Big Daddy K sits cross-legged in a plump chair that usually adorns his living room. The dining room table is pushed to the corner. Johnny is front and center with his father sitting just in front of him. Staring, gloating over what he's done. "Hello, Kyla. I'm so glad you're here."

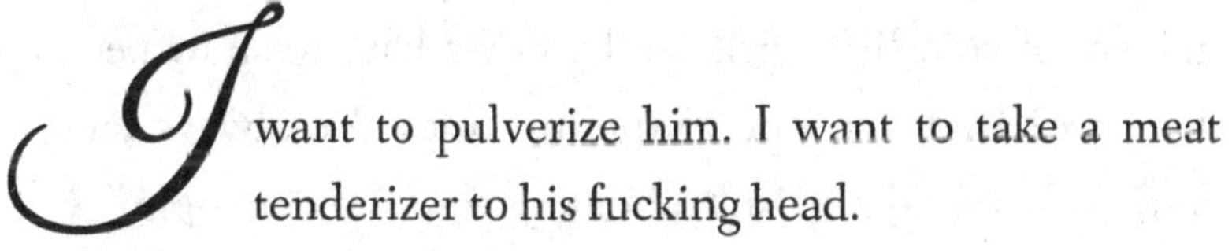

want to pulverize him. I want to take a meat tenderizer to his fucking head.

"Babe?"

Just that one, raspy word stops me. With my hands balled at my sides, I turn back to Johnny. My heart breaks. Blood trickles from his mouth, proving this wasn't just one punch. Not that that's any better, but this is a beating. Meant to hurt. Meant to inflict more than just pain.

Meant for submission.

I swallow hard, and he tries to smile for me, but he grimaces in pain instead. "Everything is going to be okay," he promises.

Can he really promise that anymore? Look what's happened.

Johnny tilts his head to the side to tell me to come stand

next to him. I do as he's asked, placing my hand around his shoulders while his wrists are tied behind him. Magnum looks on at the scene with completely veiled horror and disgust. It's in his eyes. On the surface, he appears blank, bored even. But I see it all in his eyes.

"I already told you how sorry I am," Johnny says, voice strained though he's trying to talk like he's in a business meeting. "There's no need to bring Kyla into this. It was my fault."

Big Daddy K leans back in his chair, lacing his hands behind his head. "Now, now. I know you want to save face in front of your little girlfriend, but we have to show people, don't we? Isn't that one of the top rules I've always taught you? When talking isn't enough, you show people." His glare moves to me. "You're probably wondering why Johnny's being punished."

I lick my lips, but keep my mouth shut. I'm playing so many games here that admitting to the wrong one could be catastrophic.

Johnny opens his mouth, but K lifts his hand to stop him. "I want the little whore to speak, son."

I bite the inside of my cheek. It's obvious now. He's somehow found out we've had sex. I flick my gaze to Magnum, but he's not giving anything away. We were so careful. Magnum's been checking our rooms with his bug device. Our phones. Everything.

"I love your son," I say, pressing my lips together to come

up with the right words. I don't want to have to beg this fucker, but if it gets Johnny out of any more punishment, then I'll do it. I'll fucking get on my hands and knees at his feet. "We didn't mean to go against what you said, but I—"

K's laugh swallows up all the air in the room. "You didn't mean to? So, he fell, and his dick slid into your cunt? Is that what you're telling me happened, Kyla?"

"No," I say through clenched teeth. It's not as if I have to have the "when two people fall in love with each other" talk with him, do I? "I love Johnny, and I wanted to share that with him. We didn't do it to disobey you. We did it because we care about one another."

"But I told you not to. In fact, I even think I moved you out of his room and sent him a bitch, so he could get over you."

I nod, even though I'd love to castrate the fucker for referring to women as bitches and because of the overall power he thinks he has over us. "You did, and we kept our distance for a while."

He slams his hand down on the wood armrest. "But not long enough!"

"Dad," Johnny says. "I'll take the punishment. Please just let Kyla go back to her room."

"Go back to her room? Her room? The one I gave her. The one where we saved her from that fucking shithole she was living in, and this is how she repays us? Is that the one you're talking about, son?"

Is he for fucking real? I was perfectly fine at my fucking shithole apartment.

"You said you wanted her here, so she could be kept safe, and we did that for her. But what do we find? Blatant disrespect."

"It was me," Johnny says. "I talked her into it. I practically held her down because I'm sick like that. You know, like how we play with the whores, Dad. We take what we want. I wanted her pussy, and I took it."

The venom in his voice sends ice through my veins. He doesn't mean those awful words. He's just trying to get me out of this mess. I appreciate the sentiment, but I'm not the one tied up with blood running from my face.

"As much as I wish that was true, I know you wouldn't do that to your precious Kyla. Since she showed up, you've gone soft." K stands, striding toward Johnny.

"Move," Johnny whispers, and even though I want to stay there and stand my ground, Magnum reaches out to pull me to the side just as K punches Johnny in the face with a closed fist.

Johnny's head whiplashes back. He stretches his jaw out and then looks forward again, meeting his father's gaze. Indignation roars inside me, but I gulp it down. Sometimes, the hardest thing we have to do is sit back and watch.

"Since she showed up, you've cared more about her than the Crew. What have I always taught you?"

"Crew before everything," Johnny says, voice slurring.

"Exactly!" K gets in his son's face, his pallor as red as a firestorm. "*Everyone* is the property of the Crew. I am. You are. She is. She's not yours, Johnny. She's *all* of ours."

K turns toward me. I meet his gaze with a stony one myself. He takes a step toward me and reaches out, placing his hand on my tit. He squeezes until it's painful.

"Don't you touch her!" Johnny roars.

K laughs, his hand fondling now. "I'm going to have to beat that possessive streak out of you."

He gives my nipple a pinch right through my shirt and acid fills my stomach. In a flash though, he uses the same hand to punch Johnny again.

Magnum's hands bite into my hips. He steadies me, rooting me to the ground because right now seems like the absolute perfect time to just grab the knife from my damn pant leg and end this fucking thing.

The guards, though. They're everywhere. And Johnny probably can't even walk. There's no way we would get out of this unnoticed. Free.

"Breathe," Magnum whispers in my ear. "Fucking breathe, beautiful. You can do this."

His strong words bring tears to my eyes. I blink to hold them in.

"Kyla was supposed to be your prize for when you took your rightful place beside me. Do you remember that deal you made, boy?"

Johnny nods. He keeps blinking, and I cringe thinking of the pain he must be in.

"Now what am I supposed to do with that?" K turns and strides back to his chair in a huff. "I already told the whole Crew. Should I announce to them that the successor to the largest organization in the area can't even follow simple fucking instructions? You can get ass whenever you want. Wherever you want. I explained that to you as soon as you started jerking off. No reason to use your hand," he scoffs. "No reason to ruin anything because of a little piece of pussy." K waves a dismissive hand toward me. "You're putting me in a fucking position, son, and I don't like it. I'm supposed to be able to rely on you more than anyone else. Anyone else," he grits out.

"You can," Johnny says.

I move my gaze toward him and recognize the determined look in his eyes. He's trying to regain his father's trust instead of thinking of different ways he could blow him to pieces.

I've never had a parent turn on me. I don't know what that's like. I've always said I would give anything to have my mom and dad back here, but I also like to think if they treated me this way, I'd know where to draw the fucking line. Big Daddy K has Johnny by the balls. I get that. He has shit on him. He uses the parental card. He has his manipulation down to a T.

"You're forcing me to come up with another way to

punish you. I can't let everyone else know you defied me. What happens when people defy me?"

"We eliminate them," Johnny says, voice dark. He inches his chin higher in the air.

K nods slowly. He picks at the fabric on the chair he's sitting in like it's a lazy Sunday. "I don't want to do that to you. My only son." He lifts his gaze. "But you also know I just can't let you get away with disrespecting me, don't you?"

"I know," Johnny says. He forces his shoulders back as if he's going to face whatever his dad has in store for him head on.

Inside my head, I'm screaming, *The beating isn't enough?! Fuck you, you fucking prick! You got your point across.*

"And you know it has to involve Kyla, too," K says, like it's the last thing he wants to say. His voice is contrite. His face even looks as if Johnny is forcing him to do this. This is manipulation 101.

Johnny's throat works. His pulse triples in time until it looks like the rapid flutter of a hummingbird's wings. "I'll take it all. I deserve it."

K shakes his head. "Unfortunately, I don't think that's true." His snide glare slides to me. "Kyla's new, and she needs to understand what exactly she's in for now that you've chosen her."

I swear I can hear Johnny's teeth grinding from here. He so wants to say something, but wisely keeps his mouth shut.

K shrugs. "So, I thought, what better way to treat a whore than to treat her like a whore?"

My stomach clenches, and Magnum's fingers bite into my sides again. To K, it probably looks as if he's holding me back from him, and he is, but for different reasons than he might believe. Magnum doesn't give a fuck about K, but he does give a fuck about Johnny and me.

"What are you saying, father?"

"Jiko!" K calls out.

In the flurry of shit since we walked in the door, I'd forgotten he was supposed to be here. A door opens behind Johnny, and I glance over at the figure striding in. His gaze meets mine, holds it, and doesn't look away as he moves opposite us. He's dressed in his suit still, perfectly tailored, perfectly ironed. Shoulders back, chin out. He has the look down. That post, rich boy, I deserve everything look. Johnny usually has that down, too.

"Another thing you should remember, Jonathan," K says with a smirk. "Sometimes your friends aren't always your friends."

The look I give Jiko should incinerate him on the spot. I don't even have to hear K's next words to know that Johnny confided in Jiko, telling him we had sex, and now Jiko's used that against us. He's told Big Daddy K our secret. The secret that got Johnny looking like this.

I'm going to murder him.

"Jiko came to me earlier to tell me what happened between you two. The fact that you'd had sex despite my implicit orders. He came at great risk, considering it wasn't easy to convince me my own son would deceive me."

I keep staring at the lowlife, willing him to look at me, but right now, he's preening under K's words. I'm going to chop his dick off. I'm going to beat him until he's just as bloody as Johnny and then more, until he's choking on his own life force. I only wish I'd kicked his ass earlier in the ring. Knocked his teeth out. Broken his trachea. That would teach him to talk. To betray his friend.

I glance down at Johnny who's looking at Jiko with sad eyes. One of Johnny's only friends. Everyone in his life hurts him.

"What's the punishment?" Johnny asks, sounding bored. I worry for his mental state right now. Will this push him over the edge? Will it do what K wants it to do? Follow in his footsteps to the depths of hell no matter the circumstances?

K licks his lips, gleaming at me. "To teach Kyla that she's the property of the Crew, not yours and definitely not her own...and to teach you that you can't deceive me and get away with it, I've come to the perfect punishment. To prove Kyla isn't yours, you're going to watch Jiko fuck her."

I gasp. I try not to, but the intake of breath happens before I can steady myself. When he said he was going to treat me like the whore I am, he wasn't kidding.

My stomach rolls again, and my knees tremble. Magnum's hands on me keep me steady on my feet, but they don't make me feel safe anymore. Can I even feel safe here, this close to my sworn enemy? I was stupid to think I ever could.

"You want him to rape me?" I ask, incredulous determination pouring from me. Because fuck that. I will start chopping dicks if that's what it comes to.

"Trust me," Jiko says, a glint to his eye. He licks his lips. "It won't be rape because you'll be begging for it."

"You make me sick."

Jiko turns a twinkling eye to K. "I like them feisty. I think this is going to be fun."

"Fuck you," I seethe.

"Watch your mouth, slut," K growls. "As far as I can tell, Jiko is the most loyal man in the room. Loyalty goes a long way."

"He won't touch you," Mag whispers. "I promise he will not fucking touch you."

How can he promise such a thing? If I don't do this, K will probably just murder me right fucking here. If I don't play their game, he'll put a gun to my head and pull the trigger. He doesn't give a fuck. There's no reasoning out of this. There's no playing on his good side because he's the devil. He doesn't have a good side. The space where his heart should be is cold, dark, and vacant.

"I think you'll have fun," K says, smirking at me. "I

might even have to try that cunt out myself one of these days."

Revulsion slithers through me. If it comes to that, I'd rather him put a bullet in me. There's no way on this Earth I'm getting raped by my parents' murderer.

He leers at me as he stands. "She certainly looks like she's good and tight." He trails his gaze over me, and I stand frozen in place. I'm too scared to move. Too scared to think, even. I don't want anything I do to provoke him.

"I'll need proof, Jiko," K says as he walks from the room. "Preferably of the photographic kind." He moves into the kitchen to pour himself a glass of deep, brown liquid. "One with some tits will do." He winks at his new buddy. "I'll give you guys the room. I won't be back until late, so don't think you have to stop at one, Cardinale. Make her yours. Over and over and over."

Big Daddy K moves forward, throwing the alcoholic contents in his glass on Johnny who grunts, baring his teeth as the burning alcohol seeps into his cuts.

Fucking asshole.

"Magnum," K says as he immediately looks away from his son. "I expect you to make sure this happens. If she fights, hold her down. I don't think my son will give you any trouble, but if he does, call me."

"Yes, Sir," Magnum says.

I want to vomit. If I vomit, maybe Jiko won't fucking

touch me. Maybe I'll gross him out so bad he'd rather fuck the chair.

K waltzes toward the door. With each step, my heart beats louder and louder. By the time the door opens, the buzz in my ears is so pronounced I'm reeling from it. Magnum's whispering to me, I think, but it just all collides in my head like a tornado with no possibility of dying out.

The door closes, leaving us trapped in here. I kneel on instinct, pulling out the knife Magnum gave me and brandishing it in front of me. "You messed with the wrong fucking people." And then I lunge at Jiko Cardinale.

29

$\mathcal{F}$ury and rage blind me. My training along with a hefty dose of self-preservation kicks in because before I know it, I have Jiko in a chokehold, the blade of the knife at his throat.

I can see myself doing it. How much pressure would it take? Just a little? A lot? I've never slit someone's throat before, but there's a first time for everything.

I'm shaking. I want so badly to pull the blade across his taut skin, and I don't even care what kind of person that makes me. He betrayed us. He betrayed Johnny. And his laughter at raping me sickens me to my very core. Someone that cruel doesn't deserve to live.

He grabs my arms, yanking at my hold. "Wait," he chokes out. "Please, wait."

Mag takes a tentative step toward me, catching my attention. I lift my gaze to meet his. As usual, his look is impenetrable. Does he want me to do this? Does he want me to stop?

"I can explain!" Jiko rushes out.

I close my eyes. They still burn with unshed tears as if I could let loose at any moment. If I kill him, K will just think of some other punishment. Maybe with someone else. Maybe with him.

"Please!" Jiko pleads.

I release my hold on him, then stomp kick him in the ass. He sprawls out on all fours, choking and spluttering. Mag takes his gun out of his waistband and holds it on the traitor.

Johnny moans, and I run to him, quickly untying the good old-fashioned rope K used as restraints. Deep burn marks mar his wrists. He must have fought like hell to get away. To do something.

Johnny tugs me over weakly, but I come willingly. "Are you okay?" His good eye darts around my face.

"Am *I* okay?" I bite my lip because I am seriously close to losing it. "Are you okay?"

"I'm only okay if you're okay."

My lip wobbles, and I hate how weak I feel at this moment. Adrenaline courses through me, and I know that logically that's making my reactions heightened. Everything is ten times as bad or ten times as good. Right now, every-thing is ten times as shitty.

"I'm sorry," Johnny whispers, so only I can hear, then he gets up on unstable legs, leaning onto me for support. "You better speak now before Magnum puts a bullet in your brain," he commands, turning right back into the gang higher-up he is.

Jiko sits back on his haunches. He runs his hands down his face. "I had to, J. I'm so fucking sorry. Your dad has shit on my dad, and I had to find a way to make that go away."

"By stabbing him in the back?"

Jiko doesn't even look at me. He just stares right back at his friend, begging and pleading him with his eyes to understand. "You know I would never touch her," Jiko said. "I had to say that to get him out of here and to make it seem as if it was going to be awful for you guys."

I knew I hated this fucker. "Shoot him," I tell Mag.

Mag pulls the hammer back on his gun with an audible click.

"I had to!" Jiko screams, looking around wildly. "You know how it is, Johnny. You know."

"So, you sacrifice your friends for your family?"

"I do what it takes," Jiko says, thrusting his chin into the air.

"Is it all good?" Johnny asks. "With my dad and your dad?"

Jiko nods.

"It better have been fucking worth it."

"I wouldn't have done it if it wasn't."

"You could've fucking warned me," Johnny scolds, relaxing a little.

I gawk at him. We're just going to let him get away with this? I turn to stare at Magnum, my gaze burning into his. He still holds his gun to Jiko's head, and he doesn't look as if he's going to pull the trigger anytime soon.

"Johnny," I hiss.

He turns to me. My heart breaks as I look at him. His dad did a number on him. "I've had worse," he says, trying to smile for me like that's going to make me change my mind.

"That doesn't make me feel any better. That bastard's a traitor." His words still ring in my ear about him enjoying fucking me without my consent as I point a trembling finger at him.

Johnny pulls my hands up, just like he used to. He drops kisses on my knuckles that soothes some of the tension. "If he hurt you, he knows I would fucking kill him."

"He hurt you," I growl.

Johnny takes my face in his hands, moving in to kiss me. His lips linger over mine, but I press into his split lip, blood and all.

When Johnny pulls away, he rubs his thumb over my lips, probably smearing his blood over me. "That's part of this life."

"That doesn't fucking make it right!"

"I said I was sorry," Jiko mumbles tersely.

I turn fiery eyes on him. "Sorry? You think that's enough?" I pull Magnum's blade up again. "Enough would be to see you suffer in the same way. Maybe I should tie you to the chair and beat the shit out of you." I tread toward him like a predator, only kneeling next to him when I'm close enough to reach. I place the blade of the knife on his cheek. "Enough would be to see you bleed like him."

Jiko licks his lips. "I'll make it up to you. To both of you. I promise. You have my word."

Johnny moves up behind me and places a hand on my shoulder. He gives me a quick squeeze, and I stand. He takes the blade from me and then crouches, feeling my legs for the holster. When he finds it, he lifts my leggings and places the knife back inside. "Magnum, let him up. We all need to put our heads together to figure this shit out. Can you do a bug sweep? My dad usually doesn't have cameras running in his own suite because he doesn't want evidence of the shit he does in here, but it would be like him to have them set up to catch this. If there is, we'll figure something out about doctoring any video footage."

"Figure something out?" My voice breaks. "Your dad is expecting pictures of Jiko raping me. How are we supposed to pull that off?"

"Don't worry," Johnny says, squeezing my hand. "I've got this."

He looks like he's far from having control of the situation. He's bloodied and bruised. He can barely walk, and he can only see out of one eye.

"If he doesn't usually have cameras, we're probably good," Jiko comments as he stands and straightens his suit coat like he wasn't just begging us to forgive him. "We went right from talking to pulling you in. He didn't leave the room, and he didn't get on the phone with anyone."

Magnum finishes his sweep and corroborates what Jiko's said. No bugs. No cameras, and no listening devices.

Thank fuck. I don't doubt they could figure something out, but that's one less thing we have to worry about.

Magnum and Jiko face Johnny and me, and I have a feeling Magnum is staying close to him because he still hasn't decided whether he should take him out for what he's done. We're on the same wavelength in that respect. I didn't trust him, and I was right not to. I don't care that Johnny feels otherwise. They've had similar upbringings, so he gets it, but what Jiko's done is wrong. You don't hand over the people you care about to the monsters. The fact that this monster is Johnny's dad makes it that much worse.

Johnny stares at Magnum and Jiko while I just pierce daggers into Jiko's forehead, my mind trying to come up with a solution to the situation because there is no fucking way I'm letting Jiko put his fucking cock inside me. No fucking way. If anyone even suggests it, I will cut their dick off, too. Guys do not get to decide what a woman does with their own body.

"I have an idea," Johnny finally says. He tears his gaze away from the other two to look at me. With one eye completely swollen shut and the dried blood mixing with fresh blood, I wonder how he can even keep a sound mind at all.

"We should clean you up," I say, reaching out to touch his face.

Johnny shakes his head and stops my hand before I can touch him. "Not until we figure this out. Dad will expect Jiko to be fucking you right now, and if I end up in any of the pictures, I can't be clean."

I swallow. "Jiko's not fucking me unless he wants to end up with a knife buried in his chest and his dick cut off and shoved in his mouth."

"Fair," Jiko says.

I glower at him, and he shuts up.

"Hey," Johnny says, returning my attention back to him. "Look at Magnum and Jiko. They have similar builds. Similar skin color. Jiko even has a red tint to his hair."

My mouth dries, and I lower my voice. "What are you saying, Johnny?"

"I'm saying what if you have sex with Magnum?" he whispers as if this is a private conversation and the other two aren't even in the room. "We'll get a couple of clever shots. Nothing with faces and nothing with your body parts." He sighs. "He needs evidence to let this go, Kyla. I'm so sorry."

He leans over and whispers. "And you care for Magnum, right?"

"So, you're asking me to have sex with another guy?" It doesn't sound like him at all. Of course I want to have sex with Magnum, but not like this.

"I don't fucking like it," he says, voice dejected, "But I've already assumed you've done something with the others."

"Jiko, leave the room," Magnum demands.

Jiko opens his mouth.

"I said leave the fucking room." For good measure, Magnum reaches for his gun, but Jiko is smarter than he looks.

He walks toward the door he came out of. "Just let me know what to say. I'll be waiting back here."

As soon as the door clicks shut, Magnum says, "We haven't had sex yet, Johnny. This isn't—"

"There's no other option." Johnny's jaw clenches after cutting him off. "He needs proof, and Jiko isn't going anywhere near her. My skin coloring is all wrong, plus, I have dark hair, I'll never pass. Plus, let's not act like you don't want to fuck each other."

"Not like this," Magnum and I say at the same time.

I can barely look at him.

"Obviously not like this, but if we don't do something, he could come up with a worse punishment. If not Jiko, then who? He picked this for a purpose. He wants to show me Kyla isn't really mine and what better way than to have someone fuck her in front of me. He could get multiple someones if we don't comply. It'll be ten times worse. You know it, Mag. You know what he's capable of. Next time, he'll demand he's in the room, and there's no fucking way we'll be able to get out of it then. It has to be this way."

"This isn't something for us to decide." Magnum scratches his scruff. "It's Kyla's body. I'll do whatever she wants. I'll still go into the back room and put a bullet in Cardinale's skull if that's what she wants."

Finally, I glance up, meeting Magnum's gaze. The look there is indescribable, and it immediately softens me. The two guys here, right now, only want what's best for me.

Johnny's right. If we don't handle this now, it could get worse. It's not as if K's just going to drop it. He wouldn't.

"Okay..." I say, holding Magnum's gaze.

Relief sags Johnny's shoulders. He presses a kiss to my temple. "I'm so sorry." When he straightens, he says, "I'm going to get Jiko's phone for the pictures. You guys talk or whatever you have to do," he says awkwardly.

Johnny strides toward the back room. Magnum moves forward. "We can leave," he says. "Right the fuck now. I can get us out of here. We don't have to come back."

I wrap my arms around his neck, loving that he's still thinking about me. He really meant what he said earlier. *I think it's time you let someone take care of you for a while.* "We can't leave," I tell him.

"I don't want our first time to be this," Mag says, jaw clenching. "It's not fucking right."

"Then let's not make it this." I don't even know what I'm saying, but I agree with it as soon as it leaves my mouth. I pull him down to kiss me.

He moans into my lips, taking control. I open for him, and his tongue thoroughly assaults my mouth, obliterating any bad thoughts. This, I can handle. Jacob and I are an eventuality. He wanted to take it slow, but this was going to happen.

"I'm so sorry you have to do this," he breathes.

"Sex with you won't be a chore," I tell him, my core already heating in response to his demanding kiss.

He yanks my hips to meet his, and I'm greeted with his erect cock, lengthening right through his tactical pants. "Never," he says. "But I'm not used to an audience."

My nipples peak. The experience I had with Oscar and Brawler in the strip club flashes through my mind. "It can be fun," I breathe.

He groans, nipping at my neck, turning my body to molten fire in the process. I grab the hem of his shirt and pull up. He grabs the material in the back and helps me take it off, the typical guy move that's hot as fuck. I work my hands over the hard planes of his chest. He's been putting that weight set in his room to good use because this body has been labored over. Cut with long training hours and sweat.

I kiss the dip between his pecs, and he moves my chin

up to claim my lips again. His grip settles onto my hips, his touch just shy of biting as he pulls me toward him with needier movements.

He growls as he grabs my shirt and pulls it from my head. He reaches for me again, moving his hands down to cup my ass. It isn't as if Magnum hasn't seen me naked before, but this time, it's for him. He has the control. He's the one who gets to touch me, and if his cock is anything to go by, he's enjoying every moment of it.

I am too.

The door to the back room clicks, and Magnum freezes. I kiss him back with more fervor. We can't stop this now. It's done. Plus, I don't want this to stop now.

For Johnny's part, he's quiet as he moves back into our space. The bubble that Magnum and I have made for ourselves. The back of my neck tingles, so I know he's in the room, but he's not making himself known. He's giving us this.

"I want you," I whisper to Jacob.

He moans, and my words do what kissing him couldn't. He ignores Johnny and pushes my leggings down my thighs. I kick my shoes off and then step out of my leggings and socks, so I'm standing there in my bra and panties. His hands come up to cup my breasts, and I gasp at his firm touch.

The chair Johnny was sitting in creaks.

I undo the button on Magnum's pants and push them to

the ground while I kiss him with everything I have. It's a desperate kiss. A hundred emotions I tried to keep at bay swim to the surface, and I put them all into the kiss, sweeping my tongue over his like we're in a private duel.

He teases my nipple through my sports bra, and I moan. "Yes."

With a hand tight around my back, he pushes my shoulders back as he trails his lips down my chest before capturing my nipple in his mouth, sucking it right through the fabric of my bra. He gives it a sweet bite, and my pussy clenches.

With one hand, he unclasps my bra, and I don't think I was ever so happy to take it off in my life. Now bare-breasted, he plays with each peak until I'm taut with want.

"Jacob," I breathe.

He moans into my skin, purring his approval at my use of his real name. He dips his hand over my stomach and under the band of my panties. He caresses my slick pussy before pushing a finger inside. I grab a hold of his upper arms, moving in tandem with his touch.

The chair creaks again, and I wonder if he's getting any pictures of this. Or if he's upset or—

Jacob presses into my clit, and I gasp. *Fuck, fuck, fuck.*

"I want to come on you," I breathe.

Jacob bends, picking me up by the backs of my thighs and takes me over to the arm of the couch. He sits me on it, then tears my panties down. I grasp to balance myself as he yanks his boxers down his thighs. His dick... Fuck, his dick. It's impressive. Thick and straight.

Behind him, Johnny rises to come closer. I watch him as Jacob lowers a condom over his cock.

The anticipation has me groaning. Johnny's face is unreadable, masked because of the blood and bruising, so I don't know how he feels about this. Knowing him, he would never let it happen if he didn't want it to.

Or if he knew there was no other way.

I reach out, gripping Jacob's dick, stroking him until his body clenches. He pulls me forward, lines us up, and then plunges inside of me. My mouth falls open at how thick he is. "Fuck, Jacob. Oh, God."

"I've waited for this. I've wanted this."

I open my eyes to find Johnny lifting the camera. I tilt my head up and then wrap my hands in Jacob's hair as he pumps inside me. Short pumps, testing. As if he's unsure still.

I wrap my legs around him and pull him toward me. He grinds against my clit, and the moan that escapes me encourages him.

"You feel fucking fantastic."

I'm lost for words. I'm surprised there's enough room for Magnum to bury himself inside me. I can barely move against him without pleasure ripping through me at the spot he's reaching.

Johnny moves to the side, cell phone still raised. I must

be into dirty shit because my body ratchets higher and an orgasm hits me out of nowhere. I hold on to Jacob as a scream tears through me, my walls clenching around him.

He pulls back to watch me, which I don't notice until I'm spent. But the look he's giving me, warms my body. "That was beautiful," he murmurs, reaching out to move a stray hair off my face.

He goes to pull out, but I tighten my hold on him. "What are you doing?"

He glances to the side, eyeing our watch party. "Are we good with pictures?"

Johnny drops his hand and licks his lips. His irises are huge, a telltale sign he's aroused. "I took a lot. I'll have to go through them to pick the perfect ones."

Jacob smiles and kisses my nose. "You did good, beautiful."

He tries to pull out again, but I hold him there. "Then this is about us," I say. "That's done, and now it's about us."

He untangles my legs around him and pulls out. He feathers his thumb over the line of my jaw. "Not right now. Not here."

He removes the empty condom and steps back.

"Jacob," I call after him. "I want you to come."

His jaw tightens, and he moves forward. The look he gives me holds me in place. Johnny steps back, giving us space. "One day, I'll come inside you. One day, I'll lose control, but today's not that day, beautiful girl. Trust me, I want to. You felt too fucking good. I could've lost myself, but what kind of man would that make me? You deserve better." He kisses my forehead before walking away, stiff cock still hanging out as he moves to pick up his clothes. "Let's get Jiko back out here and wrap this up."

ohnny goes through the pictures. Magnum and I refuse to look at them, but I trust him to pick out ones that simultaneously show what we were doing, but also don't show anything too revealing. Johnny's smart. He's been living in this world a lot longer than me, so he knows what will appease his dad and what won't.

Jiko is only allowed to see the pictures Johnny wants him to send to his dad. The others, he deletes off his phone. He taps Jiko's phone against his palm as he eyes his friend. If that's what we're still calling him. "Send him the pictures and then call and tell him it's done. Play the part," he warns Jiko before tossing him back his phone.

Johnny loops his arm around mine and leads me from the room. I still can't believe we're just letting Jiko get away with this. He's the whole reason we had to do that. He takes me straight to the elevator while Mag lags behind. He nods at the guards, and I doubt any one of them even realize the shit that just went down in that room. They're just there to make sure there's no outside threat. The threats are inside though. Hell, they're on the outside too. They're coming at me from everywhere.

"Take care of him," Magnum says, right before Johnny lets us into my apartment and shuts the door behind us. He leans his forehead against the wood, smashing his fist into the door several times, yelling at nothing and everything at the same time. The roar that comes from his mouth squeezes my stomach until it feels as if it's in a blender.

I grab his arm, holding it back so he doesn't do any damage. "Babe," I say, voice cracking. He turns toward me, and the fissures in his exterior aren't the only things bleeding through. His eyes tell me all the heartache he feels underneath.

I thread my fingers through his and lead him into the bathroom. Gingerly, I undress him. First taking off his blood dripped white shirt and then his pants. Stains of crimson have leaked through the fabric and brushed his beautiful skin in copper. I turn to start the shower and then undress myself under his intense stare.

This gang life is a rollercoaster. One moment, I'm being threatened with rape. The next Magnum has me by the pussy, and now, I'm dealing with a bomb about to detonate, and I'm fairly sure whenever Johnny combusts, it won't be pretty.

Sticking my hand into the shower spray, I check the temperature and then step in myself, dragging Johnny in after me. Water just this side of scalding cascades down our bodies. I move him into the spray. Water sluices off him, tingeing pink as it swirls down the drain. "How's your face?"

"Hurts like a bitch," he says, reaching his hand up to touch it gingerly.

"It's swollen," I tell him, inspecting it now that the blood is running off.

He shrugs. He said it wasn't the first time he's been beaten that bad, and I wholeheartedly believe it, but I'm anxious to ask him when? Why? How long ago?

Johnny dips his dark hair back into the spray, running his long fingers through it. We switch positions afterward, and I let the water run all over me, coating me in more warmth. It isn't just Johnny's heated gaze setting fire to my skin, it's the water, too.

"You liked fucking Magnum, didn't you?"

I lick my lips. I can tell he wants me to say no, but I'm not going to lie to him. There's no reason to anymore. "Yes."

He presses his lips together. He's just finished lathering his hair with shampoo. Soap bubbles line his hair, giving him a child-like look. "Can I tell you something?"

I nod.

"Watching that turned me on." He gives a quick shake

of his head as we switch positions again. He lets the water wash the soap from his hair, and I wait for him to talk, sensing he'll get this out on his own time. "I thought I'd want to kill anyone who touched you, and I think I would. I *know* I would. If it had been Jiko who was doing that, and I could tell you weren't comfortable, I would've killed him right then and there. This was different though. You like Magnum."

I nod, blinking away some of the water that runs down my face. I've told Johnny this before. I've used those same words to describe my feelings for Magnum, but I wonder if it's the sex aspect that made him see it. His father has taught him that the gang and sex is all he needs. Maybe it was how I was with Jacob when we did it. Maybe he saw us in there and discovered not just two people fucking for the fun of it. Which is fun, too, but that's just not what this is. It's something different. He saw two people coming together because they care.

Johnny cups my face and brings us both under the spray. His head blocks the pulse of water from hitting me directly in my face until it's just a nice coating of droplets. It's as if we're under a waterfall, spray coating us.

"Do you feel the same way when you're with me? You looked like you wouldn't want to be anywhere else, Kyla."

I reach up, threading my fingers behind his neck. "The absolute same."

He lowers his mouth to kiss me. It's soft and comforting.

Not usually the type of kisses Johnny gives, but I kiss him back with the same slow tenderness. "My mind tells me you're breaking me." He hovers his lips over mine. "But my heart tells me you're fixing me."

He moves me until my back is against the shower. With as beat up as he is, his dick still works. It's hard against my stomach, poking my belly. Johnny deepens the kiss, then lifts me until he's at my entrance. He slides inside, holding me against the shower as he fucks me nice and slow. It's a quiet torture. A beautiful, maddening pleasure that builds over a simmering heat. We cherish one another. We make promises until the water runs cold, and eventually, we come together in a perfect moment amid dual gasps and moans.

He pulls back, and even though his face is marred and broken, he holds me steady in his gaze, and I'm absolutely certain that just meant something more than just reaching for the climax of pleasure.

He guides me back to my feet and pulls out. His cum drips down my leg as he steps back into the shower spray, washing himself, rinsing away the evidence of what we just shared. He steps out, and I replace him, standing under the showerhead, rinsing a final time under chilled water before turning it off.

Johnny waits for me with a fluffy towel, wrapping it around me as he scoops me into his arms and carries me to the bed.

I giggle like I'm a little girl. "You shouldn't be carrying me around. You're hurt."

He smiles down at me, but the look is all wrong with his swollen face. It's a contrast to the swollen cuts.

"I should get you some ice."

"I'll get it," he says, pushing my shoulders back to the bed.

He moves to stand, but I hold back on his hand. "Let me take care of you." I pull back with more force when he doesn't immediately listen and then give him a wink as he falls to the bed. I get up, wrapping the towel around myself and head out to the kitchen to grab the ice pack. I knew these would come in handy, I just didn't think they would be used for something like this.

A knock comes on the door as I close the freezer. "It's Jacob," Johnny calls out.

I go to the door and open it. Jacob peers at me in my state and gives me a half smile. "Is our boy better?"

"I hope so," I tell him, holding up the ice pack. "I was about to give him this. Come on," I tell him, nodding toward the bedroom.

Magnum and I reach the bedroom to find Johnny sprawled under a sheet. He looks up at Mag lazily. "Is it done?"

"Done."

Johnny sighs as I hold the ice pack over him. He takes it from me and shoos my hand away. "I'll probably be getting a call soon." He looks toward the bathroom, and my gaze falls to his pants.

"Got it," Mag says, holding Johnny's phone out. "I found it on the coffee table when I went back to make sure Jiko did what he was told."

"I forgot," Johnny says. He holds his hand out and Magnum tosses the phone to him.

"I called Oscar and Brawler."

I nod.

"They're coming over."

I flick my gaze to Johnny, but he doesn't balk at the information. In fact, he looks relieved. "Good. We all have some strategizing to do."

Since we're about to have even more company, I slink to the closet.

Johnny chuckles from his spot on the bed. "I promise you Oscar and Brawler will be more than happy to see you in a towel."

I give him a wink over my shoulder and let the towel drop, shaking my ass for them both before pulling on a pair of Johnny's sweats that I've commandeered and one of Oscar's football shirts.

When I turn, Magnum and Johnny are both staring. At this point, they've all seen me naked, so why bother? Also, if I spearhead the clothes are optional campaign, I'll see more skin, and I'm all fucking over that. "Wipe the drool, boys," I tease, which lets air fill the room again. There's so much tension holding it back. It might be sexual or real-life danger heaviness. Take your pick.

On my way back to the bed, I take Jacob's hand and lead him there. He's not just going to hover in the background anymore. He's one of us. He's one of mine.

"Are you going to be okay?" he asks Johnny, searching his injuries.

"He didn't break anything," Johnny mumbles. "I'll just have a fucked up face for a couple of weeks."

I lean over, kissing his cheek. "Not possible. Nothing about your face is fucked."

He gives me a look like he doesn't believe me, and yeah, sure, he's messed up right now, but nothing could detract from his hotness factor.

Magnum's phone pings. He pulls it out of his pocket. "They're coming up the elevator right now."

I heave myself off the bed. "I'll go let them in."

I hurry out of the room before either one of them protest and get to the door when the knock comes. I open it, and Oscar pushes inside first. He captures me in his arms, lifting me off my feet. He's wearing his hat backward again. A look I love on him. He doesn't say anything, just hugs me until he sets me on my feet, and Brawler's arms surround me from behind. His hot breath hits my ear as he presses a chaste kiss to my neck. "You okay?"

I nod, feeling myself relaxing already now that we're all together. "Come on," I tell them. "We're all in the bedroom."

"Meeting in the bedroom? I could get down with that." We walk inside, and Oscar stops. "Dude. Fuck. Are you okay?" His concern strikes me, considering they'd just fought earlier. Though, you'd have to be heartless to see Johnny's face and not care.

"I'll get over it," Johnny mumbles.

I can tell he doesn't like being singled out as being hurt, but he's going to have to get over that. We're a team.

We all take spots on the bed, and I size them up. If this is going to be a regular thing, I'm going to need a bigger bed. We wouldn't fit on here if we were all lying down. Not that my mind should be headed in that direction, but if you're surrounded by four hot guys and your mind doesn't go there, there's probably something off with your libido. Just sayin'.

Brawler's hand traces down my back. Magnum's on my right and Johnny and Oscar are across from us. "Tell us everything."

Johnny reiterates the story since he's the one who was involved in most of it. The shock and anger that splays over Bat's face warms me. "I hope you killed the fucker."

I scoff. "I wish."

Johnny continues, confessing to everyone that he didn't kill Jiko because he knows what it's like. He tells us his friend isn't a bad guy, and I want to disagree with him, but I see where he's coming from. He was between a rock and a hard place with the devil the only way out. I've been there before. Made decisions I didn't want to but had to. That's why I'm here.

"What's going to happen now?" Oscar asks. "Do we have to worry about any more repercussions from K?"

Johnny shakes his head. "No, he's done. He dished out the punishment, and for all he knows, we complied. He won't even bring it up again."

"Easy for him. He wasn't the one beaten to a pulp or made to screw someone." I reach for Magnum's hand on the bed, so he knows I don't mean anything against him. I wanted that part. Sure, I would rather our first time be more personal, but it is what it is. Hopefully, we'll have a lot of time to make up for it.

Mag squeezes back.

"Alright, so..." Oscar says. "We got the fight coming up. Brawler's initiation tasks, whatever they may be. And we still have to worry about the next move Gregory might make. Did I get everything?"

"We need to keep Kyla away from my dad," Johnny says.

"Right. Because that will be easy."

Johnny lets out a breath. "I want her to move in with one of you guys. I want her as far away from here as she can get."

I sit up. "What?"

Johnny finally takes the ice pack away from his swollen eye. "It's not safe for you here. I'll tell him I thought it was best, so we don't fuck anymore. I don't know. I'll make up some excuse."

Brawler's hand drops to the bed, leaving a trail down my spine. "Maybe she can get her apartment back? I'd say she can live with me, but..." He shakes his head. "...my mom."

I rub his shoulder. "I know. It's okay."

"She can live with me," Oscar says, capturing my gaze. "My mom hasn't been home in a couple of months. I haven't heard from her. I don't know where she is."

"But is that really the best idea?" Magnum asks, speaking up. "She has more security here in the tower than anywhere else."

"Right now, her biggest threat is inside these walls," Johnny says, voice growing darker. "I'll take Gregory's guys over my dad any day. We'll sneak her out of here in case anyone is watching. For all anyone else will know, she's still here."

No one agrees with Johnny. We sit in silence and mull it over.

"We can just try it," Johnny says. He's a bit forceful because he's used to people just agreeing with him. "If it doesn't work, we'll figure something else out, but I don't trust my father around her. Magnum, maybe you know some guards we can trust." He shakes his head. "Scratch that. No one outside of us knows where she is, okay? No one."

I frown at Johnny. I'm used to being here with him, so I don't know how I feel about this. Plus, it's taking me away from K. That was never the end game.

Though, even I can understand that's probably a good thing right now.

"Now that that's settled," I say, knowing this will piss off more than a few people in the room. "We need to talk about how Brawler has to kick my ass in this fight."

## 31

Oscar's bike revs underneath me. I tighten my grip around his hard stomach as he pulls away from a stop sign on our way to his house. The last half of the meeting with the guys was tense. No one likes my idea about losing to Brawler, even though they eventually conceded that it was our best avenue. Even Johnny.

Yep. Even Johnny.

My hair sneaks out from under the helmet and whips around my shoulders. The city blurs by as he drives. The thrum of the bike underneath me lulls me into a sense of relaxation. He doesn't immediately take me back to his apartment as planned. Magnum and Johnny will be pissed, but Oscar does what he wants. He drives me out of town, taking the backroads where he can open up the throttle. We fly down the pavement, nerves skittering through me at the dangerous excitement of it all. Driving like this is like the predicaments I keep finding myself in since coming to the Heights. It's scary here. No doubt about that, but it's also thrilling, and that's not even counting the fact that I've found the guys who complement me here. A whole new round of fear and energy tingle my limbs at that thought. It's been so long since I allowed myself to feel love and be loved. So. Damn. Long.

Oscar takes a turn a little too sharply, and even though my stomach bottoms out, I laugh. He chuckles underneath my hands, his abs tightening as he increases the speed a tad. The guy is crazy. He gave me the only helmet he had, so he isn't even wearing one. I'm holding his ballcap in my hand because the helmet I'm wearing kept hitting his brim when we first started out. His raven hair flutters free at the sides. His tan forearms ripple with movement as he steers the motorcycle around another bend in the road.

I press my helmet against his back and watch the side of the road flip by like perfect pictures in time moving in quick succession. There's something so peaceful about this. Almost like we're flying. A sense of freedom wraps me up in a warm blanket.

We stay out on the roads a little longer until he eventually turns the bike back toward the Heights as the sun starts to set. By the time we head down his block, I'm shivering from the cold. He pulls up next to his door around the corner from the store and helps me off the bike. He turns the key and throws his leg over, dismounting with more grace than I've yet to accomplish. I help hold the bike steady as he opens the small storage area. After walking the bike in, he kicks the kickstand down before reaching back for my helmet. I undo the clip and yank it off. He gives me a smirk as I run my hands through my hair to tame it.

Once he has everything inside, he locks the garage up, takes his hat back from me, and then leads me up the narrow staircase to his upstairs apartment.

My phone vibrates in my back pocket, and I'm sure it's a text from one of them, wondering what's taking us so long. I pull it out and send a group message letting them know we arrived at Oscar's apartment safely.

Oscar quickly runs through the place, picking up stray garbage as I chuckle at him. "It's fine," I tell him. Though, Johnny did threaten to send a housekeeper here. He must think Oscar lives in filth, which he doesn't.

"Gotta have the best for Princess," he mocks.

There's one thing I love about Oscar and Brawler's places that are missing from mine, Magnum, and Johnny's. That lived-in feel. It's homey. Things that have been used recently are out. A pen. A pad of paper. A book. A can opener sits on the kitchen counter. There's never anything like that in mine or Johnny's suite because the housekeepers come by and pick it up. Don't get me wrong, that's nice too, but it also makes our places a tad sterile. Almost like it's not a home.

"I like it, Oscar. Don't bother."

He grunts. "Yeah. I'm sure you like it better than the tower."

He comes back out to the main living area, and I stop him, blocking his beeline to whatever else he thinks needs to get picked up. "Don't be silly. This place is your home, and I would like it no matter what."

He arches a brow. "What if I lived in a cardboard box on the street?"

I narrow my gaze. "Can we both fit in the cardboard box?"

His dark eyes flare, and he nods.

"Then I would like it," I tell him, giving him a quick kiss on the lips. "Now, can we do something normal? Like binge TV and eat candy?"

Oscar chuckles. "That's your idea of normal?"

I shrug. "That's what I would be doing if I was home."

He shakes his head but leads me to the sofa anyway. He hands me the remote and tells me he'll search the kitchen for junk food. I turn the TV on, but I watch him instead. He pulls down some Oreos from the cabinet, sitting them next to a bag of chips on the counter along with a loaf of bread.

"Can I ask you something?" I call out.

He comes out from around the kitchen. "Anything."

"How do you make money?"

His gaze burns into me. He tosses the chips and the Oreos down on the coffee table in front of us.

"I was just curious because your mom—"

"Doesn't work?" he supplies. "Doesn't give me money? Doesn't do anything?"

I bite the inside of my cheek. "Yeah. All that."

"I get money from the Crew. I fast-tracked my way in, so I could start earning a wage. When we got back to the Heights and Mom started back into her drug nonsense, I knew things were going to go back to the way they were, only worse. I burned bridges when I left. I used to work at the grocery beneath us, but Heights people didn't trust me like they used to. I joined the Crew for protection and for the money. I couldn't wait to go through the regular initiation tasks like most, I needed to start making money right away, so they agreed to push me through as long as I did what they said. They pay me to watch over the high school recruits. They pay me to keep my ears to the ground. You'd be surprised what you can learn in the school. I write them weekly reports that sometimes have information they need and sometimes don't. I also help them with various other things occasionally."

"And it's enough?" I ask.

"Am I Uncle Scrooging it in money? No," he says, looking away. "But it's enough to get by."

I cup his cheek, making him look at me again. "You are something else, Oscar Drego."

He shakes his head. "I did what I had to to survive."

"But you *did* do it," I tell him. Not everyone does. His mom, for example. She checked out. She's not helping. She's not doing anything. Brawler's mom, too. Hell, Johnny's mom left him as well. Not everyone does what they should do. Even if you just do that, you're doing okay. Sometimes it's enough just to do enough.

Oscar leans forward to gesture toward his offerings. "Which first?"

"Chips," I tell him, already salivating. He hands me the bag of Doritos, and I open them, holding them between us so we can share.

We decide on a movie and start to watch. Minutes turn into an hour and an hour into three as we put in another movie and snuggle on the couch together. It's so comfortable being here. In fact, it's so comfortable I fall asleep and Oscar wakes me with a kiss to the crown of my head. "Let's go to bed, Princess."

I play groan at him, and he smirks. "Do you want the bed to yourself?"

I stand, wrapping my arms around his middle. "Absolutely not. I want to wake up in your arms."

Oscar and I undress once we're in his room. He shucks his clothes off until he's in his boxers while I'm in his football shirt. He teases the fabric between his fingers. "I love that you wore this."

I shrug it off like it doesn't matter, but I love wearing their clothes. Is that strange? There's just something about wearing their too-big t-shirts. Letting them—their smell—wrap all around me is like having them close to me all the time.

Oscar has just wrapped his arms around me after we get in bed when his phone rings. He breathes out. "If that's one of them, no promises I won't murder their asses."

I smirk, but when he turns over, he answers it without any venom. The sheets gather at his waist as I play my hands up and down his back.

"Really?" Oscar asks.

The tone in his voice makes me stop.

"Yeah, thanks for telling me." He breathes out, displeased. "No, no. I'll take care of it."

He hangs up the phone, resting it against his forehead.

"What's up?"

"Another body found." He pulls the phone away to scroll through his Contacts. He stops on Johnny's name and presses Send. Whatever he answers with, Oscar says, "No, she's fine."

I smile at that, though Oscar doesn't seem to think it's sweet or cute or funny. "Body found in the alley just south of the boulevard. Candy in the pockets." He pauses. "Yeah, one of our guys. My guy tells me it looks like it's been there a couple of days. He called us first."

Without another word, Oscar hangs up with a shrug. "What?" I ask.

"He said he'd take care of it."

"Who is it?" I ask, mind already filled with nasty images of a ghostly white, decaying body. And bugs. I shiver.

Oscar pulls me close to him. "One of our low guys. A grunt."

"If he died a couple of days ago...?"

"I know," Oscar says, rubbing my arm nonchalantly. "Then that's only a couple of days after Farmingham, and a level up, too."

I finish his thought. "So, we could have another dead body on our hands shortly..."

"In theory," he says.

We lie there, my mind working over what's happened. Eventually, Oscar brushes a kiss over my temple. "Shh, Princess. Get some sleep. There's nothing we can do right now."

Oscar's a sound sleeper. The next morning, I wake before him. Each movement I make on the bed doesn't rouse him, so I start playing a little game. I trail my fingernails over his body. Still, his breathing is steady and even, eyes twitching under his lids.

I take it a step further, fingers brushing over his cock. In the middle of the night, he must have shed his boxers because he's naked under the sheets. His dick twitches and grows. I swear, his heart pumps louder even though he hasn't fully woken yet. I grip his dick in my hand, giving him small pumps. He rouses even more, moaning like he's having a very good dream.

I bet he is, and I'm going to give him the best dream.

I push the covers away and scoot down the bed. I've already had a taste of Oscar, so I know what it feels like to have him in my mouth. My core clenches at the thought. Before he wakes up, I pull my shirt off and shimmy my panties down my legs, leaving us both bare. If this turns out the way I want it to, I won't be needing these clothes, anyway.

I lick Oscar like a lollipop, swirling my tongue over his head. His hips jerk, and I grip him tighter, working him toward my lips. I take him all inside, humming.

"Ahh, fuck," Oscar says sleepily. He tangles his hand in my hair, giving my head pressure. I glance up to meet his eyes, and his mouth is open in a silent "O" of surprise as I work him. "Fuck, Princess."

I let his dick pop out of my mouth and grin at him. "Sorry. I wasn't tired anymore."

I push his hips to the bed and take him in my mouth again, running my lips down his length and back up.

"You undressed for me?" he asks huskily, reaching out to tweak my nipple.

I nod, the movement working my mouth over his cock.

"You're moving in and never leaving," he breathes out.

He's so serious that I can't help but smile, ruining the rhythm I had going on, but Oscar doesn't mind. He takes my chin and moves me up to claim my lips. He groans as if he enjoys tasting himself on me. Liquid lust burns through me hot and needy. I crawl over his body, so turned on that I can barely think. His cock presses against my center, and I ease myself over him.

He lets me go, eyes shooting wide. "Kyla." His surprise turns into a groan as I move over him. He lowers his gaze to where we meet, watching his cock disappear inside me. "You're so tight," he grinds out. "Fuck me."

"I thought that's what I was doing," I tease.

He reaches up to play with my tits. "Take whatever you need from me, Princess."

I grind down over him, my walls clenching around his hard ridges. "Fuck, Oscar."

He grips my hips. "You like my cock inside you."

"Yes, your bare cock." I swallow, my mouth suddenly dry. Being this close to him without any barrier is a drug. I could shoot up with it and be high on life.

His dark, wild eyes watch my every movement. We

grind against one another, and I lose myself in the chase of pleasure. I'm not quiet. I give Oscar every little piece I have inside me.

"Yes, right there." I grind down over him, and he meets me, anchoring me with his hands on my hips.

The bed rocks and the frame hits the wall as I ride him. The rhythmic pattern of the thumps match my cries. "That's right, Princess," Oscar encourages. "Tell everyone."

A low, throaty moan escapes me. I can't wait until I can share my feelings for all of them with the world and not have to worry about the consequences. I don't want to hide.

He cups my breasts as I increase my movements, slamming down on top of him as he spears me. "God, Oscar, I'm going to come," I breathe.

His fingers curl into my skin. "Come on my hard cock?" He snakes his arms around to my ass, digging his fingers in while I thrash over top of him.

"Yes, right on your hard cock." My orgasm hits, and it takes a heart-stopping moment before it slams into me full force. I cry out, and Oscar takes control of my hips to ride my orgasm out.

He flips me to all fours, entering me from behind before I've had a chance to fully recover. "Hands on the wall," he commands

I crawl up the bed, reaching up to place my hands on the wall. Oscar moves with me until we're at an all-new angle. "This tight hole is mine." His strokes are relentless. A barrage that never stops until I scream his name as my core squeezes him. He takes a few deep breaths while I come, waiting until my own breaths even out before he starts again, his movements much slower this time, as if he wants to take his time.

"You like that dirty talk, Princess," he practically coos.

I moan in answer. He has no idea.

His thighs start to shake, but he keeps the same pace, pulling almost completely out and sliding in to the hilt in a dramatically slow fashion. Even when his breathing hitches and I can tell he's moments away from spilling, he keeps the same pace, grinding into me before pulling almost all the way out, fingers tightening against my skin. "Fuck, Princess. Can I come inside you? I want to fill you."

I move back against him in answer, and Oscar loses it. He yanks my hips against his, holding me there while his cock jerks inside me again and again, a seemingly never-ending climax that he breathes harshly through, finally biting my shoulder playfully.

You couldn't pay me to move from this position. Oscar coming inside me, the tight hold he has on my body like he doesn't want me to move away. The warmth that fills me and surrounds me.

The ultimate acceptance.

Oscar doesn't pull out. He covers me with his body while we get our bearings until he eventually falls out. As soon as he does, he reaches around, drifting his hands down my stomach and pushes two fingers inside my sensitive cunt. He plays in his own cum, whispering dirty thoughts in my ear about leaving pieces of himself inside me. Branding me. Claiming me. I eat it up, thrusting against his fingers and rubbing my clit over his palm until I come so harshly, I fall to the bed, exhausted and worn out. He moves to my side, pulling me against him, his hand cupping my sticky mound and the mixture of both of us just dripping there onto his needy fingers.

He kisses my back. "You're never leaving."

## 32

Oscar and I lie in bed together until I have to get ready for training. Soon enough, Johnny will be calling, wanting to pick me up to take me to the gym. Oscar told everyone he could take me, but they agreed that the car was safer than Oscar's bike. Plus, I'm all for the car since more of us can be around each other that way.

Johnny sends a text five minutes before he knocks on the door. Oscar lets him in as I finish up in the bathroom, pulling my hair into a high ponytail for training. There's nothing worse than having your hair get into your face when you're trying to knock someone out.

I walk out to find Johnny looking around the apartment, nose curled up. I shoot him a look when he glances over at me. His lips curl into a smile though, and with that panty-melting look, who can stay mad at him?

He places his hand around my waist and kisses my temple. "Magnum's in the car making sure no one's walking by."

"We're in the Heights," Oscar says. "They'll look away. Especially now with bodies showing up. They won't give up Kyla to anyone. Especially not until her fight tomorrow. They've been waiting months to see her fight again."

The usual anxious nerves I get pre-fight don't swamp me. If I was fighting anyone else but Brawler, I'd be ecstatic.

I want to get back to my regular life. I want to get back in the ring. I just don't want to get in front of him, someone I care for.

"They're going to be unhappy," I breathe out, not looking forward to the shitshow that will follow this.

Johnny looks away. He was the hardest to convince that Brawler had to win. He knows his father though. He knows how evil he can be. Since he mandated this as one of Brawler's initiation tasks, he can't just not win.

"Did you talk to your father?"

"Let's get in the car," Johnny says, thrusting his chin toward the stairs leading down.

Oscar follows us out, locking his door behind us as we head down to the waiting black car. Instead of sitting in the back with those guys, I slide into the front seat. Johnny gives a short growl behind me, but Magnum's lips tip up at the corners. Magnum's driving us in one of the regular cars today, so we don't have to talk through the small window the divider usually leaves when it's not up.

I click my seatbelt in place and then turn around in my seat, catching Oscar's eye while I do. He's also grinning, which makes me think everyone's content to gang up on Johnny. I mean, a little. And I wouldn't call it ganging up on, maybe just showing him how I want it to be, so he can get an idea of what he's in for if he chooses this.

"Well?" I ask.

Johnny runs his hands through his dark hair. "He was pleased with the pictures," he says, jaw ticking. It sounds as if there's a whole other story to that, but I don't need details. Johnny's face still looks terrible this morning even though he should be able to see out of his eye better.

Fucking bastard.

"Jiko gloated, so he did his part perfectly. Dad's looking forward to your fight tomorrow."

I roll my eyes. "I'm sure he is. Looking forward to money is more like it."

"It makes the most business sense," Johnny says, nodding, easily slipping into the gang business persona.

I stare at him blankly.

"What did he say about the body?" Oscar asks.

"He asked me if I'd figured out who did it yet."

I turn back around in the seat, facing the windshield again. Magnum reaches over to thread his fingers through mine. I've had about enough of Big Daddy K. We're talking about one of his guys' lives, and he isn't taking it seriously.

My phone vibrates, and I take it out. **Here**, Brawler texts.

Since no one has figured out what to say back to Johnny after that remark, I tell everyone Brawler's already at the gym. I'll have to have a private talk with him today. I need him to actually fight me. It has to be believable. This route might put me in harm's way, but I'm already on K's shitlist. Brawler isn't.

I'll have to physically and mentally prepare myself to get beat up. It's not like this won't hurt, I just understand it has to be done.

Oscar reaches out to place his hand on my shoulder. "You okay?"

I place my hand over top of his, playing over his fingers. "I'm good."

He gives me a squeeze and then removes his hand, sitting back in the seat once more. It doesn't take long to get to the gym from Oscar's apartment. Magnum does his usual watching the area thing as we walk in, and then he heads through with his bug detector as Finn and Jax come to greet us.

The mood is pretty somber in the gym already. Brawler's off hitting the punching bag in the corner. It swings on its swivel hooks, the chains clanging as he puts all his energy into hitting the bag. It's taking a beating, too.

My eyes bulge out of my head. I'm going to be staring that down tomorrow. He's going to hurt me. It's not that I can't inflict damage either, but his fists are like cement blocks. He's one of the most skilled fighters I've ever met, and that's not to mention the fact that I care about him. I don't want him to hurt me, and I don't want to hurt him, but I have to separate the two. At least tomorrow, I do.

"This is a terrible fucking idea," Jax says, eyeing the big man taking out all his rage on the poor leather-wrapped punching bag.

I try to shake myself out of the fear swallowing me. I can't let Brawler feel worse than he already does. He'd rather rip out his right arm than fight me, but we're left with no choice.

I yearn for a day with choices. Opportunities. Moving around at my own discretion. It's why I'm here after all. Freedom. I just had to give some up for a little while to gain a lot.

I yell at myself internally to get over myself. I've been in fights before and this will be no different. I have to treat it like any other.

Brawler moves around the bag. He sees me out of the corner of his eye and stops, lowering his guard. His chest rises and lowers. The ink creeping up his neck stands out like a Picasso on a muted background. I drop my water bottle and towel and move toward him. He waits for me where he is, the bag swinging to my right.

"Kyla..." His voice is a desperate plea, as if I have the power to stop this. As if I have the power to tell him this doesn't need to happen. None of us have the power right now. We're all just puppets on a string until we can take it back.

"Let's give them a moment," Mag says in the background.

My eyes fill with salty tears.

"That's it. I'm not doing it," he says, moving forward to cup my face.

"You have to," I say, checking the tears as best I can.

"It's not worth it," he growls.

I move my hands up his neck. I trace the angel wings, one light and one dark. "We don't want to become these people, right?" One sacrificial lamb, and one wolf. We have to play the game and play it smarter than them.

"I can't hit you," he seethes. "It's not in me."

"Tomorrow, it will be. Tomorrow, pretend to be a different person. You're not you, and I'm not me."

"Impossible," he says, shaking his head. "I'd recognize you anywhere. What's in you is in me, and when two people like that find each other, they can't just wish it away."

"You know you have to," I say. A tear finally escapes, tracking down my cheek. I never thought I'd be begging a guy to kick my ass. It's true you can find strength in anything. This might be the moment I need the most strength. For both of us. "Then think about the future," I tell him, grabbing onto that thought and holding it closely. "It's a means to an end."

"I thought I was helping you!" He turns and slams his fist into the heavy bag, sending it flying.

"I'll never forget that," I tell him. I hold out my hand to steady the bag. "How you walked into that room with no thought of your own well-being. You sacrificed a part of yourself. I get it."

"And I'll be giving up another tomorrow the first time my fist lands. I might as well just carve myself into pieces right now, Kyla. There's no way this is going to work."

"It will," I argue, trying to make myself believe it as much as him. "It has to. For the same reason you walked into that room and sat at that table with the people you despise is why I'm going to stand in front of you tomorrow and beg you to hit me. Because I'm doing it for you. If you're good enough to sacrifice yourself for me, then I'm good enough to sacrifice myself for you. I want to. Do you hear me? I *want* to."

His jaw tenses. It works over and over, his Adam's apple bobbing up and down. Eventually, he nods once, conceding with slumped shoulders.

I can't congratulate myself over this. Both Brawler and I know that crawling back from this will be a feat, but I owe it to him. He gave his all for me, and now I'm giving my all. That's how relationships work. They're not one-sided. They're a mess of love and heartbreak. Of destruction and building back up. After all, the only person who can truly break you is someone you love. If they weren't, you wouldn't care enough to get hurt.

I walk away. I can't stand to look in his pained eyes anymore and know I'm putting it there. I plead with Magnum with my eyes, and he walks over to Brawler while I slip inside the office. Jax stands, but when I lean against the wall and slide to my butt, he sits back in his chair and wheels over. The chair creaks in its quest to get closer to me. He pulls a tissue out of the box on the combined desks and hands it over.

I catch the tears falling and then drop my head back against the door, staring up at the tiled ceiling. Water stains cover the surface. Jagged, brown circles in various sizes. Marked there from who knows how long ago. A memory of a moment in time when something unexpected happened. "Your ceiling is gross," I choke out.

Jax follows my stare then glances back at me.

My breath hiccups as I try to keep from bawling.

"I love this place. Shitty ceiling tiles and everything."

I nod, knowing the feeling. That's why I'm still in the Heights because even though I know things aren't good right now, I'm better here than I was out there. Because of them. All of them.

"Don't come to the fight tomorrow," I tell him on a shaky breath.

"You'll have to convince Finn, not me."

"I mean it," I say, my voice hardening. "Just find a way to make him stay home."

He tilts his head. "I hope this isn't because you don't want us to see you lose."

"I don't give a fuck about that." I wad the tissue up and use a dry section to wipe my eyes again. "It's not safe. I don't want you guys near the gang. Promise me?"

"Promise," Jax says. He leans back in the chair. He's fiddling with a pencil in his hands, but he tosses it onto his desk, and it rolls over the shiny veneer surface. "For the record, I already thought you were badass, but what you're doing makes you the strongest woman I know."

I choke out a laugh. I'm sitting here bawling in his office while running away from something that hurts too much. That doesn't sound strong at all. "Yeah, right."

He shrugs. "Suit yourself, but not many people would do what you're doing. Taking a loss for someone else. Hell, it's not even that. You're throwing yourself away for him. To help him."

"To save him," I say.

"Well, that diminishes it then," he says, teasing.

I groan, wondering how I got here with Jax of all people trying to comfort me. It's so backwards. I mean, I guess he's trying to comfort me. If he doesn't mean to, he's doing it, anyway.

I wipe at my face again and stand. I take a few deep breaths. I know I have to go out there and face reality again even though it would be so lovely just to hide back here. Even if Jax was my company. I throw the used tissue in the trashcan and look at him. "How do I look?"

He observes me, gaze never straying from my face. "Like a beautiful soldier, an avenging warrior."

"So, Wonder Woman basically?"

"Basically," he says, and I swear he almost laughs.

He stands from the chair, pushing it back under his desk and then moves forward. He spins me around and then puts his hands on my shoulders. He massages my muscles there. "Now you're going to go out there, put your Wonder Woman face on, and tackle everything head on. I've never seen you do anything less, so there's no reason to stop now."

He gives me a hearty shove, and I walk back out of the office, lifting my chin into the air. Brawler is in the ring with Finn. He has his game face on. We all do. I peer around the gym, catching on each of us as we watch Brawler work. Tomorrow's going to suck for all of us, not just for Brawler and me. We're the most directly affected, but what affects us impacts them too.

But like with everything that's happened, we'll get through this, too.

Oscar swaggers over to me, never missing a moment to make me smile. "If you want, we can just go back to my apartment. I'll sink myself so deep inside you you'll forget everything going on."

I chuckle, almost letting loose a few more tears. "You're sick, Drego."

"Too soon?"

I shake my head and then pounce on his back. I wrap my legs around his middle and hug his neck. I give him a sloppy kiss on the side of his head. "To the ring, please."

"Oh, so I'm your horsey now?"

"You wanted me to ride you, right?"

He chuckles. "Not quite what I was thinking, Princess, and you know it."

I throw my head back and laugh. I catch Johnny watching us and smile at him. He looks away right after as if I'd caught him doing something he shouldn't.

I might be losing it. I might be looking for things that aren't there. However, I could swear he wore a half-smile while watching us.

Maybe. Possibly. I bite my lip and hold on for dear life as Oscar springs to the ring.

## 33

On the way to The Ring, I have flashbacks. I asked Oscar to be with Brawler, but Johnny and Magnum are with me while we drive to the Crew's new fighting venue that never got to see its opening night. It's as if time has rewound, and I'm replaying the chapter in my life that should've happened a couple of months ago. Only this time, Brawler will be staring me down from across the ring, not the girl whose name I can't even remember.

Everything must be working out for the Crew because as we pull up, the amount of bodies waiting near the building to get into the fights triples. They're coming in hoards, as if a concert is about to go down in the middle of the Heights. Girls dressed in skimpy leather skirts or booty jean shorts hang off guys with saggy pants, backward hats, and t-shirts. The Heights has shown up tonight. For this.

Big Daddy K better be happy. The blow I'm about to walk into says he better be creaming his pants over what's about to go down.

Johnny and Mag have been pretty quiet since they picked me up. There was no pre-fight training meeting with Jax and Finn like there was leading up to my last fight that never happened. Oscar had already left to be with Brawler when Magnum and Johnny showed up at Oscar's place. Magnum looks almost the same. Almost. A veiled layer of tension hovers over him. Johnny, however, is tense. His foot jumps up and down in the car, gaze darting out the windows, as we pull around the back to the fighter's entrance.

"I'll be fine," I promise him.

The swelling on his face has gone down, so he mainly just looks like he got his ass kicked instead of tied to a chair and beaten. His skin is probably still tender to the touch. I've been there. Bruises like that will linger, even long after the fight is over. It'll probably be worse for Johnny though. The person who left him looking like that was someone who was supposed to love him, not a pre-ordained match to see who's more skilled.

"I'll follow you guys in," Mag says as he pulls up to the door.

Johnny shoves the car door open and then reaches back for my hand. I place my fingers in his, and he squeezes tightly before leading me out of the car and through the back door. It leads to a narrow hallway and then a back set of stairs. The building they got is practically the width of the entire block. It's huge. Once we're up the stairway, the narrow hallways lead to different changing rooms for the fighters. Johnny walks me down to the door that has my symbol on it. It's the same symbol that's on my robe. I smile as he opens the room up, and there everything is, laid out and ready for me. Brawler must have done this. My own personal training room. I finger the bra and shorts I'll be wearing in a little while. A cute set. Black with purple trim. It's too bad they're about to get bloody. That I know for sure. Glancing up, I notice two doors in the dressing room. Johnny explains that one exits out the back—the one we just came in with—and the other leads to the fights themselves. It's a cool setup.

Brawler and I didn't plan out the fight ahead of time. Mostly because it needs to look real. Big Daddy K is going to be out there, watching us with a critical eye due to it being one of Brawler's initiation tasks. I asked Johnny if he thought it was weird Brawler's other tasks weren't set yet, and he told me no. They set them in succession. So, if Brawler beats me, then he'll get the next one. If he accomplishes that, he'll get the next and so on. No sense in planning more activities if Brawler loses the first.

I sit on the small bench and Johnny walks over. "Is there anything we can do to make it hurt less? I Googled it, but I couldn't find much of anything."

I smile at his concern. "I'm going to take some Tylenol in a little bit and then just have ice ready. Lots and lots of ice. Maybe an ice bath."

"The rooms only have showers," Johnny admits, looking at the space as if it will suddenly change because that's what I want.

Behind us, the door opens, and Mag appears, shutting it soundly behind him.

Before Johnny can offer to rip the showers out and put tubs in, I tell him ice packs are fine.

"Don't let Brawler see me right after, okay?" I say, flipping my gaze between the two of them so they know I'm serious. "Get me out of there as soon as possible. I have a feeling his acting abilities suck."

"Done," Mag says.

Johnny growls. He's been bitchy and on edge all day, but there's nothing I can do about it. He knows this is all his father's fault even though he'd love to blame it on Brawler. It's too easy to do that. There are always reasons for everything, however hidden they may be. Hardly anyone or anything is black and white. Everything is made up of layers, just like nature. A predator with an alluring shell. Or an angel who looks like the devil.

I pick up the bra and shorts and head into the attached bathroom. The whole area is one space. The bathroom doesn't have a door, just a walkway into a separate room. It's also ten times nicer than what we had at the warehouse. I peel my clothes off then stare at myself in the mirror over the sink. My eyes look dead today. You ever just stare at yourself and wonder what's going on in your head? I've had years of experience of staring at myself in mirrors, searching for my parents' reflections. Searching for pieces of them they may have passed on to me. But right now, I can honestly say I don't even look like myself.

I glance away and tug on my fighting outfit. Afterward, I pull my hair back into a tight ponytail and then braid it, wrapping two elastics around the ends, so it won't let loose during the fight. My stomach tightens after I finish, realizing that every little thing I do is only taking me toward the inevitable. With a huge breath, I walk out to do my pre-fight stretches. There's no point in getting any more injured than I need to by pulling a muscle because I didn't put my all into the fight, even though I already know how it's going to turn out.

A knock sounds on the door, and Magnum opens it. A guy I recognize from the warehouse sticks his head in. "The fight before yours is about to wrap up. You'll be on soon."

I nod with a sickening twist to my insides. I'm not sure I've ever not wanted to do something so much in my entire life. Something that I knew I had to do, but didn't want to, and it's fucking killing me. I've had mini pep talks with myself all day about picking up my ovaries and doing what needs to be done, but I still come right back around to the simple fact that I don't want to.

I just don't fucking want to.

The guy leaves, and Magnum walks toward me. He moves my chin, so I look up into his hazel-green eyes. "Focus."

I nod.

"Future."

I nod again, threads of steel spreading out to harden my veins. Johnny moves to my back, pressing close to me as he massages my shoulders. I stretch my neck from side-to-side while he digs his fingers in. "Have I told you lately that I think you're perfect?"

Magnum moves in from the front, and suddenly, I'm in a Magnum-Johnny sandwich, each pressing against me, their body heat breaking through the tension and flowing through me.

My mouth parts, and Jacob takes advantage, swooping down to press his lips to mine. Johnny drops his head to kiss the curve of my neck, and suddenly, my mind is preoccupied in a completely different way. I moan, relishing in the love from all sides, not wanting it to end.

Before it can get too far, Jacob pulls away, pinning me with his gorgeous stare. Johnny works his lips up my neck. "You have a lot to look forward to, babe."

A shiver runs through me. If they're promising me an incentive, this might be... No, it's still going to suck, but I'll take it as a recuperation present.

Johnny reaches over to grab my robe off the bench and

helps me put it on. Magnum pulls it closed in front, hands lingering near my hips. "Remember how much he cares for you," he says, his voice a little off from his usual sure tenor.

"I know," I tell him, giving him a small smile. I create some space between us all, so I can continue my stretches. I get another five minutes before the same guy returns to lead me to the middle of the ring. My dry throat sticks, so I swallow the thin air as I walk out after him. My robe billows out, but I can't even enjoy it because I'm so focused on what's waiting for me when I get out there.

Johnny and Magnum follow after me, but I may as well be by myself. I block out everything I've built here and focus on the insurmountable task ahead of me.

The crowd's excitement level ratchets up when they first see me. It allays some of the nerves, but frays others. Johnny and Magnum act like bodyguards beside me, but people still get their hands in to brush against my skin. I hardly notice. The arena drowns out. I see them, their mouths open, their hands raised while I walk down the path to the middle of the room, but I don't hear them. My mind works on overtime to mute it all out.

I almost stumble when I walk into the circle to find Brawler step out at the same time I do. He's so fucking handsome. I thought so the first time I saw him. He's even hotter now that he's got fighting shorts on, a bare-chest, and fists clenched like he wants to beat the shit out of something.

I bite my lip, eerily aroused by the scene in front of me.

His eyes are more of a cobalt blue today, not the swirling turquoise I'm used to seeing. The ink on his body appears darker, more pronounced. The tribal tattoos swim up his arm as if moving while he shakes his hands out. The angel wings on his neck are alive, beating life's blood into him.

I've only ever seen Brawler fight once. From up in the Crew box in the warehouse. Sure, I've seen him train a bunch of times, but this will be something. I'd kill to have a spot front row, watching him tear into somebody.

The crowd roars. The nameless, faceless people around us are literally just that: nothing. Their faces are all striated and muted, like nothing matters but Brawler in front of me.

The guy who's taken over for Brawler for the night steps into the middle of the circled area. Real bleachers rise up along the circle, reaching all the way to the ceiling. It's so hot in here, my skin already sticky with sweat. Gone is the smell of stale beer from the warehouse, even though alcohol is still all around. They've just gotten fancier. It's not just cheap beer, it's mixed drinks and shots too. One of these days, I'll have to come to the fights just as a spectator. Wouldn't that be nice?

"For your final fight on this opening day," the guy shouts amidst a chorus of screams. "Uppercut Princess versus Brawler!" He draws Brawler's name out and goosebumps skitter over my expectant skin.

He nods at both of us and backs away.

Right. So, this is it. This is one moment that will define

my life. It's odd to know it before it even happens, and not just look back at it years later and pinpoint the very second things changed. I already know the first blow will change things. It's just up to Brawler and me to fix it later.

I treat the fight like training at first. I creep in, just as I would do if we were in Jax and Finn's boxing ring. I look for his tells. I plan my attack. When the first opportunity comes, I don't take it.

*Fuck.*

I shake it off, circle around him and start again. Brawler looks just as content to do this with me, play with each other, but it won't work. My gaze darts up. Like with the warehouse, a special boxed area for the Crew sits atop everything else. It's fancier, but what fills it is the same. Big Daddy K is front and center in the window. Johnny is next to him, fists clenched at his side, but it's K who grabs all of my attention. He's leering, a half-smile on his face is more predatory than anything. He's the perfect representation of an enemy in beautiful clothing.

I lick my lips and focus back on Brawler. I send a silent thought up, hoping he'll forgive me for this, and then I head in. I attack first because I know he won't. If any one of the guys is too good for me, it's him. Hell, it's not just me. He's too good for the Heights. He's too good for most things. He's been through the shit that has taught him who he wants to be.

He's just...fuck. He's good. Not halo worthy, obviously.

None of us are, but he's just...good. There's no other word for it.

He blocks my punches and attacks with some teasing ones of his own. Just like he would in training, telling me he could've got me if he wanted.

I smile at him, and he smiles back.

Fighting someone you train with is difficult. They know you. They know your style, and I'm not even counting the fact that neither one of us actually wants to hurt the other. It means I have to do something unconventional.

I run at him. He's stunned, pausing briefly. I plant my foot on his thigh, grab his shoulder, and glance an elbow off his head. I didn't throw it as hard as I could have, but the audience loves it.

Brawler throws me off. His gaze narrows now, and I wonder if I've poked the beast.

We circle again. Oscar yells his name, followed by, "Do it!"

He comes in, catching me in the chin. His hands are heavy, powerful, like fucking sledgehammers. I'm impressed and pissed at the same time.

Listen, taking the fight out of a fighter is a hard feat. Brawler's standing in front of me, and I know that, but that doesn't mean I want to get punched in the face.

I give him a few body shots to his perfect abs, and he retaliates with a backfist to my cheek.

I have to bite my lip, a mixture of emotions swimming

through me. Most of them contradict each other. I'm mad. I'm embarrassed. I'm...proud of him.

I grin, loosening my fists to go in for another attack. I give him a couple of jabs to the mouth. He captures my arm, kicks my feet out from underneath me and slams me to the floor. I grunt on impact. It really sucks to go down hard on a cement floor like this.

Brawler doesn't immediately pounce on me, which tells me he's doing this with love. God, I love the big guy. I blink at the ceiling a few times to get my bearings back and then kick to my feet in one movement. The spectators in the front row stand, appreciating that little maneuver. Actually, after that, everyone in the room stands in a ripple effect. It's that part of the fight where you know you're about to get your money's worth.

Brawler throws a roundhouse to my legs. It hits me in the calf and stings. Adrenaline lessens some of the pain during the fights, but for some reason, kicks can be different. Especially well-placed kicks like the one he just threw.

I stomp kick him in the gut, earning a grunt from his lips. We circle each other again, acutely aware that this fight is taking a while now. Everyone is foaming at the mouth to see what happens. Brawler can feel it too. His eyes start to change because we can no longer play with each other. We have to get this done, and it's going to kill both of us to do it.

I give him a slight nod, barely imperceptible, as I move in. As before, I know he would never make the first move, so

I crack him in the nose. When I retreat, blood drips from his nostrils, and my heart cracks in two.

He licks his lips, a different kind of armor locking into place around his body. He goes from cold mask to even colder mask. A spike of fear hits me.

Brawler moves forward. I throw up blocks to ward off his punches. I do just enough so it looks as if I'm trying to stop his attack, but the first time his fist connects with my face for real, I don't have to pretend anymore.

The room goes out of focus. He hit me in the right spot. I stumble and shoot for a takedown to make up for the fact that my brain is haywired right now. I must catch him off guard because I'm able to wrap him up. I land on top of him, but he flips me to my back immediately. He catches me in side hold, working for position. I struggle against him, but Brawler is heavy. He's bigger than me. Stronger than me. Let's not forget, he's also a better fighter than me. Listen, I'm good. I hold my own against people, but Brawler's better. Especially when my head is still ringing from the last hit he gave.

I get out of his side hold and ease into his guard. He postures, swinging his fist down at my face.

My eyes swim. I gaze up at him through fractured vision, and I catch the moment something inside him breaks.

He pulls back.

*No. No.*

I use my legs to pull him back toward me, wrapping him

in a hold like fighters do when they want to get their breathing under control. I hold him until it's just us two. Hearts crashing against our rib cages. "Don't you fucking dare," I say. "Finish it. It's the only way."

He growls into my ear, and it probably looks like a sound of annoyance to everyone else.

I give him an elbow to the cheek. It's weak though. Partly because I'm fucking tired, and partly because he's supposed to be winning this fight. He will win this fight.

Then I pull him back down, his face crashing against my chest. "I love you. It's okay."

The world goes blank after that. His fist connects with my temple, and I'm out.

I've lost consciousness in a fight before. It was one of my first ones. It lasted only seconds, waking before I even fell to the ground, but I was so terrified. This time, I must be out for longer because when I come to, I'm in Mag's arms. He drags me away from the circle.

I blink, and in front of me, Jiko faces off with Brawler.

*What the fuck?*

"*The* fuck..." I drawl, actually voicing my confusion at seeing two fighters in the ring where I should be.

No one seems to notice me being dragged off, and Magnum doesn't say a word at first.

"What happened?"

"You're okay," Jacob says.

"I know," I grind out. "What the fuck happened?"

He hauls me to my feet, his corded arms wrapped around my middle as we watch Brawler and Jiko go at it.

Jiko's dressed in a low-slung pair of joggers and no shirt. My initial thoughts about him when he held pads for me the other day were correct. Dude's good.

But he's no match for Brawler.

I glance up into the VIP box. K leans over, trying to get a

better view. Johnny's eyes are on me, and I give him a quick nod to let him know I'm okay.

"What happened?" I ask again as Brawler's fist connects with Jiko's cheek.

"He came out of nowhere," Mag answers. "Brawler was reeling back to hit you again, and Jiko just tackled him off you. Started calling him out."

The crowd around us is going nuts. They're loving every second of this unscheduled fight. They're clearly on Brawler's side. Someone in the front row even pushes Jiko closer to Brawler, who takes advantage of the situation by landing a solid knee to his midsection.

Brawler's on fire, and I might be a little fuzzy, but I can tell the difference in him. His whole demeanor has changed. He's hitting for damage, and Jiko's face complies. He splits his eyebrow open with a hook that just glances. The kind of punch that's great for opening someone up using your knuckles.

"Come on," Mag says, trying to lead me away.

I shake my head and hold back. "No, I'm watching this."

"You were just out cold."

"I'm fine," I promise, shrugging him off me.

The amount of energy coming off the crowd makes goosebumps sprout on my arms. The feral shouts switch something in me, and I'm yelling with them. "Get him! Come on!"

Okay, I might still have an axe to grind with the way Jiko

backstabbed Johnny. I am loving this. I could watch this all damn day.

Brawler gets hit in the mouth. He smiles, showing off blood-stained teeth. He looks like a killer out there, hunting his prey. He's dominating. That's not to say he's not getting tagged, but he moves through the punches. Takes one to give five.

Behind me, Magnum's low voice creeps in through the screams around us. I glance back to find him on the phone.

The crowd erupts, and I turn to find Brawler wailing on Jiko as he falls to the ground. I start jumping, excitement barreling through me. "Yes!!"

"Fuck!" Jacob yells. Suddenly, I'm being dragged away. I try to put the brakes on as Brawler gets to his feet, but Magnum stops me. "We have to leave."

I finally pull away from him right before the door that leads to the dressing rooms. "What's going on?" I grind out.

I turn to face him, and the look on his face is pure panic. Eyes wide and bloodshot. Gaze darting everywhere into all corners of the packed room.

Before he can explain, the pop, pop, pop from an automatic weapon goes off. Frightened screams fill the area, quickly turning from excitement to fear. An avalanche of bodies rush down from the bleachers and Mag pulls me just under them to shield me, making me crouch. "Stay down," he orders.

I grip part of the metal underbelly of the bleachers. "What is it?" I ask, even though I already know.

He creeps out from under the bleachers and then darts back. "Cole just called me. He told me something was about to go down. We need to get out of here."

He starts to move toward me, but I move just out of his way. "Brawler's out there! And Oscar and Johnny! We're not going anywhere."

Magnum sighs, then reaches into his pockets and takes out the keys to the car. "Take the back hallway. Get to the car and leave. Don't look back."

I stare at him, pushing his hand back toward him. Another round of gunfire fills the space amidst more cries, and we both duck. A cluster of people run by us, searching for any way out. I'm about to head toward the bleacher opening when two people come careening through the aisle, masks of terror on their face. The one closest to us falls. Dead eyes peer back at me, but the other body ducks inside, and I meet a pair of blue eyes that make my heart leap.

I can't even make my mouth move. I grab for him, and he scrambles under the bleachers with us. We crouch low.

"Who is it?" Mag asks, pulling his gun out, holding it in front of him.

"Never seen him before," Brawler says. His bare chest heaves. Red splatters adorn his side, blood spray from when the person running next to him got shot. "There are a few though. I saw three. Two started going toward the box."

My stomach turns over. If I'd eaten before the fight, I'd have upheaved everything right in front of me.

"Oscar?"

"I don't know where he went," Brawler pants. "Everyone dove for the ground. I couldn't see."

Mag looks at both of us, snarling at our fighting attire. Neither Brawler nor I have any weapons. "Fuck."

More screaming ensues, sending shivers through me. The pure terror in their voices sends panic jolting through my limbs.

"I'm going out there."

Magnum moves so fast, I can't even reach for him. One moment, he's there. The next, he's stepping out into the aisle leading to where the gunshots are firing from.

I follow after him, ignoring his earlier command of staying where I am. I crouch next to the bleachers, and Brawler follows behind me.

At the end of the aisle, I watch as Magnum stands to his full height and pulls the trigger. Three shots ricochet through the room. He starts barking orders, his gun still out in front of him. "Move!" The other gunfire has petered out and hope swells inside my chest.

I creep out behind Magnum, keeping low while he surveys the room. At the apex of losing my cover, I glance to my right. A gun sits on the bleachers. Further up, a body lies across several rows, blood dripping off it and down the shiny surface.

I sneak my hand around the railing and grab the gun. Crouching back down, I open the chamber to see how many rounds there are. Four. I guess it pays to be in a room filled with people who have no problem carrying. How he got this through Security, I don't know, but the bigger question is, how did the fucker with the semi-automatic get his through Security?

I walk out, Brawler following close behind with a hand on my back as we head toward the middle of the ring. Bodies litter the floor, scattered everywhere in varying positions as they were trying to flee. I quickly scan them and find no signs of Jiko or Oscar.

Masculine yelling catches my attention, and I stare up at the box to find a guy with a gun pointing it out the window.

"Run!" I barrel into Mag as we hightail it out of the open space, finding a place to stand just under the box. The glass explodes overhead and rains down onto the blood-coated cement. The crowd, still unable to get out, screams. Some cry as they crowd toward the exits once more.

My only thoughts are of Oscar and Johnny right now. I don't know where Oscar is, but I know Johnny's up there in the box. At least, that's where I saw him last. "We have to get up there."

Mag shakes his head. "They have the advantage."

"Johnny's up there," I grind out.

Mag swallows, glancing at the gun I was able to pick up. "You know how to shoot that?"

"Yes."

He starts up the steps to the box, keeping low. In my head, I'm thrown back a couple of weeks when we were at the warehouse looking for Farmingham's body. We didn't know what awaited us then, but we know now. Trouble.

"Follow me. Stay right behind me. If I tell you to run, I want you to run. Do not second guess me," Mag orders.

I nod Brawler forward, taking up the rear since I'm the only one of us who is armed besides Magnum. I watch our backs, making sure another intruder doesn't come in from behind, wiping us out before we have a chance to get up there.

What makes matters worse is that I don't know the layout of these rooms or the box. I knew how the other box was set up, but I have no idea what we're getting ourselves into with this one. Are there places where they could hide and shoot? What about walls? What about...well, anything?

"What's the layout like?" I whisper to Brawler.

Sweat runs down his tight muscles, mingling in blood. Hopefully, that's the only blood I see on my guys tonight.

More yelling erupts as we move up the stairs stealthily. In the distance, echoing sirens sound, signaling the police are on the way.

I must be becoming more Heights than home because to me, sirens don't mean safety. Not anymore.

"It's all open," Brawler hisses. "It's a replica of the other box."

So much for a surprise attack, but at least they'll be out in the open, too.

As soon as Magnum hits the top stair, he barges inside the open doorway, moving to his full height. He shoots, the shots ringing through the air in quick succession. As I come around the corner after Brawler, a guy falls to his knees, a bullet wound lodged in his thigh. His gun clashes to the ground, and Big Daddy K scoops down to grab it.

More yelling jolts me. Both sides give out orders to drop guns. I have my own weapon trained on a guy I don't recognize while also searching the room for Johnny. I find him in the corner, slumped to the ground. Brawler follows my gaze and immediately starts after him amid guys yelling at him to stop.

The guy I'm squaring down raises his gun, pointing it at Brawler, and I shoot. I hit his shoulder, knocking his gun out of his hand. Another shot goes off, but it's drowned out by an explosion. The building shakes, and I duck to catch my footing.

Another ear-splitting detonation sounds. I know exactly what it is because I've already been through this. A bombing.

"Kill them!" K orders, already raising his gun in front of him to point at a guy I don't recognize.

An explosion hits, and the floor of the box tilts. The braces underneath the private box whine and groan. They aren't holding. One of Magnum's security buddies grabs K's arms, dragging him toward the stairs. I scramble toward Magnum as the front of the box splinters. The guy I shot, along with the one Magnum took out, slide as the floor gives out underneath them. They tumble out of the now open box. The wall full of windows that overlook the fights just disappears, taking the men with them. I glance around to find K hurrying toward the stairs. He looks to his left just before he hits the staircase. He sees Brawler hauling an injured Johnny to his feet. He sees his fucking son there but runs off anyway.

Dirt and dust fill the air. It closes in until I choke on it. The fire alarm rings, and I realize the particles in the air might not all be from the explosion. Worry crashes into me. We're on the second story of an exploding building that might be on fire.

Magnum hauls me to my feet as I choke. We meet Brawler and Johnny by the door to the stairs and look out. The stairs are half gone. K and the last guard left standing are running toward a fire exit on the opposite side of the room.

The building seems to have settled for now, but that doesn't mean another explosion won't go off. Or that a fire won't suddenly appear.

Magnum descends the staircase until he's on the last remaining stair. He jumps. There's a five-foot gap between the floor and the last stair, but he lands with ease. The stairs are now rickety with no support, but Brawler and I are able to hand Johnny down to Mag. He's bleeding from his hip area, and when Magnum grabs him, he lets out an injured cry through gritted teeth.

Magnum sets him down on the bleacher at his feet and then turns back for me. I turn, scrambling off the edge and holding on to the very end while Mag grabs me by the waist and helps me down.

Brawler's next. The last stair breaks under his weight as he tries the same maneuver I did and crashes to the ground, taking him with it.

"Fuck." He pulls his hand away. A big gash opens up his palm, and blood pours out. He grabs it with his other hand like he can hold the two sides of his skin together, but blood seeps through his fingers. Magnum whips his shirt off and ties it around Brawler's hand before pulling Johnny to his feet next to him. We run down the bleachers as fast as we can. The alarm still blares overhead and smoke and dust cloud our vision.

"I got him," Brawler says, taking Johnny from Magnum. He hoists Johnny into his arms as Magnum takes his gun out again, searching the area when we get to the cement floor. The only people left in the room are us and the dead bodies scattered about the ground. The outside sirens get louder. Out the tall windows lining one wall, red and white lights bounce off the smoke and particles floating through the air.

"We need an exit," I choke out.

Magnum starts moving toward the door K went out of,

but the building shakes again. I can't quite describe the feeling of uneven, moving footing underneath my feet as it pitches this way and that. It's like walking on a trampoline, only worse. A trampoline that a thousand other people are jumping on.

A splintering crack splits the cement floor. In a scene you might find in a natural disaster movie, I jump to the side, slamming into Magnum. Concrete chunks fall through the center of the floor, a split opening up the room. Magnum and I scramble away from the widening crack as flames dart up through the missing floor.

Brawler and Johnny are thrown back.

"No!"

Heat washes over my face. I choke, my lungs burning from the inside out. My gun falls from my hand, and I can't find it in the wreckage. Concrete pebbles and shards litter the floor, imbedding into my palms as I move back across the floor. Then, I'm being hauled to my feet, staring back at the space where Brawler and Johnny just were but finding nothing.

"Brawler!" I cry out.

I can't see anything through the flames that are spreading up over the ceiling now. The heat is almost unbearable.

"Come on, Kyla," Mag urges. "We can't go that way."

I turn, finding a Jacob I don't recognize. It looks like he's been in a warzone. He's coated in gray and white dust. So much so that I can't even see the color of his hair or beard poking through ash.

I take one look over my shoulder to search for them again, but find my legs working to keep up with Magnum as he pulls me toward the exit. It's terrible knowing you can't do anything to help the ones you love. I don't know if they're okay. I don't know if they got burned. I don't know if they fell through the floor when it opened up. An ache starts in my chest and spreads.

I can only hope they're doing the same thing we are right now: Running for their lives.

My chest twinges with the shitty air in my lungs and the fear of not knowing who's where.

Again.

It's like the story of my life.

Through the floating ash, the red Exit sign barely filters through in front of us. Magnum and I hit the floor and crawl toward it. He checks the door before swinging it open into a hallway that's been untouched. It's as pristine as it was when they remade the building into The Ring.

A policeman darts down the hallway. "Cotton. Fuck."

I cough, my lungs protesting the clean air. It kills my throat. The sound is hoarse, echoing through the vacuous space.

"Downstairs," he tells us, waving toward the area he came from. "We have a triage area set up."

The policeman claps his back, leaving it there, and

among every other thing that's just happened, I fixate on that. This policeman's hand on Magnum's shoulder.

I walk out into the night air ahead of them. A paramedic waits for me just outside the door. He pulls me toward an ambulance, the crisp night air creating havoc on my lungs, and I cough again. They put an oxygen mask over my face, and I dart my gaze around as I'm being led down the block, away from the building, away from the fire. I look for familiar faces, but I just see curious people lining the streets as policemen try pushing them back, telling them they're unsure if there will be any more explosions, so they need to move away from the building. Roadblocks are set up just beyond the ambulances, and the further we get away from the building, the clearer the air gets.

The paramedic leads me to a triage area at the back bumper of an ambulance. Magnum walks toward me. Another paramedic asks questions at his side, but Mag waves him away, and the uniformed rescue personnel finally leaves, recognizing Magnum isn't going to give him anything or even let him help.

Jacob reaches out his hand, threading his fingers through mine. Just as I'm about to remark that it's always just the two of us after shit goes down, a chorus of yelling erupts behind him. Both of us turn to find several emergency personnel surrounding a stretcher.

I jump to my feet, tear the oxygen mask off, and push through the crowd as I make my way to the still form.

There's so many people it could be lying there. A spectator. One of the shooters. Or it could be someone I would give anything to see right now.

The guy on the stretcher pushes away one of the EMT's hands. A gasp sticks in my throat. Tribal tattoos. A hand scattered with familiar black markings. "Brawler!"

He turns his head toward us, Mag's hands feathering at my waist as we finally get to the stretcher.

"We need to get him to an ambulance," one of the paramedics scolds.

A cop gets in our way, reaching his hands out at his sides to hold us back.

"I'm his girlfriend!" I say, pushing back.

Behind the cop, Brawler struggles to his feet at the protests of all the emergency personnel. He ignores them, coming up behind the cop and nudging him out of the way. I throw my arms around his waist, resting my head on his soot-stained chest. Just feeling him breathe beneath my skin is a relief. He got out. He—

I pull away, all breath escaping my chest. "B-Brawler... where's Johnny?"

He grits his teeth and looks away.

*No. No, no.* I pull away from him, searching in the direction where I first saw Brawler on the stretcher. Johnny has to be somewhere. He has to be.

Brawler grabs my shoulders and makes me look into his swirling blue gaze. "They took him, Kyla." He swallows. "I don't know who it was. I tried to fight them, but they knocked me out." He peeks up at the growing bump on his forehead that he definitely didn't get from the fights. "He's gone."

I stumble back, and if it weren't for Magnum steadying us both, Brawler and I would've gone down in a tangle of limbs and broken hearts.

I curl my fingers into Brawler's skin, close my eyes, and make a promise just as powerful as the one I made my parents when I said I'd get revenge for their deaths. *I will find Johnny Marx...alive, even if it's the last thing I do.*

E. M. Moore is a USA Today Bestselling author of Contemporary and Paranormal Romance. She's drawn to write within the teen and college-aged years where her characters get knocked on their asses, torn inside out, and put back together again by their first loves. Whether it's in a fantastical setting where human guards protect the creatures of the night or a realistic high school backdrop where social cliques rule the halls, the emotions are the same. Dark. Twisty. Angsty. Raw.

When Erin's not writing, you can find her dreaming up vacations for her family, watching murder mystery shows, or dancing in her kitchen while she pretends to cook.